LITTLE
CAESAR

LITTLE CAESAR

Tommy Wieringa

Translated from the Dutch by Sam Garrett

Black Cat
a paperback original imprint of Grove/Atlantic, Inc.
New York

First published in Dutch in 2007 as *Caesarion*
by De Bezige Bij, Amsterdam, Netherlands

First published in English in 2011
by Portobello Books, London, UK

Printed in the United States of America

ISBN: 978-0-8021-2049-6

Black Cat
a paperback original imprint of Grove/Atlantic, Inc.
841 Broadway
New York, NY 10003
Distributed by Publishers Group West
www.groveatlantic.com

12 13 14 15   10 9 8 7 6 5 4 3 2 1

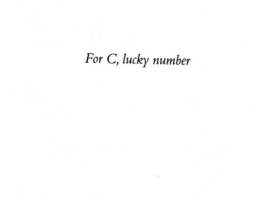

For C, lucky number

'And who,' I said, 'was his father, and who his mother?'

—Plato, *Symposium*

EROSION

At Norwich Airport I rented a Ford Focus, the only automatic they had.

'Have you ever hired a car with us before, Mr. Unger?'

She had the watery beauty of many women in these parts, the same lank blonde hair. I wasn't to be found in the system; she copied my passport and license and slid them back to me across the counter.

'And the key of course. Won't get far without that.'

She reminded me of the girl I'd seen once by Bunyan's Walk, after I'd heard something and left the path – on the mulchy forest floor I saw her, she was riding a motionless old man. He had his pants down around his knees and was looking up at her in glassy fear, at her big white breasts bouncing up and down, her glowing red face. The ferns had rolled their tongues out.

I took the key from her. Gleaming ivory were her nails.

I had left Holland because of the message delivered to me that morning.

'A telegram,' the receptionist at the Pulitzer Hotel said. 'For you.'

Warren passed away.
Funeral Monday 2 March.
Catherine

As I was packing my bags later on, I thought about how Catherine must have invoked God and all his angels in her efforts to convince the postal worker to actually send a telegram. In her world, the announcement of the death of a loved one did not take place over the phone.

Warren himself would have disapproved of that as well, amiably but firmly. Back when we were still neighbors, when I would call them because I was too lazy to walk the short distance to their house, they always answered only after many rings and in a sort of quandary, as though they thought: *what is that strange thing ring-ringing in the hall?*

The bronze urn with my mother's ashes, which I've been carrying around for a few months, I put in a plastic bag. I wrapped two sweaters around it before stuffing it in the suitcase.

The Ford smelled of new. DRIVE LEFT, the sticker on the dashboard warned. I left Norwich and drove to Suffolk. The cozy feeling of hollowed roadways, the tall hedgerows on either side. I missed the turnoff; Alburgh was badly marked. Little in the way of street lamps in this corner of the world. Just before reaching the built-up area of Alburgh, I turned. Back on Flint Road, a rubbly road full of potholes. In the cold light of the headlamps I saw slow, sick rabbits. Fountains of muddy water sprayed from beneath my tires. This road served to link together those few houses still remaining on Kings Ness. *Kings Ness!* Glorious heights on which we'd made our stand to the bitter end!

A dull smack in the rear wheel well. Coup de grâce for a myxomatose rabbit.

I stopped before number 17. The porch door stuck; I took off my shoes and put them in the darkened vestibule. Then I knocked softly and opened the door. A flood of light, women at a kitchen table. Catherine was sitting at the head; the others were her Irish daughters by her first marriage. All four of them.

'Boy,' she said. 'There you are, finally.'

She rose to her feet like a nail being levered straight, and wrapped her arms around me as if I were a lost son. My nose in her fragrant crown, I stood there, stared at by her hulking daughters.

'Catherine . . .'

4

'It's all right, boy, it's all right.'

I shuffled in stocking feet across the linoleum, around the circle of daughters, shaking hands, expressing my condolences on the loss of their stepfather. Someone handed me a glass of whisky.

'Glenfiddich,' one of them said, 'the only thing I could get at the duty-free.'

They watched as I drank. I had always kept my distance from them, in the old days, when they would come over from Ireland to visit. They would hurt me when no-one was looking, pinch me or pin me to the ground and tickle me till I started crying. I may have been only the boy next door, but the fact that Catherine seemed to draw no distinction between me and her own children made them jealous and unpredictable. They lived with their claws extended.

Occasionally one of them would bow her head and blow her sorrow into a tissue. Through the window I could see the little lights of Alburgh. Catherine smiled at me.

'Warren asked for you at the end. He wondered whether you were going to come. It was hard to reach you, boy. Promise me you'll never disappear like that again.'

I was touched to know that he had thought of me on his deathbed. It was the kind of thing one had to deserve. I wasn't sure I did.

'Your mother,' Catherine said. 'It must have been terrible for you. I got your card.'

'I had to let you know,' I stated.

'How long ago was it?'

'May. Almost a year already.'

'So young,' she said. 'Far too young.'

The daughters stared. I wondered whether they had already reproduced, helped to swell the ranks of blunt objects in the world. Two of them had their heads together, mumbling in that guttural Gaelic of theirs. Another one filled the glasses.

5

'This is a heathen land,' Catherine said. 'They wanted to keep Warren at the funeral home. We were only allowed to see him by appointment. Then they arranged him for us. But we keep our loved ones with us, at home, till the very last day. And then we play music and drink.'

A flurry of disgust crossed her face.

'So cold, the English, so cold.'

'Heathens,' a daughter said.

Catherine produced a hypodermic and a vial from a drawer in the table and prepared a shot of insulin. One of her daughters stood up. Catherine lifted her sweater a bit and pointed to where the shot should go.

'All those years Warren kept track of my blood sugar levels in a notebook. You could see every little fluctuation. Now I have to learn how to do everything. Like a child.'

'You'll learn,' one of her daughters said. 'We'll help you.'

'Do you want to see Warren?' Catherine asked me.

I shook my head.

'Tomorrow morning,' I said. 'When I've prepared myself for it.'

The dry rasp of the metal cap screwed off the bottle. The single malt seared my gullet, and from my numb mouth there now tumbled questions about the cliff, its inhabitants, the damage caused by winter storms. The erosion that never stopped.

At the end of the Alburgh pier, where the Belle Steamers full of London holidaymakers once tied up, two fishermen were leaning over the balustrade. They each had two lines in the water. Below them the leaden gray waves washed around the pilings; the sea was cold as a corpse.

From here you could clearly see Warren Feldman's titanic accomplishment, and how those efforts had already been almost obliterated by the sea. Over a length of about one kilometer he'd thrown up a wall of turf, earth and clay − the wall was four meters high and stood out darkly against the yellow sand of the much higher cliff against which it leaned at Kings Ness. A primitive bulwark against erosion. Since time began the land here had been eaten away by the sea, during storms, when the North Sea threw its clenched fury at the cliffs of eastern England. Far away, at the extreme northern end of Kings Ness, stood the home of John and Emma Ambrose. All the house needed was a wee push to be drawn into the abyss.

My mother and I had known the falling feeling that went with living on the edge. The inhabitants of the medieval town of Castrum had known it too, the water had driven them further west all the time. Now the sea flows where the city once lay, Castrum no longer exists, her name sounds like Atlantis. She was lost to the North Sea, which gobbled her up storm after storm, bite by bite. The western edge of the vanished town had snuggled all the way to Kings Ness. You could say that we, the people of Kings Ness, are the final inhabitants of Castrum, the last of the Atlanteans. Our house too, on that night long ago, became a part of the ruinous street plan of Castrum which stretches

7

some three miles eastward out onto the seabed, and is visited only by divers and sea creatures.

The teashop at the entrance to the pier was open, the bookmaker's and souvenir shops closed and, according to a note on the door, remaining that way until Saturday, 21 March.

On the parking lot at the pier the beach cabins were in winter storage. An introspective ghost town. In May, when the storms were past, they were arranged in a long, colorful ribbon along Alburgh beach.

I went down a flight of steps in the concrete seawall to the beach, where the tide was making its advances. Along the narrow strip between cliff and sea I walked to the northern end of Kings Ness. The cliff here was brittle and sandy, not like the chalky walls of Sussex. There was wind erosion as well – on summer days with a brisk east wind, tons of sand and pebbles would sometimes stream down onto the beach. The sand martins that built their nests just below the edge damaged the cliff that bit more.

The seawall had not been worked on for some time; huge chunks had been bitten from it. The layer of cloud above the sea opened up, a sinkhole in the gray dome of the heavens; the sparkles on the waves far offshore made it look as though silver dolphins were breaking the surface there. Suddenly I knew how I had once believed in phantom ships of light that plied the horizon, and the old, shell-encrusted sea god who rose up off the coast. Overpowered by the memory I stood there and saw how the hole in the clouds closed again, how everything was reduced to the gray of a spring that would not come.

This was where our house has stood, ten meters above sea level. I could tell by the broken pipes sticking from the cliff up there, the mains that had provided us with gas, water and light. Rusty pipes: anti-aircraft guns, trained on an empty sea.

I headed on. The bed of pebbles creaked beneath my feet. Anyone bothering to walk for hours with head bent, staring at the beach, could find here million-year-old amber from northern European forests.

The Ambrose family's fence was still dangling from two posts. One gentle push of a foot and the whole thing would come tumbling down. Somewhere up on the cliff was a dog that barked hoarsely and without stopping.

I had reached the end of the seawall, where the hill of Kings Ness ran down and sank a little further into a labyrinthine landscape of creeks and swaying reeds, a place where only thatch cutters and barking Chinese water deer found their way. I climbed the hill, back in the direction of Alburgh. Long ago, someone had planted a post here with a sign on it: UNSTABLE CLIFF. DANGER OF COLLAPSE. Upon the cliff itself I experienced the spaciousness of sky and water, here the world crumbled and disappeared into the waves without a trace. Higher up, Terry Mud's caravan still stood, a few meters from the edge. You could move right into it, at least if you could tolerate the hot-pink velour curtains, the enormous floral armchairs, the imitation wood paneling and the mordant dieffenbachia in the window. The whole caravan could have been embedded in a Perspex cube, like Damien Hirst's shark, and saved as a time capsule for future generations: looking through the windows, they would be able to see the 1970s. At a single glance they could take in the style and the mentality of those years, and thank their lucky stars that they were gone for good.

I walked past the Ambrose house. A woman in a turquoise bathrobe was leaning over the fence, calling her dog.

'Ruffles! Ru-ffles!'

Behind her, in the doorway, stood a stark-naked girl. Her face bore the signs of Down's syndrome. She stood there pale and shivering, her watery eyes followed me in vacant curiosity. She had a prominent pubic mound. I didn't recognize the woman in the bathrobe, she couldn't have been Emma Ambrose. Caught by surprise, she greeted me with a scowl.

I turned up the way to Warren and Catherine's house, along the same potholed road I had taken the night before. There were flattened rabbits everywhere. The road surface was a worn blanket of steam-rolled rabbit fur. In the distance, a rifle cracked. A cock pheasant flew cackling into the bushes.

You could tell the sick rabbits in the field by their listlessness. The disease caused the animals' eyes to swell, they developed lumps, went blind and died a slow, painful death. A weasel undulated along the side of the road, diving into the brown ferns and brambles for protection when he noticed me.

In dreary fields, crows hopped through the soaked corn stubble. Amid the hills to the west the occasional old, truncated steeple stuck out here and there above stands of oak. The crows and the steeples, as well as the rabbit plague at my feet – the Middle Ages had never ended here.

Catherine was hanging out the washing behind the house, I could see her through the kitchen window. Black garments flapped in the sea breeze. I walked out through the pantry. She took a clothes-peg from between her lips and clamped a sock onto the line. She brushed a few locks of hair from her face.

'Only a couple of weeks ago I washed and ironed his good shirt for Mrs. Hendricks' funeral.'

The cold was seeping up through my socks. In Warren, Catherine had lost the love of her life. I knew the story of how they had met, Warren was the one who had told me, it was very romantic. It made your heart writhe just to think about it. We went inside, Catherine said it was time for her shot. She opened the drawer and took out the little case containing her arsenal against roller-coasting blood sugar levels.

'I don't understand his system completely,' she said as she opened the little notebook containing his insulin schedule. 'What are these red and green squares? Even my illness is in his hands. Even that. Help me, would you?'

She handed me the needle and pulled up her sweater. I saw the old, white skin and shuddered in spite of myself.

'Where do you want it?'

She pointed to a spot close to her spleen, an island of pinpricks. The needle was pointed straight at the skin, Catherine clucked soothingly. The tip jabbed through the resistance of epidermis and slid into the subcutaneous layer of fat. The shiver passed down to my scrotum, it was an unbearable intimacy. I pressed the plunger all the way down and withdrew the needle.

'Let's go now,' she said.

Warren's study, the war room in his struggle against the politicians and the bureaucracy. Before we went in, Catherine asked if I'd be willing to play something at the funeral service on Monday.

'Have they got a piano?'

She nodded.

'Of course,' I said. 'At Marthe's cremation I played Beethoven's "Funeral March". Well known, lovely.'

'Fine. Please, do that.'

Dark and cold the room, the windows were open behind the curtains. Big candles burned at both ends of the bier, the wicks had eaten their way deep into the candle-grease. Catherine leaned over the man in the coffin and stroked his cheek. In the dusky darkness it looked like my own father lying there. It took a moment until the dead man and the one in my memory clicked together to form a single image, that of Warren Feldman. Catherine was whispering to him. All the color had left his beard, he looked wilder than before. Why was he still wearing his glasses? It was a pathetic sight. I wanted a little Viking ship for him, the king on a bier of kerosene-soaked wood, his fingers folded around the hilt of his sword, to launch the ship with the wind from offshore and then set it aflame with a burning arrow – but times were different now.

His big hands folded on his abdomen. Lovely, straight nails. The hands touched me – I thought about the things he had made with them. The home of his ex-wife Joanna, the new roof on the pantry of our house, his seawall. They had whetted knives, ground axes and written letters to the district committee from which the splinters of his congealed rage had spilled out on the desk when opened. They had loved two women, first Joanna for almost twenty years, and then Catherine for the rest of his life. The smell of candle grease carried me back to that other catafalque, the one on which my mother had lain in the crematorium's mortuary. My head felt hot, I had to get out of here. I thought she was crying, Catherine. My clichéd hand on her shoulder felt like an unseemly interruption of her last moments with him. I wanted to count for nothing in that final contact.

On Flint Road I saw them coming towards me, the daughters. Russian farmers' wives. They had been off shopping at the Somerfield in Alburgh. I raised my hand in greeting. They didn't reply, their arms were hung heavily with carrier bags. I had greeted them too early, too many meters had to be covered with eyes averted. It took a long time for us to reach each other. I said, 'Hello, how are you this morning?'

They said, 'Oh, fine, thank you,' and asked whether I was coming from Catherine's. I said I was. We walked on. Fifty meters further I looked back and saw them scraping down the road, shoulder to shoulder. Sometimes a gap arose in the phalanx as they skirted a pothole.

I went down the hill and passed Joanna's house in the curve, the house Warren had built. Like last night, no-one seemed to be at home. Warren's land extended all the way to the bottom of the hill, to the parking lot by the pier. I wondered whether Joanna would be at the funeral, whether the war between Catherine and her would be called off for the duration of the ceremony, a fragile truce.

I had taken a room at the Whaler. Catherine had offered me a bed; I thanked her but said no. Too many women, too much mourning.

Behind the taps in the Schooner bar I saw a familiar face: Mike Leland. We had played rugby together, he had been our second-team captain. He grinned broadly.

'So it's the piano man, well well!'

He stuck his big hand out across the bar and pumped my arm back and forth. Mike Leland had been working as a waiter at the Whaler before I left Alburgh. I had played the piano, afternoons in the lounge and evenings in the bar – I could still remember the expression on his face when he heard how much I earned.

'I work,' he had said in aggravation, 'and you . . . you play.'

He had worked his way up to manager, but looked as misplaced as ever with his number eight's body in a barman's uniform. He still played rugby, of course, these days as weight-bearing wall for the front five. Mike put a half-pint down in front of me and asked what had brought me to Alburgh.

'The old Knut,' he said then. 'The folks up there won't have long to go now. How long you staying?'

I told him I didn't know, no fixed plans, but that I enjoyed seeing the hill and the village again. He frowned.

'Not married are you, Ludwig?'

I shook my head.

'Children, regular job?'

When I kept shaking my head he whistled softly through his teeth. Went on rinsing glasses mechanically.

'Not married, no regular job. What on earth has become of you, piano man?'

'Just the piano, that's all. It's a useful trick.'

Mike shook his head and laughed, a bit in spite of himself.

'Still not an honest day's work in your life. I must be doing something wrong.'

My room looked out on the little market square. On a pedestal in the middle of it was a WWII mine, painted fire-engine red, with a slot in it for contributions to the families of sailors lost at sea. I recalled the quote from the Book of Jeremiah that was engraved on the mine – *There is sorrow on the sea.*

My cell phone showed two missed calls.

★

'Hey, Liberace, where are you? The bar's full. We're waiting for you.'

'I asked nicely if you'd let us know where you are. At the desk they said you'd checked out. Christ, Unger, answer your phone. Stop acting like some kind of prima donna, goddamn it.'

There were a few battery stripes left. I dug around in my suitcase looking for the charger, and carefully lifted the urn in its plastic packing, until I saw before me the image of a wall socket. My battery charger was still in the Pulitzer Hotel, which I'd left the day before.

I kicked off my shoes, rolled myself up in the counterpane and, without a further thought, fell asleep.

It was early in the evening when I awoke. At the Readers' Room, along the esplanade, I looked at old photographs of seamen from Alburgh – captains in the merchant marine, sailors on wartime frigates, herring fishers casting their nets at the Dogger Bank. By the glow of the opaline-glass reading lights I looked at ships that had run aground or been blown in half by dastardly submarines. The display cases contained clay pipes and braided epaulettes.

Some devout Christian had left money in his will to the Readers' Room, to ensure that seamen would waste their time not in cafés but under the reading lamps. I had never seen a seaman in there. In fact, it was even doubtful whether there were any seamen left in Alburgh. A fisherman or sailor would have seemed as quaint there as a thatcher at a county fair. Yet the Readers' Room still stood, and someone came every day to open it and close it again around eleven each night. That weird space, a mini-museum and public library rolled into one, had in some mysterious way escaped the ravages of time.

At the Lighthouse Inn I asked the waiter to take away the little bowl of chips. There are moments when I cannot bear the sight of chips. It has something to do with the ecstasy of loneliness. Years ago, whenever I felt that way, I would fill my pockets with pebbles to keep myself from blowing away. That lightness still took hold of me at times, when I had been alone and out of contact with people for a long time. I scraped off the cod's silver-gray skin and paid no more attention to my *freischwebende* condition. I knew it wouldn't be long before an end came to that weightlessness.

Later that evening Mike Leland asked me again how long I was planning to stay, and then, upon the incessant vagueness of my replies, he cast his nets.

'Wouldn't feel like playing here a bit, would you, when you've got the time? That's what that thing's there for.'

That thing: a Brinsmead grand I had played before, now as false as a compliment to your mother-in-law.

'It needs tuning,' I said.

'I could have someone come in tomorrow, it'll be fixed in a jiffy.'

He was drawing in his nets.

'Last summer we had a fellow here by the name of John Whittaker,' he said. 'Used to play on the *Queen Mary*. I heard he's dead. Found him in his room, at the Seagull in Lowestoft.'

'The way of all lounge pianists,' I mumbled.

'It's a service we'd be pleased to offer our guests,' Leland said, as though he'd just come back from a marketing course. 'And of course it doesn't have to be an act of charity, does it, Prince Charming?'

He was referring to my former hourly wage of twenty-five quid, as established by Julie Henry, the manager at the time. She'd had a weak spot for me, there was no denying that. The affrontery of twenty-five pounds an hour was etched in Leland's memory. Perhaps he still figured there was some corrupt connection between the level of my wages and Julie Henry's smiles whenever she walked past the piano in her barmaid's uniform, which I believe she ordered to fit as tightly as possible. Sometimes she would run her hand slowly across the lacquered frame.

We agreed to thirty-five pounds an hour, Leland and I did, and dinner beforehand. In twelve years' time my value had risen by an additional ten pounds an hour. During the first week I could stay at the hotel for free, after that I would have to find lodgings elsewhere; a room was too much to ask.

And so within the first twenty-four hours I, who had come to town for a funeral, had found work, food and a place to stay.

When I came downstairs the next morning, there was a piano tuner at work.

'An old workhorse it is, guv,' the man said. 'All those children's hands.'

I came closer and peered into the cabinet.

'First they look at it for a little while,' I said. 'Then, carefully, they try out a key. When no-one comes over to yell at them, they try the next one. There's a magic idea in their head that says they can suddenly play the piano, just like that, a miracle. I remember the days when I stood in front of the piano and thought I had Beethoven in my back pocket, that all I had to do was hit the keys.'

'If you ask me, they just like to bang on the thing as hard as possible,' the piano tuner said.

'Will you be able to get it back into shape?' I asked.

'Oh yeah. You the new pianist?'

I nodded.

'I'll fix it for you as well as I can, but the pads are pretty worn. I can't do anything about that right now.'

'Probably doesn't matter too much for "My Way",' I said.

The palm trees in the gardens had been bound up for the winter. I shook off that night's dream, about a woman from long ago. Early in the afternoon I went into a shop and bought a bottle of whiskey. The beach cabins on the parking lot by the pier breathed dull endurance. They were, like me, built for a different season. I walked up the hill. Warren had put up signs. *Private. Authorised vehicles only. Please keep gateway clear.* For years this was the road taken by trucks loaded with sand, clay and rubble for Warren's infamous 'soft seawall'. Through the streets of Alburgh they had thundered down to the sea front, past the pier and then up Kings Ness. The road was reinforced with debris and concrete plates, and in clouds of dust they raced uphill, downhill. Every day Warren had stood, clipboard in hand, counting the trucks, listing their cargo in code and mumbling things like 'glorious clay'. When it was raining he would sit in his Land Rover, wipers on, clipboard on his lap. There was something cheerful about him, about the way he would say 'it's all a game', or smile knowingly at adversities and call them 'a new challenge to dialectical thinking'.

For a long time, Warren had worked for a company that made water-purification systems. After a traffic accident he was forced to convalesce for a year, and when he was finally able to work again there was no position for him. He was almost sixty at the time, he received financial compensation, and so he dedicated himself to the preservation of the cliff and the houses he still owned.

A few mornings a week a retired crane operator from Kessingland would park his moped at Joanna's house. Then he would walk up to the dragline parked on Warren's supply route. From our house we could hear the engine fire up, and often I saw the black smoke pressed from the pipe atop the cabin, the deep shudder that ran through the machine. I always thought that pieces of it would start to fall off. He would remain there like that for a while, letting the thing idle. It seemed as though the motor were mustering the strength to leave its spot, after which it started to move, slow and cold as a reptile. He moved the loads the trucks had dumped, bringing them to the far end of the seawall. In that way the barrier shifted further and further along the cliff. But for us it was already too late.

Warren would not be buried until Monday, three days from now. The smell coming from the study reminded me of my mother's death.

Not all of the daughters were there. One was sitting at the table with Catherine, another was making her presence known by the sound of clattering dishes in the adjoining kitchen. Catherine smiled in the unbearable way of women who are keeping there heads up. I sat down at the table and proffered the bottle of Tullamore Dew I had bought that afternoon.

'Irish whiskey,' I said. 'I hope it's the right one.'

'That's sweet of you. Mary, fetch glasses, would you?

The daughter stood up and set out on her slow course into the kitchen. I wondered how Catherine, dianty and light frame herself, could have produced these.

'Maureen and Mary are the only ones who could stay. Kathleen and Jane had to get back. Maureen's staying another week. After that I'll be on my own. I came to England for Warren. I don't like England. But I never regretted it a day in my life, following him. Now there's nothing for me here anymore. Only his grave. They' − here she nodded towards the kitchen − 'say I should come back. But that's exactly what I ask myself, boy: should you stay where your love is buried, is that where your home is? Or is it with your children?'

Mary came out of the kitchen with glasses and put them down carefully, as though they were eggs that could roll off the tabletop. I jiggled my shoulders, made nervous by the question.

'I don't know, Catherine. Since this thing here, since the house diappeared, I'm not sure anymore about places. I don't think I'm the right person to ask. My tendency would be to . . .'

'Go on.'

I was thinking about people whose days are like grass, like a flower of the field and the wind passes over it and no-one knows where it stood.'

'Isn't that a psalm?' Mary asked.

I nodded and screwed the cap off the bottle.

Catherine said, 'Say that again.''

That's all I know, just those lines.'

'So recite them again.'

I smiled and shook my head. It was a psalm that had been read at my mother's cremation, I had felt the meaning of every single word, the grass, the flowers, the wind. All of it so fleeting, so fragile. Above her glass, Mary's eyes flashed back and forth between her mother and me. She was not going to break the crystal of silence.

'Marthe,' Catherine asked me then, 'was she cremated?'

'Ashes. What she really wanted was to be burned beside the Ganges.'

A searing trail down my gullet.

'But Winschoten was good enough in the end.'

'Mother,' Mary said, 'without Warren this house won't be here in a few years. In ten years everything will be gone. Are you going to wait for that to happen?'

Catherine didn't respond. She stared into space, her gnarled, weathered hands around the glass, as though warming herself at the fire inside it. The second hand on the plastic clock thumped like a piledriver. We sat there and breathed.

When I sang 'Summertime' in the bar that evening, it made me feel more melancholy than bright and breezy. Summer and youth overlapped in the lullaby, as they did in so many people's memories. But it wasn't the right moment for 'Summertime', the bar was in relieved, Friday-evening mood. Leland worked the beer pumps as though racing a handcar down the trackes, you could tell he was born for the publican's life.

I kicked in to 'Candle in the Wind', which has always made the English go all melty ever since Elton John transposed it from Marilyn

Monroe to Lady Di – by that time the average Brit has already traded in his solid matter for something more liquid.

I peeked out of the corner of my eye and saw a woman at one of the tables. She wore a black turtleneck beneath her fitted jacket. Her head seemed somehow to float independently of her body. I studied her pale, sensitive face, the portrait of a Catalan princess. She let the fluid in her glass rock like an ocean swell. Round eyes, cornflower blue like a baby doll's, with those heavy eyelids that open and shut when you shake her. She was the girl who is left, of her own choosing, once all the other girls have been taken home. She says, 'It doesn't matter. You get used to it'

When she comes, she weeps. Not out loud, but when your fingers touch her face in the darkness you feel the tears on her cheek.

When at last I picked up on the lively buzz coming from the other side of the piano, it gradually lifted me from my low spirits. Leland grinned at me as I kicked in to 'Take Five'. My presence was his gain. I played the little tune of gratitude as easily as I did the 'Radetzky March'.

The evening slipped away, and I took two short breaks. Around eleven I finished my final set with 'As Time Goes By', something people had been humming along with for ages.

I got up and walked to the bar. The woman put down her glass and nodded at me. From behind the tap, Leland was gesturing to me. What he really wanted to do was yell, like in the rugby club on Saturday morning after the match. He put a pint down in front of me.

'Good job, Ludwig. spot on for an evening like this.'

'It was okay, I figured.'

'They were over the moon. What you do is pur cinema, man. With someone like you in the place they think they're on the *Titanic*, or in a bar in Casablanca.'

The beer sang its way through my body. Maybe I'd hang around here for a while, wait for spring to come, at home and away from home, a little cloud of dust that settles.

I ran into her the next day on the esplanade, the woman from the bar. Her name was Linny Wallace. She said I'd played nicely last night.

'Particularly Gershwin, you put a lot of feeling into that.'

I told her I liked Gershwin, his lightness, which seemed American to me.

'I've never seen you around before,' she said.

'Just got into town on Wednesday.'

She worked as an estate agent in Reading. On the beach, in the distance, people were walking their dogs. I told her I had come for a funeral, but had stumbled on this job while I was waiting. That it was, after a fashion, a homecoming, because my mother and I used to live up there on the cliff. We had left this place twelve years ago. Maybe I would stick around for a couple of months, springtime was lovely here.

'And after that, what will you do then?' she asked.

'After that I don't know. I'm a grasshopper, I play music while the sun shines.'

'But you cadge firewood from the ant when you get cold,' said Linny Wallace.

We followed the walkway south; in the distance you could clearly see the outlines of the reactor at Sizewell – its dome gleamed in the sun.

'I figured you more for someone who belongs on the boulevard at Cannes,' she said.

When she laughed, you could see that she was older than me. On Avondale Street we stood and watched an old man and his dog. The animal sat on its backside and used its front legs to pull itself across the pavement, to scratch its itching anus.

'I've never seen anything like it,' Linny Wallace said. 'As though he's sledding . . .'

I said nothing about impacted anal glands, which a pair of expert hands could easily squeeze clean.

A sort of cheerfulness settled down between us, we laughed at the many expressions of old, guttering life that could be seen around the village. God's waiting room, it was sometimes called; Alburgh had the highest death rate in all of England. Paradoxically enough, that had to do with the favorable conditions one found here for carefree sunset years. The local shopkeepers lived in the calm certainty of uninterrupted revenues from countless pensions; restaurants and teahouses offered senior citizen discounts of up to twenty percent.

I told her how, just yesterday, I had stood in the doorway of an off-license, looking at an old man standing beside his scootmobile and messing with his gloves. When I left the shop a few minutes later he was still there. He lived in a different time-space continuum, where you could take a hundred years to put on your gloves without growing impatient.

From the old days, when I had walked these streets as a boy, I remembered the man who stood still at unexpected places. He always seemed to be deep in thought, in search of who he was and what kind of life he led. When he stopped he would wave his shaky hands out in front of him, carving mysterious symbols in the air or, with a bit of fantasy on the viewer's part, conducting an orchestra of invisible mice.

Alburgh had also gained a certain fame for the large number of hardwood benches in its public spaces. They were everywhere, along the esplanade, by the golf course, beside the pub; simple benches donated by survivors for the public good. The backrests bore inscriptions showing to whose memory the bench was dedicated.

My loving husband, he loved Alburgh deeply.

In view of sea and sail.

To all those here, nipping at their pints. Think of Tom.

Ginger Tooke, a spry little woman, had once given guided tours past the benches; she knew the stories behind many of the inscriptions. For all I knew, Ginger Tooke herself might meanwhile have passed on to her next incarnation as a hardwood bench along the esplanade.

I had to get back to the hotel for my afternoon shift. Linny and I walked into the place like excited children. I ran upstairs to iron a shirt. On my voicemail I found another message from my former employer. The poison was not yet out of his stinger.

'Ludwig? This is Peter. Hope you still remember me. You'll never play here again. I sent a fax to the whole hotel chain. And, oh yeah, I've filed a claim against you. Violation of contract. I know what you're thinking, but an oral agreement counts too. In court. You'll hear more about it. Asshole.'

I opened another little text folder. *Mi amor. Where are you? I don't deserve this. F.*

I had no idea who F. was. My telephone didn't recognize her number. I thought about the Spanish salutation, but that didn't really say anything: the language of love is a confusion of tongues. I deleted the message. The battery still showed one little stripe of energy.

There were a few guests in the lounge, sitting in orange easy chairs and reading thrillers and newspapers. Two waiters had rolled the piano into the room. Linny Wallace was squatting down beside the stone hearth, poking up the glowing heart of the fire. The head waiter, a mere boy, was staring attentively at her ass. He was the liaison between bar and lounge. Children were playing on the olive-green carpet. I sat down at the piano and leafed through the bundle of sheet music. When I flagged him down, the waiter came over to me with a rather wobbly gait.

'Could you bring me a daiquiri?'

His knitted brow sank into a dip above the bridge of his nose; it looked as though he were about to ask *huh?*

'I'm not sure we have that,' he said.

'It's a mixed drink, you can make it.'

Finding out whether this was within the realm of possibility was something about which he didn't seem particularly keen. The word itself, I suspected, would disappear from his mind halfway between here and the bar, like a copper falling out of your pocket.

'Could you tell me the name again. Perhaps Mr. Leland knows what it is.'

'Dai-qui-ri. I'm sure he does.'

The boy shuffled over to the door, his shirttail hanging out of the back of his trousers. The look of his backside was as lifeless as the one on his face.

I had copied the music onto A5 sheets, so I didn't have to turn the pages as quickly. A few bits from Tchaikovsky's ballets, for starters, 'The Waltz of the Flowers' from *The Nutcracker*, then a waltz from *The Sleeping Beauty*. My shoes creaked on the pedals, I really hated that sound. After Tchaikovsky I swung out into Mozart. In the pause between two *Sonatines Viennoises*, Leland came into the lounge.

'What did you ask the poor lad for?' he whispered. 'A do-re-mi?'

'A daiquiri,' I whispered back.

Leland shook his head.

'A daiquiri, bloody hell.'

He nodded deferentially to the guests who were peering at us over newspapers and the tops of reading glasses. A few minutes later the boy came in with a daiquiri in a cone-shaped glass, with a layer of sugar around the rim, just the way I liked it.

Linny was thrilled by how I brought Mozart to life. Outside, the darkness slipped into streets and doorways; in the lounge, the dry logs crackled on the fire. I remembered a similar afternoon, long ago in Vienna. My mother and I had stayed there for a few weeks while she was doing *Josephine Mutzenbacher's 1000-and-1 Night*. On that gray December afternoon, I had left our hotel on the Kärntner Ring and took the bus to the Sankt Marxer Friedhof, in search of Mozart's cenotaph. I wasted so much time trying to find the right bus that it was growing dark by the time I reached the graveyard. The gate was already locked. Through the bars, the only living thing I saw amid the graves was a little white dog. Going around to the side of the cemetery, I scaled the low wall with the help of an elderberry bush. I wandered at random between the trees, with dark webs spun in their crowns. Here, somewhere, was where they had buried him after sunset, on 5 December 1791. The official burial act spoke of an *einfachen allgemeinen Grab*, but which plain grave it was, they had apparently forgotten right away.

At an open spot where the last daylight was lingering I found a stone pillar, artfully carved, against which a mourning angel leaned its forehead. It was a friendly angel, one which, when I was gone, would lift its head and quietly sing *Der Tod, das muss ein Wiener sein*.

The gray paving stones outside the inn shone in the soft drizzle; I took an umbrella from the stand by the door. As I passed the restaurant I looked in. It was still early, only a few of the tables were taken.

Many of the little fishing cottages were empty, they were only rented out to tourists during bathing season. The occasional window was lit. There was no one else out on the street, the sign above a shop door groaned in the wind. I smelled coal burning, and sometimes

28

wood smoke. The fishing cottages of Alburgh, piled up against the slope, gave the impression of gradual, organic growth – like a shelf fungus or a colorful fantasy design by the Viennese decorator Friedensreich Hundertwasser. The little houses looked as though a couple of strong men could pick them up, just like the beach cabins down by the pier. From a distance, Alburgh looked like a *mille-feuille*, pastel-colored structures growing on top of each other in layers. Two towers stuck out above it all, the conical white lighthouse and the belfry of St. George's.

The esplanade was covered in orange streetlight. The cold metal of the balustrade above the beach bit into the palms of my hands. This was the decor of my teenage years, it made me feel like a tourist at Pompeii. When I did come across people on the street, I avoided their eyes; I didn't want to have to guess at what the good people of Alburgh remembered about Marthe Unger and her son, Ludwig.

What I missed when I knocked on Joanna's door was the deep woofing of Black and White, the one so black and the other so white that they looked like a single dog with its shadow. Instead, angry barking came from the other side of the door. When it opened, the little dog flew at my legs. A Jack Russell, his little teeth flashing frighteningly.

'Down, Wellington!' said the woman at the door. 'Down!'

Wellington was going wild. He leapt up against me and seemed bound and determined to sink his sharp teeth into my balls.

'Oh, bleedin' Jesus . . .'

She seized the animal by the scruff of the neck and, in an outburst of fury, threw it into the yard.

'I'm very sorry,' she said, 'Welly is so . . .'

Then it clicked into place.

'Ludwig!'

29

'Hello, Joanna.'

She spread her arms and wrapped me in a musty embrace.

'Ludwig, it's so good to see you. My lord, come in, come in. Welly, go fuck yourself!'

She slammed the door. On the other side, Wellington was still going out of his mind, scratching his nails against the wood.

'He's such a dear,' she said, 'but so jealous. The children gave him to me. That way they don't have to worry much about their old mother, they figure. I'll let him in when he calms down a bit.'

But on the other side of the door, Wellington was not giving the impression of a dog soon tuckered out. Joanna led me down the pine-paneled hallway to the tiny, low-ceilinged living room. It was hot inside. No windows were open.

'Would you like some tea? Or is it already time for something more fortified? Would you . . . ?'

I saw that she was doing her best to keep moving, to keep up the cheerful tone, not to drop a single stitch for fear that otherwise she would come tumbling down, once and for all.

Before the window was an ironing board, on the TV screen the anchorwoman on Channel 4 spoke to me intently without a sound crossing her lips. I leaned down to look at the proliferation of picture frames on the sideboard. Three sons and a daughter, decked out with good saintly names, surrounded by their partners and children. I'd never had much to do with them, they were older than me; two of them had already left home by the time we moved to the hill. One photo showed Warren and Joanna with three children around them; a fourth one, still a baby, lay in Joanna's arms. Warren had a short black beard and dark-framed spectacles – no trace yet of the tattered Viking king I had known. He only became that once he left Joanna for Catherine, and moved to number 17. Since then Joanna had flown the Union Jack, never at half-mast, never lowered. It was a minor diplomatic provocation, Joanna knew that 'the Irishwoman' could see the flag from her window.

The war between Joanna and Catherine knew neither surges nor truces. It simply lasted as long they both would live. I knew that Catherine, who did not have a driver's license, never allowed herself to be driven past Joanna's house on her way to the supermarket or Alburgh's Catholic church, but always went via Flint Road and on to the back route. I suspected that during the years they had both lived on the hill they had seen each other at close range no more than two or three times, and that they otherwise remained phantoms in each other's eyes. Their jealousy was in perfect balance, and had to do with the factor of time: time that both of them had not spent with Warren. Catherine grew feeble with rage whenever she spoke of the time during which Joanna was married to him.

'Twenty-five years she stole from me,' I once heard her say.

Every word of it was true. Warren reveled in possessing a woman who fought for every atom of his being.

Joanna in turn would not have hesitated to poison the Irishwoman for letting Warren give her the rest of his days. That was the bitter heart of their conflict: time. About the days they had not woken up beside Warren, not heard him gargling with mouthwash, not heard the door click shut when he left for the office, not seen him cut the cold roast or seen him slurp down his infamous homemade jellied fish. (My God, sometimes as many as twenty jars appeared on the table at once, each one containing something different from what the label promised, each one preserved with his own hands. 'Eat,' Warren said, and you ate. What you were eating you didn't dare to ask, you chewed with bated breath and swallowed it all down. That's what you did.)

'Oh, Ludwig,' I heard her say behind me, 'it's so sweet of you to drop by and see me. I was dying to know whether you had come, with this situation and all. Where were you when you heard?'

She put two mugs down on cork coasters. Through the smoked glass of the dining table I saw a pair of mangled slippers, newspapers Wellington had torn to bits.

'Would you like some milk, love? I didn't put any in it. You always did like my tea, didn't you, Ludwig? Pour the boiling water right onto the leaves? And only first flush? You haven't forgotten, have you?'

I was startled by the dog, that suddenly jumped up against the window outside. It drew its nails down the glass, it looked as though there were a little trampoline beneath the window. A horrible thing to see, that leaping dog trying to wrest a position of honor among the humans.

'Aw, poor thing, I'll just let him in.'

She left the room. The dog came storming in. Right away the animal resumed its animosity and began barking so shrilly that it hurt my eardrums.

'Welly, stop that immediately!'

Wellington moved back a few steps and shut his mouth. Joanna put the milk on the table.

'Good dog, that's a good boy, good Wellington.'

I reached out and petted him gently on the head.

'Don't touch his ears!' Joanna said in a fright.

I yanked my hand back.

'He's very touchy there,' she said. 'I think it's something traumatic. You can pet him wherever you like on the rest of his body, with the grain as it were, but he's ever so touchy about the ears, aren't you, Welly? Does Welly want a biscuit?'

At the word *biscuit*, the animal rushed forward and leapt at the biscuit in her hand. The height of its jump, the perfect timing with which it snapped shut it jaws, was a wonder of precision. The biscuit disappeared without chewing. I tried to get a conversation going, about how she was doing, about the children, whether she still played golf, but Wellington never let me get a word in edgewise.

'He demands a great deal of attention,' I said. 'You must be careful that a little dog like that doesn't cut you off from the rest of the world.'

Joanna nodded. From her eyes a river of love flowed in the little dog's direction.

'He must have been awfully lonely,' she said. 'Otherwise he wouldn't act this way. That's what they all say. He's overcompensating. The Jack Russell is such a people's pet, they forget that sometimes. But it's all in here.'

She lifted a booklet from the top of a pile. *Think Like Your Dog.* Underneath it was a booklet from the same series, *What the Dog Thinks of Its Master.* Even more gruesome was *Your Very Best Friend: Jack Russell.*

'Do you read all of that stuff?'

Joanna nodded vigorously.

'I think you need to know what you're bringing into the house. Most people have no idea at all, they just act.'

'What happened to Black and White? Dead?'

'They're buried back in the garden. I had to put White down. That's right, you knew them, the dears. Have you already been, up there?'

The index finger pointing, not followed by the eyes, in the direction of number 17.

'Have you seen him?'

'Yesterday. No, the day before. And you?'

She shook her head.

'I don't count anymore, they've wiped my name from the books. Isn't that right, Welly? They don't want the missus around, do they? I raised his children, but there's no place for me.'

The bitter lines around her lips grew deeper.

'With all respect,' she said, '*you* didn't bear his children and *you're* allowed to see him. So unfair, so cruel. They don't want us around, do they, Welly? What they don't know is how often he came down here, and not just for a cup of tea, oh no . . .'

'Joanna . . .'

'Would you like some milk? The English way, right, darling?'

I couldn't stand to watch this life in free fall any longer. After the tea, I left. Around my heart was a hand that squeezed.

'Can you play something from *Schindler's List*?'

I looked up at the middle-aged woman. She was tapping her ringed fingers rhythmically on the piano's frame. I raised my eyes to the ceiling and pretended to be turning an internal searchlight on the archives of my memory. Then I sighed deeply and said, 'I'm sorry, ma'am, but I can't seem to find anything from *Schindler's List*.'

She smiled as though I were a thing to be pitied. When the same woman came over later to ask whether I knew anything from *Titanic*, I was able to satisfy her with 'My Heart Will Go On', and asked her to forgive me for not sounding like Celine Dion. She looked at me as though the scent of my irony was not pleasing to her.

Linny Wallace came back from the ladies' room. A pair of blue jeans and a white blouse that shone like silk, with a high collar. Her lips gleamed like a polished apple. She had bound her straight blonde hair up in a knot.

It was Saturday night, things were at their zenith. Saturday night was a ledge with on one side the week past and on the other the week to come – it was precisely atop that ledge with the steep slope of duty on either side that they felt free and came with their requests. The bar of the Schooner was transformed into a honky-tonk with the 'Maple Leaf Rag', and a cluster of men at the bar sang along with the refrain to Tom Jones' 'Delilah'. Oh yes, I was worth every penny. Linny was being chatted up by two men at the bar, they were in high spirits. Over the course of the evening the same boy who had waited on me that afternoon brought me two more daiquiris, sublimely mixed by Mike Leland. (I know there are those who say that you're no credit to your profession if you drink while you're playing. What can I say?) A nervous man came over to me and asked if I could play some Erroll Garner.

'I don't play Erroll Garner,' I said with a wink, 'I play Ludwig Unger playing Erroll Garner.'

Then I played 'Misty' for him. He looked around triumphantly from atop his bar stool, ready to tell anyone who would listen about his proclivity for Erroll Garner, but Linny was already engaged. One of the men she was talking to fetched three pints of Guinness; maybe they were hoping to have sandwich sex with her later on in their room. English girls do the weirdest things when they've had a few.

After Leland had served the last round, I launched into Randy Newman's 'Lonely at the Top'.

> *I've been around the world*
> *Had my pick of any girl*
> *You'd think that I'd be happy*
> *But I'm not*

I got up from the piano and slid onto the barstool next to Linny's. Leland mixed me the final daiquiri of the day. The bar was emptying out. The man who'd asked to hear Erroll Garner said *goodnight, all*, but too quietly; I was the only one who heard.

'You disappointed someone terribly this evening,' Linny said. 'A woman. I heard her tell her husband: *he's got to be the only pianist in the world who doesn't know anything from* Schindler's List.'

'A couple of weeks ago a woman stomped out of the bar because I didn't launch into something from *The Lion King*. "Hakuna Matata". Jesus Christ.'

We drank in silence. The lime juice snapped at my gums.

'Piano man . . .' she said.

I laughed quietly.

36

She asked, 'Is that something you become by mistake?'

'By mistake is pretty much it. And it's not hard to imagine that one day, by mistake, you stop being one too.'

'So how does a boy from Alburgh mistakenly come to play piano in a bar?'

I mulled that one over.

'That's a magic question,' I said then. 'The answer is a bridge that runs from then to now, from my very first memories to this very moment.'

I told her about the city where I was born, Alexandria. Dutch mother, Austrian father. We lived in Kafr Abdou, a district popular with expats because it lay out of the way of the roar of hundreds of thousands of cars and millions of people – that infected larynx from which rose the hellish scream of sirens and honking and cursing. One day my father, an artist, failed to return from a trip abroad. Cut and run, halfway through the first verse. His shoes still beside the door, cigarettes still on the table. Not all failed marriages dissolve in strife and pain, sometimes it goes with a single sweep of the sword. I couldn't remember any real split-up or any major sorrow. It had flown noiselessly, an owl in the night. It took five more years for my mother to fully realize that her husband had left her with a child and a house in Alexandria, and that he would never reply to the telegrams she sent to every corner of the globe where he happened to show his face. All that time she waited for him, living as though nothing were amiss, as though at any moment she might see him standing out there in the garden, that he would come up the steps at a single bound and take her in his powerful arms. Going on as though nothing had happened was her way of protesting against the unfairness of fate. The situation called for, no, it cried out for weeping and wailing or perhaps the racking of silent sorrow. But she gave in to neither, and lived her life in a grand display of denial.

37

★

Mike Leland closed the bar. I asked him for a bottle of Rémy Martin and the keys to the lounge, so that Linny and I could carry on the evening there. A little later he turned off the spots above the bar. At the front door he lifted his duffel coat from the hook and swung his heavy body into it. His wink was slow with fatigue.

'Behave yourself,' he said.

A few coals were still glowing in the hearth, I blew away the ash around them. With strips of bark torn from the split logs beside the fireplace I brought the fire back to life.

'Careful you don't blow it out,' Linny said.

I had blown too hard, the little flames had sunk back into the orange glow.

'People have a hard time letting a fire be,' she said.

'I've done this before,' I said as casually as I could.

Her voice, laced with delicate threads of mockery: 'You'd rather I didn't get involved?'

I nodded.

'That's always a touchy thing with men, isn't it,' she said. 'Cognac?'

From the ashes there grew an orange blossom, shivering in the gentle flow of my breath. When the fire had acquired enough strength I fed it with a few thin logs of birch. I sat back in the easy chair beside hers.

'Alexandria,' she said, 'that's where we left off. Please continue.'

Up from my memory loomed Mrs. Pastroudis, my first piano teacher. My mother had signed me up for lessons, she felt that an instrument would allow me to better express my emotions. At the end of each session, Mrs. Pastroudis noted my achievement in a hardbound ledger: finger positioning, finger exercises, scales, harmonics. She wrote *excellent!* and *outstanding!* beside all of them. Her warm, heavy hand lay on my head throughout most of the lesson. The piano was in the basement, in her living room. She talked a great deal about the past. Once her family had owned the entire building, now she possessed only the lower floor. She remembered the parties in the salon above her head, the beau monde of Alexandria. On the breath of a sigh, a name would sometimes cross her lips.

'Constantine Cavafy even came here sometimes.'

Along with the wave of nationalizations set in motion by the young Colonel Nasser, her family had lost almost all its holdings. Revolution is redistribution. Most of the Greeks had left Alexandria, but Mrs. Pastroudis had stayed in order to write *excellent!* and *outstanding!* in my ledger.

My mother and I lived alone in our big house. The servants' quarters were occupied by Eman, the maid. A forest of bushes and trees encircled the villa, overgrown fences separated it from the other homes. The gardener sprayed every day, the leaves were hung with sparkling droplets. No ray of sunlight ever penetrated to the lowest layers, it was damp and dark there, crawling around beneath the growth the red soil clung to your fingers. The trunks were overrun with epiphytes, fleshy, ineradicable. Before the windows were wooden shutters, a guard kept watch at the gate.

The rooms of our house were separated by thin sheets. During the day, blocks of sunlight slid across the tiles, cats lay napping on the warm stones. Beyond each curtain you were lured further into that Byzantine temple. An emerald-green, submarine glow: you could hear your own heartbeat. Voluptuous, I'd call it in retrospect, the *One Thousand and One Nights*. Perhaps my father had lost his way in my mother's veiled world of shadows, where eunuchs and odalisques haunted the corridors. His world was that of the barracks, the rectangle.

They called me Caesarion, little Caesar. My pet name. Caesarion was the son of Cleopatra and Julius Caesar. He and I had both been born in Alexandria. In his case, the priests had hastened to announce that he was born of the union between Cleopatra and the god Amon-Ra, in the earthly incarnation of Julius Caesar. Didn't my mother know that Caesarion was the mocking nickname people gave to Ptolemy Caesar? *Little* Caesar?

It was my pet name for special occasions.

'Caesarion, play what you play so well, darling . . .'

Then I would take a little bow and climb up onto the piano stool with its pile of cushions. Caesarion was the name of the theater production we performed together, with me as wunderkind and she as the mother who had hatched that golden egg. I played *Für Elise* and the *Moonlight Sonata*. A mazurka by way of encore, and that was pretty much my entire repertoire. I slid off the stool, received the cooing and the clapping and let myself be pawed at length by the ladies present. Little princes must be buffed until they gleam. This was Circus Wunderkind, a handful of rickety old pieces I had learned from Mrs. Pastroudis and my mother, who acted as though I were Wolfgang Amadeus himself. Sometimes I shirked the duty of putting myself on display and hid in that gigantic Roman villa. Eman's slippers would hiss across the tiles as she searched for me – Lewd-week! Lewd-week! It was easy to disappear in that house, built as it was entirely of shadows and bound together by the thick veins of ivy growing outside along the sandy stucco: an exoskeleton turned to wood.

She takes me often to Le Salon Trianon, the Palace of Heavenly Pastries. I am allowed to order my own Douceur Surprise, an Om Ali aux Noisettes or the Trois Petits Cochons. She corrects me when I mispronounce the French. That is her principal contribution to my education. All those pies and pastries revolving in a lighted display case, my nose pressed to the glass I behold the orbits of those galaxies of sugar – the friendly crème caramels! The cheerful Banana Brasiliennes!

The prim Tarte aux Fruits! My mother sips at little cups of coffee and smokes cigarettes. She comes here all the time. Beneath the lacquered wooden ceiling she dreams she is in Europe, but then a weird, distorted Europe. An outpost where people try to remember exactly what Europe was, and do their best to make it resemble those memories as closely as possible. At Trianon, air conditioners imitate the coolness of northern Europe, loudspeakers drip the saccharine stalactites of Mantovani. The uniformed staff act as though we were at the Hermitage in Monaco. My mother sees the tatters and spots on the vests of the waiters and the restroom attendants, but the maître d's impeccable black suit makes up for a great deal.

'And the handles on the toilets don't stick either,' I hear her say whenever she sings the praises of Trianon.

The restroom attendant hands her a tissue after she's washed her hands, then cleans the sink with a cloth. That is my mother's idea of heaven: a gossamer web of services rendered.

'Draw the things you see on the walls, my prince,' she says whenever I get bored.

I trace out the lines of the murals, copy those mysterious, tobacco-tinted women with expressions of promise on their faces: figures from One Thousand and One Nights, turbaned women with their breasts bared, illustrations of the dissolute Orient. The colors have disappeared beneath the sediment of sticky dust and nicotine.

We spend a few afternoons each week in that high-ceilinged salon, our backs turned on the gnawed-down world outside with its smell of rotting and the eternal desert dust crumbling down from the sky. Again I hear that name, for he once visited Trianon as well – Cavafy has been here. Little wonder that he had been everywhere: the city is an island, jammed in between sea and desert; freedom of movement is limited here.

The espresso machine hisses and blows clouds of steam. The loud hammering of the handles when the coffee grounds are knocked out, the machine's red casing, fitted with sparkling silver parts, manometers and thermometers, the trumpeting of the steam pipe: the machine is the living heart of Le Salon Trianon. My mother stares out the window, a mirror from the outside so that no-one can look in. On the other side Alexandrian life shuffles by, the entire impoverished society of the masses, that anthill of nerve-racking fiddling about without cohesion. Sounds from outside penetrate faintly into the salon, the zooming of myriad carrion flies on the cadaver of the city.

One afternoon a man pauses at our table, he is pleasantly surprised to see her and bows with the grace of an Arab nobleman. He takes her hand and kisses it.

'Miss LeSage,' he says, 'this is a very great honor.'

Behind his moustache, his teeth are splendid, between the two front ones is a little gap. All Trianon watches him as he disappears through the revolving doors.

'He's turned gray,' my mother says.

I ask who he was, and why he called her that.

'That was Omar Sharif, darling.'

It doesn't occur to me to press on with my question, I am at the age when everything is both a miracle and implicitly accepted.

My father I remember only as a sound. He disappeared from my life before my active memory started; the auditory remembrance is all I have. It is a rhythmic, rasping sound that I can't quite place. It is devoid of body or face and defies explanation. That rasping sound is all I can think of at school when they ask me who my father is.

I attend the Schutz American School, not far from tram station Raml and Trianon. There, one day, I again hear the sound that is my father. That *rasping*. The classroom door is open, the sound is coming from the hall. I freeze. The thought: *he's looking for me, he's come to get*

42

me . . . The sound comes to a halt at the door: after a knock, Mr. El-Fahd, the janitor, comes in. He speaks a few words to the teacher, then leaves the room. I ask if I may go to the toilet.

'Next time you go at recess, Ludwig.'

I follow Mr. El-Fahd down the corridor, *he found me, he was this close to me all the time!* In the central hall I realize for the first time what is causing the sound, the *whoosh whoosh whoosh* of his trouser legs brushing together as he walks. Mr. El-Fahd asks me what I'm doing out of the classroom.

'Do you have to fetch something?'

I shake my head.

'Are you my father?' I ask.

He laughs.

'No, boy, you've got your own father. Now get back to the class, quick.'

He disappears into his cubicle beside the entrance and doesn't turn to look at me again. Over my head hangs a nagging cloud of sorrow; for the rest of the day I live in the conviction that Mr. El-Fahd really is my father but that he's lied to me for a Top Secret Reason – but slowly the cold light of logic penetrates into my misty fantasies and I understand that my father is not the only man in the world with knock-knees. The trousers of men with straight legs don't make that sound. Not like that.

I float in the vacuum left by a father who isn't there and a mother who is absent, whose sole pedagogical premise consists of laissez-faire, laissez-passer. Behind her eyes, dreams go floating by. Sometimes she's so quiet, that mother of mine, you'd almost think she wasn't there. I love her the way Mr. Cavour loves Mother Mary, about whom he tells us stories in an annex of the Alexandria Community Church. He convinces us of his boundless love for the mother of Jesus, even though

43

he's never met her. We see a movie about the Holy Family in the desert, and when it's over Betsy Pearlman says, 'I'm in love with Jesus.'

I sit on my bed, my mother is applying her makeup at the dressing table. I look at her reflection, my blood roaring from the scent of her mascara. The little brush rolls along her lashes, that intense gaze, there's nothing else in the world she looks at in that same way.'

'Do you want a little too?' she asks.

She highlights my cheeks with rouge and paints my lips red.

'Ludwig, so handsome, so handsome,' she sings quietly.

He doesn't have to come back, that father of mine. I am a painted prince, I live with the queen in a palace with a fence around it and a guard in his little house beneath the eucalyptus trees along the street, we have no need of rasping trouser legs in this house. She paints my nails with polish, blows warm air on my fingertips, she's so close and so physical now that I lean forward and fall against her – she loses her balance and grabs hold of the dressing table. She pushes me away.

'Now look what you've done, it's all ruined,' she says.

A few minutes later, frowning angrily, she cleans her nails with acetone one by one and applies new polish. Her jewelry tinkles softly. She has lots of jewelry. Whenever she eats or drinks or applies nail polish you can hear her bracelets tinkle. The rings on her fingers make a tapping sound like a dog's claws on a wooden floor.

'Flap your hands now, then it will dry faster.'

But before long she drifts back into her absent-mindedness and becomes unreachable for me again. Her veiled look, a mirror clouded with age. A barrier hangs between her and things, one you run into like a sliding glass door that's just been cleaned until there's no more difference between inside and out. Behind that door she sits, I leave greasy fingerprints on the glass.

★

One day they left a huge wooden crate on the pavement, big as a house, and the next day another. That evening at dinner Eman didn't say a word: she was grieving. Only a few days later did I see my mother again.

'We're going back, little prince,' she said.

And when I asked where we were going, she replied, 'To Europe.'

She was not going to wait for my father any longer, in a city where she didn't belong. She had sold the house and ordered the crates. There had always been a powerful magnetic attraction between my mother and the world of objects – over the course of time the house had filled up with the ten thousand things. During the weeks that followed I watched as our life disappeared into the crates, everything we had, every chair, every cushion, every Bedouin carpet. When I saw how her temple was desecrated by the mover, I didn't know whether to feel relief or sorrow.

The walls bore the pale shadows of vanished cupboards and rugs. When the workmen suddenly appeared in my room, it was Eman who bore the message that I was to pack my little red suitcase. I was to fill it with clothes and the things I absolutely could not do without; there was no knowing when the crates would be reunited with us.

We left Alexandria early in the morning. The taxi raced across the crumbly asphalt to Cairo, what I remember is the right side of the road.

'We have to go back!' I shouted suddenly. 'I forgot something!'

But all we could do was go on, the road back was sealed. She didn't ask what I had forgotten. I asked when we would be coming back.

'I don't know, Ludwig. For the time being, we're going away.'

Then I understood the meaning of parting, I cried without making a sound. Another boy would come to live in my house, he would be drawn blindly to the spot where I had buried the forgotten treasure, a plastic box containing yellowed dog's teeth I had found beneath the bushes, and crystals I had collected from the streets. Eman claimed they were pieces of car windows, but I knew better – crystals, from the depths of the earth. The dog's teeth were full of scratches and grooves, and covered in a dark brown patina. Teeth and crystal, that was what was left of me. We were moving quickly away from my treasure, and there was nothing I could do.

Our first stop was Holland. Waiting for us at the airport were my mother's sister and her husband: Aunt Edith and Uncle Gerard. They took us to the north of the country, a long trip by car; my mother and I sat in the back seat, the two people in the front didn't say a word. My mother was wearing her sunglasses and seemed used to this silence.

'The two of you would have been better off flying to Hamburg,' my aunt said at one point. 'Or to Bremen.'

'No planes fly there from Egypt,' my uncle said.

He spoke in a dialect unfamiliar to me. They lived in a rambling farmhouse beside a canal, not far from Bourtange, close to the German border. In Egypt I had seen the irrigation works maintained by farmers – canals, sluices, an increasingly intricate network of interlocking ditches, but never a canal like this one. Its straightness was intimidating.

It was summer, a few times I heard my aunt sigh *goodness, it's so hot.* The heat to which I was accustomed was exceptional here. A few days after we arrived, my mother said she was going away for a little while. The evening before she left she came and sat on the edge of my bed. As she spoke, her eyes remained fixed on a point just above my head, on the light blue cornflowers on the wallpaper.

'I thought maybe we could be at home here,' she said. 'My family close by, your uncle and aunt, but I was wrong. I can't live here. There are a couple of places I need to take a look at, I'll try to come back as quickly as possible, okay, sweetheart? Will you be nice to Uncle Gerard and Aunt Edith?'

And so I remained behind, for I don't remember how long. Long, dry days flowed together endlessly. Motors pumped water out of the canal to quench the land. Teetering columns of dust above the flat fields bore up the azure-blue dome of sky.

In the villages I saw, the houses were all built of red bricks. It oppressed me, the darkness of it, the square staunchness – there was no resemblance at all to the orderless festering of the city where I was born.

At the kitchen table I tasted vanilla custard for the first time. Custard from the bottle, yellow and glutinous and almost as delicious as the pastries at Trianon. Uncle Gerard scrimped the last bits from the bottle with a thing he called a 'bottle licker'. After meals Aunt Edith went to the kitchen and used a scraper to remove the final remains from the pans.

Uncle Gerard took an old scooter out of the shed, pumped up the tires and showed me how the thing was used. He was good to me, Uncle Gerard, not as strict as Aunt Edith, who gave me the feeling that I even *breathed* wrong. The scooter expanded my world. My forays along the straight canal became longer, I would get as far as the locks where children sometimes swam and dove from the wall into the water. From the shade of the poplars, I watched them. I didn't approach them, they left me alone. They belonged together, there was no room for outsiders. I looked at the shimmering curtains of water when they did cannonballs, one of the boys was the king of the 'atom bomb', the column of water that shot up then was higher than ever – and that was how I became invisible of my own accord, a pale spot off beneath the poplars, dreaming away the summer there – I watched, I drank deeply of paradise there and even though I didn't take part it still seems to me a flaw in the fabric of creation that one day you stop cycling to the locks, stop doing cannonballs in a pair of floppy swimming trunks, stop wrestling with the others and swimming underwater, smoothly and fluidly as sea lions, to give the girls a dunking – that you grow out of that, become too old for that, is something which I have always seen as a sign that the soul exists, and that it can be ruined.

And then, suddenly, the whole troupe comes to life, the disorderly pile of bikes is untangled, they take off.

'Nice scooter you got there,' one of them says in passing.

That really makes them laugh, and impresses on me that I am too big for it, for this scooter, just as they will soon be too big for the locks, for bare feet on pedals, for the sand between their toes.

At the table I say nothing about my daydreams. My face, my body exhale the light, the heat that my skin has breathed in during the day. I wonder whether Uncle Gerard, somewhere in one of his sheds, might have a bicycle that would fit me. I'll ask him when she's not around. I ask for more potatoes. Aunt Edith dishes two onto my plate.

Not long after dinner I put on my pajamas and watch TV in the front room. Then it's time for me to go upstairs. The runner on the stairs muffles my footsteps.

'Good night,' says my aunt in the doorway.

The light worms its way in through the curtains, I toss off the sheet and walk to the window. It looks out on the canal, the poplars, on the farms and fields beyond. Uncle Gerard is watering the lawn in front of the house. When is my mother coming back? Since she left, no-one has said a word about her. I don't know where she is; the thought that she won't come back and that I will have to stay here forever carries me to the gates of panic. Shadows crawl over the road, nestle down between the trees and bushes, the water turns dark. She will come back, she would never leave me all alone. I'm in her thoughts the same way she is in mine, she will come to get me. I fall asleep only after I hear my uncle and aunt talking quietly on the landing, after I hear their bedroom door open, the discreet click of the key in the lock.

★

'A bicycle?'

Uncle Gerard claws at the stubble on his chin.

'No, boy, I don't have one of those. Ours, but it'd be too big for you. Do you know how to ride a bike?'

I figured I did, that was just something you could do, wasn't it? The kids at the locks rode bikes as though they'd been born on them.

'When's my mother coming back?' I wanted to know.

'Oh,' Uncle Gerard says.

He shrugs. I don't receive an answer. In me that day rise up the first words that have to do with the great parting. The choral response to the requiems I will write for her down through the years. *Oh beautiful mother, who art in heaven, hallowed be thy name* . . . the wreckage of prayers from the Alexandria Community Church becomes part of the lesser Office for the Dead. While I scoot furiously along the canal, the words well up, *farewell Mother, don't leave me alone, Aunt Edith is a bitch, come back, come back* . . .

One evening a taxi pulled up in front of the house, I had already put on my pajamas. The door flew open, I ran barefoot down the garden path, through the gate, and rushed into her arms.

'Ludwig! You've gotten so much heavier!'

At that moment I'm suddenly filled with poison and rage, it had all lay hidden behind the missing and the fear – *she left me alone. She'll do it again. Again and again.* My embrace weakens. The kiss dies on my lips.

'How was it, sweetheart? Did everything go well? Did you have a nice time?'

She didn't even call me once. If she had, she could have asked me all those things. Not once. Shivering, I sink into a pool of accusations. Later, at the table, my aunt says, 'The way cats are too. Until they remember who puts the dish out for 'em.'

She had traveled all over northwestern Europe. She was enthusiastic about *darling little coastal towns* in northern France but found Picardy depressing and decrepit. The Danes were friendly but so bourgeois, it was only in England that she thought there might be possibilities for us. She hadn't found a house yet, she wanted to go looking along the east coast. In Alexandria she had known lots of English people with whom she got along well.

'The English understand eccentricity,' she said.

The next day I pack my red suitcase and descend the noiseless stairs. I walk into the front room.

'That's the way we see it,' my aunt was saying.

My mother's voice.

'The beam in your own eye, Edith. You've overlooked that one again.'

They catch sight of me too late to cover up the hardness in their voices. My mother says, 'Then I think it would be better if we didn't see each other again.'

She grabs me by the arm and pushes me forward.

'Say thank you to your uncle and aunt, Ludwig.'

I stand on tiptoes to kiss Aunt Edith; she doesn't bend over far enough and so the kiss lands on the wattles under her chin. I kiss Uncle Gerard too, the uneasiness growling in his throat.

'Goodbye, fella, it was fun.'

We leave the room; in the hallway she seizes her suitcase, we walk out of the garden, onto the brick-paved road. The open sky, the raging sun overhead. She clamps my hand in hers, in the other she's clenching the suitcase, its wheels rolling half over the bricks and half over the dusty verge. We're heading towards the locks.

'Hurry up a little, damn it.'

My arm holding the suitcase is on fire. At the locks in the distance there are no children to be seen. Breaths of wind rustle in the poplars'

crowns, the world is keeping its head down in the motionless afternoon heat. Only when we get to the locks does she let go of my hand.
We stop. There are plucks of sweaty hair at the back of her neck,
transparent spots of perspiration shine through the body of her dress.
There is little left of the stately rage with which she stamped out of
the farmhouse. Melted. Now she is hopping on one foot, taking off a
slip-on pump. Then the other one. She reaches around behind her and
gropes until she finds the zipper. In one fluid motion she bares her
back. It's impossible to imagine deep red blood pulsing beneath that
smooth, marble-white skin, to imagine her consisting of anything but
gleaming skin. She gives a little shrug, the dress slips off. It's as though
she's stepped out of the shadow. Snowy white underthings. She un-
hooks her bra. Across the skin on her back and shoulders a pattern of
stripes. Crouching down a little she descends the sandy bank step by
step, until the slope becomes too steep, then she straightens up and
dives into the water. She re-emerges, she laughs, pushes the hair back
out of her eyes.

'It's lovely! Come on in, Ludwig!'

Not me. What if the children show up? She rolls onto her stomach
and swims to the far side in a few strokes. A car is approaching in the
distance, Uncle Gerard's orange Opel. He stops at the locks. She swims
back over and climbs up the bank. Uncle Gerard stands nailed to the
spot, he forgets to reach out and give her a hand.

'Hello, Gerard,' she says.

She stands in the road, tilts her head to one side and wrings the
water out of her hair. His eyes follow the lines of her body like a hand
that caresses. (Only much later, in the Uffizi, did I see what Uncle
Gerard saw that day at the locks: Botticelli's Venus, born of sea and
foam, never in his life has he seen anything lovelier along that canal. I
look at the poor man, his reddened face, his eyes flashing hunger and
shame – so much and all at the same time, for the first time I catch

sight of how complicated these things are.) She asks why he's come. He tears his eyes off of her and looks back in the direction he came from.

'Wanted to give you two a lift to the station.'

My mother slips her arms through the straps of her bra and fastens it. She steps into her dress and turns her back on Uncle Gerard. Looking back over her shoulder she asks, 'Would you?'

He holds his arms out as though to keep her at a distance. His rough fingers pull up the zipper.

'Thank you.'

She takes off her wet panties and stuffs them into the suitcase. Uncle Gerard puts our suitcases in the trunk, we drive to Groningen in silence.

'Where are you two headed?' he asks before we get to the station.

'To England,' I say quickly from the backseat.

My mother nods.

'Too bad,' she says, 'it had to go like this.'

'Yup,' he says.

She climbs out, he takes the suitcases from the trunk. He waves to us as we walk away. My mother doesn't look back. But I do.

It was winter and we were standing in a low-ceilinged living room. The living-room window looked out on the sea. On the horizon were ships that seemed to be standing still, but had advanced undeniably whenever you took another look.

'The view, that's the great plus,' the owner was saying. 'You live here, as it were, in your view.'

Rabbits darted out from beneath the gorse, there was a whole maze of holes in there.

'And of course it's not winter all the time,' he said.

Hanging beside my ear was a mummified spider on a thread; whenever I moved it spun in the current of air. The man hadn't done much to make the house presentable. We heard the murmur of the waves and something else, above our heads, quiet and persistent. An endless gnawing. My mother peered up at the dark beams.

'Little holes,' she said after a moment.

The man looked as well, and said, 'Woodworm.'

He ran the flat of his hand over a sideboard.

'They eat everything,' he said. 'Little bastards.'

He dusted off his hands. Thousands of tiny jaws, grinding the woodwork to fine powder.

'I'll have to get around to treating the whole thing.'

'It seems like a lovely house, for the two of us,' my mother said.

The man shook his head.

'One problem,' he said.

We looked at him.

'Erosion.'

'Oh, really?'

'The whole thing's slowly sinking away.'

He pointed outside, at the edge of the cliff.

'With every storm we lose a little bit more. The politicians aren't doing a thing, neither is the district council.'

'I don't understand,' my mother said.

'Two or three meters a year. All my land, all gone.'

'So don't buy it, is that what you're saying?'

'Ah!'

He raised his index finger and said we should follow him. We went outside. A surreal amount of rubbish was piled up around the house. Someone who couldn't throw away a thing, who even saw an ice-cream truck in an old dairy van, with a few modifications here and there. That draughty dairy van, faded to old ivory, was the biggest of the objects that had ground to a halt there. For the rest it was cement mixers, rails, crossties, building materials. A hill of petrified sacks of cement and the overgrown remains of what looked like a crane.

'It's all going out,' he said.

He waved his hand casually, as though those tons of scrap iron could be carried off by a magician's sleight of hand. Amid the thorns and the old iron was a kind of goat path which took us to the edge of the cliff. My mother's mantilla caught in the thorns, the bushes were taller than I was. Then, before us, opened the panorama of sea and sky.

'Look,' the man said.

My mother's hand was resting on my shoulder; we peered over the edge, down where he was pointing.

'I'm making a wall,' he said. 'To stop the sea.'

In the distance, a low, dark barrier had been thrown up against the foot of the cliff.

'What the sea washes away during a storm, I put back the next day. If I didn't, we'd soon be standing in the water here.'

He was talking to the horizon.

'Not a meter of the cliff gets lost down there anymore. A soft seawall, made of building debris. A closed system.'

'But . . .' my mother said.

She pointed to where his wall stopped, a few hundred meters to our right.

'On its way,' the man said. 'By next winter, I'll be here.'

He pointed to the spot below our feet.

'Once the foundation's been laid, it's just a matter of keeping it filled. Every year I lose thirty-five to fifty tons of material. On a good day I can have a thousand tons added. At a pace of forty to fifty truck-loads a day. In two years, once the wall's reached the northern end of the cliff, all I'll have to do is keep it up.'

A utopian. It was seductive to listen to. We stepped back from the edge. The house was about fifteen meters from the cliff.

'It's lovely here,' my mother said. 'Does it all belong to you?'

He nodded.

'And you really want to sell this?'

'None of the children are using it. An empty house is an unpleasant thing to look out on, that's what the wife and I think.'

His house was located back behind ours, further inland. It had white plastered walls and a pointed roof that stuck up above mountains of scrap and the wild growth of thorn bushes. The houses were thirty meters apart. He would be our neighbor. If he and his wife were nice, a path would be worn through the bushes; if they turned out to be bastards I knew my mother would start thinking about a fence. She was quite solitary, I had never seen her try her hardest to make contact with others. Vast towers of cloud parted, sunlight came gushing between them. We looked at the house.

'Tudor,' the man said.

His name was Warren Feldman, and he had just sold us a house.

★

56

A few weeks later we were able to move into the house, which was being eaten from the inside by wood-boring insects and threatened from the outside by erosion. These factors were accounted for in the price. It was not an expensive house. The taxi took us there slowly, the driver swerving around the potholes in the road. Warren Feldman was just coming out the front door, in overalls, a paintbrush in one hand and a blue jerrycan in the other.

'Well folks,' he said.

Then he fell to the ground. Boom, just like that. In the same taxi, we took him down to the doctor in Alburgh. Without ventilating the place, he had been slapping some poisonous substance on the beams to stop the woodworms and the long-horned beetles. He was sick for a week, and we couldn't enter the house for a few days. We took a room at the Whaler.

'At least he's a man of his word,' my mother said.

The scrap metal around the house was gone, it had been moved to his own backyard. March came, the gorse blossomed, before long we were a raft in a sea of yellow flowers. They smelled overpoweringly of coconut. The days turned warm after a cold winter, we slept on bare mattresses, happy refugees in our own house.

Then the crates arrived. At an invisible signal they had been loaded onto a vessel in the harbor of Alexandria, sailed across the sea and unloaded at Norwich. The house was flooded with the ten thousand things. I had watched them being packed with regret, now I watched them being unpacked with reluctance. This house was so much smaller than the other one, yet still everything fit in. I didn't understand my own reluctance. Perhaps, having grown accustomed to temporary addresses, I had realized that it is no shame to live without a history. Since leaving Aunt Edith and Uncle Gerard we had stayed at hotels, we had seen Venice and spent a long time in London; it had been difficult for her to find a house that was suitable and not too expensive. Hotel rooms, I had noticed, can serve as an antidote to melancholy.

The house was now overrun by the past. The piano was in the living room. Pathways had been cleared between the cupboards of dark, heavy wood from Rajasthan, the glass chandeliers, between artworks by Bedouins from the Sinai, camel-hide lampshades, floor lamps of chased copper – a museum in which only she knew the origins of things. With the arrival of the crates, the light had been pressed out of the house. A tomb full of magic objects for a highly individual mystic religion.

I fled into the summer. Skylarks soared up to higher spheres and sang in religious ecstasy. Farm machinery growled through the rolling fields. I loved the *flowing* life on the beach. As soon as the weather even slightly allowed, the English tossed off their clothes and surrendered to the sun. How on earth could people be so white? I received mugs of tea from women sitting in front of their beach cabins. The cabins were smaller than the crates from Alexandria, and furnished with home-made cupboards full of glasses and a counter with a stove. The women sat in deckchairs all day, wearing their floral bathing suits and exchanging high, sing-song noises.

Usually I was alone. I didn't mind being alone. Sorrow and happiness had a deeper hue then. Sometimes I looked up suddenly, at the edge of the cliff, and saw my mother there, gesturing to me. She never shouted. She waited until I could feel her eyes burning at the back of my neck.

She almost never went into the village, and the beach was a place she rarely visited. Sometimes she would go for a swim very early in the morning, or later, once the bathers had gone home. On very rare occasions she would sit in the shade of a windbreak, wearing her big Dior sunglasses and wiggling her toes in the sand. She established no bonds, exhibited no social behavior.

★

We found a housekeeper, Margareth. Her boyfriend, an unemployed Arsenal fan, brought her and fetched her again each day around noon. Margareth polished and dusted the objects in the house, slowly and carefully, and when she got to the end she started all over again. She did the shopping for us in Alburgh and prepared the evening meals.

I grew up in a world of women. I developed an unhealthy interest in bath oils. Sometimes my mother got the urge to cover me in make-up. I never put up a struggle. There was no masculine counterpressure, no male role model. Warren was too far away for that. I understood girls very well indeed, in fact I shared their interests and pursuits. I wrote in a diary with a little golden padlock and burned incense in my room. On my thirteenth birthday my mother gave me olive oil shampoo and a pot of Lancôme facial crème, and I was *pleased*. That's not how it's supposed to be. That's not normal. It was a wonder that I wasn't teased about it at school. It was perhaps only because there were girls who were in love with me that I avoided the suspicion of homosexuality. From my very first day at that school I was awash in excited whispers. That never stopped.

Virtually all my father's possessions had been put out on the sidewalk in Alexandria, except for the scale model of a tower he had been building in the harbor of Alexandria, a few rolls of blueprints, his sketchbooks and the preliminary models for a group of statues. Those statuettes were in my mother's bedroom. They depicted my father and my mother locked in the act of mating. From the shadows of her boudoir they came out to meet me, fantastical creatures of rough clay, half-human, half-beast. It was only now that I began to notice them; they had been around all my life and had simply become a part of things.

The first time I asked where the models came from was during one of our sessions before the mirror at her vanity. She was doing my face.

Painting me, that might be a better way to put it — first she applied a heavy foundation of Pan-Cake that obliterated all expression, then drew a new face on top of that. She looked at me so intensely while she worked, the way she usually looked only at herself in the mirror; I loved that undivided attention.

But I wasn't to be put off: once again, I asked why he had portrayed them in that way.

'Your mouth, Ludwig, you moved!'

But she knew very well that there was no getting around an answer. And so it arrived by fits and starts. During the first year they were in love he had immortalized them countless times. *As man and woman*, was what she called it. That answer didn't satisfy me.

'As we were making love,' she said then.

He had photographed their coupling from various angles — material for *Blind*, a group of what was to be seventeen life-sized porcelain statues of my copulating parents, in a host of positions. Some overlaid with mosaics, others with cloisonné, they had long stood in the Guggenheim at Bilbao. A Kama Sutra built to scale.

'But if I wasn't born yet,' I said to her face in the mirror, 'then it could be that I was being conceived right there, at that moment, right?'

Her shy laugh, the hand reaching for the mascara.

'Now just sit still for a moment.'

She brushed the mascara onto my lashes, I kept my eyes fixed on the clay figure of the woman on her knees, the bearded man behind her. The satyr taking her from behind. I thought: *Here you come, Ludwig Alexander Unger, here you come!* and laughed — straight through all the makeup, the face of innocence, the laugh burst forth like a new day.

'Oh, damn it,' she grumbled, 'I was almost finished.'

We spent a lot of time in front of the mirror. Gradually my eyes opened wider. I loved the narcotic sweetness of her bedroom, the heat of her body close to mine. It excited me. Sometimes I masturbated afterwards.

I was her makeup doll, she would tell me things from before my memory began. I had the impression that in making her historical sketches she used the eraser more often than the pencil. While she was painting me, my eyes opened to her icons as well: a pen and ink portrait of the Maitreya, a pastel of Jesus of Nazareth, a photograph of Bhagwan torn not entirely intact from a magazine. These were the fixed points in her personal pantheon.

'They look like him,' I said.

My geisha face was expressionless.

'Hmmm?'

'Those men, they look like him. Like my father.'

Her smile wavered. Mentioning him caused her pain. Physically.

'No they don't,' she said.

'Yes they do. They all have beards.'

'But that doesn't mean . . .'

'And those piercing eyes, like they want something from you.'

She shook her head. I pushed in the knife and twisted it.

'Why are all of them hanging here on the wall, but there isn't a picture of him in the whole house?'

'Stop it, Ludwig. Those are examples to me . . . universal teachers . . . inspiration. Call it whatever you like. But it doesn't have anything to do with your father.'

I pointed at the statue of them mating.

'They look like him,' I said.

'I don't know what's got into you today, but I want you to stop right now.'

But I didn't stop. There was a pleasant sort of wakefulness in my head, something related to hunger. What can be seen, will be seen.

61

We lived at the edge of the world and could fall off at any moment. We knew that when we moved in. That the house was a risk. That although Warren was building a line of defense, there were unknown factors. Our preservation depended on the pace at which the wall progressed, the quantity of material he could obtain. We didn't know that in the month before we arrived *five* meters of the hillside had been lost. Warren did the best he could, we never doubted his trustworthiness.

'Put everything inside,' he said once during our first winter there. 'Make sure everything's battened down. Seriously.'

From my bedroom window on the first floor I saw it coming. First the gusts of wind. The playful nudges. I heard it crack. In the sky above the sea psychedelic colors flowed together, bursts of rain lashed our house. I saw sulfurous skies, then watched as everything turned *green*, the green of sunglasses – the sky had fallen on its side, the rain was coming in horizontally. Clouds of dark blue ink curled in on themselves, like an animal writhing in pain. The storm came closer, the light was sucked out of the world in a vortex.

'Ludwig!' my mother shouted from downstairs. 'Stay away from the windows! Don't get close to the windows, that's what Warren said.'

The wind grew stronger, I remember my amazement at the power of something that was invisible.

The storm lasted a day and a night. Its voice made our ears ring. Everything shook beneath the pounding drumbeats. We lit a fire in the hearth but the smoke came back through the flue. We had put some things in the shed and fastened down others, but we had thought too much about the word *storm* and too little about a sky that was turned against us. The roof of the pantry was lifted and ripped off, we found it later in the bushes. The house felt like it was being torn from its foundations. Everything clattered and whistled. My mother went outside with a flashlight to fasten a shutter. She came back inside in a frenzy.

'The wind,' she panted. 'So strong. Can't breathe.'

We sat up for part of the night, wrapped in blankets, and finally fell asleep in the living room. We knew: when we awoke, the sea would have come even closer.

Looking out the window in the half-light of morning, I saw the dark figure of a man out there. His coattails were flapping. I pulled on my boots. The wind knocked the air out of my lungs. Along the path between the thorn bushes I walked to the cliff's edge, where Warren was leaning into the wind.

'Here . . .' he shouted. 'And there.'

A huge breach had been knocked out of the seawall further up. Under our feet the waves were washing up all the way to the cliff. His hand on my shoulder, *don't get too close, boy*. The cliff could have been undermined, it could collapse, we would drown in the foaming sea. We looked at the ragged edge, and I saw Warren's concern. A new boundary had been cut out. I tried to stand beside him like a man sharing his concern, I knitted my brows and let earnestness take possession of my body.

When we bought the house, Warren had said that by the next winter his wall would extend all the way in front our house – he hadn't made it, not by a long shot. We saw his struggle, the great effort; my mother didn't want to remind him of his promise already, not now. Besides, there was no use. It was painful. He was doing his utmost.

During the storm flood of 1953, Alburgh had been almost entirely surrounded by the sea. Six people drowned. At Dwight Busby's café you could see how high the water rose: on the wall, Busby had painted little waves at the height of a man's shoulder. A storm surge of that caliber was rare. The North Sea was a shallow bowl, the water flowed into it from the north and back out again through the Strait of Calais. During that storm the wind had pushed more water into the bowl than it could take, ebb and flow were disturbed, the water from one high tide had not yet disappeared before the next came rolling in. The tides piled up: the volume of water in the bowl had now doubled. And all that pent-up energy exploded against the coast – the cliff was eaten away at from below and ultimately collapsed.

During our first winter at Kings Ness, a great deal of land was lost as well. There was not enough filling material coming in, the work some-times stopped altogether. When it started again, sounds of protest were heard from Alburgh about the trucks driving up and down the cobble-stone streets. A letter to the editor of the *Alburgh Chronicle*, grumbling among the citizens. They felt sympathy for *Mr. Feldman's War*, but the village wasn't built for such heavy transport, its rustic charm was being violated, people came here for the quiet and natural beauty.

On one occasion the work on the soft seawall was halted for six months. Chemical waste had been found amid the debris. The contaminated section was dug away, and since then Warren had kept careful track of what was dumped where, so that polluted ground could be traced back to a source. Warren had a shipment of concrete WWII tank traps placed at the bottom of the cliff, in front of our house. This served to slow the erosion somewhat. We started looking at the sea differently. Its aesthetic and recreational functions began waning in importance. Before us lay an element that was out to destroy us; we interpreted its indifferent destructiveness as an act of aggression.

Warren Feldman wasn't the first person to try and safeguard the coastline, and he wouldn't be the last. It was inevitable that large parts of East Anglia would one day be under water again. People would continue to struggle against that, just as the inhabitants of the lost town of Castrum had once thrown up walls of mud and twigs against the tide.

Sometimes, drawn by the romanticism of that drowned city, tourists came to look from our garden. You had to have a good imagination, for there was nothing to see. Looking east from Kings Ness, out over the sea, you looked out across the empty space where the town had once been. From the murky waters, divers sometimes brought up chunks of church wall and coping stones; it was this marine archeology that told us what Castrum may once have looked like. Spread across the sea floor were the remains of at least eight churches, four abbeys, two hospices and an unknown number of chapels – where crabs and fish now lived, as well as sponges, lobsters and the occasional eel.

Castrum had been a port town even in Roman times. The pride of Alburgh's museum was a scale model of the city, which also illustrated its gradual disappearance. Dotted lines showed how the coastline had run in former times, how it had kept moving up – Kings Ness was now its extreme western border. Each of the dotted lines was marked with a year: 1286, 1342, 1740, 1953. Hundreds of storms had raged through the centuries, but that handful of dates was important, for it was then that storms of exceptional violence had taken place. Great damage had been caused in those years, the coastline had changed drastically. Starting in 1740, the dotted line ran outside the western limit of the town and one could no longer really speak of a Castrum at all.

It had been a large town, covering more than a square mile at its peak. There were four gates, protected by palisades and reinforced earthen walls. Castrum owed its prominence to its harbor, the largest in eastern England. At the height of its prosperity it had served as home port to eighty trading vessels, its fishing fleet went as far afield as Iceland. The town's elite wore clothes of Flemish linen and drank French wines. Wood for its ships came from the Baltic. The streets were peopled by merchants from Antwerp, Stavoren and Kiel. It was a city one visited to go to the market, to get drunk down at portside and exchange blows with a boatswain from Jutland. Down there were also the workshops of master guildsmen and tanners and smiths. The houses of Castrum were made of wood, its houses of prayer and its abbeys of stone. Outside the town were the fields and the herds, but Castrum's lifeblood was trade – the multilingual, noisy trade of the North Sea.

On New Year's Eve in 1286, a powerful northeasterly storm blew in. It was spring tide. A thick embankment of gravel was forced up by the waves at the mouth of the harbor; the entrance was blocked, ships could only make port at high tide. The people were unable to dredge a new channel. Castrum lost some of its importance to competing harbors. For the first time, the city saw more people leave than come in. Its inhabitants were seeking their fortunes elsewhere. And maintenance of the seawall, that work of many hands, was neglected.

Then came the night of 14 January 1342. Masses of water, whipped up by the wind and the moon's pull, crashed against the east coast. The storm shoved the water out in front of it. A town lay in its way. Houses in the port district were torn apart, their inhabitants escaped to the upper city with whatever they could carry. Waves leapt up meters high, as though the sea were tossing lassoes after them. By the moonlight breaking occasionally through the coursing cover of clouds that night, the people watched all their earthly possessions being lost. The wailing storm blew in their faces salty rain and sulfurous yellow clots of foam, churned down below in the vaults of hell.

By morning light they saw the ruins of houses, customs sheds, inns, warehouses, wharfs – all of it shattered by the incessant pounding. All that was left of St. George's were the walls and the belfry; graves had been washed open, their horrific contents now revealed to the light of day.

In the centuries that follow the city's role dwindles steadily. By the seventeenth century, Castrum is only a quarter of its original size. Many of the original inhabitants have moved to a nearby hill, where they have founded a town by the name of Alburgh. Old Castrum and new Alburgh become locked in a bitter struggle for scarce means.

December 1740 arrives. A powerful northeasterly wind has been blowing for days. It is very, very cold. The wind swells to storm velocity. Masses of water again pile up before the coast and come thundering down on the cliffs on which Castrum's last remains are standing.

A priest, William Mason, who led his last service in St. Paul's a few days earlier, documented the consequences of that storm. St. Paul's, Castrum's largest church, is torn apart by the waves. Its eastern wall collapses. A few days later the belfry falls as well. When the sea calms at last, Mason sees that the waters have laid bare the foundations of buildings long forgotten. Old wells hidden by the soil till then rise from the ground like chimneys. What is left of the town is strewn with stones, crabs and fish. Rivulets of water race down the streets on their way back to the sea. Mud everywhere. The penetrating stench of rotting. The parade grounds are flooded, and that spring the sea asters blossom inland. Freshwater springs have turned silty. The Church of the Holy Trinity, atop the cliff, has lost its nave. The bell tower is all that remains standing. Bones stick out of the cliff, human skulls are found on the beach.

The belfry of the Church of the Holy Trinity is a story in itself. For decades it stood miraculously alone, then sank slowly under its own weight from the cliff onto the beach, where it remained *upright* – a wonder documented in the annals, paintings and drawings of the day: a lone, arthritic index finger, warning of a fate that had happened long ago.

In nasty weather they say you can still hear the bells of the Holy Trinity ringing in the waves.

When my mother had finished doing my makeup, I would go to my room. The cloud in my chest hot and blood red. I lay down on the bed and unbuttoned my trousers. My head on the pillow I tightened the muscles in my neck – fluttering images on my retina, up to and including the spasms. The minor shame afterwards, mild as a shake of the head.

There was a life before and a life after the discovery of sperm. I masturbated as though possessed. I ejaculated into dirty socks, towels and the insides of trouser legs, I even ate it when there were no jack-off rags to be had.

The obscene thoughts about my mother, her role in my fantasies, ended one week after my fifteenth birthday. A postcard, with stamps from a faraway country, in a hand I did not recognize, landed in our letterbox. Addressed to me, albeit with the wrong surname. *To Ludwig Schultz* it read, as though the card was not written but dedicated to me. Schultz was my father's surname; in England my mother had had it replaced with her own. The text of the postcard consisted of one line, only two words: *Love me.*

I brought the card to my mother. She took it and read it. In any icy voice she said, 'From your father.'

My father had sent me a card! I now deciphered the scribble beneath the text as *Bodo.* He knew I existed, he had spoken my name! And he had given me an assignment. Love me. That was the when the shame fell like an axe. Love *me*, it said. Not her, his wife, but him, my father. With that barebones message Bodo Schultz had renewed his claim upon her. From far, far away he had read my filthy thoughts, he had looked into the secret chambers. With the postcard, taboo suddenly stood like a pillar of lead between me and my mother. Those two words were his warning, but with the warning also came the absolution: were I to mend my ways he would requite my love with his own. All this lay encrypted in that *Love me*.

My father's card gave me a father. A man with handwriting, a hand that wrote, an arm with which he waved to me from a distance, a torso in which beat a heart that might just have kept a place for me.

The front of the card showed a statue of a man. A copper pirate, he had one arm and one leg and was brandishing a cutlass above his head. He was cleaving the deathly blue sky in twain. The yellowish cardboard on the back bore the imprint *Cartagena de Indias*, and *Estatua Blas de Lezo*. That must be the pirate's name, I realized, Blas de Lezo. The postmark told it had been mailed two weeks earlier, one week before my birthday. Perhaps my father had intended it as a birthday card – an assumption that made me happy. He had gone to the trouble to find out where I lived; who knows how many cards he might have posted throughout the years? To Alexandria, for example? Perhaps there was a pile of them waiting for me there, bound up with a red ribbon?

I went to the library and looked up the man whose picture was on the card. I found Blas de Lezo in a number of places, but most useful of all to me was a book entitled *The War of Jenkins' Ear*. It dealt at length with Blas de Lezo y Olavarrieta – no pirate, but a Spanish naval hero who had fought from Sicily to Oran. In consecutive order he had lost a leg at Malaga, an eye at Toulon and an arm at Barcelona, and was therefore referred to as *Mediohombre*, the half-man. His statue stood in Cartagena, Colombia, because he had defended that city against the English admiral Vernon.

Vernon had tried to take Cartagena, the point of departure for the Spanish treasure fleets, with one hundred and eighty-six warships, with two thousand cannons and an army of twenty-four thousand men. Blas de Lezo defended the town with only three thousand soldiers, a couple of hundred Indian archers and a handful of frigates. It was one of those battles that captures the imagination, in which what would seem to be a hopelessly outnumbered band of men defeats an overwhelming army. Blas de Lezo, however, paid for his victory with his life.

I detected no real meaning in it, in the name *Mediohombre*. The half-man was simply a half-man on a postcard, plucked by Bodo Schultz from a rack in Cartagena to send to his son in England. Behind the hero of Cartagena one could make out a dark old fortress, a wall, the roundels. On the wall a slender metal cross. What was my father doing in Colombia? What wind drove the restless waves?

The face with which he had until then occupied my fantasies, that of a janitor at the Schutz American School in Alexandria, was replaced by that of a Spanish naval hero who, judging from his portrait in copper, had a prominent lower jaw and fleshy lips that pouted angrily.

In my imagination, my father and I never looked alike. I was my mother's child, as confirmed when I was little by shop girls and little old ladies on the beach who always tousled my hair and said what a *handsome little fellow* I was.

I don't know whether my mother was aware of the connection between the postcard and the end of our makeup sessions. Sometimes she tried to lure me in.

'Oh, come on, just for me, just one more time?'

One winter evening, the house fat and round with the smell of wood smoke and cooking, I let myself be drawn in. One more time, as she'd asked, because I longed for the intimacy between us, which had never been more powerful than when she was doing my face. It smelled so lovely, so heavy, in that shadow chamber of hers, where she slept on a raised bed amid an ocean of pillows. Feathery light veils hung from the ceiling – the holy of holies, shielded from the eyes of the impure. Her atmosphere settled over me like a voile, her smell crept into my nostrils and made my knees weak. She studied my face intently in the glow of the lights on her vanity table.

'You'll have to start shaving soon,' she said. 'A little reddish, it looks.' She applied a layer of foundation cream.

'But your complexion is perfect. You have my skin.'

She had the skin of a young girl. Old skin has no light, it doesn't reflect it the way a young, tanned complexion will, but absorbs it. Old skin sucks up light the way a wall sucks up basecoat. You can tailor away wrinkles and folds, vacuum away fat and shoot yourself full of Botox, but the gleam of young skin cannot be imitated.

She picked up a brush and tapped it against her hand, the silken soft bristles slid over my face. It was waxen and pale now, a porcelain doll. With steady hand she drew lines beneath my eyes, her breath brushed my cheek. A message blinked on and off like a dying neon light inside my skull – LOVE ME LOVE ME. The mascara brush stroked my lashes, she held her face close to mine and smiled. To my lips she applied Chanel, the bright red lipstick she sometimes wore when she left the house.

A little later, as I was jerking off in the bathroom – Caesarion Philometor – I caught an involuntary glimpse of my own face in the mirror above the sink, just as I reached orgasm, my feminine, corpse-pale likeness, and was overcome by a feeling of such horror and filth that I had to close my eyes to myself.

That next Wednesday evening I went to the field where the rugby club held its practise sessions. It was dark and cold, but the little wooden clubhouse was warm. Out on the field men and boys were tossing a ball back and forth. A tall mast cast out nets of light over them, beyond that was the darkness. From a changing room at the side of the clubhouse came a big man, who asked what I was doing there.

'Coming to see whether I like it,' I said, 'rugby.'

'Have you got gear with you?'

'No.'

'Next time bring your gear,' he said.

He jogged out onto the field. The training started, they ran laps. Standing at the edge of the dome of light, I watched them. Plumes of white steam came from their mouths and nostrils. A halo of steam hung round the head of one older, bald player. When they started running through their set moves, I soon lost track. After a while, though, I realized that you had to throw the ball behind you, preferably to a player in motion. I discerned two groups: the gang of tall, heavy men who together formed the scrum, and the faster attackers, who spread out across the field. I entered into conversation with another spectator, a boy on crutches. He was captain of the seconds, he had broken his shin during a match. His name was Michael Leland, *call me Mike*. He explained the basics of rugby. It seemed to me to be a sport of the clenched fist and the open hand – the fist symbolizing the clenched power of the forwards, the open hand the speed and agility of the three-quarters. It looked interesting and hard, it seemed to me fitting for the assignment I had given myself: to become a man.

I bought boots with metal studs, socks and a rugby shirt in yellow and black, the team colors of the Alburgh Rugby Football Club. Was I planning to play rugby? the old saleswoman at Fraser's warehouse asked. Then I would also need a mouth guard, and shin guards and sports tape.

At home I dropped the mouth guard into a pan of boiling water and, while it was still soft and screeching hot, pressed it around my upper teeth. It felt like the enamel was shattering.

My mother tried to talk me out of it, she was afraid I would break my fingers and no longer be able to play the piano, but the very next Wednesday I went back to the clubhouse. I changed uneasily in the presence of strangers, in that cold changing room with its rampant outbursts of fungus, the brown rings on the ceiling and the odd hole in the wall. The smell was unfamiliar to me, but countless changing rooms would follow, and all of them smelled the same.

What I remember of that first training: biting cold, and the moment I found myself facing the man who had asked me last time where I'd left my gear. The top of my head reached his chest, I realized I needed to tackle him, and that meant: hit his upper legs hard with my shoulder and throw him to the ground – which I failed to do. I sort of hung on to the hem of his shirt till he shook me off casually and continued on his way to the try-line.

Not long after that I played my first match with the juniors, at wing, a position where I couldn't do much harm. I heard a gray-haired cynic on the sideline say that the winger was the only spectator allowed to get involved in the match. For the time being, I showed no special talent for any other position. On my team was a boy named Selwyn, a god-given athlete who scored three tries that first day. He was a fly-half and a joy to watch. His body contained power; when he went in hard and low you could hear the opponent's suffering. His tries were almost ruined by my clumsiness along the line; I let my own man pass on two occasions. I was still afraid of the clash, of bodies running at me, and clawed halfheartedly at shirts and shorts.

'Your man! Your man!' the coach screamed.

But I was lying on the ground and my man was on his way to his try. The boy on crutches was standing on the sideline as well. I avoided his eyes. The second time I let my man go I was saved by Selwyn Loyd – who came roaring in from halfway across the field, grabbed the boy who had passed me from behind just before he reached the line, and smacked him to the ground.

74

The Wednesday after that I was given tackle training.

'And eat more pork,' the trainer said. 'Or don't you eat meat at home?'

Apparently I had the aura of a vegetarian.

'We eat meat, Mr. Gorecki,' I said.

'Steve.'

He approached me, zigzagging.

'Go all the way through with your tackle,' he said.

After he stiff-armed me, I found myself lying on the grass, looking up at him.

'You didn't go all the way through. Hit him with your shoulder and finish it. Don't let go till your man's on the ground. Concentrate on the thighs, not the ball.'

Fleshy tree trunks, those thighs, pig's bristles and mud. I could barely get my arms around them. Still, I succeeded in tackling him a few times. He wasn't too enthusiastic about my technique, but my perseverance pleased him more.

The field, where I learned that I had a body, was beautifully located. It lay atop the rise beside Alburgh, the golf course began below it. Behind the eastern goalposts lay the sea, behind the clubhouse was the water tower in a rolling landscape of grass and gorse. The wind was almost always blowing hard.

That spring I noticed that my body had grown stronger, harder, and that I had started enjoying standing around in the canteen after training or matches and laughing stupidly with the people around me. I drank beer for the first time, because they always forgot to bring along Coke for me. From rudimentary kitchens came an endless flow of hot pork sandwiches on which we squeezed out rusty-brown HP sauce. I liked the stories and anecdotes told by the older players, men who seemed to me to have been not so much born but sprung full-blown from dragons' teeth. I kept a keen eye on their matter-of-fact, alert manner, and imitated it. The windows of the canteen were always steamy, I remember the eternal rain and the sea in the distance. And that Mike Leland drank from a mug in the form of a tit, with a hole in the nipple from which he sucked his beer. After the match songs were sung beneath low ceilings; when I joined in my individual identity slowly grew fluid and passed into something communal, a place where things were light and easy.

Sometimes I thought about my father, about how I was being faithful to his assignment, and imagined that he could see me in the midst of that rugged, jovial crowd, and that he approved.

It's almost four-thirty, an early Sunday morning in Suffolk, and I've just walked Linny Wallace to her room. Both exhausted, the bottle empty but for the last two fingers. The point of hesitation, the uneasy moment at which people sometimes become lovers, that first kiss, the hungry rustling of fingers over cloth, the magnetic card slipping into the lock and the door falling closed behind everything else that follows. I know that I have seen many such nights of hasty, aggressive sex, but at this moment I can't remember any of them individually.

The cell phone is dead now. The screen lights up for a few seconds when I turn it on, then falls back into the yawning darkness of an empty battery. I stand there looking at the phone in my hand with a growing feeling of isolation; I am now beyond reach of the accusations of women and badmouthing hotel managers. Hate mail is also a form of attention.

I wake up with my clothes on. It's already past ten. I drink three large glasses of water, take an ibuprofen and undress. Then I sleep on, until early in the afternoon. I have lunch in the restaurant: bread, bacon and eggs, two double espressos and big glass of orange juice.

As agreed, I meet Linny in the lobby at one-thirty. Her eyes are fresh and bright, not misted-over like mine. I'm glad we didn't go to bed together, even though I'm accustomed to the uneasy contact that tends to follow that. I know the way. Questions remain hanging in the air, hints. Sometimes you feel like it, sometimes you don't.

We go outside, I want to show her the cliff.

'You're not a grasshopper at all,' she says. 'You're a storyteller on a square in Marrakesh.'

I feel ashamed. I've been bending her ear with my life story, a madman who grabs you by the arm on the street and walks along as he relates his gruesome history. Then, when it's all over, he asks you to buy him a gravy roll.

'I'm sorry,' I say. 'I let myself get carried away.'

The desire to tell her about my parents, the things that happened only so recently, confuses me. So much floating around inside me, all that debris in orbit. The reason for my confession, as far as I can tell, lies in the desire to impose order, something that overcomes me sometimes at restaurant tables when I pile up the dirty dishes after the meal, the knives with the knives, forks with the forks. It's hard to refrain from doing that, even though I've noticed that in some circles the piling up of dishes is not viewed as a sign of good upbringing.

'How far along are we in the story?' Linny asks.

'Halfway, more or less.'

'Your story was a dream, last night. I couldn't remember my own life anymore.'

'I don't know what got into me.'

'It was hard for me to let it go. You are going to tell me more, aren't you?'

'You fell asleep.'

'I was so tired. I couldn't keep my eyes open.'

'You stuck it out amazingly long in that madhouse.'

Her bright laugh. Her voice would be perfect for telemarketing.

'A madhouse, yes, it is *that* a bit.'

We walk up onto the esplanade. I point out to her House Avalon, along the walkway. A deep front garden, from the drawing room the inhabitants can see the sea.

'English eclectic,' Linny says. 'I'm awfully fond of that.'

I know the white house from the inside. In front of the low hedge was a bench. *Misty season*, the inscription read. We look at the house behind its white picket fence. The memory splinters behind my eyes.

Selwyn, the rugby player, lived here. He became my friend. A boy who sailed along this coast as in a painting by Hopper. His father was a physician, his mother played cello with the Norwich Philharmonic Orchestra. There was a Blüthner in the drawing room; the first time I visited them I did my very best on a couple of Chopin waltzes. I liked Selwyn's mother. She was mildly eccentric. A chocolate fondue fountain after a dinner could move her into a state of disquieting rapture. Selwyn had an older brother as well, who came home sometimes at the weekend. They didn't look much alike.

Linny and I head towards the pier. She has pretty hair, I notice that as she walks in front of me, down the steps to the beach. It's very soft, when it's just been washed she might say *it sticks out all over the place*. I feel like laying my hand on it.

At Kings Ness she stares at the crumbly earthen barrier, the remains of Warren's sea wall.

'I've read about it,' she says, 'about how the coast is eroding, but I had never imagined it this way. So . . . romantic.'

I ask what she means by that.

'It reminds me of Caspar David Friedrich. Maybe because of what you've already told me about it.'

Involuntarily, the image arises of her as an art-loving single girl. Perhaps she even uses the word *unattached*. Perhaps she goes on group tours to ruined cities in Jordan and cloisters in Georgia, exchanges photos and reminiscences on the Internet for a time afterwards, then she's alone again and no one thinks about her anymore.

I tell her about Warren Feldman and how he, when the district council decided not to extend the concrete seawall from Alburgh to Kings Ness, took things into his own hands. He wrote to construction companies and road builders, offering them the opportunity to dump their rubble along his cliff for half the price they would pay elsewhere. In that way he obtained both income and the material he could use to protect Kings Ness against the sea. At the time, fourteen houses were still standing there. During the war there had been twice as many.

Warren Feldman had powerful opponents. The most grief was given him by Natural England. According to their particular conservationist doctrine, the sea was to be given free play on the coast around Alburgh; the huge quantity of fossils that appeared from the cliffs after heavy storms was purportedly a topographical novelty. The cliff was put on the list of SSSIs, Sites of Special Scientific Interest.

'First people, then fossils,' Warren said, and commenced a struggle that would last the rest of his life.

It started with ninety thousand tons of peat from the South Lowestoft Relief Road. That was the basis for his seawall. It had to be spread out along the entire foot of Kings Ness, over a length of almost a kilometer. Trucks carrying sand, clay and stones dumped their loads on the cliff, a dragline pulled the debris from all those building projects out across the seawall and piled it into a grim barrier. Chunks of stone protruded from it, boulders of reinforced concrete, sometimes an old shoe. I remembered Warren up there, on the cliff, overseeing the work on the wall down below. The wind blew tears in his eyes and crumbs from his beard, which served as the archive of many meals. He leaned on his walking stick, a thin raincoat flapping around his upper body – he never bothered to zip it shut. He had a mysterious preference for wearing layers of two or three T-shirts, with two sweaters over that. He never wore anything but outdoor sandals. In the summertime his unusually big toes stuck out of them.

King Knut, they called him, based on a legend that is usually misconstrued. It was long ago that Catherine had told me the story of Knut, who ruled over England and Scandinavia sometime around the eleventh century. It started with the courtiers flattering their king, telling him how all the world would bow to his will.

'The sea as well?' Knut asked.

'The sea as well,' the nobles echoed.

Upon which Knut had his throne carried down to the beach and waited for the tide to come in. The water approached. Knut ordered the sea to withdraw. The water rushed in around his ankles, and again he called on the waves to obey him. The courtiers retreated to safety, and only when Knut was up to his knees in the water did he stand up and wade to the beach. Throwing his crown onto the sand, he said to his followers, 'There is only one King worthy of the name, and that is He whom heaven, earth, and sea obey by eternal laws. Reserve your praise for Him.'

I remember finding that a strange, Christian ending to a story about a Viking king and the sea, but Catherine – serious-minded Catholic that she was – was taken aback by my skepticism.

'If you were my child, oh, oh, oh . . .'

Later I learned that a wading bird, *calidris canutus*, otherwise known as the red knot, takes his name from this same legend.

A couple is walking towards us down the beach. Hand in hand, both wearing orange body warmers. I once walked with someone hand in hand, on Venice Beach, after I had left Kings Ness. I don't know how I would react if Linny would suddenly take my hand, as one of my own sort in search of warmth.

I show her the place where the broken pipes which once led to our house were now sticking out of the cliff. Erosion having continued unabated, we might even be standing where the house once stood. She looks at the surf, you can hear gravel rolling in the undertow.

'So here England disappears foot by foot,' she says.

We walk on and climb Kings Ness from the north. Dull yellow light is filtered in downy spots across the water. On the horizon we can see a mirage, a flat, glistening surface, as though an ice floe were sliding in this direction.

'Oh, yuck,' Linny says when we get to Flint Road.

'Via Dolorosa,' I mumble.

She hops to avoid the dead rabbits and potholes.

'And I cried so hard at the end of *Watership Down*!' she shouts.

After number 17 we leave the road and climb the overgrown path that once led to our house. In my memory it still stands there. I can walk up to the door, open it and smell the furniture wax and cleaning fluids that Margareth keeps in the cupboard beside the back door. It comes as a deep, never-ending surprise to find that things that no longer exist still live on inexorably in my head, and will remain there until the end of days. I understand now, better than ever, why people put up memorials and place inscriptions on benches. Our life's work must not come to dust.

The gorse has stretched its tortured limbs across the path. The little shock at the emptiness along the edge, where memory has placed a house.

'This is where it was,' I say.

'Which number?' she asks.

I don't understand what she means.

'The house number.'

'Fifteen. Over there is where it was. And there' – I point to a spot even further away, across the sea – 'there lay Castrum.'

The bar is quiet that evening. I knock off early. Linny is the only one in the place, except for a man who takes a sip of whiskey and a sip of water by turns.

'Hello there, old night owl,' Leland says.

I sit down beside Linny, the only person in the world now who really knows anything about me. She's drinking a kir cocktail, I eat the cherry. She says, 'I'm leaving tomorrow.'

I nod and realize that Warren's funeral is tomorrow as well. That I'm supposed to play in the church. I don't even know what time.

Later, in the lounge, a bottle of water and a bottle of Chivas Regal within arm's reach, we slip back into our conversation like a hand into warm water. I tell her about Selwyn, who opened my eyes. It was with him that things started.

I'm impressed by his physique and his handsome head of blond hair, he finds me interesting I believe because I am *hors categorie*. We both play in the reserves. In the shower after matches I can hardly take my eyes off him – Michelangelo's David, but then with a bigger cock. During the match, when we're attacking, I tend to stay close to him; by means of sheer force or a fluid sidestep he's always able to force a couple of breaks, it's worthwhile to operate in his wake. A few times I even score after he gets tackled just before the line and passes the ball to me as he falls. Scouts from Bath and Leeds come to see him play, but his parents have forbidden him to take up a professional career; he can play rugby at Oxford or Cambridge as well. It's easy to imagine him studying economics or medicine, rolling right through it and then going on to lead a smooth and easy life. In amazement I see how an

83

even-tempered, friendly person like Selwyn can also be merciless – on the playing field, but also during the hunt. He owns his own rifle, a Mannlicher-Schoenauer with a walnut stock; I've watched him shoot wood pigeons, grey squirrels and magpies without blinking an eye. His ruthlessness contains no rage, not even cruelty – it is as even-keeled as the rest of his personality.

One frosty February morning we go out with a group of hunters, including his father. They're decked with bandoleers, a tractor with a trailer full of hay takes the nine of us from one hunting area on the estate to the other. We comb the woods in search of vermin. That's what they call them. Selwyn blows a grey squirrel to pieces and says that it's an exotic species, a kind that doesn't belong here. I glance over to see if it's a joke, a sly reference to yours truly, but I see nothing of the sort. Norvie, the game warden, says grey squirrels are harmful, they eat the bark from the trees. I can't avoid the feeling that we're more harmful to these animals than they are to us, but I keep such soft thoughts to myself; I will be like them, and laugh loudly at their jokes.

'It's open season for pigeons, rabbits, hares, blackies and deer.'

'Blackies, Norvie?'

'Pakis, wogs . . . I'm no racist, mind you, I just can't stand the blackies.'

I will not bat an eyelid when Selwyn asks me to take a photograph of him with that animal in his hand, the top of its body dangling by a few shreds from the rest. Gun smoke and a lacy mist hover between the trees and sometimes, when we step out into the open field and see on the horizon a row of Scots pine with flattened crowns, it's like being on the savanna – Africa, just before the sun breaks through the clouds.

The tractor takes us to Bunyans Walk, the hill on the coast just north of Kings Ness. The erosion is eating the land away there as it is at our place, but more dramatically, taking heavy old trees down with it. When you look up from the beach you can see the web of roots clutching naked and panicky at the yellow sand.

The forest seems to cringe when we enter. We work our way in a long line through dead brown ferns, break off branches that get in the way. The men shoot at the bends in branches, someone shouts, 'That's no tree, that's a hotel!'

A series of shots follows – loud, dry cracks and an explosion of activity amid the leaves and branches on high. I cover my ears and see Selwyn smile.

'There!' a man screams at the tenth squirrel.

The animal hides on the side of the trunk where we're not. The men circle the tree and keep firing until they hit it. The squirrel is stuck between two branches, its head hanging, blood dripping onto the forest floor. Selwyn's father shoots a jay, someone else kills a woodcock, others magpies and a pair of grey squirrels. We move on in a long row towards the edge of the cliff, a roebuck bursts through our lines. In the surf ahead bobs a heavy tree trunk, the kind you find on the beach sometimes, soaked and heavy as lead, who knows how long it's been floating across the oceans.

We leave Bunyans Walk to the south, moving into the reed flats that separate the hill from Kings Ness. The reeds grow here behind a sort of dyke of sand through which the sea breaks at times. In the pale light of the February sun, the reed stems look like a million strokes of a single-haired brush. A slow, fluid shiver spreads across the flats, an invisible hand petting a cat's back. Here amid the reed is where the barking Chinese water deer, muntjacs, hide, another exotic species. At dusk, when I walk the secret paths through the reeds (I know the hidden thatchers' spots, I know where the poaching goes on), I'm sometimes startled half to death when one of them suddenly goes racing off. I've never actually seen one, but you can hear them splashing away for the longest time. In China they think the muntjac has magic powers, because of its lightning speed.

Selwyn asks if I'd like to shoot some; I don't feel like it much, but I let him hand me the gun. I turn to face the wood's edge, and he points to a crow's nest in an oak tree. I aim and shoot, but hit only branches. Shrugging, I hand the rifle back to him – not cut out for it, see? In the distance, the game warden shouts that we're moving on. We're the last ones to the trailer, where they're smoking and talking about a bachelor party in Amsterdam.

'All you need's a pair of clean shorts and a suitcase full of condoms, hahaha!'

The undisputed highpoint of the trip was when the groom-to-be ate a peeled banana from a Thai cunt. Selwyn's father says they should keep their filthy talk to themselves, there are young people about, but he laughs too loudly for anyone to believe him.

The decisive story, the one in which Selwyn played a role, took place in late winter. It had been foggy for days. Going outside in the morning on my way to school, the wet, gray dampness would seep into my clothes and finally into my head as well. After seeing nothing but diffuse gray for days on end, you start to feel like you've turned into fog yourself. I wrote little notes to myself, things like *We have been in the mist now for six days; whether anything is still alive outside this we do not know.* Sometimes, when you heard a plane flying overhead, you knew the world had not yet come to an end. The sea could not be seen, only the surf could be heard. The window was a blind square, luminescent as a picture screen.

One ash-gray afternoon I was out looking for amber amid the thick gravel on the beach by Bunyans Walk. I could see little more than the stones beneath my feet. The mist was blowing around me in tatters. In the distance I saw a phantom approaching, a tenuous, shivering pillar.

86

Slowly it changed into a human, into Selwyn with the family dog, once they came close enough. But without the friendliness. I had noticed it in the canteen recently as well, something was weighing on him. And it had to do with me. Out of sight now, the German shepherd sniffed and growled.

'Kaiser!' Selwyn shouted.

The dog appeared from the mist. It jumped up against me and left sandy footprints on my trousers and coat.

'So are you going to tell me about it?' I asked.

'What?'

'About what's up.'

He peered into the fog. Then he said I should come to his house at three. I stared at his back until he dissolved.

A little later I climbed the path to Kings Ness. The field to my right had been recently plowed, the soil was gleaming. Further up the fog turned thin and yellowy, above it at last the sun was shining. I heard the jubilant song of a lark, but the pounding in my chest was produced by a sense of impending calamity.

I arrived at three o'clock sharp. Selwyn led me into the TV room. He pointed to a chair. From beneath his jumper he then pulled out a videotape, without the box. He slid the tape into the recorder, the television jumped of its own accord to AV.

'This is what I want to show you,' he said with his back to me. 'My brother came home with it.'

A metallic-sounding jingle, the logo of a film company, warnings concerning the unauthorized screening and reproduction of the material, then the first images. A landscape somewhere in Southeast Asia, the camera panned over a bay by morning, canoes being poled along by standing fishermen in reed hats, then across a beach to the patio of a villa on a green hill. A company of Caucasians, colonial and bored. The camera's eye rested on the individual players. This was where the cast of characters was pointed out, who mattered and who would remain unimportant. It zoomed in on a young woman holding a cigarette between her long fingers. She exhaled a thin stream of smoke. The smoke curled into the title of the film, LILITH, then the letters faded into butterflies and hummingbirds that flew off screen one by one. We were back at the beautiful young woman – in whom by then I had recognized my mother. Or rather, a woman who resembled her to a tee, an extremely young version of her. She was Lilith. I edged up to the TV to get a closer look, but behind me Selwyn had pressed the fast-forward button and events were rushing past at a baffling speed. Men, women, intrigues and searching looks, the villa amid the dark green hills, a swimming pool and a hairy-chested man in a loin-cloth . . .

'Stop the film!' I shrieked.

And there she was again, at the edge of the pool, resting languorously on a divan. I knew that body, it had figured in my erotic fantasies. Now there it was beside a swimming pool in god-knows-where, and that guy with the loincloth was up to something – you could see his cock plainly behind the fabric. She didn't react, only lay there challenging the gods stoically, a pair of large black sunglasses on the bridge of her nose. He said something to her about the temperature of the pool. She said there was nothing wrong with it. Things began picking up a bit after that, when the man said, 'Now that you've gone to bed with Richard . . .'

'Oh, Henry, please. It didn't mean a thing.'

'You're a slut. And you know what we do with sluts.'

'Oh?' the woman said ironically.

He dropped the loincloth, the camera zoomed in on his organ, a big one with thick veins. I looked around in desperation. Selwyn was leaning against the wall, the remote in his hand.

'*What is this?*' I exclaimed.

'What do you think?' he said tersely.

She had her slender fingers around the penis and pulled back the foreskin. Her gaze was ironic as ever. He straddled, oh horror, the divan and pressed his cock to her mouth. It disappeared into it almost completely. Slowly, he fucked her like that. She sniffed and gagged. Spittle was forced from the corner of her mouth. I vomited on the carpet. I clenched my teeth but it shot out my nose and from behind my molars; I held my hand in front of my mouth and ran for the toilet. For a moment the immediacy of vomiting displaced the flashes in my head, the knowledge that it was my mother, *my young mother*, being fucked in the mouth. Something came to a close there, at that moment. Nothing would ever be the same. Because it was her. No doubt about it. Not just the face. The hands. My mother's hands.

I hung over the pot, everything swirled, the world a washer drum. Sweat dripped from my forehead. I remained kneeling there, because I didn't know what else to do. There was nowhere for me to go. I knew of no better place than the toilet floor. The veils had been ripped away, I had seen what had been concealed from my eyes. It wasn't a lie, it was worse than that. I had been blind and deaf, this had been hidden from me behind continually shifting backdrops – new pieces of decor had been slid between me and the truth, again and again. Who knew about this? Had they all been whispering about it behind my back for years?

Selwyn was down on his knees; a tub of steaming water beside him, he was scrubbing the contents of my stomach out of the carpet.

'So it is her,' he said to the carpet.

'Sorry about the mess,' I said.

'You didn't know about it?'

'No.'

'Nothing at all?'

'No.'

The screen behind him was dark. I turned on the TV again. Selwyn stood up.

'What are you doing?'

There she was again, the mother-from-the-girlish-photos, naked now, with a camera's eye between her legs, zooming in on little curls of pubic hair and a pouting cunt in between, nothing I hadn't already seen in hundreds of other pictures – except this was my mother into whom the man was wedging his way.

'Christ, Ludwig, turn that off!'

But I wanted to see what there was to be seen. This was the time and the place for it, another opportunity would not soon present itself. My head in my hands, I watched the stranger mating with my mother, but without the sound on, sound was too much to bear. Selwyn was standing beside the door, nervous, perhaps listening for the sound of his parents coming home. Minuscule drops of sweat on her upper lip, the irony had now made way for an expression of all-consuming pleasure. She had her hands clasped behind his little buttocks and was drawing him in deeper. I ran the tape forward. The events followed each other at a lightning pace. It was about the rivalry between two men, and it involved four women: a lady meant to represent the upper classes; an Asian beauty with little breasts; a blonde, nondescript girl; and then my mother, the star of the film, who emanated a certain unassailability. At the end she was taken by both men at the same time, who seemed in this way to have laid aside their conflict. It was raw, no-holds-barred porno, in garish, heavy color. It was hideous, every erotic tingle was snuffed out by shame and confusion. My heart pounded wildly in my chest. I fast-forwarded to the credits, then hit play. The names rolled down the screen, hers first.

LILITH – EVE LESAGE

I stood up too quickly, a flash of dizziness almost knocked me to the ground. I waited until the snowy interference went away, then walked out of the room without a word to Selwyn. I went outside like a narcotized man – the son of. The earth might open up and swallow me, I would be grateful. Eve LeSage. Marthe Unger. Porn star. My history was in need of rewriting. All my life I had been walking down the street with a bell around my neck. I bore the brand of shame. The rumors would seep through the walls like moisture, they would whisper behind my back, the suffering would have a name.

A watery sun shone through the grey vapors, the weather was clearing up quickly now. Silver stripes pulsed on the sea's surface. In the distance, further than I had been able to see for days, a lonely white wave rose up; for a long time I had been hoping to see a whale, I longed for those great souls of the sea who spoke their mysterious sonar language under water.

At home I went up to my room and sat down at the desk. I couldn't imagine a life beyond that moment. Every once in a while I was caught by an unexpected fit of retching, eruptions of slime and gall. I kept the wastebasket close at hand. I could have taken my diary and scratched out my feelings in letters of blood; instead I closed the curtains, lay down on the bed and fell asleep.

The next morning the sun had returned, the weather was blustery. Before my window, gulls fought their way into the wind. They hung above the edge of the cliff, great black-backed gulls, and continued to flap their wings stoically, even when being blown backwards.

I hurried out the door and stayed away all day. For some time, I don't believe my mother even noticed that I was avoiding her. I slept a great deal. I slept my way through the shock. I looked up Eve LeSage on the Internet. There was plenty to be found. She had acted out her roles alongside Linda Lovelace and Sylvia Kristel, for a time she had been a cult figure. *Lilith* was viewed as *artistic* in its day. She had played in six films. *Lilith* was the very first, and it made her a star. I found photographs and interviews; websites where her memory was kept alive – she had suddenly left the sex industry behind, various rumors circulated on the web about the reason why.

One evening I was sitting with her at the table. We were eating jacket potatoes with crème fraiche, beans and chili sauce; I sculpted a landscape of snow and blood in my gouged potato. I could hear her chewing. Swallowing each bite. Her cutlery scraped across my nerves. This time, when she looked up, I didn't lower my eyes.

'Is it possible that something's bothering you?' she asked.

I shrugged.

'Ludwig?'

'Yes?'

'Is something wrong?'

'Something wrong. Does the name Eve LeSage mean anything to you?'

She raised the fork to her mouth and chewed slowly, cautiously. She nodded almost indiscernibly.

'It had to happen sometime,' she said.

Silence followed.

'I didn't know whether I should let you find out yourself,' she said, 'or whether I should tell you about it.'

So you just did nothing.

'I was grateful for every day you didn't know.'

I slid my potato to one side.

'It's so . . . *filthy* . . . I've never seen anything so *filthy* in my life.'

'I'm really sorry,' she said '. . . for you. You're the one I feel sorry for. For you, I wish it hadn't . . . that it could have gone differently. That I could have spared you this.'

'Too late.'

'Too late, that's right. I tried to keep it from you. I've always dreaded this moment. Later, someday, I'll tell you how . . . how it went. If you

92

want to know. There's more to it than you see right now. Than you *can* see. My life, back then, it made sense. I don't know how to say it . . .'

'Six films. *Six.*'

'It wasn't a crime, Ludwig.'

'Prostitution is illegal.'

'They were films. I'm not proud of it, not at all, but I've never regretted it terribly either. I can imagine . . . for you it's different, it doesn't have anything to do with you. You weren't even . . .'

'How could you?'

'I'm not my body, Ludwig, it's just a vehicle . . . I didn't hurt anyone, on the contrary. Except for you, now. But you weren't even around then, you can blame me for it but you mustn't hate me for it, sweetheart. Okay? You mustn't hate me for it.'

I had no words left. Not one.

'Ludwig, would you please not look at me that way? Your father used to look at me that way. So . . . full of disgust.'

Two tears, the one beginning its descent before the other.

'I don't want you to look at me that way, do you understand?'

In the days that followed the subject came up a few times. She didn't ask for understanding, she explained the circumstances under which it had seemed more or less normal to her to act in porno films. I noticed that knowing about the background to it watered down my rage. It reduced the distance between me and that gross blunder. In other words, life went on. It sought a balance between extremes, and kept on doing so until a certain degree of everydayness returned, a way to go on. It wrapped itself around the alien irritant like an amoeba around a bacteria.

At the club, they already knew about it. I was sure they talked about it when I wasn't around. Sly jokes were made on occasion, but I learned to live with it. A well-known saying has it that football is a gentlemen's game played by thugs, while rugby is a thug's game played by gentlemen. Among footballers I would have suffered social damage, but at the Alburgh Rugby Football Club I was given consideration, and not condemned – something I have always credited to the degree of refinement that goes along with rugby.

On the field I became more reckless. The technically perfect tackle is one thing I never mastered, so I simply threw everything I had at my opponent, sometimes with surprising results. I played in the second row and was injured as often as I was not. One recovers quickly at that age. While making one of those insane tackles, I broke my collarbone. They said the boy I hit came from Sizewell, home to the nuclear power station whose dome we could see on the horizon on clear days, like a pale, setting sun. It felt like smacking into a bus. The boy could not have been older than seventeen, but he already had a bushy moustache. An injury bears the signature of the one who caused it – for the rest of my born days, I will never forget that boy from Sizewell.

The English have a useful expression: 'adding insult to injury'.

A letter arrived at our house from the district council, signed by the local secretary, A. Brennan. In it we were summoned to leave 15 Flint Road before 21 October. If we left within the time allotted, the council would see to the razing of the house, the removal of the debris and the cleaning of the plot. If we did not comply, the damages – including the cleaning of the beach below – would be recouped from us. If asbestos had been used in the house, the damages could be even more considerable. The tone of the letter was bland, as though we were being asked to no longer put our rubbish out for collection on Tuesday, but on Wednesday. The date, 21 October, was repeated in the final paragraph; on that day, gas, water and electricity would be cut off.

We had landed in the danger zone, there was no denying it. All those years the abyss had been stalking us in a slow, creepy dream, now it was about to pounce.

The day the letter arrived, the outside eastern wall of the house was still four meters from the edge. It could take years, but it could also happen that same winter. My mother was at the table, the letter in front of her.

'They don't waste any time,' she said.

I read the letter twice and found no reassurance in it anywhere, nothing about replacement housing or compensation. We were caught between erosion on one side and official pragmatism on the other. My mother was sitting straight up in her chair. The memory of her, copulating.

'What about the insurance?' I asked.

She smiled grimly and shook her head.

'What do you mean?' I asked.

'Nothing.'

'Come on.'

'You can't insure yourself against things like this. I tried everywhere, almost every insurance company there is. Their argument was that we were aware of the risk when we moved in. We . . . I . . . accepted the risk.'

'So what now?'

No reply came. I more or less understood what was looming over us: no house and no escape route either; family and friends were nonexistent. We were consigned to each other. She had bought this house with the proceeds from the house in Alexandria; we had been living off the remainder, and off her savings. Now her investment was crumbling quickly. The letter from the district council reduced the value of our property to a debt. I wasn't sure she really saw the extent of the catastrophe. Her composure was outrageous. In the privacy of her bedroom, I suspected, she turned to her mentors for support; the bearded men with piercing eyes to whom she went for counsel. She was convinced that there was a higher plan behind everything. Events like this were learning moments. The assignment of meaning, favorable or not, provided comfort. The bitterest reality could be borne as long as you saw meaning in it. The primeval defense against the void. Her conviction had nothing to do with God, she said, but if you looked carefully you could make out his shadow on the floor.

I went upstairs and kicked my desk. Framed by my window was a kite, veering wildly. Behind it the glistening sea.

That evening I shoveled Margareth's fish pasties into my mouth in huge chunks.

'I've been thinking, Ludwig . . .'

'Hmm . . .'

'. . . but we're not leaving. We're staying here. This is our house, and they can't force us.'

I frowned in puzzlement.

'Without gas? Water? Light?'

'I showed the letter to Warren. He says it would be no trouble putting in a few pipes and cables between his house and ours. And we can buy bottled gas in the village. See it as a sort of camping. Warren will give us all the help we need.'

'Yeah, because he feels guilty.'

It was around that same time that the first layer of sand and clay was dumped along the base of the cliff below our house. Pending the verdict of the court of appeals, Warren had resumed work. From the day the letters began arriving, we lived in limbo. There were letters from lawyers, from the power company, the waterworks, municipal summons – my mother used a clothes-peg to clamp them to the lamp above the table, thereby giving fate a festive touch.

It often takes a long time, but once the powers-that-be bundle their rays into a searchlight there is no escape. The linkage of information is a steel fence that slowly closes in. An all-encompassing authority, impersonal as a chemical process, had nestled in our life. The date was written on our lintel. The day would come – and distant as it seemed when the first letter came, just as quickly did 21 October arrive. It was a Saturday, however, so nothing happened. But on the very next working day the flame died in the geyser. The heating went off. A few weeks later, a van from Eastern Electricity pulled up and parked along the road. Then the lights were gone too. Water no longer rattled in the pipes. Warren dug a trench to our house. Switches and wall plugs suddenly became useless ornaments, the telephone stopped working. Within a few days Warren had seen to all these things, a strip of churned-up soil bound his house to ours. My bedroom window was now permanently misted over because of the paraffin stove I used to heat the room. Margareth cooked with bottle gas. But no matter how skillfully our lives skirted these obstacles, we were aware that – however you looked at it – these were the *final days*. That lent them a certain beauty and significance. Time possessed a degree of urgency for which I would later search in vain.

There were three storms that winter, none of them with the force of the legends of 1286, 1342, 1740 or 1953. Warren's seawall was battered away at a few spots, it was only below our house that a piece of the cliff was actually lost. A severe chasm now extended inland. Grass sods hung over its edge. Things were starting to get *personal*. Whenever the water struck, when the shivers rang through the house, we sat bolt upright. Then the silence drifted in like the fog.

At the end of that next spring I finished secondary school. I was eighteen, older than most of the pupils in my class because of the year I'd missed after Alexandria. Despite the urging of my tutor and the headmaster, I refused to consider university. As I walked out the door of the latter's office, he said to me, 'You have a good mind, Ludwig, it would be a pity not to use it well.'

I played piano at the Whaler and earned a lot of money for a boy my age. I was one of the first to buy a cell phone, and I had a computer in my bedroom. For the rest, I played rugby. Whenever I put in my mouth guard the sand would crunch between my teeth; lying in my bed at night, after the match, the grains of sand grated beneath my eyelids. I enjoyed the armor of aching muscles that girded me up for days after a match, the satisfied frisson of the body sorely tested. Someday, far in the future, you'd pass a rugby field and feel the painful yearning for Vaseline on your eyebrows, sports tape around your vulnerable spots, the pre-match nerves in stomach and fingertips that caused even the best, most experienced players to pop off again to the loo beforehand – and you would ask yourself how in heaven's name you had ever become locked up inside that old body, and when you saw the bodies out there smacking together and scrambling back to their feet as though they had merely tripped, you would shut your eyes.

My mother and I live together in elegant separation. There is no reason to go into things any deeper. Sometimes I am able to see her the way I used to; that is to say, without the things I know now. The fact that things are ambiguous, not clear-cut, has been peppered into me. My mother has led so many lives already, her life with me was merely one manifestation. That makes you unsure of yourself. You can imagine suddenly being all alone, all the rest falling from you like wilted leaves, the skin of an onion.

It is our last summer on the hill. I have been excused from the assignment of having to belong anywhere; my mother's past has everything to do with that. Now I am a freak, and therefore free. I could walk around naked, my skin no longer a shield against heat or cold but a permeable membrane – my body glides through the mild outdoor air like a paraglider above fields of corn. Along the wooded banks, trees stand like congealed forest fires, the dust of Flint Road covers my shoes. Even though I'm amid the lush nature of Essex, the cedar-like crowns of the Scots pine in the distance still remind me of Africa, my image of the savanna, a sensation so powerful that I can let it roll on for minutes at a time. The farmer's binder has been shuffling back and forth across the fields for days, spitting out black bales of straw. The undeveloped plots between the road and the cliff's edge are choked with head-high thistles, tansy, poppies big as a fist and daisies radiant in their simplicity. Butterflies waver above the polyphonic buzz of a field of flowers. The telephone poles along the road breathe creosote vapors, sparrows and sand martins sitting on the wires like notes on a staff. The borders at Warren and Catherine's are exploding with voluptuous blue hydrangeas and then, suddenly, seen from the corner of my eye, the sparrows fall from the lines as one and dissolve into the mulberry hedges at the side of the road.

That winter our house was lost. At last, I would add from this vantage. A storm just before Christmas put an end to the wall, granting the second flood tide free access to the cliff. Warren never got the chance to fill up the lost earth; those were the first weeks of the new year, weeks during which almost no building was going on and no rubble was available.

Factors, circumstances.

When the forecasts began speaking again of bad weather, Warren appeared at the door with a face like iron.

'I need to talk to your mother,' he said.

I traipsed upstairs like a little boy and tried to listen in, but by the time they reached my ears the words had become unintelligible. Once he had left, I asked, rather casually, 'So what's the news?'

'Oh,' she said. 'Warren thinks . . . the forecasts are bad. He's afraid, I mean, he thinks this might be the end.'

But still. The weight. The irreversible. It hasn't made itself known, it was simply waiting for you all that time in the dark.

'What are you thinking, love?'

I blinked back tears and said from the doorway, 'I'm going to pack my things.'

What a house means. The walls around a cavity. It means inside, it protects you against the outside. Now inside was about to become outside. The roof would be ripped open, the dark sky would force its way in, the cold, black sea. I looked around my room, pondering over what should be taken and what not. There was no plan, no destination; the best thing was to pack as lightly as possible. I had a brown cardboard suitcase, found along the street, with stickers from a Rhine cruiser and the Lorelei. Two pairs of trousers, shirts, underwear, a bound-up packet of letters and postcards. For the rest, those valuables I thought I could probably hock should life turn against me: mother-of-pearl cufflinks, the automatic Tissot watch that had belonged to my great-grandfather, Friedrich Unger. (He, Friedrich Unger, had crossed the border from Ostfriesland to east Groningen province to marry a Dutch girl, Aleida Wanningen – ancestors immortalized in photographs in which time seemed recalcitrant and stiff, you couldn't imagine people laughing out loud or cheating on their spouses. My mother got her beauty from Aleida; even the fashion of that day and the sepia print couldn't hide her regular, noble features. Friedrich and Aleida's son, Wilhelm Unger, known as Willem, was the father of my mother and Aunt Edith. I had never seen my grandparents; my grandmother died early on of heart problems, my grandfather had turned his back on my mother after *Lilith*. As far as my mother knew, he still lived with his second wife in the brick colossus close to Bourtange, the farm I knew from pictures in which my mother wore cotton dresses and walked barefoot through the dust of dry summers. When we were in Holland, the stopping-off place between Alexandria and here, he had refused to see us. That's what his second wife, Aunt Wichie, said; he himself refused to come to the phone. At the time I had noticed nothing of that, that I had a grandfather not so far away.)

I took along some sheet music and three books, *Moby Dick* (my loveliest book), *The Painted Bird* by Jerzy Kosinski (from my mother's bookcase, the promise of grown-up literature) and *A History of Western Philosophy* by Bertrand Russell; still unread, but impressive after our English teacher, Mr. Dowd, told us that Russell had written the book during a passage by steamer to the United States, from memory, almost without reference works.

A quiet knock on the door, my mother. Her arms folded across her chest, she leaned against the doorpost. I asked what she wanted.

'There's a truck coming the day after tomorrow,' she said.

I looked around, the posters on the walls, the computer, the metal bed, the cupboard that listed to the right because it was not screwed together well.

'That's what I want to keep,' I said, pointing to the things on the bed.

The howling of the wind, only the beginning.

'It's just a forecast,' she said.

'Dream on.'

'We do have to be prepared,' she admitted, 'you're right.'

We talked about the end, my mother and I. It was our best conversation in a long while. We were not melancholy or dramatic, those were moods that had gone before; in the cold light of the fait accompli, the evacuation and the loss seemed easier to bear.

'And afterwards?' I asked.

'When this is gone, you mean?'

She nodded at the window, outside which the chasm had approached to within a single bound.

'There has to be something then,' I said.

'I have faith that something will come along.'

Faith was her secret charm, the abracadabra of holistic magic. For a moment there was the wrenching feeling of irritation, but I let it pass. She said, 'I can always get work cleaning houses, or . . .'

'Or at a roadside garage, then we'll be white trash and we can live in a mobile home along the highway! And we'll drive around in a van full of junk and neglect our teeth, okay?'

She laughed. The tinkling sound of ice cubes in a glass.

'So, the day after tomorrow.'

She nodded and said, still in the doorway, 'We have to be strong, okay, sweetheart?'

'Strong . . .'

'You already are, you always have been. I don't know anyone else like you, Ludwig. In fact, you don't really need anyone anymore.'

Gently, I pushed the door closed behind her.

Sometimes the final notes of a song will go nagging on in my mind. For hours, until a new melody arrives to replace the old one. The same happens to me sometimes with the final words before a silence. They nestle in my head and echo there for a long time. A mysterious, internal repetition. That evening it was my mother's voice. *In fact, you don't really need anyone anymore.* Later, as I was playing the piano as well: *In fact, you don't really need anyone anymore.* It summoned up an entire world view. The crowning element in personal development was to not need anyone, to be alone, a mote in the darkness. The final consequence of this view of life, of course, was that she didn't need me either, anymore.

On my way home I noticed that the wind had picked up. The foam on the surf glowed in the moonlight. The waves were already washing up against the sea wall, but still lacked the force to do it any harm. But it would swell, gather momentum, bubbling and hissing, to strike at our Achilles' heel. I would sleep poorly in my bed beside the chasm.

Movers arrived. She pointed out the things to them. That needs to go with, that one doesn't, careful with that lamp, you're going to dent the copper if you do that. I remembered the house on the Rue Mahmoud Abou El Ela, the faded negatives of cupboards and tapestries on its walls after the dismemberment, and felt the brief stab of loss when I thought about the treasure buried in the Eden of roses, bougainvillea and blue-blossoming jacaranda.

There were three of them. The driver was the boss. He shook his head as he worked.

'I can have them bring a bigger lorry,' he said a few times.

They wound their way amid the ten thousand things, an elephant ballet. Outside the wind mocked our efforts. The mover drove back and forth twice between our house and Warren and Catherine's shed, where we could store our things until further notice. A double row of moving boxes was piled up against the back wall, full of objects swaddled in soft tissue paper, starting in on their period of waiting in the dark.

★

The walls shuddered. So close, you could see the waves from the window. The gray masses of water being pressed up along the cliff and shooting three, four meters in the air, to the top of the roof, where they seemed to pause for one brief, ghastly moment in order to eye us, their prey, before collapsing back into the sea. The end game. The whirlwind of snippets in my head, the age-old questions: where are we going to live? Who will take care of us? An all-embracing *what now?* But I also knew I would be disappointed if it didn't happen now – I was tired of dawdling, of pacing the waiting room until the doctor returned with the verdict. Downstairs I heard the vacuum cleaner, my mother trying to undo at least a little of the ravages the movers had left behind. The state in which she left the house behind, I realized, would determine her memories of it. The arrangement and cleansing of that which is doomed to perish is a crucial act, a paradoxical expression of how to live.

A premature brand of disaster tourism had begun. Heads popped up from behind the bushes to observe our evacuation. It was impossible for them to get any closer to the house without standing right at the window, so they watched from a distance, sometimes with binoculars. We were *the house that wouldn't last long now*, we were *the sea reclaims its own* and we were also, as the headline in the *Norwich Evening News* put it: CASTRUM'S LAST HEROES. One caption read that this, it was rumored, was the house where former porno star Eve LeSage lived with her son. By the time the *Sun* latched onto the juicy story – SEX GODDESS LOSES HEARTH AND HOME – we were no longer available for comment; they had to use old pictures along with their story, my mother on her back with Wills Horn on top. A team picture from the year our second XV won the championship. In it, I am kneeling at the front, my arms resting on one knee. A circle has been drawn around my head. Selwyn is standing behind me, his arms crossed, beside him you see Leland wearing his scrumcap. Bailey and Dalrymple have just burst out laughing – it's a cheerful photograph. I had no idea who had been accommodating enough to pass it along to the paper.

In the same way my mother did her vacuuming, so I performed my duties that evening in the Whaler. I played as though the sand were not being washed away from beneath our house at that very moment, I sang as though no block of basalt lay on my heart.

'It's gonna happen now, isn't it?' Leland said when I took a little pause between sets.

There was no stopping Miss Julie Henry. Her empathy went beyond the bounds of decency; I could picture her deflowering me in the walk-in cooler. Leland asked where I was going to sleep. First at Warren and Catherine's, I said, we would spend the night there, after that we weren't sure.

The hotel was busy, a crowd had been drawn by the spectacle of the storm, the waves shooting up meters above the jetties. I took off earlier than usual and ran to Kings Ness. The tempest had now thickened to more substantial stuff, I had difficulty making headway. Torrents of rain. Salty globs of foam were being blown across the land, grains of sand and grass and leaves lashed me about the ears. The sky was open and clear. Over there the dark contours of the house. I stormed into Warren and Catherine's. The three of them were sitting around the lamp.

'It's still there!' I shouted.

As though something had fallen to the floor and shattered.

'Take your shoes off,' Catherine said.

I slid up to the table.

'Your shoes!' Warren said.

I went back to the dark vestibule and kicked them off. A glass was waiting for me, the windows rattled in their frames. The substance in my glass was pungent and brought tears to my eyes – I had learned to drink beer in rugby canteens, but whisky was new to me. A hard and unrelenting master. I couldn't quite get a hold on the mood around the table, I was locked out of the circle.

'We've been talking about it, Ludwig,' my mother said. 'Warren and Catherine have offered to let you stay here for a while until things are a bit clearer.'

I didn't say a word. I waited.

'I'm leaving for London early tomorrow morning,' she went on. 'I don't know exactly how it will work out, I want to talk to some other lawyers. Warren agrees that this is a case that might go all the way to the European Court of Justice. Because it's about – a kind of protection. How did it go again, Warren? The right to defend your home? A basic human right, that's what you said, wasn't it?'

I was too excited to pay attention. I asked Warren for a torch; he handed me a Maglite heavy enough to brain a cow. The light blazed a trail for me through the bushes. I moved towards the edge and stopped about ten meters from it. The waves were slamming against the cliff with the dull, punishing blows of a heavyweight. A haunted house, lonesome and forlorn. It made you feel the kind of pity you might feel for a mistreated pony. My eyes fixed on the darkened house, I ducked down in the bushes to get out of the wind and bid welcome to my memories. It was cold, so I crouched down further. Hissing fountains came rocketing up from the depths. Scuds of rain were whipping down on me. It must have been past midnight, I had visions of our house as a ship, of the listing and the floating away, of how it would forget us on its journey.

Then a voice, my name. LUD-WIG! I stood up. Stinging needles in my flesh as the blood started flowing again. A beam of light close by, Warren, his spectacles dotted with rain. He screamed, 'WHAT ARE YOU DOING?'

He stood there for a moment, looking, shouted *CAREFUL!* and moved back towards the house, shoulders hunched up around his ears. Waves broke over the edge, white shapes scaled the cliff like enemy soldiers. Foam flew through the cone of light from the streetlamp. I couldn't take my eyes off the water's rise and fall, the towers collapsing one by one. Even if the house survived this, its eastern wall would be badly damaged, the water must be in the front room already. Sometimes I thought I detected motion, the shiver that came before the collapse into the depths – an illusion. The house was still standing, perhaps it would be spared! A twinge of absurd hope. I ran and screamed at the wind, the sky – I was the loneliest, oh joy, the loneliest of all! I danced like a demon in the beating rain. A noise made me stop, I pointed the torch at the house. The groaning of a nocturnal animal, an inexpressible pain. With amazing lightness the house spun low on its axis and slid moaning, screeching, into the chasm. The music of my nightmares. A sound like an underground explosion – then it was over. I stared agape at the void where the house had been standing just a moment earlier. I had never experienced such lucidity. A chosen one. At this very moment, even as I had the thought, things were going as they had always gone on, first a house, then no house – true erosion wasn't about losing a house but about time; I had seen time in action, the being, the not-being, the glorious indifference. I fell to my knees and clawed at the earth, let it run through my fingers like a farmer. Cold rains washed over me, on the back of a whale I traveled to the ends of the earth, nothing remained hidden to my eyes.

That was how I'd always imagined it, the slow-motion image of a house sinking into the depths, like the opening up of the earth's crust, but that was not how it was. It tilted and disappeared into the turbulence below. Strangely enough, the version I actually saw never supplanted the imaginary version. Even now they exist side by side in my head, they are both equally real. Sometimes I have to tell myself *oh no, that's not how it went.*

I stayed with Warren and Catherine for two weeks, and it drove me crazy. I was brimming over with destructive energy. There wasn't enough room for me under one roof with two old people. I moved in with Cameron Fitzpatrick, a boy from my team. He had a flat of his own above Webster's greengrocer's. It was a little place. During the daytime I rolled up my sleeping bag and stowed the mattress in the cupboard. I remember cigarette butts everywhere and the exhausted furnishings from the second-hand shop. Cameron's father had disappeared from sight, his mother couldn't handle him anymore. He had been to a few boarding schools. Rugby sort of helped to keep him in line. Now he worked in the stockroom at Fraser's. He was lost. A boy who would only make it with a lot of good luck, which he didn't have. Cameron had once smoked a joint on the steeple of St. George's. God knows how he got up there. He talked about it to anyone who would listen. He lacked the class to keep quiet about things like that.

I tried to let things run their normal course, but things got in the way. The article appeared in the *Sun*, with that disgusting picture of my mother and the one of my team. In which I played piano in that *respectable hotel on Alburgh's quaint market square.* You'd be surprised how many well-heeled people read that rag. I became that boy with *some kind of problem.* The moles had dug deeply, their burrowing had even unearthed Bodo Schultz. They wrote horrible things about him, horrible in the sense that they might have been true. About his destructive art, the riots it provoked. I bore the dubious patina of fame, my origins were a myth. I tried to be unyielding and distant. I thought about my mother's words, the sentence branded on my skin: *In fact, you don't really need anyone anymore.* The evil spell that pushed my life in a certain direction. The future looms up before me like the mouth of a smooth metal tube, nothing to grab hold of: I slide, I fall, nothing sticks to me, just as I stick to nothing. My fingers glide across the keys, a Chopin nocturne in G-minor, opus 15-3, I nod politely at the quiet applause. I am a good little monkey.

My mother took a room at the Belfort in London. I called her once a week. I couldn't quite pin down what she was doing there. When we spoke she put on her long-distance voice, the voice of people who aren't alone in the room. A claim was being prepared, she said, she had a lot of confidence in the new lawyers. And she had to go to Holland for the reading of a will, but she didn't say whose. She was behind her veil and she wasn't coming out. I had the feeling that the house was the rind that had held us together, and that now we had fallen apart into two clean halves. I was worried. I couldn't imagine her alone in the world, doing everyday things, I had experienced so little of her dealings with anyone other than me.

Twice a week I ate at the house of Selwyn's parents, Paula and Ashley Loyd. Selwyn had indeed gone off to study medicine at Cambridge, he came home with stories about nightly scrambles across the slate roofs of the city. About vomiting in the dean's front garden. He played rugby for the university's first team, and punted on the Cam with stunning girls. His life had taken on an infectious dynamism.

It was with a feeling of relief that I left Cameron's perspective-free cubicle on those evenings to dine with Paula and Ashley. They didn't make me feel like they were doing me a favor, they enjoyed having company now that their children had all left home. They asked no prying questions and would never blame you for something you couldn't do anything about. When we watched TV I could see the old barf spot on the carpet.

Paula had something carelessly aristocratic about her. She wouldn't have been caught dead wearing a crazy hat at Ascot, but carrying a butterfly net in the jungles of Belize was perhaps a different matter. Ashley was a slyly humorous, good-natured man, a man with see-through, innocent secrets. A general practitioner, he was preparing for retirement by fixing up old furniture in the garage. Hunting was his real passion. He always asked whether I wanted to take a nice piece of venison, a haunch home with me. *A leg of hare, perhaps?* Sometimes Cameron and I, when we were stoned at night and had the munchies, would fry up the contents of the package I took with me and attack it with blunt cutlery.

I took the train to London. She picked me up at Liverpool Street Station. She laughed a lot, people looked at her. We walked down the street side by side, sometimes she took my arm. We were going to have a nice day together, she had decided that already. She talked a mile a minute about her plans, the progress in the court case. There was no way you could tell we were tragic, not by looking at us. We ate pastries at a tearoom and looked at ships on the river of lead. She wore elegant little white shoes, when we left the tearoom she tossed her mantilla around her shoulders. She held the key to the city. It confused me; after burying herself alive all those years on the coast she now moved along as though the streets were supposed to bend to her will.

'And what about you, Ludwig? she asked during lunch. 'Tell

me, how are you getting along there with your friend . . .'

'Cameron.'

'Cameron, I don't believe I know him, do I?'

It was a senseless question, she didn't know any of my friends, the people I went around with. I told her about the graciousness of Paula and Ashley Loyd. That I sometimes went to visit Warren and Catherine and, irrational as it might seem, to see whether the house was still there, whether I hadn't awakened from a dream to find that everything had remained unchanged.

She turned her head away when I told her that I had seen two bulldozers on the beach after the storm, scraping together the debris and dumping it into the bed of a truck. The remains of the house were skimpier than you would have thought. A chimney with chunks of wall attached to it, a large, broken sheet of concrete. Sections of walls, roofing tiles. Shards. Wreckage. I had watched from up on the cliff, and it felt as though I were the one being swept together down there, a ragbag that would never again be whole. No trace of our possessions – tribute, carried off by the hostile army. I stood up there watching the bulldozers' dance and, in almost mystic fashion, knew myself to be a part of history; in exactly the same way I stood there, with the now innocently cooing surf in the distance, countless others before me had let the destruction of their lives sink in and weighed their possibilities.

That same evening I took the train back home. It got dark early, I bought a single to Darsham. The fact that I had taken a single to London that morning had apparently escaped her. I had assumed that I would spend the night in the city, but her buoyant *I'll just walk you back to the station* had set a different scenario in motion.

As the train bored its way through the darkness, I knew that I hadn't got through to her. I looked at my reflection in the window, a boy closer to tears than to laughter.

I left a note for Cameron, thanking him for his hospitality and explaining that I had found a room of my own. We would see each other at the club. The little apartment I moved into was beside the Readers' Room, on the esplanade. It was usually vacant in winter, so I could rent it for two months before the season began. My clothes were permeated with the caustic smell of smoke, and I was glad to be able to leave that hopeless mess behind. I was my own master now, and things were in the offing. It wouldn't be long before I would hand over to Julie Henry that which she wanted so badly. Her sexual aggression repelled and excited me. The difference in our ages was considerable, and then there was also the imbalance of power; factors charged with eroticism. There had been moments when things could have happened. A hotel consists of many spaces perfectly outfitted for love. One time, when I passed her in the kitchen between two stainless-steel counters, she positioned herself so that I couldn't get by.

'Sorry, Miss Henry,' I mumbled, and squeezed past.

Her body, its imprint glowed against mine as though we were naked. For the first time I was exposed to the sexual appetite of the female of the species, and realized that it essentially differed little from that of the male. That was a lesson I would remember. The moments after work, the staff sitting together in the bar, tired and satisfied; the collective fatigue lent the alcohol added wallop. Julie Henry remained commandingly close, and I didn't quite know how to deal with it. Drunkenness seemed a safe enough strategy, it was like handing over the tiller to a more experienced pilot than yourself. This, all this, was nothing but a misunderstanding. That misunderstanding continued out on the street, where I waited for Julie Henry after she had closed the bar and the night clerk had locked the glass door. After asking where I lived, she said, 'Then that's where we're going.'

Her heels clicked down the hollow street, clenched together inside me were the cold and warm hands of fear and excitement. There was a glistening at sea and the lights of ships in the distance. The trembling of my hands was something I noticed only after having bounced the key off the sides of the lock a few times. She stepped into the hallway behind me and closed the door. Then she pushed me against the wall and kissed me. Concerning the rest I can say that I was not coerced into making any decisions. Her body was a command.

Next morning she was gone, and that seemed to apply to what had happened as well: the body bears no memories of lovemaking, there is only the river racing between the darkened banks. But one walks down the street like a different person, the world has revealed to you a few of its secrets, you alone know what that smile means.

Worth recounting perhaps is that, that evening in the Whaler, I thought I needed to act like a lover – as though required to publicly account for what had happened. That Ludwig Unger had lost his virginity to Miss Julie Henry. Hear ye! Hear ye!

'Act a bit fucking normal, Ludwig!' whispered the woman whose anus had shortly before been suspended above my face.

It was all very confusing.

I phoned my mother at the only number I had for her, the Belfort in London. The receptionist said she had checked out a few days ago.

'You must be mistaken,' I said.

'I'm sorry, sir, but Mrs. Unger is no longer a guest at this hotel.'

I hung up. The helpless feeling, as though a loved one were on their deathbed on another continent and would die before you could get there. Disgust at the prima donna facet of her character, the irresponsible whims, the way she took for granted that the world would forgive her her fickleness; the way she acted like a little girl.

'A bit irresponsible at that, yes,' Paula Loyd ventured.

Ashley was humming. I looked at the cell phone in my hand, the screen that had stayed black for days.

'What will you do now? Wait till she calls?' Paula asked.

'I don't even know if she still has my number.'

'Would you like to take a cut of something or other along with?' Ashley asked.

'I can't remember her ever calling me at this number.'

'I'm sure she'll be in contact soon. Maybe she'll try to phone here, or to the Feldmans. She'll always be able to find you. As a mother, believe me.'

I was ashamed of these things, around the Loyds, the impression of coming from a poor social environment. But the need for comfort, for reassurance, was stronger.

Yet another day. In principle, nothing special about it, like so many other days it disappears beneath your feet like a treadmill. It assumes meaning only later on, when you think back on it in the knowledge: that was the last day.

It starts in the dressing room, where Samuel Titterington says, 'Did I tell you lot that I swallowed a 5p piece last night?'

And then the rumor that John Davies, our club Negro, had fucked Harriet Tooke in a beach cabin. John remains silent, smiling beatifically. We're playing against the second XV from Lowestoft & Yarmouth. A low, cold sun is shining on the grass. I'm flanker, a nice position, you hang at the edge of the scrum so that you're the first one off when the ball is scrummaged. There's always a great struggle amid the forwards, it's physical and aggressive. Bodies, shoulder. I pick up the ball from a ruck and charge a hedge of opponents – sometimes the wall gives, sometimes it doesn't. Then you're knocked to the ground with six or seven men on top and every last bit of air knocked out of your lungs, this is the end, the grass against your lips, flesh and swathes of sport tape in your field of vision – they don't notice! Not enough air to scream for them to get off you!

So you drown in that sea of bodies.

A little later you're walking around again in a daze, you're still there, they rolled that oxcart off your chest and you sucked up oxygen like it was medicine. The relief at finding that everything still continues for the moment, the chalk on your knuckles and the wind from the sea that blows the last brown leaves across the grass.

A little later I was smacked in the eyebrow. Blood ran down beside my eye, a rip.

'Wipe it off,' Leland said.

If I didn't the game would be stopped for a blood bin. We'd already run through all our substitutes. It was a hard match, but we won easily. Everyone did what he had to do, we played strongly, plainly. In the showers the elation, the flushed bodies covered in abrasions and bumps, flattered by the steam rising up from the cold floor.

'I think it's going to need two stitches,' Ashley Loyd said.

He'd been watching the match from the sidelines. In the fading light outside the canteen, he looked at my eyebrow. Then he went in and rummaged about in the silver-colored first aid kit behind the bar, until he found a packet with needle and thread that was still intact. He grumbled about how we needed to replenish the kit. In the beer closet, beneath the light of a bare bulb, he peered at my brow.

'Jungle medicine,' he mumbled.

And, a moment later, 'This will sting a bit.'

The long, calm glide of the needle through my skin, the doctor is a god making me whole again. Outside the door people were shouting orders to the barman, rashers hissed in the pan. From the little kitchen,

Mrs. Packton shouted *I'm not a bloody magician, you know!* And just as I was retrieving my wallet and cellular from the crate of valuables, the phone went. A long, foreign number. My heart leapt. I answered it.

'Hello?'

'Ludwig? This is Mama. Where are you? What a horrible noise.'

I walked outside, her confusion in my ear.

'Ludwig? Are you there?'

'Where are you?' I asked once I was outside the canteen.

She laughed.

'It's so nice to hear your voice, sweetheart.'

'Where are you?'

'In America, California, I'm in Los Angeles! What time is it there? Here it's . . .'

'What are you doing there?'

'Do you know Rollo Liban? Haven't I ever told you about him? Rollo's an old friend, a good friend, he invited me to come here.'

'You haven't been in touch for more than a month.'

'You can't imagine how busy I've been!'

'You're in America . . .'

Her giggle.

'At a hotel on the beach! Everything's changed so much here, but somehow it's still the same. You'd hardly believe your eyes.'

'When are you coming back?'

'Oh, I have no idea, angel. For the time being I'm just taking things as they come. I'm sitting on my balcony now, in the sun. The first few days were very gray and somber, but the weather's been beautiful lately. Maybe someday we can live here, I think you'd find it very special too. Of course, it's still America, but . . .'

A little later, after we'd hung up, I realized she had not answered the essential questions: where she was exactly, and what she was doing there. I thumbed back to *calls received* and punched the last number. A woman's voice, with the enthusiasm of good news.

'Loews Hotel, can I help you?'

I hung up and looked around the canteen. The windows were steamy, the walls seemed to bulge a bit from all the light and life inside there.

I tore my eyes off it, turned and walked towards the lighted edge of the village in the distance.

'THE GREATEST COMEBACK IN THE HISTORY OF PORN'

The triumph of that first journey! As though you were piloting the aircraft yourself and setting it down, light as a feather, on the black sheet of tarmac! A little later, carrying my old suitcase, I walked out the sliding glass doors and into the world. I had drawn dollars from the ATM in the arrivals hall, the banknotes called me a man of the world. Fully confident, one strolls through the screen version of one's own life, no one can see your heart pounding like a puppy's. Look at him climb into that taxi, the casual air of authority, a man who has pulled so many cab doors closed behind him and says, 'Loews Hotel, please.'

The cab driver turns around.

'Hotel what?'

'Loews.'

The irony tugging at your lips shows him his proper place.

'Where's that, man? The Lois Hotel? Never heard of it.'

Well then, if this poor immigrant lives in such dark ignorance you'll have to help out a little, serve as his missionary, a lamp unto his feet. You spell out the name of the hotel for him and lean back; now everything will go according to plan. But the man doesn't know when to quit. Now he wants to know *where* it is, this Loews thing of yours. Suddenly you lose your composure, it shatters into a thousand pieces; *he's* the driver, I tell him, but if he doesn't know anything I'm perfectly willing to take the wheel. His indifference is like bedrock, he doesn't even seem to have picked up on my slur. Los Angeles, he explains to me, is a multiplicity of towns: Beverly Hills, Compton, Venice, Santa Monica, Palisades . . . And I have to listen to all this. I fall back in my seat and mumble Santa Monica. The taxi moves away from the airport, into dissolving sunlight. The afternoon is drawing to a close, the glory is a lie, the bitter taste in your mouth at the end of the binge.

The streets had something distinctly shabby about them. Sometimes in the distance you could see a bundle of skyscrapers, all in a clump, as though smelted together by thermonuclear heat. I looked at the screen on my cell phone, which didn't work in these parts. The road beneath the cab rolled by in slow waves. Palm trees stood in blunt silhouette against the turquoise billboard of sky. Big black cars slid by, introverted chunks of steel with darkened windows. I lacked all curiosity about the life inside them. Between the houses I sometimes caught a glimpse of the ocean.

'This must be it,' the driver said at last.

I said nothing, simply handed him the fare from the backseat. There were long, drawn-out limos at the entrance and men in weird tailcoats. Once inside, the enormous space of the atrium came crashing down on me. I made my way between rows of life-sized artificial palms, a cathedral of light and openness, past the reception desk. Through the huge glass panels at the end of the colonnade you could see the quiet ocean. My tattered cardboard suitcase marked me as an intruder; ducking into the lounge, I tucked it away between the little table and the easy chair. A waitress served me a Budweiser and slipped the bill under the bowl of pretzels. When she left, I glanced at it. Eight dollars for a beer. Ten beers and I'd be broke. I was impressed. Never had I drunk anything so expensive. At the Loews, the balance between price and performance had vanished completely, the hotel was a discreet piece of machinery designed to shake as much money as quickly as possible from its guests' pockets. The guests didn't care much. The bronzed floozies in their gold slippers, the noisy middle-aged men with barrel chests and spindly legs, the elderly couples with failing bodily functions but a portfolio full of reduced-risk investments; the price of things was an abstraction on the statement from the credit-card company.

I had hoped to catch my mother at something, perhaps merely to catch a glimpse of her life without me, but after an hour I went to the reception to ask for her room number. A young man tore himself away from the crowd loitering behind the desk, his smile broad, his cordiality obscene. Mrs. Unger was not in her room. I went back to the bar. My chair had been taken, so I settled down beneath a giant TV screen showing a silent basketball game. Suddenly I felt nothing but disgust for Loews, this temple of whores and hucksters. The window dressing of the lie.

'*Ludwig!*'

I looked up. The tight iron band of my thoughts pressed against my eyelids.

'Ludwig, where on earth did you come from? How did you ever find this place?'

'*Vade retro.*'

'Who's that?' asked the man she was with.

'Ludwig, darling, what happened to you?'

'I came to see how you were doing,' I say then.

She shakes her head. I see that she's thinking about becoming annoyed, saying that it was stupid of me to come here, but you don't say things like that to someone who has traveled halfway around the world for you.

'Could I ask . . .' the man says.

She turns and looks at him, scowling in irritation.

'This is my son,' she says.

Her finger approaches the sutures on my brow, she tries to touch them but I turn my head away.

'What have you got there, what is that?'

'Ah,' the man says, 'so that's it. How you doin', Ludwig?'

His eyes shift from me to the game going on above me.

'Say hello to Rollo.'

'Hello, Rollo.'

'Hello, Ludwig.'

'Okay, but who's this Rollo Liban?' I shouted to her a little later, from the bathroom.

I was sitting on the toilet, but conversation remained a possibility. The bathroom was filled with the smell of her body, the perfumes with which she tried to mask it; lotions, oils.

'An old friend,' said the voice from behind the door.

'What kind of friend?'

'A friend-friend, never anything more than that. Perish the thought.'

'So where did you meet him?'

'Listen, grand inquisitor . . .'

The smell was an intimacy, you inhaled someone. To smell her, the maternal scent, made me nauseous.

When I closed the bathroom door, the humming of the ventilation stopped. She was standing at the window. Below was the silent swimming pool. A flat, blue stone. A thin fog had moved in, along with the dusk.

'Why don't we take a little walk?' she said. 'The pier is lovely.'

In the distance I could see the Ferris wheel on the pier, bathed in shimmering light.

'You can have your name written on a grain of rice.'

'I'm not a little boy anymore.'

'I know that, darling.'

'You haven't told me what you're doing here.'

'You can't imagine how depressing London was.'

She turned to face me.

'Come on, let's go out. Stop staring at me like that, would you, sweetheart?'

★

There was gym equipment on the beach, with a low wall around it; in the semi-darkness a man was practicing on the bars. She took off her low-heeled shoes and we walked through the sand to the pier. The words were burning in my mouth, but I couldn't spit them out.

'People surf here during the day,' she said. 'Boys with those boards, what do you call them . . .'

'Surfboards.'

'It's amazing, the things they can do with them. They're completely at home on the waves, they know exactly what they're going to do. You should take lessons while you're here.'

A few good moments were all that remained. Who would want to go and spoil them?

'First I want one of those grains of rice with my name on it,' I said.

We crossed the heavy timbers onto the boardwalk. Along the way there were people fishing, and others offering useless services. The man who wrote your name on a grain of rice was there too. There was a Latino girl selling Disney balloons, a little stand where you could buy soft drinks, magazines and cigarettes. The Ferris wheel was deserted. It was almost dark, except for a deep purple stripe along the horizon. We stood at the railing. A ring of buoys with bells attached had been set around the end of the pier: an audible warning to those approaching in the fog, which had a way of coming up suddenly here. They made a lonely sound. She said, 'The pier at home didn't have bells like that, did it?'

We walked back. The rice-grain man was still sitting close to the entrance. A light-skinned Negro, his hair hanging in matted strips.

'Lookie there,' he said in a voice that could make heavy objects shiver.

My mother smiled.

'This is no woman,' he said, 'this is a story. I'll write it for you on a grain of rice.'

'It's for him,' my mother said.

She nodded in my direction.

'His name is . . .'

He held a finger to his lips.

'Your name is enough. I'll be gentle, I'll write it between heartbeats.'

He bent over and took a grain of rice between thumb and index finger. The hand holding the thin fountain pen moved under the lamp.

'But it's for him,' my mother said, 'Ludwig.'

'Magic formulas first,' the man said.

We stood and waited, curious and ill at ease. The shaman made a zooming sound as he wrote. Beneath the timbers, the water was slapping against the pilings.

A little later he held up the prize triumphantly, and put it in a little glass tube.

'A grain of rice for you, from your humble scribe on the banks of the Nile.'

He added a drop of oily fluid and sealed the tube with a silver cap on a string. She took it from him. We looked at it. The name was magnified by the curve of the tube and the oil in it: Eve LeSage.

'What does it say?' asked my mother, who wasn't wearing her reading glasses.

'Can't you read your own name?' the Negro asked.

Then she got it.

'Oh,' she said coolly.

'It's all here in black and white,' he said, 'look!'

Reaching around behind him into the box in which he carried his things, he produced a magazine. *LA Weekly*, with my mother on the cover: EVE LESAGE BACK IN THE LIMELIGHT. A come-hither pose, her forearms crossed beneath her breasts, her face held up alluringly. The snakes hissed on the Negro's head. My mother, sustenance for the poor.

I took the glass tube out of her hand and slid it back across the table.

'Don't believe everything you read,' I said.

We walked beside each other without a word, away from the pier. I was thinking Eastern thoughts, fortune-cookie things like *he who wishes to hide the truth must beware even the grain of rice*, which was comical, but not right then.

'You knew,' she said.

'More or less.'

'That's why you came.'

'Maybe. I don't know.'

'I had the feeling you knew.'

'I'll never not know anymore.'

'That's life, sweetheart. That's part of growing up.'

'Don't give me that horseshit. Please.'

It was silent for a bit. We plowed on through the sand.

'That's no way to talk to your mother, you know, I deserve a little ...'

'Don't say *respect*. That's not one of the matching words.'

'We've talked about this before, Ludwig. I can't make things any better for you, this is how it is.'

'And so now you're going to say you didn't have any choice in the matter?'

'Did I?'

The words caught in my throat. From far away I could hear the bells at sea. My voice was thick with frustration.

'You didn't have to do this.'

'You know, I earn ten thousand dollars for every day on the set. That makes up for a lot, okay? Not for all of it. But for a lot.'

'A well-paid whore is still a whore.'

'Ludwig, I don't want . . .'

'But isn't that the way it is? Do I have to call it something else, just so it's easier for you to take? Get used to it: the world sees you as a whore. For what you are. For what I am.'

'Oh please, don't make such a production of it,' she said, suddenly calm.

I reach out and grabbed her arm.

'But that's the way it is, isn't it?!'

'I respect your feelings, Ludwig, but I also have a life of my own. I don't have to take you into account in all my decisions anymore. I spent twenty years . . .'

'Oh, I see, a sacrifice. Of course. You made a sacrifice, for me . . . I was an inconvenient interruption to your life as a whore.'

'That's not what I am,' she said quietly, 'so please stop it. I have a contract for three films, and Rollo's trying to arrange a show for me in Las Vegas, along with Annie Sprinkle and one of these new girls, Holly Cranes or something. I've heard that Linda Lovelace got thirty-five thousand a week in Las Vegas. We could make a new start, Ludwig, start something new.'

'So this Liban is your pimp.'

'My agent.'

We had arrived at a broad channel that ran down to the sea. We couldn't go any further, we had to go up, to the paved path used during the day by cyclists, skaters and pedestrians. An asphalt road through the desert.

'They dump straight into the ocean,' my mother said. 'Swimmers get sick from it.'

The water was covered in thick foam. It moved. I couldn't help but think about puréed shit.

She walked on, back to the hotel; I went looking for something to eat. I was not pleased. There were certain words. Whore. Pimp.

They bothered me. It was pathetic. I crossed them out of my vocabulary.

On Appian Way I saw a big man screaming into his cell phone. The man's voice cut through the darkness.

'No, now you're gonna listen! We're talking here, you and me. I buy a drink, you buy a drink, and that's it. No, I'm talking now. No! First you're going to let me finish . . .'

He was giving someone hell. It was all completely revolting. Before I even reached the corner, a woman came running past me. She was holding a cell phone to her ear as well. She screamed.

'I wanna fucking die! Do you hear me?!'

She slalomed through the cars waiting at the light on Ocean Avenue. A shopping bag fluttered wildly on her arm. She ran into a parking lot and was gone.

Russian cabbies on Colorado Avenue were chewing on seeds, spitting out the hulls. A couple of blocks further along I went into a restaurant. The realization that it was a vegan place arrived with the menu. The mint tea, pumpkin soup and spring rolls all landed on the table at the same time, *because*, the boy waiting on me said, *we're closing in a minute*. He put the bill on the table as well.

'Maybe you should have told me that before I ordered,' I said.

The look on his face changed. The hatred with which restaurant personnel talk about us behind the swinging doors. Sometimes spitting on the plates.

'It says so on the door,' he said curtly.

Still lightheaded from the flight, I slipped into that buzz of estrangement that the world sometimes produces. I left the restaurant before finishing my meal. Out on the sidewalk I saw sheets of thin, parchment-like paper, torn from a book. I picked up some sheets that were still glued together. Someone had ripped a Bible to pieces. The pages rustled between my fingers. The final pages of Genesis, a large chunk of Exodus – the portent was not lost on me.

My mother was in bed when I came in, she looked at me over the top of her reading glasses. I suggested asking for extra sheets and blankets and sliding the two halves of the bed away from each other.

'I don't want you to do that,' she said determinedly, 'that would clutter the place up right away. The bed is big enough as it is.'

I was too tired to enter into another conflict, to work up the energy needed to get my own way. She went back to her book about force fields and how a secret world government had covered up the discovery of an internal combustion engine that ran on water. Esoteric literature was all she read anymore. I took my toothbrush and pajamas out of the suitcase. A fast shower to rinse off the trip, my gums bled when I brushed them. I tried not to think about the future, about a life full of temporary addresses.

Sleep was long in coming. On the other side of the bed there was someone else's body. It breathed, it made a choking noise and then, two hours after the light went out, it began to snore. Sucking in air with a rattle, letting it escape again with a soft burble. Disquieting intimacy.

'You're snoring,' I said in the dark.

A little later, again, louder this time.

'Hey, you're snoring!'

She awoke with a start.

'Oh, sorry,' she murmured. 'I'll roll over.'

She fell back asleep, became body once more. The body that would again play a role in people's fantasies. Men's. Millions of men. It would be lusted after, it would summon up burning desires – her likeness would be reproduced countless times, she would be a star again, for that is what a star is, the result of uncontrolled, eruptive proliferation, a metastasis. But now, because it was a comeback and she was much older than back then, there would be the nudge-wink of camp, of bad taste taken ironically, perhaps she would become the patroness of homos, who had more or less invented camp. But how ironic could it be, I wondered, commercialized sex: you could fuck in front of the camera in a derby or a Minnie Mouse mask, but it remained pornography: the portrayal of penetration, intended to stimulate masturbation. The way it had appeared to me in *Lilith*. That body beside me. That had already caused me so much painful confusion, and that was now snoring. The thought: what if I raped her? Then it would all be over and done with, then the sin would be manifest and my life would have purpose, it could consist of penance. I would long for what didn't exist: forgiveness. I can't turn my thoughts to anything else, it's all equally filthy. And she sleeps on, like a baby. A very noisy baby. In her dreams there are no demons. I am standing guard. This is how our lives will be, I suddenly see it all clearly: she will give herself away, and I will save her. With me she will re-find herself and remember who she was. The life of a porn star is her point of departure, I will be her return. All night long, that is the only clear moment, the moment when I realize what our life will look like. I will stay with her, wherever she goes to do whatever she does, I will be there with all the inert patience of a confession box. I also know that she will push me away, that she will say I should lead my own life and that I don't have to be her keeper; words I will tolerate purely and passively, with the smile of one who knows better.

Halfway through the night, I'd had enough.

'Why did you turn the light on?' she moaned.

'You're snoring, goddamn it.'

I climbed out of bed and began pulling away the sheet on my side. I pushed the beds apart.

132

'I have earplugs in the bathroom,' she said, 'in my sponge bag.'

'Forget the earplugs.'

Now I had a single bed, but not enough sheets and blankets. In trousers and a T-shirt I went out into the hall, took the lift down and asked at the desk for extra sheets and a duvet.

'Which room number, sir?'

'I'll take it up myself.'

'We'll have it brought to you, sir, that's no problem. What is your room number?'

A little later a knock at the door, a black boy with sleepy eyes behind a pile of linen. My mother had turned onto her side, a sleep mask from the plane over her eyes. She had fallen asleep again.

The next morning she had gone out, without leaving a note. A big breakfast, the fruit aglow with freshness. I could get used to this life. Dozens of snowy white gym shoes wandered back and forth through the dining room, a procession in all directions. Outside the windows an oceanic heaven full of immaculate light. To be honest, I didn't quite know what to do. The day spread out before me without direction. I tried to summon up the feeling of a traveler who, after journeying on foot for two years, finally arrives in California.

'California, here I come,' I said to myself quietly a few times, but couldn't hold on to the feeling for long.

At a little breakfast place on Ocean Avenue I pulled a copy of *LA Weekly* from the pile. After taking a walk, on a bench outside an alternative coffeehouse I sat down and read the cover story. The article was in two parts, an overview of her career and the account of a press conference. My eyes skimmed back and forth over the lines, *Mister Rollo Liban, Miss LeSage's agent . . . major deal . . . Watchtower Productions . . . high-class porn . . . return of porn-chic . . .* Autumn would see the release of her first film in twenty-four years. Yes, she was older, she must be close to fifty now, the journalist wrote, but she was still absolutely dazzling. If she had been preserved so wonderfully without the benefit of plastic surgery, he noted, then it was nothing less than a miracle, comparable to the wondrous conservation of the remains of the nineteenth-century saint Catherina Labouré in Paris.

'Do you think your body can still stand up to it, to all that tumult?' was one of the questions asked during the press conference.

She had smiled and said 'This body *is* the tumult, Mr. Journalist.'

Concerning what she'd done between then and now, where she had been, she spoke only in guarded terms – Europe, a family, life on the sidelines. And why had she chosen to make a comeback now? Three reasons, she'd said: for the money, for the money and for the money. And the fourth reason: for the light. The light was her metaphor for attention, the fame she had left behind for a man. That explained the text on the cover: EVE LESAGE BACK IN THE LIMELIGHT.

It amazed me to see the matter-of-fact tone in which they spoke of a comeback in the world of porn: no sniggering, no moralizing. Perhaps it didn't matter what you were famous for, perhaps politics, entertainment, criminality and pornography all enjoyed the same status here.

A contract had been signed with Watchtower Productions for three major productions: First *Lilith, The Second Coming*, then *Josephine Mutzenbacher's 1000-and-1 Night*, and finally *Testament*, a delirious, pornographic reconstruction of three sexually laden stories from the Old Testament: the tale of Tamar, Onan and Judah, the story of David and Bathsheba and that of King Ahasveros and Esther.

The film about Josephine Mutzenbacher would be shot on location in Vienna. The director was Jerry Rheinauer, the Cecil B. DeMille of pornography. The article referred to her, Eve LeSage, as the Grace Kelly of porn; it was a universe of derivatives, of quasi-artists trying to gain status through references to real artists, to other stars who had shone without the rancidness of smut.

I was dressed too warmly, the sun was scorching now. This was not a place where one could do without sunglasses. The light was too bright, it made my eyes water. Through the blur of tears, my gaze fell on a review in the *Must See Art* section: a new exhibition, *Abgrund, by Bodo Schultz, at the Steinson & Freeler Gallery*.

Bewildered, I took the paper inside and read the article there. In an exclusive move, Bodo Schultz's agent has offered the gallery new work. The art critic describes what he has seen: a film made by Schultz, ragged and intense. Schultz leads us along the brink of an *Abgrund*, a chasm of his own making, not the chasm of the soul but a physical one, somewhere in the jungles of Panama. He himself does not appear on camera, except for one moment; the camera is fixed on a single point, we see a man approaching and then, behind his back, there is a huge explosion. The camera is knocked over by the shockwave; a few moments later someone picks it up, it's still running, the camera's eye slides across a man's torso, his face: Schultz. The charge has gone off prematurely. A slow, silent film, for the rest; each time Schultz launched into his poisoned litanies, the viewer was shocked. It was a video report of his project in the jungle – he was destroying a mountain. A mountain. The critic was impressed by the ruthlessness, praised him as a man of extreme consistency. A 'must-see', in other words.

There was more of Schultz's work on display at Steinson & Freeler, but that movie, that apparently was what it was all about.

I had found information about my father on the Internet, at the terminal in Alburgh's little library, articles about the moral implications of his work, but nothing that had interested me much at the time. To me he was the man from the postcard, *Mediohombre*, the one-armed, the one-legged. I often had the feeling he could see me.

I walked back to the hotel along broad avenues. The gallery was open from eleven to six, and closed on Sunday. La Cienega Boulevard, I had to find out where that was.

'Where were you?' my mother asked. 'You mustn't just go away without telling me where you are.'

We were in the Ocean and Vine restaurant at the Loews. I put the *LA Weekly* on the table, with her picture facing down.

'They're exhausting, interviews,' she said of her own accord. She waved her hand to dismiss the world.

'Rollo hired a suite on the top floor. I think there must have been ten interviews in all. I barely had time to eat breakfast.'

She stuck a porcelain spoon into her decapitated egg, the soft yolk welled up, gleaming like an abscess. A little egg white was clinging to her lower lip. The droll voice of our biology teacher, Mr. Bonham Carter, when we stopped beside the *Amorphophallus titanium* during our tour of the botanical gardens at Cambridge: *Associations drawn at your own risk.*

The toast crackled between her teeth.

'This is a lovely hotel,' she said.

'Who's paying for all of this? It's insanely expensive here.'

Her glance shot back and forth between the egg and me; she was trying to hide her uneasiness, to decide what she could tell me and what she couldn't.

'Darling,' she said, 'I don't know . . .'

'It doesn't matter,' I said, 'it's already in print somewhere.'

I turned over the magazine and found the review of the exhibition. Jabbed at it with my finger. She looked, her head tilted slightly in order to read it better.

'Aha,' she said, leaning back in her chair.

'Don't you want to read it?'

136

'Tell me what it says. I forgot my glasses.'

'That's weird,' I said.

'Well?'

I read aloud to her. She sat there, motionless. She didn't touch her brunch after that. And when I was finished, 'That man is becoming more deranged all the time.'

She flagged down a waitress.

'Would you like something else, Ludwig?'

I passed.

'Everything on the bill of room 304, please.'

She had no desire to go to the gallery. In the elevator she said, 'That man destroys everything he touches.'

'But aren't you curious? I bet you're dying of curiosity.'

'Let him pay his back alimony first.'

La Cienega Boulevard was too far to walk now, I saw on the city map I'd bought that afternoon. I would have to wait until tomorrow. I hung around a bit on Main Street and was amazed by the number of holistic services on offer there. I seemed to have stumbled upon a marketplace of karma-yoga, Ayurvedic consumer goods and glass capsules filled with ionized water to help against jetlag, hangovers and all sorts of radiation, for sixteen dollars and fifty cents apiece. From all those little shops wafted the odor of incense and aromatic oils. The hippie dream had become an industry, supported by vegan surfers and Buddhists wearing flip-flops. I hissed *fuck off* at a girl who tried to press on me a flyer announcing a meeting with Yogi Amrit-something-or-other. *Experience love beyond words*, I read in passing.

It was easy to see why these surroundings and this climate were so suited to the sort of ironclad hedonism expressed so abundantly here – you couldn't imagine this kind of bullshit in Djibouti or at sub-zero temperatures. It was a delicate lifestyle that could survive only in highly industrialized surroundings where others did the real work, or in artificial biotopes in the Second or Third World that relied on the monoculture of tourism. The hippies' kids had grown up, this was their world – their egoism seemed even more monstrous than that of their parents.

I realized why my mother felt attracted to the West Coast. For her this was where it had all started, after a disappointing study of classical song at the conservatory in The Hague. She had a nice voice, it had been her diva dream to become a singer. But polyps on her vocal cords and, in the long run, not quite enough talent had been her downfall. In the course of her study they made it clear to her that she would never be more than a middling choir singer. With her boyfriend, she had left for the United States. He, Jelte Boender, was a rocker from Groningen province who wanted to travel Route 66. After two weeks on the road they drove into Los Angeles; the sparkle, the party everyone was talking about. They performed on street corners, he played his guitar, she sang – 'Nights in White Satin', 'Bridge over Troubled Water'; slow, maudlin songs that made his skin crawl but that fit her voice, a bit sing-songish, without much power behind it. One day they saw Richard Burton and Liz Taylor walking down Hollywood Boulevard; she felt the old ambition flare up, the burning scar of the semi-talented. *She* should be the one walking there, stared upon, untouchable – handing out the occasional autograph like a benediction.

She and Jelte Boender slept at a boarding house in Culver City and lived off the pittance from their busking.

One day she was meditating on the beach when a man approached her. The paraphernalia of a photographer: tattered camera bag, Leica around his neck, the words, 'Hello, pretty lady, could I ask you something? I hope I'm not bothering you?'

To make a long story short, he wanted to take pictures of her. Topless.

It was a Sunday afternoon, Jelte Boender was auditioning for a new rock band in Venice (which would later meet with modest success as St. Vincent and the Grenadines, albeit without Jelte Boender, who failed the audition). The man introduced himself as Gene Howard. She thought about the story she could tell later on: *I was meditating on the beach when a photographer came up to me, he looked a little bit like Kris Kristofferson, but his name was Gene Howard – that was before he became* the *Gene Howard – and said to me . . .*

She went with him to the studio at his house, and as she was taking off her blouse, her bra, she did her best to summon up a sense of destiny unfolding. Gene Howard didn't even try to get her into bed, all he wanted was her beauty. She was flattered and not nearly as shy as she'd thought she would be. Even when he asked her if she minded taking off the rest, whether he could see her naked, she didn't experience that as a violation of her physical integrity, *all those things that people like Gloria Steinem tried to make of it*, as she told the journalist from *LA Weekly*. She had felt pretty and wanted, this was her calling; being born and growing up in east Groningen province had been a mistake. This place was her home, this light and this promise.

Gene Howard told her that he sometimes worked as production assistant to Abby Mayer, producer and director of films such as *Ride Me High* and *Harem Keeper*. She had never heard of him or his work. Howard said he would arrange a meeting.

'Oh my God,' Abby Mayer said when he saw her, 'you're . . . fresh cream and apple pie . . .'

She thought he was a bit of a creep, but she sensed that he had power. He was preparing an ambitious production, his biggest yet, and she *was* Victoria Wagner, Mayer said, the woman around whom the story of *Lilith* revolved.

'What do I have to do?' she'd asked. 'What does the role involve?'

'All you have to is be yourself — I absolutely forbid you to do anything else. To act, for example.'

She still didn't get it, a movie in which you didn't have to act?

'Your body, girl, your body, that's your means of expression. We're going to make a gorgeous movie, the most beautiful sexy movie ever. My God, I feel like Roberto Rossellini when he saw Ingrid Bergman for the first time!'

Mayer wanted to do some screen tests. When the taxi pulled up in front of the boarding house one evening, there was no way around it: she had to tell her rocker from Groningen that she had *a kind of audition*. She explained quickly, he snorted loudly.

'Just a skin flick, don't let them kid you.'

He had not tried to stop her. The resignation of a man who knows that when it comes to love, he's been living beyond his means.

Beside the pool at a house in Beverly Hills, Mayer had shot a loop with her, a sort of preliminary study for *Lilith* – just her and one man, the one who would probably be her leading man in the film, Llewelyn Reed. She thought he was attractive, he was funny.

Less than two weeks later the 8mm film hit the market and the buzz began. A spectacular new girl, Abby Mayer had discovered her. They were going to make a big movie in Thailand.

The loop has been lost, but the stage name Mayer dreamed up for her remains: Eve LeSage. No one knows precisely what was to be seen in that preliminary study, but one thing is certain: she had glorious sex with Llewelyn Reed.

The camera never got in her way. That was important. Some people froze in front of the camera. Not her. She had never noticed this certain kind of exhibitionism in herself before, but she didn't try to deny its logical conclusion. When it came to her body, she knew no shame.

In those years the ideals of hippiedom are rapidly becoming commercialized, free love has paved the way for a deluge of pornography. It's an easy way to make money, and the profession poses no academic requirements, it demands only sublime bodies. This, she thinks, is the start of something bigger – from here she will be taken up into the legitimate world of moviemaking, the red carpets, the cover of *Rolling Stone*. Porno and Hollywood will become one, no doubt about it, it is only a matter of time. It's so close, a hop, skip and a jump really. The resemblance is already so striking, the infrastructure, the hierarchy on the set, the star of the film, everything the same – only the one is called an art form, the other smut.

★

She flew to Bangkok with Gene Howard. Slowly but surely he had assumed the role of her manager – she liked that, business matters couldn't hold her attention for long. The crew had flown out ahead, the waiting began. Waiting for the sun, waiting for the cases of food poisoning and collective dysentery to pass, waiting for permits – and when the waiting was over, the movie was shot in about three weeks. For the genre, the screenplay was fairly elaborate, a story about the eternal triad of power, jealousy, revenge.

Llewelyn Reed had fallen in love with her and courted her with little gifts. Gene Howard, who was the production assistant and had the room next to hers, warned her about it: Reed always fell in love with his co-stars, then broke their hearts. It was thirty-two degrees in the shade. During the sex scenes, Reed's makeup dripped onto her body. Gene Howard said, 'You lie there like a cold mackerel. Move a little, even if it's only your hands. And try not to look like you're getting raped.'

But it was precisely that lack of expression, that stasis, which would become her trademark. Abby Mayer was enraptured, from behind the camera he shouted, 'You might not win an Oscar, but you're gonna be some kind of love goddess!'

Marthe Unger's hotel life began. She grew accustomed to room service. In California, after a while, she consorted only with Europeans and New Yorkers.

'It's like the Californians' brains have been fried by the sun,' she said.

She tried to develop an addiction to vodka and cocaine – everyone around her, after all, was addicted to something – but it only exhausted her. She couldn't summon up the energy for it, she was too *tired* for an addiction. Norman Mailer wrote about her in *Esquire*, or rather, about *the most lusted-after body in the world*. She drank champagne with

Hugh Hefner and denied rumors that she had gone to bed with him. And finally she left for New York, because the people there seemed more interesting. She met Andy Warhol and later Mick Jagger as well – the photographs of their flirtation, young people thirsty for life, bathing in their careless beauty.

She had earned only three thousand dollars with *Lilith*. Gene Howard had forgotten to divvy up the principal. There was no lack of men with plans for her. A lot of people had a strange way of laughing, she'd noticed that already, too adamant, a tinkling laughter that echoed with self-interest. Rollo Liban didn't laugh. She had met him at a party at the penthouse of one of the bigwigs at Atlantic Records, a fabulous suite with a rooftop garden at the St. Regis. Rollo Liban was a large man, he still had all his hair back then. He had an agency, he *ran girls*, as he put it, but it was worth your while to work for him, you got at least half the earnings. That was exceptional, that was a miracle; you had the feeling he was protecting you, that he was standing behind you. Rollo Liban was credited with having defined the difference between erotic art and porno.

'Erotic art,' he said, 'is tickling a cunt with a chicken feather. Porno uses the whole chicken.'

Marthe Unger wanted someone she could count on, and Rollo Liban had a Levantine nose for the right time and the right place. He got her into movies that made money, and saw to fringe benefits that included cool, quiet hotel rooms, vodka and cocaine. He wanted his trade to look 'classy', the association with criminality and the abuse of women was bad for business. Actors and producers in the adult industry were being taken to court, the FBI was running major under-cover operations against the producers of pornography, but there was no stopping porno. The contours of an industry emerged, today's star made way tomorrow for a new one.

'It is a little depressing,' she told Al Goldstein in *Screw*. 'Every week

143

there are a hundred new starlets waiting to take your place, especially in Hollywood.'

But Rollo Liban took good care of his star, she appeared mostly in the more *aesthetic* productions; the real raw smut, he felt, was something for Linda Lovelace or C.J. Laing.

It was the golden age of porn. The genre was subversive, hip: syphilis and gonorrhea were easy to treat, abortion had been legalized after *Roe vs. Wade*, and the only contraceptive was the Pill. The word AIDS began making the whispered rounds only a few years later; at first the disease limited itself to homosexual men.

As Eve LeSage she plays in six porno films before the dark stranger of the threepenny novel makes his appearance. The umpteenth party, scenes of fatigued excess. Then, suddenly, there is someone who doesn't fit in; he stands a bit to one side, smiles when spoken to, but keeps his distance. Atypicality as a mark of character. He keeps his coat on, a bomber jacket. Heavy work boots on his feet. She asks who that is.

'Mmmm,' growls Price du Plessix Gray.

Du Plessix Gray, aging queen and theater critic, is a friend. He says, 'Hmmm, mmmm. A wayward laborer, perhaps?'

An artist, she hears later: a European like her. Would she like to be introduced? It turns out not to be necessary. Like a boxer he comes out of his corner, straight at her; she feels the room shrink to become his presence.

'I know who you are,' he says. 'I've read about you.'

A German accent so thick she feels at liberty to say, '*Ach wie gut, dass niemand weiss, dass ik Rumpelstilchzen heiss.*'

'*Sie sprechen Deutsch?*'

'My grandfather was German. I grew up close to the border.'

'You are Dutch, I assume?'

She nods, amused. His name is Bodo Schultz, he's from Austria, a village in Carinthia. Like so many Austrian artists he hates his father-land. You can tell from looking at him that he was raised on *Knödeln* and *Rostbraten*, a hulking farmer, boulder-like, a massive neck and shoulders. She feels like running her fingers through his coarse hair.

His studio in Manhattan looks out on the massive pillars beneath the Brooklyn Bridge. The building itself looks like a shipwreck washed ashore, wind and rain have free play.

She goes to visit him. He talks about his work, but only with difficulty. She wanders past monochrome sculptures, human figures in hideous postures, twisted, suffering. She is reminded of frozen battlefields, the casts of bodies at Pompeii.

He has just returned from Okinawa, where he designed a pavilion for the World's Fair: a column of ice forty meters high, a tower veined with deep-freeze elements. Corridors, stairways and rooms had been hacked out inside the tower, when the sun shone you found yourself at the heart of a diamond. Its arches, arcades and suspended stairways caused his tower to be compared to the phantomlike interiors of Piranesi. The reference to such romanticism had thrown him into an uncontrollable rage. He is working on a new design, another tower, for a *concours* set up by the city of Alexandria. Marthe Unger finds him surly and gracious, the latter in spite of himself. It moves her to see him do his best on her behalf. They sleep together on a mattress in the far corner of his studio.

'Happiness,' he says, 'is this.'

She is proud that she can elicit such feelings in him, it gives her a special status, like making friends with an animal in the wild.

Southern Belle is her final film. Abby Mayer punches a hole in the door, he screams, 'I'd rather lose you to a car wreck than to . . . to love.'

She says that sex with anyone else is out of the question as long as she loves this man. It's that simple, and with the same ease with which she started, she stops. To Schultz she says, 'Those were my fifteen minutes. They dragged on a little.'

They marry quickly. There is no family at the wedding. Price du Plessix Gray is her witness, the owner of the Greek grocery around the corner is his.

Schultz works on a statuary group he calls *Blind*, dozens of life-sized sculptures of the two of them in the act of coition. Everyone, it seemed, felt the need to portray her naked, copulating; life's demands on her were limited. The legend of her beauty was fed by her sudden disappearance. From being the fantasy of countless others she now became the muse of a single man. She left New York for Alexandria. Schultz began preparations for *Wachturm*, his tower in the city's harbor, the shadow of the Pharos. I entered the world at the Egyptian British Hospital. When I was baptized, her artificial eyelashes fell off. For the rest, nothing special.

The treasure trove of the ancient world, the library at Alexandria, was destroyed by fire. A tragedy beyond bounds. In the 1980s a new library was built, a huge and prestigious project. It was meant, by way of compensation, to be one of the largest libraries in the world. At the same time a plan was hatched to rebuild the Pharos, the legendary lighthouse that has been shining in the eyes of civilization since time immemorial. The Pharos was one of the Seven Wonders of the World, and was destroyed by a series of earthquakes. At its feet there arose an Arab fort; archeologists still search for its remains on the seafloor. For the design of the new tower, the city government organized a competition among artists and architects. Scores of plans were submitted, breathtaking reminiscences, but in the end my father received the commission. His tower was to be built in the harbor of Alexandria, the city would look out upon it, the antique glory would be revived. Bodo Schultz, master builder, would follow in the footsteps of Sostratus. But Bodo Schultz's tower would produce no light: his would be black as obsidian. Every bit as tall as the old tower, one hundred and thirty meters. But the Pharos, according to legend, had been built of white marble, three storeys high, with a huge fire at the top that could be seen miles out to sea. That tower was an invitation to come ashore, to Alexandria, backdrop to that marvelous history play of old revolving around Cleopatra, whose own loins had been a haven to Julius Caesar and Marc Antony.

Bodo Schultz's tower broadcast a different message. *Avoid this harbor while ye may*, it said.

Alexandria lies between the desert and the Mediterranean Sea. The city encompasses its eastern harbor and bay like a womb. The bay is protected by two forts; between them, an elongated artificial island was once thrown up to break the waves before they reach the city. The island is a few hundred meters long, and ships can enter the bay on either side. There, on that island, was where Schultz's tower would rise: *Wachturm*, an obelisk black as a shadow, his tar-drenched middle finger held up to the world. The tower was closed on all sides, there was no telling whether it protected the city against intruders or actually held it hostage.

Schultz spent most of his days on the island. Many months went into laying the foundations. In my mind's eye I see him amid the cranes, cement mixers and bulldozers, while shiploads of building materials keep coming in. He acted as the classic artist-builder, the way Daedalus had, bringing his dark vision to life with his own hands. The island is easy to see from the Corniche, the seaside boulevard that encircles the bay in a lazy curve. In bad weather one sees the sea rising high and dark behind it, while the calm surf in the harbor hardly changes.

After dark my father took the boat back with the last of the workers, arriving home only after I had been put to bed. My mother once made a home movie in the garden, perhaps with the idea of sending it to his family for Christmas – greetings from the outlands. I am sitting on a little orange tricycle with a sort of pickup bed at the back and staring the whole time at my mother, who is holding the camera. I forget to move the pedals. A hand against my back pushes me along, then we see the rest of the man, but only from behind, a bent figure. I look at my mother again, and the scene ends there.

The second part of the home movie must have been made that same day, I'm wearing the same clothes. I'm sitting on a swing at the back of the garden, behind me stands my father. He is wearing a white T-shirt, it fits tightly around his torso. He is strong, a Carinthian farmer.

He is built for adversity; if the ox dies, we'll just pull the plow ourselves. Picasso had a body like that.

'Are you having fun, Ludwig?'

My mother, operating the camera again, but I don't answer, because the swing is going fast and high.

'Bodo, it's scaring him.'

My legs fly higher and higher, the little doll's feet sweep helplessly.

'Bodo, stop it, he's frightened!'

The film stutters and goes black. Not suitable for sending to the family. The mysterious thing about those images is that his face is never seen, only that hand, that arm, that torso. Even during the swing scene, his face remains in shadow.

'Now that you mention it,' my mother said when we looked at the film many years later.

She told me how frustrated he was; he hadn't counted on the conditions in Egypt, which were tough and resulted in messy delays. I imagine it as having been something like the *Tower of Babel*, by Pieter Brueghel the Elder: little men contributing stone by stone to an arrogant, godless project. He cursed the inefficiency and the leisurely way they lifted their hands to the heavens when the wrong building materials were delivered. He incurred the workers' wrath with his brutish treatment, his frequent shouts of *Scheiss doch auf Allah!*

Winter came, a bitter west wind delayed the work, and two storms in rapid succession finally brought it to a standstill. People say he beat laborers, those little fellahin in their djellabahs who had come in from the countryside to earn a few piasters in the big city. In the light of later accounts, that is not unlikely. It is commonly known of disturbed, narcissistic characters that they regard all adversity, even when imposed by inanimate factors such as the weather or natural disasters, as a personal insult. These things provoke a deep, impotent rage, everything is conspiring against them, that is why they shake their fists at heaven and flail the waters of the Hellespont. Or, as Captain Ahab said: *Speak not to me of blasphemy, man; I'd strike the sun if it insulted me.*

I think my mother was deeply shocked by the dark storm clouds that gathered over her. She had never seen him like this, a tense and enraged Austrian out to build a tower in the harbor at Alexandria, a barbaric ruler over a ragged legion of day laborers, an obsequious throng, his subjects.

Wachturm sprang from the soil like a poison toadstool, decked out with an intricate network of wooden scaffolding on which countless little men made their way up and down. Medieval! Medieval in the sense of manual labor, bond service and feudalism, those same conditions – in other words – which still pertain in large parts of the world, so that *medieval* perhaps describes not just a historical era, but also a packet of conditions that floats around the world, regardless of time or position, and is unpacked here or there. Whatever the case, the Pandora's box bearing the label MEDIEVAL had now been delivered to that elongated barrier island.

The tower was not completed. After three years my father went away and never came back. He left many things behind, unfinished, a tower, a marriage, an upbringing.

(Later, in Alburgh, I was eleven or twelve at the time, I was given a box of Playmobil. I built a castle with it. The good guys lived in that castle; the bad guys gathered in a black tower that was not made with plastic building blocks. Only much later did I realize that that black tower and *Wachturm* were one and the same; it was the scale model of *Wachturm* that I had played with all those years.)

It was a good two-hour walk to La Cienega Boulevard. The Steinson & Freeler Gallery, it turned out, was located in an old, single-storey commercial building, a bright orange oblong. Before the entrance, marked by a set of smoked-glass doors, a little crowd had gathered. These were not art lovers, it seemed to me; the dreadlocks and clothing daubed with political slogans were too much in evidence for that – the fashion statements of left-wing activists. They unrolled a banner, a girl was taking flyers from a shopping cart and handing them out to passers-by. Someone was toying around with a megaphone.

I crossed the street and took a flyer. Stop this maniac from dese-crating holy mountains. The maniac portrayed was Bodo Schultz. I wormed my way through the activists to the entrance, but that wasn't supposed to happen – they lined up between me and the door and began chanting, as if in a dream

'IT AIN'T NO ART TO TAKE MOUNTAINS APART. IT AIN'T NO ART TO TAKE MOUNTAINS APART.'

As though by magic, their looks became combative – from a gaggle of freeloaders they had been transformed into a militant cell. Their arms were locked together, it looked like experimental theater, with me as the sole member of the audience. Behind me, two of the demonstrators raised the banner, you could read the words through the back of it: VIOLENCE AGAINST NATURE IS VIOLENCE AGAINST MANKIND. A voice beside me said, 'Immoral art is a crime, that's how we feel about it.'

It was the girl with the flyers, and her words were spoken in complete earnest. I had to bend over to hear her.

'That's what we're trying to tell you. If you'd like more information, come with me.'

Her friends kept droning the same words, IT AIN'T NO ART TO TAKE MOUNTAINS APART. We walked over to the shopping cart.

'What interests me,' I said, 'is exactly what you people have against Schultz.'

It looked like she was about to roll her eyes or start clucking with her tongue, but she restrained herself. She asked, 'Are you familiar with the work of this Mr. Schultz?'

'Not particularly. I mean, I don't know much about it.'

'There's something very wrong with that man. And with a world that views him as an artist . . . His work as art.'

The words were like bitter rinds in her mouth. Behind us the mechanical cadence of the chorus halted. She said, 'Mr. Schultz acts out his vandalistic urges on nature, which can't defend itself.'

From the cart she dug out a few photocopies, I saw a pile of folders marked PRESS – this kind of activism was, in its own way, highly organized. I pointed at the press kits.

'What are those?'

'Are you a reporter? Foreign? You sound foreign.'

'England,' I said.

'Well then, would you write down the name of the publication or network you work for, and your email address, so we can keep you up to date on our activities?'

The *Norwich Evening News* was the first newspaper that came to mind. She handed me a press kit, in which I hoped to find more substantial information about Schultz.

'But now I'd really like to go inside,' I said.

'Oh, but you can't do that. We're not letting anyone in. Usually we wait till the police come . . .'

She looked at the others, then at her bright red Swatch.

'They're a little late today.'

'Who?'

'Yesterday they were here before noon. Come along, I have to . . .'

'Who are you talking about? The police?'

'What do you think, that we're going to go away voluntarily?'

A man came out of the building. A clipped gray beard, neatly dressed. The gallery owner. He was trying not to yell.

'Go away,' he said, 'get out of here, you people.'

'You know we can't do that,' one boy said.

'You people are obstructing the freedom of expression. Fascism. Deplorable.'

'You could also see it as free publicity,' the boy said.

The natural leader, handsome, gangly, maybe the son of a judge. Stenciled on the back of his jacket was a portrait of Che Guevara.

'Guys,' he said, 'could I . . .'

'This is art, damn it. Not politics. You people are turning it into politics. Wrong! Wrong! If you want politics, go to city hall. Go bother them. This is a gallery.'

'Everything is politics, I'm afraid,' the boy said.

Behind the man, in the doorway, I saw a young woman wearing heavy-framed glasses. The lenses were ponds of contempt.

'Fuck off,' the man said. 'All of you, fuck off!'

Now he had starting yelling despite himself.

'You're the one who chose to display his work,' the boy said.

At a sign from him the others began chanting again. Loud and monotonous, you could easily hate them for it. The man and woman disappeared. The chorus stopped.

From my vantage point across the street I watched things develop, but there wasn't much to hold my attention. They passed out flyers, smoked cigarettes, grew bored. The girl who had given me the press kit looked over a few times, waved once. I was sitting with my back against a tree. A position of strength. This was the same way I had watched the children at the locks, dissected the group dynamics of the strong and the weak, long ago in rural Groningen. A bottle-green memory.

Lethargy settled on the protestors across the street, there was at the moment nothing to feed their identity as activists. I opened the folder and started reading.

Schultz had bought a mountain in Panama's Darien province, the borderland between Central and South America – an impenetrable jungle region, no roads; the world began again only on the other side, in Colombia. He used Emberá Indians as laborers, hired them to help him carry out *Abgrund*, the destruction of his mountain. He was tearing it to the ground bit by bit. The report said he was already almost halfway there. There had been protests, conservationists and anti-globalists had joined forces against him. I found a sheet of paper with a summary of the activities carried out against *Abgrund* – petitions, protest marches in Panama City, before the Panamanian consulate in Geneva, the embassy in Brasilia, accompanied by the dates, the names of the committees and the estimated number of demonstrators; picayune detail lent the efforts an official air. And there were lists of endangered animal and plant species in the region. The picture slowly emerged of a reckless hater who squeezed the life out of all those little animals with his own two hands, who crushed rare flowers between his fingers.

Mitchell Rhodes, a fellow at the Smithsonian Tropical Research Institute, had tried to visit *Abgrund*. He got as far as the boundaries of the terrain itself and was stopped there by guards. FARC militiamen, AK-47s slung over their shoulders. Rhodes and his companions, two guides and a biologist from the University of the West Indies, had been assaulted, shots had been fired in the air.

The press kit contained copies of aerial photographs of a clearing in the jungle, the dreary wasteland of a mining operation. A steep, lonesome mountain in the middle. I thought I could make out conveyors, bulldozers, barracks. Smoke from bonfires. Down there, somewhere, was my father. Concerning Schultz himself, his motives, I found little. Speculations, no facts. Words like 'demonic' and 'fascistic' reflected the authors' opinions, but clarified almost nothing. I was disappointed. I had hoped to find him, or at least get a little closer.

The girl crossed the street.

'Hi,' she said once she was standing in front of me, 'you were sitting there reading so quietly . . .'

'Not a lot happening, is there?'

'A boycott calls for a lot of patience.'

'Is that what you call it, a boycott?'

'That's what we're doing, a boycott. With a high degree of public agitation.'

'Straight out of the Demonstrator's Handbook?'

'Sort of. But if you're a reporter, I probably shouldn't tell you too much.'

'I'm not a reporter. I only wanted the press kit. Sorry.'

She had something awkward about her, a kind of beauty which I could imagine that only I might be able to appreciate.

Two police cars stopped in front of the gallery. We crossed the street, I kept my distance in order not to be confused with the demonstrators. The tall boy was handcuffed, the girl with the flyers kept pushing her way up to the front, it seemed as though she *wanted* to be arrested. Five protestors were taken away, the others were chased off with batons.

'You can go inside now,' she said as she passed.

The wheels of her shopping cart rattled on the concrete. The incident seemed to have made no impression on her. She smiled in a way I couldn't figure.

You could call it my introduction to my father. In the flesh. I strolled past his work slowly, trying to see in it the world of his thoughts. The mind of a man turned inside out. A series of paintings on rough wooden panels, all unevenly sawed. They looked like dark landscapes, uprooted as though by war. Each had a vanishing point, a darkness where the earth seemed to swallow itself. Once that black hole had caught your eye, everything seemed to move towards it like a mudslide off a hill. The catalog noted that the works were displayed behind Plexiglas; in view of the maker's controversial reputation, vandalism could not be ruled out.

In the middle of the gallery a black square had been cordoned off, made from tarps hanging from ceiling to floor. *Abgrund* was being shown inside it. I struggled with the tarpaulin until I found an opening. Flickering images on the screen, vibrating blue light. Wooden benches had been arranged in close rows, as in a church, and I was the only visitor. The film ran in a loop, I came in somewhere in the middle. Heavy thuds like mortar fire, a cloud of dust in the distance. The camera, perched on someone's shoulder, moved towards it. Then that voice, rambling amid a landscape of boulders.

'The absolute core . . . cracking the shell.'

It was the first time I'd ever heard his voice. My breath caught in my throat. Hello, father. His English was like that of the SS officers in war movies. I tried to figure out what I was looking at. A man in a ruin of his own making. His mumbling.

'The West. Oh, how we laughed at the West!'

He aimed the camera at the mountain in the distance. I was squinting, trying to make out whether there was anything worth seeing, looking for things camouflaged, when an explosion tore away the mountainside; dust, grit, chaos. The voice guided the viewer to the earth turned inside out. A rumbling, the camera's eye looked up, more stone rolling down the slope.

'How does one become a god, I asked them. How. By defeating the old gods. By reason of overweening pride. By not being the possessive slave. Weakened, smitten by the tiniest violation of his slavish happiness. Let us be butchers. Bear witness to our predilection for a universe of blood and bones. Create a cosmic slaughterhouse . . .'

Close to the end of the film: that mountain again, the camera fixed now, a man approaching from the distance, a bulky shape. Then the explosion, premature, the fraction of a second it takes for the shock-wave to knock down man and camera. The screen whirls, the camera like a dead man's open eye staring at the sky. Raindrops fall on the lens. Someone picks up the camera and its glides over a man's legs, registers for a moment his face seen from below – a short, grizzly beard spotted with gray. The flashing whites of the eyes, like those of a dog suddenly appearing beside you in the dark. *Mediohombre*. My father. Immeasurable loneliness was his task and his fulfillment. He created nothing but emptiness around him. It was a nuclear longing, the things shall never rise up again, he will rule over his grave for a million years. Schultz walked towards the place of the explosion, a climb. The camera swerved, a view of treetops as far as the eye could see. Higher. You could hear him panting. Sometimes he paused and pointed the camera at the destruction. Around it nothing but jungle, green and feverish at the edge of an open wound. That he had been there all those years . . . I tried to imagine the volume of stone, the mind-boggling effort needed to move it all. The hollow gaze of the Indians as well, that comment on the futility of yet another hallucinating gringo come to bend the earth and the people to his will. They were used to this, their history was a litany of defeats and subjugation, their fate was hereditary.

'Only the proud know what falling means, the chasm. The abyss at your feet. That one little step. That longing.'

The hissing of the wind, sometimes an animal noise like a dentist's drill. His snorting breath. Far below, people were moving, forming chains; obedient ants.

I didn't watch the entire film, at least not to the point where I had come in. Going out the door, I felt nauseous. The searing light – sunglasses, I needed a pair of sunglasses. From the glare of an over-exposed photo, the girl I'd just met suddenly appeared. I was not surprised.

'So, are you convinced?' she asked.

'Wait a minute.'

I squatted down, with my hands covering my watering eyes.

'Hey, can I do something?'

'Could I borrow your sunglasses for a minute? I think that would help.'

I let some light in through my fingers to get accustomed, then accepted her glasses. Colored lenses, a comfort to my eyes. I stood up. The girl in rosy light.

'I needed to sit down for a minute,' I said, 'I was completely blind.'

'Are you allergic to light?'

'Not that I know of, no.'

'Your eyes are watering really bad.'

'Did you come back to demonstrate a little?'

'No. I just came back.'

A confident smile. Little teeth, the moist pink gums. To take my tongue and feel how smooth that would be.

Her shopping cart was parked in front of the diner window. She was drinking tea. She pointed at the stitches on my eyebrow and asked

158

what had happened. Concerning the milkshakes going to other tables, she knew the quantity of sugar, colorants and fat they contained; the hamburger I'd ordered she commented on in terms of the origin of the meat, labor conditions in the meat-processing industry and the issue of waste. It was like clutching a landmine. She said, 'That's true, in the long run. That's why it's so hard to convince people, because it doesn't pose an immediate threat. We're not made to see long-term threats. We jump to our feet at a rustling in the bushes, that's what we're made for; a disaster fifty years from now doesn't matter much to us. In evolutionary terms, we're not prepared for the solutions to the problems we've created ourselves. We act as though nothing's wrong. Our day in the sun is more important.'

'You're certainly well-informed,' I said.

'That's right, joke about it. While you still can. So what did you think of the work of our Mr. Schultz?'

'*Mister* Schultz?'

'Um-hum . . .'

'Lonely. It's lonely. I've never seen anything that lonely.'

'A strange choice of words. For something so criminal, I mean.'

'Have you seen it?'

'No.'

'No?'

'I don't have to.'

'You go out demonstrating against something you haven't even seen? That's ridiculous.'

She shook her head stubbornly.

'You don't have to crawl into the sewer to know that it stinks.'

'Nicely put, but it doesn't mean anything.'

'I look . . . well, you can look with your principles too, if you get what I mean.'

'Pretty blue principles.'

'Excuse me?'

'Just kidding.'

'I'm serious.'

'Yes, I noticed that.'

'You didn't finish what you were saying, about Schultz.'

'There's no way we can have a conversation if you haven't even seen it.'

'Now you're angry.'

I grinned at this strange creature across from me. The tip of her tongue between her teeth. We knew. I got a hard-on.

'Let's go buy you some sunglasses,' she said.

She had been born in Augusta, Montana, left home at eighteen. Boulder or Seattle, that's where she wanted to go. Boulder was further away, she figured *I'll go there first, I can always go to Seattle later.* I couldn't quite follow her line of reasoning, but it made me laugh. Boulder hadn't felt like home, so she went west, to Los Angeles. Her apartment was in Venice. She had never made it to Seattle.

She pushed the shopping cart along, talking the whole time with an exuberance that did me good. Her soul may have been drenched in activism, but there was little that was grave about her. She wore striking clothes, wide linen trousers, a black blouse that reached to her knees, on top of that a knitted something, maybe what they call a stole, purple, sometimes she stopped for a moment to fling it over her shoulder again. Flip-flops on her feet. Glistening rings on toes that were long and slender, no helpless appendages. Thin, sensitive wrists.

Her car was parked at a supermarket. She put the folders, press kits and bottles of water in the trunk, then walked off to return the cart. I shouted after her, 'What's your name, anyway?'

'Sarah!' she shouted back over her shoulder.

When she walked everything about her moved in a private current of air that tousled everything, her curly dark hair, her clothes.

'What about you?' she asked when she got back.

I told her my name.

'German?'

'Yes.'

'Where are you headed, Ludwig?'

She pronounced my name as though tasting a new dish. I shrugged. She said, 'I live close to the beach.'

'I didn't bring my swimming trunks.'

'Trunks aplenty,' she said.

There was nothing wrong with the way she drove, it was just that she never stopped doing all kinds of things while sitting at the wheel. A dust mote that she tried to remove from her eye while looking in the rearview mirror, something in her bag, a piece of chewing gum, lip gloss that suddenly demanded her complete attention.

'You don't have to look at me when we talk,' I said. 'Just look at the road.'

'You're scared, ha ha! I've never had an accident, so don't sweat it.'

'That only hastens the day when you *will* have one.'

'You're drumming up bad karma, Ludwig.'

At a gas station I bought a pair of sunglasses with dark green lenses. Broad, bleached freeway interchanges slid past below us, the road a track of bone. When you're driving towards the ocean you can feel it, a kind of reassurance. Occasionally the sparkle of water between roads and buildings. And further away, on the horizon, the vision of Schultz's lacerated mountain, in sharp silhouette like Mount Fuji.

The hubcaps scraped the curb as she parked. We walked along the side of a house, climbed a set of metal steps in the backyard to her apartment. It was small, she mumbled something about not paying any attention to the mess, but it was impossible not to; the innards of a closet lay scattered across the floor, the couch, the bed. While she was digging around in a wooden crate, I looked at her backside.

'Swimming trunks,' I heard, 'must be here somewhere . . .'

A triumphant yelp, she held up a little black *slip de bain*. The bathroom was so small that your body acted as the lock on the door when you sat down on the pot. The hips of the man whose trunks these had been were even narrower than mine. I preferred somewhat roomier beach fashion, trunks in which you didn't stand out so much. She was sitting on the bed, a sarong around her hips. The cups of her bikini top closed around her breasts like a pair of hands. There would be no resistance. We were living in a state of delectable deferment.

We walk to the beach, it's not far. Sarah. Her flip-flops make a clapping sound. The sun has permeated the pavement with heat, it seeps up through your soles. To touch her, to give her a little shove – it's allowed, she is free in her conduct, without a word she has let you know that you may be as well. To give a little shove to someone you have known for only a couple of hours, call it playfulness but the seriousness of desire burns in your throat. The start of something. An encounter like this, those sparkling little teeth, the lovely dark hair; all it demands of you is participation, the willingness to leave your murky life story behind.

She asks about you, who you are, where you come from, but your biography suddenly seems so leaden.

'I'm going in for a dip,' she says. 'I have to pee.'

Shameless creature, I thought, with your delicious tits. I watched her go, her ample butt and thighs. I kicked off my own clothes and followed. I thought about her urine when I dove, in the state I was in everything was charged with sex. She was already out to where the waves were breaking. Surfers lay in wait for the big rollers. I couldn't catch up with her, she was the better swimmer. Bobbing around a bit, I waited for her to come back. The water was cold and stinging, I imagined the journey a drop of it might make, touching land again only at Sydney or Osaka. I also thought about a song by David Bowie, 'Space Oddity', about the wayward astronaut Major Tom who leaves his tin can.

The rise of an approaching wave toppled me from my floating position, I resurfaced and rubbed the water out of my eyes. I found myself looking straight into her smile, behind her a wave rising up like a wall of steel. The surfers were lying on their boards, paddling full speed before the curl. Then it crashed.

We found each other close to the beach, stinging water in my nose, Sarah rising up from the bubbling foam, laughing, coughing. She stuck her fingers under the hem of her bikini top and pulled it into place. Water glistened on her skin.

'Come on, up onto your feet, you.'

She slapped her palms on the water's surface, the way boys do in a swimming pool. We walked back to our clothes. I saw the dimples in the small of her back. She spread out her sarong for us on the sand and said, 'The water along the coast is actually too polluted to swim in. Around here it's a little better, but people often get sick. Surfers develop sores. Seals and sea lions develop problems with their immune system. We do everything we can, but it's tough.'

'We?'

'Clean the Bay, an organization I'm involved in. We've had some success, but it takes such a long time!'

She rolled her eyes.

'And you, you, could stand a little sun.'

She poked her finger at my upper arm and chest. I said, 'So you demonstrate against an artist and in favor of clean water, and what else?'

She glanced over, as though to check whether I was poking fun at her.

'Oh, a couple of other things. The Venice Beach Tree Savers ... the city's plans for the neighborhood are completely ridiculous. And an organization called Save the Holy Peaks, the protests against Schultz are actually related to that. We work with Native American organizations to counter the commercial exploitation, the disfigurement of holy mountains in Arizona, Hopi territory. Ski resorts have already been built there, but because there's been so little snow the last few years they're talking about pumping polluted water up from the valley and using machines to turn it into snow.'

Sarah shook her head.

'Perverse,' I said.

'You wouldn't believe the things people come up with.'

'I guess it keeps you pretty busy,' I said goofily.

'In a couple of weeks there's going to be a march on the Court of Appeals in Pasadena. If you come along you can see what we do, and why.'

With a simple gesture she opened a perspective that went beyond today; in a few weeks' time we would be together again, or still together. I was relieved to find that there were things that happened that had nothing to do with my mother. Her name admitted light into the picture. Sarah. She lay on her back, her arms folded behind her head. Short black hair in her armpits. I lost my way in the details, the little golden hairs on her tummy, darker on her forearms. I knew how the dried salt felt on her skin, that it tugged slightly, sometimes chafed a little.

It was cool in the shade along the streets. Young families behind windows with wrought-iron bars, the clattering of pans and voices calling out to each other. She looked at me. Heat expanded in my throat. We stopped, she came one step closer. The warmth of her body, exhaling sunlight. I smelled her hair, she raised her head, her breath against my armpit, my neck, her face brushing lightly against mine. Our bodies dovetailed. I was embarrassed by my erection pressing against her thigh.

'Are you coming with me, Mr. Ludwig?'

She pulled me along, I drew her back and wrapped my arms around her. We kissed greedily, quickly, she pulled away again. Could they see it, the people in their houses, were we passing by in the fiery glow of a comet . . . ?

She closed the door quietly behind her, latched it. Our coming together bristled with electricity.

'Do you want to take a shower?'

Clumsy mouths searching each other's shape, imprinting them. Our hands went their way. The slow waltz towards the bed, I felt her hand on my member. Her giggle, light as a feather.

'I noticed already, back on the beach.'

She stepped back, the sarong slid off her. She reached around behind her, unhooked the bikini top, slid the straps down over her arms, it fell to the ground the way everything fell to the ground here. She stepped out of her bottoms. The stripes from elastic bands on her skin. The shadows. I pulled off my T-shirt. She unbuckled my belt. I struggled out of my trunks and my cock, the uneasy third party in this company, sprang to attention. Her cool hand closed around it, led me to the bed. She fell back, I knelt between her legs, spread my fingers to seize her breasts, lifted my head and kissed her hard, cold nipples, the bikini top had still been wet. Her hand felt its way down, took me into her, her eyes wide open.

'Oh, Jesus.'

I had never known purer rapture. She took the lead, the most experienced one.

'Now, now!'

165

★

Her bed, the two of us lying on it with eyes open, looking at the different shades of blue coloring the room, and wondering aloud why most of them had no distinct name of their own but referred to something else of that color – sky blue, cobalt blue. The blues with Antwerp and Prussia in their names.

'They have codes,' I said. 'Color codes. BI58CC. C378NB.'

'Cold,' she said.

'Exactly,' I said.

I slipped off, into sleep, my face nestled against her throat.

'Ludwig?'

'Hmm.'

'Forget it. Go to sleep.'

The room was dark when I awoke. From the sounds around me I figured it was still evening, not night. A television, cars. She was lying with her back to me, her hand on my pelvis. I slid out of bed; when I came back from the toilet she was lying on her back, looking at me.

'Are you as hungry as I am?'

Outside – the amazement that everything had gone on the way it always did, as though we were standing on a still point, a stone in the stream – there we stood and there went everything. I thought: heaven, that can't be anything except this day, and then forever.

We ate at a Tibetan restaurant close to her house, photographs of monasteries on the walls. Cold, hard mountain landscapes. Boulders hung with colorful pennants. I ordered something with black-eyed peas and rice, she had something with pumpkin. The food arrived with surprising speed, in ceramic bowls.

'It's easy to be a vegetarian here,' she said. 'This city is keyed to vegetarians. But the rest of the country . . .'

There were things running through my mind. Questions.

'Would you rather be alone, later on?' I asked. 'I mean, I have another place I can sleep.'

She leaned across the table.

'What do you think, Ludwig? I'm not finished with you that easily.'

I'd expected a different answer, poignant phrases. I caught a glimpse of love as a conspiracy, the attractiveness of it. How quickly you became attached to someone whom you hadn't even known existed that same morning. I thought about my mother's omen, *In fact, you don't really need anyone anymore*, the contrast with this assenting little predator.

In her bed that night as well, in the soft, flickering glow of the metropolis, her body was a loud affirmation of life – chasms and heavens opened up to me at the same time, we climbed and fell, before my eyes floated visions of Schultz at the edge of his abyss, he and his woman, embracing each other in their fall.

'Goddamn it, Ludwig!'

It had been a long time since I'd seen her so angry.

'Where were you? What have you been up to?'

'The same as you, actually,' I mumbled, but she wasn't taken with the joke.

'I didn't sleep a wink all night. This is one thing too many for me right now, do you hear me? I need my sleep. Where were you?'

I shrugged.

'A girl?'

Sarah had dropped me off at the hotel. We kissed through the open window, she had driven on to her work – at the UCLA cafeteria. Trays full of food, trays full of garbage. Sometimes she thought: this will all be shit soon. She described her work as a maddeningly endless series of removals.

My mother asked, 'Who is it?'

'Someone I met.'

'That's fairly obvious. Please, Ludwig.'

I ordered a double espresso with a side of warm milk.

'Have you had breakfast yet? Order whatever you like, they have lovely things here.'

I was brimming with sensational memories. An invincibility that I owed to her. I'd never known that love was like this.

'I think we need to establish a few rules,' my mother said. 'I don't want this anymore. I want to know where you are.'

I struck out like a serpent.

'You were gone for a whole month without letting me know where you were.'

'And this constant lashing out of yours, we need to talk about that too, I consider it . . .'

'Consider it talked about. Period. So much for the family business. And now, what are you going to do today? Who are you going to get naked with today? In exchange for ten thousand dollars?'

'Ludwig . . .'

She smiled helplessly at the girl who put my cup down in front of me.

'I don't know why you came here,' she said a little later. 'Just to make me feel rotten? If so, you would have been better off staying in England. This way all we're doing is getting in each other's hair.'

'Do you want me to go away? I can do that. No problem, really.'

The hopelessness – there was no way out. I knew she was right; I was a punitive element and nothing more. Whenever I saw her I wanted to vent my hatred, to torture her. I never missed an opportunity to vomit my gall all over her. The war of words was one I would always win, but the battle against the reality in which she moved and breathed, that never. Once she was out of sight, the rage made way for feelings of loss.

'I'd like to know what your plans are. Ludwig?'

I tried to summon up Sarah, *sarahsarahsarah*, but she eluded me. One future had made way for another. Lightness for gravity. My mother may not have known it, but she needed me in that life of leaping-before-she-looked. One checkpoint in the course of the entire day. Our lives were two hands, one filled with uncertainty, the other with which we held each other tight. Or I held her, that was more like it. The lame leading the blind.

'So you either accept it, or . . .'

'Or? Or what?'

Quietly now.

'Or then I really want you to go back to England. You can apply at the conservatory, I know they would accept you.'

Her oldest dream concerning me: her son, the concert pianist, the old music temples of Europe. The straight world of culture at last. Caesarion, the fusion of the sex symbol and the artist, beauty and creation. Just as the son of Julius Caesar and Cleopatra was supposed to have been the union of both their talents, their genius. But what did the historians have to say about Caesarion? Not much, according to the Alexandrian Cavafy: *Behold, you came with your vague charm. / In history only a few lines / are found about you, / and so I molded you more freely in my mind.*

Caesarion had only one striking talent in fact, and that was for hitting upon the wrong moment. When Alexandria was besieged by Octavian and the city seemed about to fall, Cleopatra sent her son to India at the head of a caravan laden with riches. But for reasons known to no-one, he tried to return to the city where his mother had already committed suicide; the primal tale of the queen and the serpent, how she clutched it to her breast. She died along with her maidservants Iras and Charmion. En route to Alexandria, Caesarion – aged seventeen – was murdered, probably by Octavian's henchmen.

A dismal footnote to the story of his parents.

My mother herself had failed at the conservatory, yet it would be overly cheap psychology to assert that I was meant to mend her broken dreams. In any case, though, she was unrealistic in her estimation of my talent. Middling. She had never accepted that, not back then, not now either. That was painful to me, for it meant that whatever I did she would always see it as something unworthy of me, while in fact it was the best I could do.

'The Royal Academy of Music, I'm sure they'll have you.'

'About as likely as you someday playing Mary Poppins on Broadway.'

'Oh, Ludwig, but you've never even tried! Of course you can. I'm so sure.'

I grimaced.

'I'm afraid your being sure doesn't mean much. I've told you before, I talked to Mr. Fisk about it. He thought I would be admitted to the first year, but after that, he said, that's when it really starts. And no, he didn't think I would make the grade after that.'

'What does a man like that know about it? He never made it any further than piano teacher in some country town. Everyone always thought you played so beautifully, that counts too, doesn't it?'

It must have been that she had suffered so miserably under her own lack of talent, which she'd had to compensate for with hard work. The semi-talented need so little confirmation to continue down the beaten track. An encouraging nod, an applause that lasts a fraction of a second too long – that was enough to evade self-insight for yet a little while.

A shadow fell across the table.

'Hi, girlie,' Rollo Liban said. 'Hello, Ludwig.'

I said nothing, I still didn't know how to deal with him.

'You ready to roll?' he asked her.

She dabbed at her lips with the napkin and nodded. The top buttons of Rollo's shirt were open, showing a mass of gray chest hair. He was tanned and about thirty kilos overweight. The fat had accumulated around his torso, the white canvas trousers flapped loosely around his legs. When he looked down, his head rested on a pedestal of two or three chins. She stood up.

'Please think about what I said, Ludwig. It's up to you. Will I see you this evening? Will you be there?'

'I'll leave a message.'

'Do you have enough money? Here, I'll give you . . .'

'That's not necessary.'

'Take it, sweetheart. And now we really have to go, I believe. An interview with, what's his name again, Rollo?'

'Jay Leno.'

She giggled.

'Well, we can't make *him* wait.'

A kiss on my forehead, Rollo Liban was already halfway to the door. She followed him, people turned their heads and watched them go. Before me on the table lay a packet of dollars. My economy would become entangled with hers, with the money she earned with her body – that was my bread and butter as well. I put it in my pocket, it seemed warmer than the things around it. The waitress came up to me with a black leather notepad.

'Could I ask you to sign here, please?'

I climbed the stairs to the next level of the hotel, where I had seen a piano. My fingers slid across the keys; it was tuned. I did enjoy playing, but the love and ambition my mother hoped for were things I didn't possess. I could earn my keep with it, which seemed better than a life in which you had to call someone 'boss' or sat in a conference room with four hundred men and women under the supervision of a painfully facile moderator.

Behind the reception desk was a photo of the hotel manager, Berny Suess. One day soon I would look him up, but first I went outside, into sunlight, in search of the queen of my night before.

The journey went from bus to bus. My fellow passengers were, with the exception of the occasional Latino, black. It was very hot, I had the astounding sense of being on a journey that that would never end, that the bus drivers would forget to warn me of my stop and no-one would ever ask for my ticket, like a forgotten article of clothing, a glove slid down between the seat and the backrest. There were lots of traffic jams, we stood idling for a long time. Blacks entering the bus looked up in surprise, as though I were a white man who had come to claim his seat at the front, a Rosa Parks in reverse. The final bus took me into the shady hills, it was cool there, snippets of fiefdoms amid the trees. I climbed out at the campus gates, the terminus; from here the bus drove back into the city, the heat and the grime.

I walked onto the grounds, which had the eminent air of an old park. Eucalyptus trees raised their pale arms to the sky, piles of bark lay at their feet. Under the trees students were sitting eating their lunches, their books beside them; others were wandering across the soft lawn and talking quietly to themselves, perhaps learning a role by heart; this was a spot for the elect, here you could become whatever you liked, and be the best at it. The things were veiled with a remarkable calm, the nervous haste had remained behind in the city; in these gardens the tone was set by time and reflection. It took hold of you easily, just as the neurosis of mass society did outside these gates. For a moment I reflected favorably on my mother's suggestion that I go to college; I would be able to spend a few years of my life in a sheltered space like this, with its calm heartbeat. Gray squirrels ran across the lawn, climbed the trees, the kind Selwyn Loyd had referred to during the hunt along Bunyans Walk as an *exotic species*. The faculty buildings were connected by pillared walkways and broad paths, I saw a Moorish palace, something that looked like the Roman Senate, libraries in the style of the Italian Renaissance with cypresses in front, and everything so clean, so sparklingly fresh that it seemed as though it had all been put there just before I arrived. I followed the trail of students with pre-packaged sandwiches and cups of soft drinks, and entered a covered shopping mall. In the restaurant I was prepared for the shock of reunion, I had imagined seeing her bent over a table, wiping crumbs and rings off the Formica top, but the only personnel I saw were sitting at cash registers or handing out food from behind the display cases.

Once again I found myself wandering through the eclectic architectural gardens inhabited by young people from all corners of the world, like in the color tracts handed out by evangelical Christians, with lions and lambs lying down together at the feet of an Asian girl, who is looking up in rapture at a perfectly symmetrical young Caucasian man with blue eyes: the born-again Arcadia.

At last I located the next cafeteria, where the customers took their food from trays piled high for them along a runway of display cases and heating lamps. It was busy. Espresso machines were running at full speed, the hammering of filter holders against waste containers reminded me of the joy of Trianon. Then I saw her. She was wearing a white cap, like a nurse's, it was pinned to her hair. She was nice to the people whose tables she cleaned. She was someone who believed in reciprocity, someone who might say things like *what you give comes back to you*, but I wouldn't let that irritate me, I wouldn't let it come between us.

I shook myself awake from the daydream. She vanished through the swinging doors, toting trays full of cutlery and dishes. The girl from Augusta. The girl who demonstrated for mountains and trees one day, and the next wore a white uniform and shouted as she came back from the kitchen, 'Number 28!'

She glanced at the tray.

'Meat loaf and potato salad!'

At one of the tables, hands fly up. Two careless boys, they take their own presence here completely for granted, they have never lacked for a thing – if one day they should discover that they have some filthy disease, they will be incredulous, they will feel betrayed. Selwyn was like them, I used to envy him the good fortune to which he seemed born. And also for his parents, their hospitality, the orderliness they had created. They had made sacrifices to get that far. Considerable sacrifices. They had done without things, limited themselves. They had offered themselves up with no prospect of personal gain. Their children had parasitized upon the flesh of that sacrifice, and it had made them big, strong. They lived in the certainty that, in principle, life would be good to them. The investment of time and effort on their parents' part expressed itself in that basic conviction, which would not be easily shaken. Life without sacrifice is a mess of shards, a ruin. It was because of his parents that Selwyn had become what he was, a person who didn't ask himself what his place in life might be, but who claimed the room he needed calmly and unbendingly, like a tree.

Loss was part and parcel of sacrifice. With sacrifice, you acted counter to your own interests, and gave up the right to bemoan that fact. Complaint sullied the offer, it amounted to taking back that which you had given. Yesterday, at the gallery, Sarah had wanted to be arrested; the arrest was the sacrifice. Only in that way could the act of resistance finally be awarded a crown.

I looked at her, her light-footed, chaotic dance amid the tables, the landscape of waste, and waved until she saw me. She was startled. She put her tray down on a table and walked over to me.

'You can't come here, Ludwig! You can't see me like this . . .'

She shrugged in dismay and looked down at the white cafeteria uniform.

'I figured, I'll go take a look . . . see how you're making it through the day.'

She looked at her watch.

'I've got at least another five hours. I'm exhausted.'

I nodded.

'But it was . . . it was worth it,' she said. 'With you.'

We were silent, embarrassed suddenly – we'd known each other for such a short time, still knew so little about each other. I got up.

'I'm sorry, I shouldn't have come and bothered you.'

'It's okay,' she said.

'I have to get back. Maybe I'll see you later.'

'Yeah,' she said. 'What are you going to do?'

'Oh, things, this and that. Play the tourist.'

'I have to get back to work,' she said, suddenly agitated. 'Rush hour!'

On my way out, there was a tap on my shoulder, and a question accompanied by a nervous smile.

'Will you come to see me tonight?'

Happiness, pouring out like light.

'Yes, I'd love to,' I said.

I walked all the way back to Santa Monica, to the hotel at the seaside, lighter than I had ever walked before, immune to dust and heat, actually running at times. Hamburger joints and car washes and shoals of Latinos in the shade of a taco stand; I clenched my fist and choked back an ongoing shout of triumph. This was not the world as I had known it. This cascade of sensual delights that came tumbling into my soul. Back at the hotel, beside the pool, I witnessed the glimmer of splashed droplets, their sensational beauty. If this too was the world, alongside the one of drabness and habit, then which one of them was the exception? Why was this beauty usually hidden from our eyes? Why all the veils, all the trouble it took to remove them? I thought about *Abgrund* – was that what he was doing, tearing aside the veil? Revealing the holy of holies? Was my desire to see everything, to reduce mysteries to riddles and riddles to answers, akin to his? Was that the message ghosting about in my blood? I had to backtrack, to return to the whispering that accompanied his act of violence, to experience that which perhaps could not be understood, but which *could* be seen.

The cabbie who took me to my father I paid with dollars my mother had given me, making me a child of both. Brightly colored flyers lay on the pavement before the gallery, the remains of this morning's demonstration, the daily boycott. The dark tarpaulins hung motionless, as though they surrounded the black stone of Islam. It had to be irony, a joke on the part of the gallery owner, to exhibit a work of extreme desecration with the trappings of a shrine. The cleaving of the stone. The space which served as the office was in the back of the gallery, bathed in caustic light. At a desk was the man I had seen yesterday. An old, bedraggled Labrador lay at his feet. I wanted to talk to that man, but first I had to work my way past the bespectacled secretary, who had adorned herself for the occasion with all the disdain in the world.

'Ma'am, could I . . .'

She raised her hand.

'Just a minute,' she said.

She rose from her chair and slid a folder back into the rack above her head. Then she looked at me over the top of her glasses, which struck me as a strange habit, looking at people over the top of one's glasses.

'There's something I need to ask that gentleman over there. Mr. Steinson, is it, or Mr. Freeler?'

'Neither, actually,' she said. 'And you are from . . .?'

'I'm not from anything. I just have a question.'

The man looked at us.

'What can I do for you?' he called out.

The secretary resumed her position at the Mac, her fingers with their long, painted nails hovering over the keys like a pianist before the concert starts. The man slid his chair back and came over to me. The dog lifted its head with a sigh.

'You wanted to ask something about the show?'

'About the maker, actually.'

'Have you seen the catalog?'

'Yes. But it didn't say whether he's still working on his project, on *Abgrund.*'

'As far as I know, he's still there.'

'But how do you get hold of his work? Does he bring it himself, or do you go and fetch it?'

The dog came up behind the man, leaned against his legs. The look on the gallery manager's face changed, became cautious, distant. Why did I want to know all this? he asked. Perhaps he suspected that I was a demonstrator, a disturber of the peace. I asked, 'Is it possible to meet Schultz, as far as you know? That's what I'm interested in.'

'It would be easier to schedule a meeting with the President, I'm afraid. I can't remember . . . no, no interviews, nothing.'

'I saw the film,' I said, 'yesterday. I . . . What I'm curious about, actually, is how you should look at something like this, about what kind of art you'd call it.'

He nodded.

'I remember a happening,' he said, 'sometime in the late Sixties. It was the first time I saw an artist destroy his own work. A funny guy, very mild-mannered, really. Wolfgang Stoerchle, he drove a car over his own work, his paintings. Died quite suddenly. Otherwise . . . well. It's fuck-you-work, in fact. About ten years ago the guys from the Survival Research Lab did a show at Joshua Tree. They blew up things in the landscape, accompanied by deafening music from Einstürzende Neubauten. A bit of a failure, really. A pile of debris went "blooey", and that was pretty much it. Mark Pauline still likes to blow up things, he even lost a hand in an explosion, but that was by accident. I don't know whether Schultz saw the stuff at Joshua Tree, whether that gave him the idea. And, of course, you've also got Roman Singer's Action Sculptures . . .'

'The Chinese,' the girl behind him said without looking up from her terminal. 'The Chinese do explosions, too.'

'Fuck-you-work, all of it,' the man said. 'But anything like Schultz, there's never been anything quite so, so grand. And so malicious.'

'You think it's malicious?'

'Oh yes, definitely. No doubt about it.'

I thanked him for his time and said I was going to watch the film again.

'No problem.'

I parted the tarps for the second time and went in. Sitting on the front bench, bathed in blue light, was an older couple. Again I submitted myself to his prophetic rage, cryptic as a language without vowels. The camera homed in on the workers far below as they carried off stones, the wind rasped in the mike. He ridiculed them.

'Created for obeisance. To have gods above them, not to be gods. The radical imperative. Every man is an abyss . . . but the audacity needed to be *someone else's* abyss . . . Unflinchingly. That's what it is to have backbone, to be someone else's abyss . . .'

He began making his way down, gray sky above, the exhausted greenery lurching below. Schultz was humming, you could hear the gravel crunch beneath his shoes. He sang a line of the song, repeated it at intervals. *Denn alle Lust will Ewigkeit, will tiefe, tiefe Ewigkeit.* He stopped, aimed the camera at a higher spot. The lens slid across the lesions.

'All that remains is what is gone. Deep, deep eternity. But they want a Creator. To have their existence confirmed. Oh, the cowardly sanctification of Creation. The emotion! The ideals! The piss-ants! Their *mysterium tremendum*! But destruction is the only thing with permanence. The future belongs only to the anti-Creator.'

The laughter of someone who has been alone too long. I felt like running away or weeping, how could this jousting with the gods and with people end in anything but self-destruction? I didn't run, however, I remained seated until the film came back to the moment where I had arrived the day before, the explosion of the mountain's face; only then did I leave the Ka'abah.

The street didn't help me catch my breath. This man, and I was his

179

son. *Abgrund* rolled you in the coils of a man's inner world and squeezed the life out of you. Now I had two parents in need of saving.

My life of nights began. The symbiosis. Nights during which her face beneath me against the white sheet flowed into other, all-too-familiar faces. Perhaps it was the fatigue, perhaps the ecstasy, but I often saw those faces rise up through hers like air bubbles – when we made love, or afterwards, when I lay on her like a gravestone and felt her heartbeat gradually diminish. Before my eyes, as they searched for a grip in the dusky darkness, I saw my drawing teacher Eve Prescott appear, and once, to my surprise, that of Daisy Farnsworth, a homely girl from my class. I closed my eyes to Paula Loyd, when she came swimming towards me through the milk of the night; when I opened them again it was Sarah looking at me. Let me be frank and admit that sometimes it was my mother's face as well, and that I was powerless when it came to my brain's nocturnal projections.

And so we drowned in each other, and were washed up at the first light of day in that little room somewhere in the world.

'I have to get going,' she said. 'Stay as long as you want.'

She sat straight up in bed. She looked at me, the smile of someone still halfway in the dream. I had become a stammerer, someone who said, 'You, your back, nice.'

My fingertips slid over the curve of muscle beneath her skin.

'What are you going to demonstrate against today?'

A little sound of protest.

'You know, some people have to hold down a job too, Ludwig.'

A few mornings a week she went to La Cienega to raise her voice against Schultz's work. I had been waiting for the right moment to tell her, but the longer I put it off the more of a secret it became. I feared what might come of it. Euphoria and dread were never far apart, they took turns racing like relay runners. I was going to tell her. Soon.

She would understand that I wasn't him, that his hateful, pitch-black visions were not hereditary. I asked myself why I didn't tell her right away. Was it because I wasn't entirely sure of how they, Schultz and my mother, manifested themselves in me? Mightn't the perversion and violence smolder on in me, Caesarion, the confluence of those two egos who had sought to reproduce themselves?

Sarah sighed and climbed out of bed, picking from among the things lying on the floor what she would wear that day.

The afternoon after seeing *Abgrund* for the second time, I went to Venice to wait for evening. A bar at beachside, a hamburger and a Coke, please (I'm in America, goddamn it, I'll bloody well eat whatever I like), and inside me the certainty that I will go in search of him. Not now, not right away, but I would find him, as soon as my mother and I once again had solid ground beneath our feet. What makes me think that he longs for me the way I do for him? What makes me think that I can comfort him? That I am the only one who can enter the cage without him devouring me? In my thoughts he is always *Schultz*, never *Father* or *Papa*. *Papa* sounds preposterous, like sticking your tongue in someone's ear the moment you meet them. I whisper *Papa* to him, a few times in a row, *Papapapa*, and can't help laughing, it sounds more taunting than intimate.

'Your Coke, sir. Hamburger's on its way.'

Schultz was right, eternity belongs to that which is gone. In the same way that he, his running away, has established the course of our lives. We have lived around his absence. And then, clear as can be, the insight that she, Marthe Unger, has re-entered the light in order to be seen by him. She shows herself to the world in the hope that, somewhere in that world, his eye will fall on her. The splendor of her body, which she has kept for him, and now given back to the marketplace. The marketplace she had left because she loved him – a sacrifice he

181

hadn't asked for and perhaps hadn't even wanted. Had it excited him to possess the woman who elicited such boundless desire? Was his interest, his fire, extinguished once she had given up that role for him? There had been no great crises, no drawn-out arguments poisoning the relationship, nothing had occurred that might have justified his leaving. Perhaps, when he came up to her in New York and introduced himself, he had assumed the desire of all those others, perhaps it had fed his love for her, and he had realized his mistake only on Rue Mahmoud Abou El Ela, once the others were no longer around; they were alone together now, they had only each other to fall back on.

A ragged procession of joggers, cyclists and skaters moved past the restaurant patio. I read free tabloids till the afternoon was over. Suddenly there was the encirclement of mist. The temperature dropped sharply. I paid the tab and walked into the cloud, which seemed to drip lightly, a bedewed spider's web. I followed the trail back. I was a man on his way to claim his prize. The sensation of being able to look through walls, to see their little lives. I padded lightly down their streets, the shadow of an unstoppable predator sliding across the house fronts.

The little car was parked in front of her house, one wheel up on the curb. Two steps at a time I ascended to her castle in the air and barged into her world with a bang.

'Jesus, Ludwig!'

Candles, incense.

'I've been running all day,' I said. 'All I can do is run. I don't know what it is.'

She was sitting cross-legged on the bed, wearing a white undershirt with wide armholes.

She said, 'I spent ninety minutes in traffic and sang real loud along with Lenny Kravitz. So don't I deserve a kiss?'

Yes, that and more. We rolled around on the bed like young cats, at the center of that little galaxy. At the head of the bed a votive candle was burning in front of a photo I hadn't noticed before. Disentangling myself, I leaned on the mattress in order to get a better look. Two hands cupped to form a shallow bowl, in them something unformed, a slimy wad, black, tarlike. I exhaled loudly and said, 'What is that for a mess?'

I recognized my mistake right away, saw how she answered my disgust with even more disgust. She rolled away from under me and was standing beside the bed in the same motion. Moving to the little window, she stood there, her arms crossed, ponderous, silent. This was what I had been afraid of, the wrong word, the evil charm that signaled the start of the destruction. I gasped for air, for words. I had to undo something, but didn't know what I'd done.

'Sarah, what's wrong?'

'Don't say anything.'

Disaster was flying in on huge wings, the message it croaked was the inconstancy of all happiness. One wrong move and you find yourself irrevocably out of love. I stammered apologies and climbed off the bed. Across the twilight-blue room the severity fell from her slowly, like dry husks. The picture behind the candle, I saw now, was like a domestic altar. On the shelf there was incense, a silver rattle, something that looked a pile of herbs.

'That,' she said at last in a voice that didn't seem like hers, 'is Dylan.'

She took a deep breath. Her shoulders sagged.

'Dylan was born four months prematurely.'

The ground opened up beneath me.

'Afterwards, Denzel left me.'

'His swimming trunks,' I mumbled. 'I'm so sorry. I didn't know.'

The gratitude when she glanced at me again. The life that may have been coming back.

'Denzel,' I said, 'was he black?'

'Afro-American, yeah.'

I knew nothing about the world, a rank beginner. She was a life-time ahead of me.

Days later, when she had closed the door behind her early in the morning and left me there alone, I blushed again when I thought back on that moment. I turned onto my side and looked at the black fetus in his cloak of blood and slime.

'Hi, Dylan,' I said.

I didn't know whose hands were holding him. White hands, maybe hers. After a while she had started going out with men again, some of them became lovers, with none of them had it become anything more than that.

At night she said, 'You have soft skin. Like a girl's.'

'So do you.'

A man and a woman laugh quietly in the dark. The words: *We were together. I have forgotten about the rest.* She took my hand and pushed it between her legs. The coarse hair, the slipperiness of her cunt.

'Another one,' she groaned, and twisted her body until four fingers were in her.

They moved slowly inside her, I barely had to do a thing. She breathed loudly through her nose and made little noises, the air burst from her lungs when she came. I had never been so hard, and slid right into her – I could smell my fingers beside her face, the slight sourness, the hint of iron.

We slept between thin sheets. Our bodies slid across each other, dry and cool, sometimes half awake, the delicious sense of being alive, of feeling joy at the existence of someone else, of then sinking back into the darkness of sleep.

★

I called the hotel to see if my mother was there, and was put through. She answered. I said I'd be there in an hour.

'Oh, and Ludwig, could you pick up some sandwiches for us?'

I walked to Loews, bought sandwiches and soft drinks along the way. She knew I was spending my time with a girl these days, and no longer asked about it. I visited her a few times a week. When I asked what she was up to, she remained noncommittal. I had the impression that Rollo Liban's publicity campaign was working: I saw her in the newspapers and sometimes, when I stopped somewhere for a sandwich, she would suddenly appear on the TV above the counter, in some talk show with an exuberant host who asked her about things to which I closed my ears. Let her go her godless way.

She was sitting on the balcony, wearing a big pair of sunglasses, her head tilted back to catch the sun.

'So, here I am,' I said.

It was supposed to be a hint to her to cover herself; she was wearing nothing but a pair of black panties and a hotel bathrobe that was hanging open. I saw her breasts, and felt embarrassed. She smiled.

'Ah, room service! Get a bottle of Chardonnay from the fridge, would you, sweetheart?'

Once I was back in the room, she shouted after me, 'I had them slide the beds together again, you never sleep here anyway these days.'

The room showed signs of more permanent habitation. There was an electric kettle now and a tray with different kinds of tea. On the windowsill was a wooden plank, inlaid with mother of pearl – the white ash told me she used it to burn her incense. There was a smoking ban at Loews, but she paid it no heed. The pictures of the men with beards had followed her from the house on Kings Ness; she had them arranged beside the mirror, so that every time she looked at herself she could see them too, and perhaps be reminded of their philosophy.

In the minibar I found a little bottle of white wine with a twist-off top and took two glasses from the bathroom.

She was still sunning herself as blatantly as ever, with those glorious breasts and all. The last time I had seen them was in *Lilith*, at Selwyn's house. I stood on the threshold of the balcony, my eyes exploring her body. I looked at her the way Uncle Gerard had once looked at her beside the canal, the sweet gleam of her skin, her slender, elegant limbs.

'Put something on,' I said gruffly. 'I'm not going to eat lunch with you like this.'

She turned her face towards me; behind the dark glasses I couldn't see her eyes.

'Why not? I'm your mother, I have nothing to be ashamed of.'

'I don't feel like looking at your tits while I eat.'

'Well then, look somewhere else.'

She nodded towards the sea. I had the uneasy feeling she was challenging me. That she wouldn't bat an eye if I laid a hand on her breasts, caressed her.

'Stop acting like some goddamn hippie,' I said.

'Oh God, I didn't know you were so awfully prudish, Ludwig.'

She wrapped her bathrobe around her with a sigh.

'I brought cheese,' I said. 'I hope you like *that*.'

'Actually, I'm trying not to eat too many dairy products these days.'

She unwrapped the sandwich.

'I looked at a little house, no too far from here. I can't stay here forever, unfortunately. A cute little place, perfect for the two of us.'

'Where?'

'Venice.'

'That's where Sarah lives.'

She wiggled her toes. Light pink nail polish.

'Sarah, is that her name?'

'Sarah Martin.'

'That's funny.'

'What's so funny about it?'

'Oh, nothing in particular. It's just . . . so normal. I mean, that could be anyone's name. Is she a spy?'

She thought that was humorous. She asked me, 'So when do I get to meet her? I've never seen you so wrapped up in a girl. Are you in love? Bring her over, while I'm still here. Ask her to come tomorrow, we'll do a high tea. Lovely scones, bonbons, those little tiny cakes. Or isn't she allowed to eat sweets?'

'I'm not sure this is her kind of place.'

'This is one of the finest hotels in town! Of course, she'll love it!'

She rented the house for the remainder of her time in Los Angeles, the agent said she could move in on the first of the month. It had two bedrooms, she told me, and a little garden at the front and back. You could open the garden doors to air it out. It was a quiet neighborhood, they had assured her, with none of the violent crime you had in other parts of Venice.

After our lunch I went looking for Berny Suess, the hotel manager, to see whether he needed a pianist – one who could sing as well, a jukebox with fingers. I found him in his office at the end of a dark hallway on the second floor. As soon as I appeared in the doorway, his face went all service-minded. I told him who I was and what I had come for. He came out from behind his desk energetically.

'So show me your stuff,' he said. 'We need someone occasionally, but not real regularly.'

He trotted out in front of me. A wisp of hair had detached itself from the top of his balding scalp and bobbed along at the side of his head. I tried to keep up with him, but he remained one step ahead the whole time.

'At night we have a guitarist who sings in the bar, maybe you've seen him. The only time we need a pianist is for special occasions: private parties, presentations, you know what I mean.'

There was no stool. I fetched a plastic chair from the conference room and sat down at the piano.

'What would you like to hear?'

'"Bridge over Troubled Water",' Suess said without a moment's hesitation. 'The loveliest song I know.'

Fortunately I knew it by heart, and my voice was suited for it.

'Yes,' Suess murmured a few times as I was playing.

The song seemed attached to some memory of his, and he was visibly moved by it. When I was finished I launched right into the andante of Mozart's eleventh sonata, just to show off my eclecticism.

'Buddy,' Suess said, 'where can I get hold of you?'

I grinned.

'Room 304.'

'That situation,' he said. 'Two people in a single room. Ms. LeSage's guest. I didn't want to say anything about it yet. A splendid woman, so friendly I mean, not stuck up or anything. Truly magnificent.'

'My mother,' I said. 'It was only for a couple of nights, these days I usually sleep somewhere else.'

'Listen, have you got the right outfit for this? Tie, shirt? Blazer?'

Lovers' insomnia. Whispering, we take little bites of each other's life stories. I listen to the youth of a stranger, a girl who saw snowcapped mountains to the west and violent thunderstorms over the prairies, with bolts of lightning reaching from the clouds all the way to the ground. The word *nowhere* for Augusta, a dot on the map. Ranch-style houses, pickups out in front. The desperate longing for something else. Once a year there was a big rodeo, men in leather chaps, the gruesome shouting of 'yee-haw' in the streets. She remembers the pang of excitement when one day a body was found along the road, riddled with bullets. Later her father read aloud to her from the newspaper, about a married woman who had become involved with a Hell's Angel; she had complained to him about her husband, how he made her suffer. The plan to murder him had arisen from her lamentations. The Hell's Angel had asked two friends to help him, they had lured the husband to a strip joint, later that night they had waylaid him along the road and shot him in the chest and face. Her father read such stories to her as a warning, beware of the world, but it had served to awaken in her a desire for that world, for the romance that lay outside the straight and narrow.

Sarah tries to go home twice a year, to Augusta, for Thanksgiving and for the annual family reunion.

'My mother would like to meet you,' I say.

'Already?'

Sarah doesn't know what a high tea is, but she'll try to be there on time, after work. The moment I've been avoiding all this time. She'll have to find out before they meet.

'A while ago you asked me why my mother and I are here.'

I unroll before her a threadbare life story, catchwords, incomplete sentences, compressed until no life is left in them. Mother's side, father's side, all those things I left out. Telling it straight. Ignoring her dismay.

'Oh my God, poor Ludwig.'

She remembered hearing something about it, or reading it.

'Insane,' she said, 'completely insane.'

That sounds a lot more like it already. Then she falls asleep. She has a little over three hours before her day begins. She breathes deeply and calmly. I watch over a wonder.

A little past five, later that same day. I ask my mother whether Mr. Suess has called. She shakes her head. What I really want to know is whether the shooting has already started, whether the irony and the propaganda have already segued into the earnestness of sex for money – have the hordes already descended upon her person?

She says she'll go ahead and order. Her voice at my back, 'It takes them a while to put it together. I hope your girl gets here on time.'

Everything she says repulses me. Worse than that. A hatred that nestles high in my chest. If I were to seize her by the throat, I'm afraid I might never let go. I want to know who it is who fucks her, I want to see their faces as they go into her. Sometimes I awaken from daydreams: orgies of crime and rape – by broad daylight, I walk down the street, the events in my head are razor-sharp, the world around me is cast in weak light.

Sarah is late. I know that somewhere, back in the kitchen, the meter is running. Now that I'm paying attention, I notice that you actually hear sirens here all the time. All the time. As though people here immediately act on every bad impulse. The tea and scones must be pretty much ready by now. Maybe I should keep a parking spot open for her along the street, valet parking at the hotel costs a bundle. Don't forget later on to get a pair of clean underpants out of my suitcase.

★

She arrived just after six. I was annoyed and relieved. My mother was seated behind a silver tower of aromatic substances and flavor enhancers.

'Hello, Sarah,' she said. 'I'm Marthe.'

And then to me, a little more quietly.

'We would have been better off ordering dinner.'

She poured the tea.

'No sugar for me, thank you, Marthe,' Sarah said.

She took an egg-salad sandwich. My mother rattled her spoon in her teacup. Sarah told us that someone had spilled a plate full of pasta all over her that afternoon. The woman hadn't even apologized.

'Some people,' my mother said. 'It's not right to judge, but still . . .'

'You're very pretty,' Sarah said. 'It's hard to believe that you two are mother and son. In terms of age, I mean.'

'Lucky genes,' my mother said. 'Only our necks, ugly necks run in our family.'

'I don't see anything ugly about it.'

'You do when I do this.'

My mother bowed her head, causing deep wrinkles in her ugly neck.

'Oh, but I have that too,' Sarah said.

She bowed her head as well, a double chin appeared.

'The two of you have other interests in common as well,' I mumbled.

'Do we?' said my mother.

'Incense,' I said. 'Candles. That kind of thing.'

'Do you mean spirituality, Ludwig?' Sarah asked with a treacherous kind of amiability.

I smiled at her to confirm our bond, but was suddenly not quite sure we belonged to the same conspiracy.

'He always jokes about that,' my mother said. 'You seem so afraid to believe in anything, sweetheart. Even though . . . life would be so much richer if you weren't so cynical. Just look at your father . . .'

'Let's change the subject,' I said.

I had told her beforehand that all things Schultz were taboo when Sarah was around. But I was now no longer certain that I had nailed shut that particular fire door firmly enough.

'Is cynicism something that's passed from father to son in your family?' Sarah asked. 'It seems so typically male to me. As though you men can't tell the difference between disbelief and strength.'

A little tremor of approval played at the corners of my mother's lips. Then she started talking about when I was born, how in the hospital in Alexandria she had rocked my cradle every few minutes to hear whether I was still alive. She laid her hand on Sarah's forearm.

'Even then I was already so jealous of the girlfriend he would have someday!'

The conversation fanned out into practical idealism; I raised my head with a start when I heard Sarah say, 'And that's how I met Ludwig.'

'Oh really?' my mother said.

Sarah looked at me.

'Didn't you tell her how we met?'

'Things like that don't really interest her.'

'Oh, Ludwig! That's mean! Those are exactly the kinds of things I love to hear!'

'I want to get going,' I said.

The thought of having come out of her – to gag on a mouthful of amniotic fluid.

'One more cup of tea then,' Sarah said. 'I just got here.'

'Exactly, very good,' my mother said. 'He can be so pushy. Stand up for yourself. But now tell me, where did the two of you meet?'

This was getting out of hand. I said, 'So why didn't you ask me about it, if you were really so interested?'

'Oh, well, you're always gone so quickly.'

'I'm perfectly willing to tell you,' Sarah said. 'It's no secret.'

I saw how I could come to hate her.

'I'd rather talk about something else,' I said. 'Porn or something. Fucking for money. Prostitution in front of the camera.'

The silence around that silver cylinder full of sweetness was extremely pleasant.

'That wasn't very . . . nice, Ludwig,' Sarah said after a moment.

I was speechless. She should be standing by me, at my side! Not facing off against me! After the victory, the defeat appeared without delay; my mother was sitting with her face averted, her eyes full of tears. Tears, goddamn it. Oh, you bastard, now you've ruined everything. And Sarah is looking at you with the most painful kind of distance, and now she's moving over beside her to put a hand on her shoulder and comfort that tainted whore. A different word. The charm bracelet on her wrist tinkles softly as she runs her hand up and down my mother's back. My mother, who smiles at her and dabs at the corners of her eyes with her fingertips – all female bonding at this table, it's unbearable, what a seedy little tableau. And isn't it amazing that I, the link between those two, have now completely disappeared from the whole situation? A chemical process is what it is: after the reaction the catalyst is regenerated, unchanged, and I am alone again.

'It doesn't matter,' my mother said. 'Mothers are always a kind of punching bag, aren't they? Almost all men hate their mothers. That's just the way it is.'

Sarah slides back around in the booth to where she was sitting. She blows on her tea as though it were very hot indeed.

We drove through Santa Monica, the evening was still young.

'I thought she was really nice,' Sarah said.

'You don't know her,' I say, looking straight ahead.

Futile. You can't hand over your world to someone else. I was breathing through a screen of repulsion. She'd taken sides with her. Neutrality I could have understood; partiality in the wrong direction was unforgivable. I hadn't been expecting it, my defenses were down. My mother had seduced Sarah and simply wormed her way between us. She had become my rival for Sarah's attention and loyalty.

Sarah's room was too small for sitting around together in silence. I went outside, my disappointment in one hand, my wounded soul in the other. I felt the lack of a house to go to, wherever I went I would be a guest. The streets were lined with low, dusty trees whose leaves had curled from the drought. When ultramarine overwhelmed the sky I sauntered back and came in the door with the insouciance of a cat who has disappeared for a few days. Again the candles, the incense rising in a shaky column, the mysticism of a shaman's cave. I tried not to look at the dead child, the focal point of the room.

'You're not talking,' she said. 'Apparently you're very angry about something, but how can I do anything if you won't talk?'

The listless mantra that accompanies failure. She said, 'I don't know, but what are you doing here if you don't want to talk?'

I turned around and walked back down the steel steeps, back to the street. High, searing pride took my breath away. The unconditionality could end that quickly, that quickly you could be transformed from lover into unwelcome guest. After a fashion, I actually reveled in the bonfire of self-destruction. Behind me the sound of fast, light little footsteps.

'I'm running after you this time,' she said, 'but next time you can figure it out for yourself. What do you want, Ludwig? I don't know why you're acting like this.'

For a moment I thought about ignoring her and walking on, but realized that that would be overplaying my hand.

'I didn't mean to send you away,' she said, 'I asked why you were with me if you acted like that. It was a question, okay, a question!'

My body heavy with inertia, I let myself be led back to the house. Later on she took my cock in her mouth, which was still hot from a cup of tea. A scream escaped me when I came. A few minutes later I heard the sound of spitting coming from the bathroom: she had kept the sperm in her mouth all that time.

The Indians, a coalition of tribes, had been bused in from the mountains to take part in the march on the Court of Appeals in Pasadena. As there had been during the demonstration in front of the gallery, there was a young man who seemed to be leading the operation. He was the one who held the megaphone, he led the prayer before the procession started moving. It was just past noon, the sun was shining hotly. In the middle of the circle a blind old Indian lit a fire of dried sage and mimed a series of incantations to the heavens and the earth. A banner read NO DESECRATION FOR RECREATION. A smoking stick was handed around and everyone waved it around their head before passing it on. The stick came to Sarah and me.

'Purification,' she said quietly. 'Wait . . .'

She waved the stick, first over my head, then over her own, and handed it to the nappy-haired boy beside her. Someone screamed into the megaphone, *For the rights of Nature! Of the Earth! Of Humanity!*

The megaphone was passed around. Some people were unable to find the right button. We were called upon to free ourselves from the sickness of greed and appetite. The slogans flew wildly back and forth. A group of anti-globalists, it seemed, had joined forces with the Indians. The march began. Drums pounded.

'Tribal elders to the front!' the leader shouted.

He had a pointy nose, his skin was the color of hazelnuts. I could see why people would want to follow him, his charisma seemed like something that could be expressed in wattage. Sarah was pushing the shopping cart again, this time filled with photocopied pamphlets. She handed out bananas and water to the hungry and thirsty. She was our mother. Behind us, a group of Indians were dancing – a handsome

196

man in a red loincloth laid down the beat with the strips of bells tied to his ankles. He danced the whole way, his body gleaming with sweat. I shriveled under his sacred earnestness. What was I but an intruder and an impotent practitioner of irony? Sarah screamed along with the slogans; when she tossed her fist in the air, her top slid up over her belt. I saw her pale stomach. I knew what she smelled like, I was familiar with her taste.

From the sidewalk, groups of skeptical blacks were watching the parade go by. There could have been no greater distance than that between those grim Indians and the blacks, who just stood there grinning. How differently they viewed the soil! The Indians were demonstrating here for the preservation of their holy ground, which the blacks associated with the forced labor of their ancestors and had radically turned their backs on. Sarah asked me to take the shopping cart while she went into a Hooters franchise to pass out broadsheets to the leering men. I couldn't stand still in the current, I was pushed along from behind and in turn found myself pushing a shopping cart, amid a procession of Indians and anti-globalists, to a courthouse where a verdict was supposed to be overturned. You never saw a normal, reasonable person at gatherings like this, only the crackpots with rings in their noses, wearing their army surplus outfits and chanting slogans, the dull rhythm of which expressed, above all, a sense of stagnation.

Sarah came up behind me and I passed the shopping cart to her. I asked myself whether I would ever be capable of bonding with something the way she did, or whether cowardly skepticism would reign forever in that barren, prematurely old soul of mine. When we got to Colorado Boulevard I said, 'I'm dropping out for a minute. Going to get a hamburger.'

'Now? You're kidding!'

I gave her a quick kiss and stepped out of the parade. At a bit of a distance I let the procession pass by and shivered at the melancholy sound an Indian was producing on a conch shell – a baby whale that had lost its mother.

I walked back to Hooters. There, in those profane surroundings, I let myself be served a hamburger by a girl who barged her breasts ahead of her like icebergs. Then I used the pay phone to call Loews and ask if they had any work for me. I was put through to Berny Suess.

'Hey, buddy, good thing you called. Have you got time for me on Saturday?'

He wanted to know whether I could play at a reception, some charity thing, they were expecting celebrities.

Outside I asked someone how to get to the courthouse, and set off after the demonstrators. Sarah was standing in a circle of demonstrators in front of a Victorian building set among tall trees. There was, I was told, already a delegation inside; the stay-behinds were chanting prayers and dancing and singing. The leader had stayed behind as well. He stepped into the center of the circle and said it was time to pray and sacrifice. He put a shell on the ground in front of him.

'Which way is east?' he asked his lieutenant quietly.

Calling on the spirits of the four winds and the cosmos itself, he then made a burnt offering. The smell of rosemary.

'Brothers and sisters,' he said, 'let us pray for the misguided spirits inside this building, who are also our brothers and sisters but have been blinded by greed. Let us send them love.'

Sarah nodded. There was a devout gleam in her eye. The Indian placed dried sage in the shell, lit it and fanned the smoking fire with a white wing. The group fell silent. I looked over, Sarah was standing beside me, her eyes closed. I knew she was sending love into the courthouse, or at least thought she was doing that. I thought about other things, about how much better suited she would be for the boy now leading the prayers at the center of the circle, how the two of them could lead a life of activism and holistic conviction and fuck till the stars fell from the sky – a pang of sweet jealousy. I placed my hand on her lower back, gently, in order not to break her concentration. The Indian stood up and invited the others to lay their offerings in the shell. A black man with feathers in his hair stepped forward. He knelt down before the shell and made a few karate-like gestures. His voice was that of a gospel singer. The smell of a burning feather snapped at my nostrils.

'Oh, Lord!' he shouted, 'the time has come to destroy Babylon! Is the time not ripe, Lord? We beseech thee, bring Babylon down. Down with Babylon! Down with Babylon!'

He stood up, bowed, and rejoined the circle. A lineup of weirdos followed. When I yawned, Sarah elbowed me.

'Behave yourself, carnivore,' she said.

The prayers died out, the leader raised the megaphone to his lips.

'Concerning the toilet situation,' he said, 'if you need to use the toilet, you can do that in the courthouse, but then you need to show your ID, okay? Don't make a scene, we can accomplish more by being cooperative.'

The cooperative attitude appeared to me to be the result of an endless row of defeats suffered by his people – cooperation was all they had left.

'I admire it, I really admire it,' I told Sarah later that day.

'But?'

'No buts. You guys, you have something you consider greater than yourselves. To do that, you have to have something I don't have. The ability to cast yourself off, like a sannyasi.'

'Don't act like we're a bunch of freaks, some sect of idiots. Isn't there anything you believe in? Isn't there anything sacred to you? Not even love, Ludwig? Giving yourself away for another person?'

I knew that my answer would be important to everything that came afterwards. I plumbed my inner depths, and said truthfully, 'I don't know. I really don't know.'

The day my mother left Loews, I played in the hotel for the first time. The celebrities in the room manifested themselves as coagulations in the crowd, humanity clotted around a core. It was some kind of charity thing, sometimes someone would ask me to stop playing for a minute while a man shouted numbers enthusiastically into a microphone: so many dollars for this, so many for that. The celebrities auctioned themselves off, you could pay to have your picture taken with them. Berny Suess had come into the room twice and drummed his fingers on the piano as he looked around at the proceedings. Afterwards I went past his office.

'Well done,' he said. 'I doubt they heard much, but it was better than nothing.'

I thought that was funny, better than nothing. I could pick up my money on Monday, the safe was locked for the weekend. It had to be in cash because I didn't have a work permit.

Sarah was with the Indians – she had followed the caravan to San Francisco and would be back on Sunday night.

I walked out into the gentle evening. On the map I located Washington Way, on the border between Santa Monica and Venice, where my mother had found her rental. She had taken my suitcase along with her.

I found the house in the shade of low trees. Whispers of lonesomeness in the branches. Our possessions were stored in a barn in Suffolk, I hadn't given them a thought since the journey started, weeks ago – there was nothing I wanted more than to have them around me and to say the word *home*.

I knocked. Then again. A little window in the door opened, like in some fairy tale.

'Who's there?'

She was wearing a bathrobe from Loews. Did I fancy a cup of tea? We sat down at the table, a couple of candles, shadows. I looked around at the little house with its spare furnishings. Bars at the windows, gleaming pans on the kitchen wall.

'Sugar in your tea?' she asked.

I looked at her.

'Sugar, yes. And a dash of milk, please.'

'All that sugar is bad for you.'

'You use it too.'

'Only a tiny bit. Mostly sweeteners, really.'

There was something about her I couldn't quite place. I looked at her more closely. She seemed older. Perhaps it was the candlelight, but there were lines around her mouth, her eyes, the place where life resides in a face. Sleep had lowered her defenses and removed the mask of eternal youth.

'I played tonight,' I said, 'at Loews. I can pick up my money on Monday. The first dollars I've ever earned.'

'On to stardom,' she said.

'It went pretty well. They said Tom Cruise was there.'

'Were you all by yourself?'

'Tom Cruise was there too, I just told you that.'

'Was Sarah with you?'

I shook my head.

'Well, where is she?'

'Demonstrating with Indians.'

'So now you have time for me again.'

'In San Francisco. She's coming back tomorrow.'

'I enjoyed meeting her.'

She thought about it for a moment. Then, 'She's not particularly pretty or anything. Is she Jewish?'

I looked at her, thrown off balance. Why would she say something like that? Why dispel the timid spirit of peace flitting over the table?

'I think she's pretty,' I said. 'What you think . . . well, you know, forget it.'

She sighed.

'You always think the worst, Ludwig. I thought she was nice, I said that, she seems very special.'

'Is there any food in the house? I haven't eaten yet.'

'At this hour? Eating so late isn't good for you.'

'Not that either.'

She came back with crackers and a tube of cheese spread.

'Fruit,' she said. 'Would you like some fruit?'

She put an apple down in front of me. Unless I was mistaken, I had seen this same apple a while back on the windowsill at the hotel. I squeezed a gleaming worm of cheese along the length of the cracker and smeared it out with the opening of the tube. I kept my eyes fixed on this chore all the while as I asked, 'So what are you up to, during the day I mean? Globally speaking.'

'Globally?'

'No details.'

'I don't really feel like talking to you about that right now. Some other time, okay?'

'When's the next *Lilith* film coming out? You can talk about that, can't you?'

'In October, I believe. I'll wait and see. The shooting for the new one starts in December, in Vienna. Then I'll be leaving here as well.'

'Don't you miss your things, your personal belongings? Don't you ever think about them? Don't you want to have a house again? A real house? Not . . . this.'

She shook her head.

'Material things, Ludwig, I don't become attached to them. I've never missed them for a second. There's nothing to own, not yesterday, not tomorrow, right now is all there is – and you don't own that either. Even our house . . . it was terrible for me, a catastrophe, but do I miss it? No. We had a few wonderful years in Alburgh, apparently it was time for something new.'

Her feet shuffled across the tiles. She stood up.

'Do you want to sleep here?'

I shook my head. She said, 'Because I'm going back to bed.'

I had wanted to say that I did miss Kings Ness, and sometimes realized with a start that the house was gone, gone for good, that we had fallen out of our lives and that there was no going back anymore. I'd also wanted to tell her about the Bodo Schultz exhibition, about his abyss – that at this moment he was somewhere in this hemisphere, scratching at his insect bites in a pitch-black jungle. But I would save that for later, she would feign disinterest but absorb every word, then say, 'He certainly makes life difficult for himself, the poor man.'

But that's for later. First I'll go to her house, sleep in the bed that smells of Sarah and me. Tomorrow she's coming back. Today, in fact, it's already way past twelve.

In July and August there were fires around the city. Cigarette butts, the sparks from a grinder, everything set the hills aflame.

Sarah gives me a silver ring to wear on my pinkie, so thin it bends all the time. She says, 'If someone were to ask about the two of us, not that anyone does, but imagine they did, how should I describe it?'

She's energetic and cheerful, when we argue it's because of the tiny space we share, and the differences in temperament. She can be volatile. She starts arguing, and only asks questions afterwards.

Her body is a constant source of surprise to me. She has short, explosive orgasms, she has serial orgasms, a chain of little releases that seem without end, she has orgasms of which she says, 'I don't know, it started off real heavy but suddenly it was over.'

Rugby has given me a body that is fit for hard confrontations, only in love do I get to know and control it as an instrument of pleasure.

I lay there, my eyes open, sated, the world might be there or it might not – we had drifted off on a floe that had broken free of the earth. I look at myself from above, a boy on his back, no one wondering where he was, he knew no one and no one knew him; anonymity to the limits of nonexistence.

When I got up in the morning, later than she did, I would find the notes.

I'm missing you, at the moment you read this. Now and now and now again

Or

My heart stays behind somewhere with you (look in the bed)

While we were making love I sometimes thought about the fetus above our heads and was afraid she would get pregnant again, new life against the black death that had come out of her. I dreamed she was sitting on me, riding me; when I wanted her to get off I discovered that we had fused, our bodies had become a single organism, as though we had been grafted together – the sense of horror followed me long after waking.

I read a little book I had found among the esoteric volumes on her bookshelf. About a fourteen-year-old boy who boards a ship at Naples, he watches Vesuvius until it fades from sight, he is alone now for the first time in his life. The ship is headed for America. His brother, Ricardo, is already there, he has a job in Pennsylvania. Sabato Rodilla is following in his brother's footsteps, in the new country he uses the name Dick Sullivan in order to get work more easily with the Irish foremen. His brother is killed in a mine explosion. Sabato, who now calls himself Sam, Sam Rodia, travels on to Seattle. In 1902 he marries Lucia Ucci. They have two children. Rodia is a problem drinker, in 1912 his wife divorces him. In the transcript of the interviews with him, his heavy Italian accent is preserved. *I was one of the bad men of the United States. I was drunken. All the time drinking.* But then suddenly he goes on the wagon. *I quit the drinking in 1919. I don't drink wine, beer, if you give me a hundred dollars. No touch it.*

For a few hundred dollars he buys a triangular plot of ground in Watts, a suburb on the south side of Los Angeles. Using simple tools, a hammer, trowel, pliers, he begins work on a series of towers, open constructions of steel rods, chicken wire and mortar. He decorates the wet mortar with colorful shards and shells he finds on the beach, with the bottoms of glass bottles, broken cups, the handles of pitchers, everything he scavenges from the side of the road and drops in the bag he always carries with him.

The pictures in the book showed the angular structures lit by the sun – I wanted to go there right away.

Rodia started building his towers as a middle-aged man, he was forty-two at the time, and only stopped at the age of seventy-five. Crisis, war, recovery, through it all he sits in the tops of his towers, singing and talking to himself. *I work in the night, midnight, sleep five hours a night. Work two hours in the morning, Sunday, Christmas Day.*

I read that the entire complex formed the abstract representation of a ship, the walls surrounding the triangular lot were the hull, the three towers inside were the masts. The book didn't say towards which point of the compass the bow was pointed.

The banal but essential question was why Rodia had spent thirty-three years working on the towers. He said: *Why I built it, I can't tell you. Why-a man make the pants? Why-a man make the shoes?* The beauty of it, it seemed, was enough for him, that and people's attention. *I built the tower the people like . . . everybody come.*

When Rodia turned seventy-five he gave the ground and the towers to a neighbor and moved to Martinez, where he lived with his sister. A gesture simply and poignantly dramatic. The artistic and historical value of his work was recognized during his lifetime. When someone once showed him a photograph of Gaudí's *Sagrada Familia,* Rodia asked (and I couldn't help laughing when I read this): *Did he have helpers?*

They replied: *Of course he had helpers.*

Rodia: *I had no helpers.*

I asked Sarah to take me to see the towers. She had been there once, she said.

'After that we'll drive out into the Mojave. When you're there, you suddenly realize that we live in a desert here.'

Watts. I had never seen a more cheerless landscape. Low houses, all built of the cheapest of materials. Only blacks and Latinos, we were the only white people.

'To be here after the sun goes down,' Sarah said. 'Brr . . .'

There were lots of churches, simple wood-and-brick buildings with signs out front saying that Jesus had died for our sins and that He was the only hope of salvation. We asked for directions twice, were sent to the tracks, which we had to cross. And suddenly there we were, without warning, the Watts Towers were standing there – smaller than I had imagined, less colorful too. Sarah parked the car, I climbed out and crossed the street. First the curb, then the wall lining Rodia's lot – I looked up past the circling structure of the middlemost tower, which had much more color to it when seen from close by. It was too much to take in at a glance, I stepped back. Something so vital in such illusionless surroundings, so much concretized creative urge – it touched something inside me, something I had never known was there.

'The sun again, sweetheart?'

Sarah patted my back. I nodded and wiped the tears from my face. 'Come on,' she said.

I kept my eyes hidden behind the sunglasses when we bought our tickets at the neighboring arts center. A woman led us to the gate and unlocked it.

It was no large plot of land on which those towers had arisen. But as soon as your eyes homed in on the details, the space doubled and a world of playful shapes emerged. This was the terrain par excellence of 'ornamental man', who works without examples, without predecessors, who bows only to a mighty urge to make something huge and irreproducible.

There were many spots where he had added his initials, I saw surfaces on which he had left behind the imprint of his tools, as a kind of signature: with this I, Sam Rodia, built these towers. With this hammer, this pick, this rasp, these nails and these pliers did I perform this miracle.

We crossed the decorated cement floors, peered up and became entangled in the endlessly spiraling structures, countless rings moving up. The towers were connected by arches, graced as well with sun-bleached shells. Rodio decorated in the same way nature overruns the earth when left to its own devices. This was a place that called for loud rejoicing. This was how one entered a faith, with the shock of a revelation.

Sarah pointed out a little group of miniature stone animals on an archway. I nodded and moved away from her a bit. This was also a place to be alone, without anyone else in your field of vision, a place you should have to yourself for twenty-four hours in order to see it as he had seen it, at sunup, in the afternoon, in the evening, murmuring *come, let us build us a city, and a tower, whose top may reach unto heaven; and let us make us a name, lest we be scattered upon the face of the whole earth.*

And you realize that he had seen it only briefly in its current more or less finished state. Had that saddened him, the fact that all completion also constitutes an end? Or did he view with satisfaction the empire of towers he had built with his own hands? What did he shout when the hammer struck his thumb? You wished you could have been there to see him at work, hanging from a battlement. There were pictures of it, I had seen them in the book, a weathered man at the top of the little tower, wearing a hat, a pair of torn overalls over his street clothes.

His workshop had been at the back of the complex, but it was gone now, burned down after fireworks landed on the roof. In a kiln there he had melted his glass and iron, from the walls of the complex grew melted bottles of 7 Up and Canada Dry. Ceramic handles stuck out of the walls, the ceiling of the front gate was a mosaic of broken mirrors. Beneath my feet the ornamental urge rolled on, the wet concrete was etched with endlessly repetitive geometrical patterns of flowers and hearts. In the walls I deciphered shards of plates, oven dishes, pots, pitchers. A sign said he had used eleven thousand pieces of pottery, ten thousand shells, six thousand pieces of colored glass and fifteen thousand tiles; in total, more than one hundred thousand decorative elements. I let the details burn into my memory, the birdbaths, the fountains, the words *I had in my mind I'm gonna do something, something big, and I did.*

Slowly I came out from under the spell, signals from outside were making their way through, the silly, repetitive clanging of an ice-cream truck, very loud, very lonely, as though it were your own death knell being rung.

We left the city. I looked at the worn-down mountains, lightless, arid, with here and there a few clumps of sinewy scrub.

'That people live here . . .' Sarah said.

Stretching out at the foot of the mountains was a ribbon of tens of thousands of more or less identical houses, in camouflage, covered with dust and the shadows from the ridges. People here did their shopping and sought enjoyment in shopping centers on both sides of the highway.

'What's up?' Sarah asked at last. 'You haven't said a word for a long time.'

Schultz's abyss and Rodia's towers, they were tumbling through my mind, all jumbled together. By talking I could probably have imposed structure on the whole thing, by giving a name to the shiver of the sublime I might have been able to draw a line between the sacred and the sacrilegious, between the one who built a Jacob's ladder and the other who thrashed the gods out of their heavens, but I didn't dare. Instead I said, 'Is this the Mojave already?'

We had wound our way lazily out of the mountains, a void had opened before us. Looking at the dashboard I saw that the temperature had suddenly dropped. Little groups of clouds hurried along above the flats, the monotony broken here and there by a lone, blunt mountaintop. Plastic refuse was washed up against low shrubs. Clouds were piling up in the east.

'We're going to Europe,' I said, 'my mother and I. Maybe next month already. Or else in December.'

She didn't look over, kept her eyes on the road. I thought about my mother's words. Maybe she wasn't as pretty as I thought.

'For how long?' she asked. 'Are we talking about weeks or months?'

'It depends on where she has to work, and how long it takes.'

'And you're going along with her.'

'I have to.'

'Says she?'

I shook my head.

'Says me.'

'But why? Can you tell me why?'

From between the clouds, islands of sunlight fell on the earth. In the distance were mobile homes, tossed down at random around the desert as though by a tornado. A couple of answers were battling for primacy, but one of them seemed to stand in clearer light than the other. I said, 'She's the only one I have.'

The mobile homes were surrounded by wrecked cars, half-hearted attempts at demarcation with fences and barbed wire. Dogs lay on the cold ground.

'She's the only one you have . . .'

'I can't leave her alone, not now. In this situation, I mean, now that she's making movies again.'

'And you have to babysit for her? Don't you think she's old enough by now . . .'

'I'm afraid not. Sometimes she works herself up into such a state . . . She forgets who she is, even who I am.'

'She seemed very sensible to me.'

'You don't know her. You have no idea.'

I looked over. Sarah was staring straight ahead. Her nose looked big and hooked, it reminded me of a cartoon in *MAD* in which a prince and a shepherd girl, both very attractive, were portrayed from the front throughout the story until, in the very last frame, we see them in profile and it becomes clear that they both have hideously huge noses. I knew it: my mother's poison, entering drop by drop.

'All I was asking was whether maybe you don't make yourself too dependent on her,' Sarah said in a small voice. 'That's all.'

Your heart, Ludwig, your heart. Where is it? Where did you hide it? I looked at the landscape to my right and remembered how we had left Alexandria, how I had forgotten to dig up my treasure; something of vital importance to me had been left behind – the way it would be now. Life appeared to me as an endless process of reduction. It wasn't until then that I began to understand more about the answer I'd just given; although I had lost her any number of times, she was indeed the only one I had. There couldn't be anyone else, we were the sole witnesses to each other's lives.

I saw a freight train in the distance, disappearing behind pale rock formations. Little eddies of dust across the flats. People felt free to dump mattresses and washing machines along the road. Antennae stood atop the hills.

★

When the buildings gradually began accumulating beside the road, forebodings of Barstow, she asked, 'And what about us, Ludwig?'

I laughed uneasily.

'You'll just have to go along, I guess.'

But that convinced no one. The question remained hanging.

'God, I don't know,' I said then. 'I can't split myself down the middle.'

'But you're going, is that for sure?'

We drove into Barstow, the outskirts with their rolling streets. The conjecture of dismal lives. The end of yet another day. We drove in silence, crawling along, as though we had lost something.

On a wall beside the tracks, the origins of Barstow were portrayed in words and images. The desert town had first been called Waterman Junction, and arose here when two railroads met at the Mojave River. At that junction, in 1886, a post office was built.

A freight train roared by, its whistle screamed. Behind it, on the other side, the old hills withdrew in late, crimson light. The color sanctified them. Spotlights flashed on around the switching yard, only then did the final boxcar pass. The low sun fell beneath a pigeon-gray bed of cloud.

We drove on. A sign along the way read BRINGING THE LIGHT OF JESUS TO A DYING WORLD. The road climbed, the traffic light turned red, and then we saw it, the sky burning over Barstow. Sarah parked the car in a lot in front of a garage, we watched in the certainty that a sunset like this surpassed our powers of expression. A narrow strip between the bed of cloud and the San Bernardino Mountains to the west, that was where the light was concentrated. It scorched the bottoms of the clouds, was tossed out in beams and sparked across the car roofs of Barstow. She turned the engine off, her face was bathed in red light. I put my hand on her leg.

'Hey, hi, anybody home?'

She shook her head. Her curls of molten copper. She said, 'I always knew you would go away.'

'You couldn't have. I didn't know that myself.'

She nodded stubbornly.

'I knew. Some people have things to stay for. Not you. You have things to go away for.'

In December my mother and I moved from the wideness of the Pacific to the enclosure of a country that did not border on a single sea: Austria. My father's native country. We were soldiers in summer uniforms, ambushed by the winter. We bought caps, scarves, gloves, and thermal underwear for me, because I've never been able to stand the cold. Some snow fell in Vienna, by Christmas it had melted again. We stayed at the Hotel Imperial, a marble quarry. The room was divided by double doors into two sleeping quarters; when I had to go to the toilet at night I tiptoed through her compartment to the bathroom. Whenever I thought about Sarah, missing her made me physically unwell. It chafed, an unrelenting homesickness. Every day I thought about going back, she called to me from across seas and mountains, but I plugged my ears because of a promise. A ball and chain, the dead weight of a conviction.

I underwent Vienna in a lucid kind of stupor. The ecstatic Christmas atmosphere weighed on me. As did the obsession with Mozart, Sissi and Klimt's *The Kiss*. In the Innere Stadt I shuffled along amid droves of Asians and Arabs, tourists decked out with paper shopping bags and shoeboxes. In the streets to both sides of the hubbub the buildings rose up like box canyons. You were lowered to the bottom of the ravine and looked up past the steep walls of housing blocks, to the sky cut into squares above. Behind the walls was yet another inner city, an endless network of corridors leading to millions of closed rooms, to bedrooms, cellars, salons and attics, in all those spaces lived Man with his bacteria. In there, century after century, people had breathed, loved, laughed, died and wept, and not a one of them aware of the lives before or after them, in exactly the same spaces.

★

Darkness fell early. At nine I would dine with my mother. Perhaps Rollo Liban would be there too, he was producing the film about the Viennese *Edelhure* Josephine Mutzenbacher. The biography on which it was based, *Josefine Mutzenbacher. Die Geschichte einer Wienerischen Dirne. Von ihr selbst erzählt*, had long been considered authentic, but was later ascribed to Arthur Schnitzler and then to Felix Salten. The story had never lost its appeal to the imagination. This was not the first film to be made about her, but it would be the most ambitious – and the most expensive.

My feet carried me on and on. From the open window of a tall and narrow Greek Orthodox church, pinned in between two houses, came the sound of choral music. It rained heavens.

The table at the Restaurant Imperial was set for two. Rollo Liban had arrived in Vienna that morning, my mother said, but had lots to do. We sat beneath a portrait of the old Kaiser, the city's fourth icon.

'Adolf Hitler stayed here too,' I said. 'After the *Anschluss*.'

My mother looked up from her menu.

'You can say whatever you like about Adolf Hitler, but he *was* a vegetarian.'

'I read somewhere that, despite the good cooking here, he stuck to rabbit food.'

'In any case, the vegetarian menu doesn't amount to much,' my mother said. 'I think I'll order fish, just this once.'

'You had fish yesterday, too.'

'That was just a little bite.'

'And on the plane.'

'That was chicken. And only because they'd already passed out all the vegetarian meals.'

'You could have taken pasta, that was nothing but cream with a few chunks of ham.'

'You know how I feel about pork, Ludwig.'

'The prosciutto on the melon is pork, isn't it?'

She shrugged, irritated.

'An appetizer. Who cares. Do you know what you're going to order?'

Rollo Liban came in later, maneuvering his large body around beneath the low ceiling like an oversized cupboard. I stood up and shook his hand, to make sure no-one would think we were family. He ordered a cheeseburger with onion rings. The waiter shook his head gently and said with a forgiving smile that that was not on the menu.

'I can get a hamburger in Mecca, in Havana and Hanoi, so why can't I get a hamburger in Vienna?'

Sometimes, when he spoke, it sounded like he was spitting out a fly.

'In Vienna, certainly,' the young waiter said, 'but . . . Wait just a moment, I'll ask the cook.'

That was how Rollo Liban got his hamburger with cheese and onion rings, of which I was jealous more than a bit. He took the hamburger in both hands and didn't speak a word till the thing had been devoured. We remained silent along with him. It was your classic kind of restaurant, wainscoting, the tables close together. People here spoke in a hush, you acted as though you didn't notice the others but heard everything they said. Liban must have found my presence irksome, irksome and expensive, but his behavior reflected none of that. He was indifferent as a tractor. He seemed to consider me one of my mother's perks, and seldom spoke to me directly. He did ask, 'And you, what do you do around here all day?'

To which I answered truthfully, 'Nothing.'

From the conversation that followed between them, I deduced that Prague would be our next stop. My position was not really very different from that of a lapdog; I went where they went, no one asked me a thing. He talked about the way the second *Lilith* film had been received, which was very well indeed. It was a conversation with blank spots, the code language of parents. I excused myself and left the table.

The Maria Theresia Bar beside the restaurant was a shadowy space, brothel-like with its red velour and heavy curtains, its fabric wallpaper. The barman stood in a globe of light, polishing glasses. The object of my special attention, however, was the pianist. He marched blankly from melody to melody. You could imagine him standing at a tram stop with his attaché case, on his way to work in an insurance office on the thirteenth floor. His immovability was impressive. I drank a glass of beer and talked to the barkeeper about the lack of customers – a subject which dictated that the conversation be short. The words fell dead to the floor between us. From the walls, yellowed Habsburgs stared at us in abhorrence. We spent another half-hour looking past each other, the barman, the pianist and I, each from inside his own aquarium, then I went upstairs. I climbed the stairs past the stone Danube nymph-in-a-niche, and looked back down the stairwell. It was broad enough for two coaches to pass each other. The kind you couldn't descend without imagining a crowd down below, waiting for you with uproarious cheers, or with a guillotine.

Above the nymph was a state portrait of Franz Joseph in uniform, one hand on his waistcoat, his gaze fixed on a point outside the frame. The high ceiling was a patchwork of gilded coffers. The candelabra was unlit.

At the royal suite I turned right and went to our room. My mother was lying in bed, flipping through a hotel folder. I disappeared into the bathroom and heard her say, 'I don't understand why they put us in this room. Just look at all the things they have. If you ask me, they only gave us a Deluxe Junior . . .'

A few minutes later I closed the double doors and crawled into the freshly made bed. The pillow propped up beneath my arm, I began my third letter to Sarah, on hotel stationery.

Our farewell had been torment. She said she would never see me again. I remained noncommittal about everything important.

'Then it's over, Ludwig. You can't just come back some day and expect everything to be the way it was. That's impossible. That's not fair.'

I tasted tears in a kiss, but couldn't allow myself any feelings, otherwise my entire plan would be scotched. I had withdrawn from the course of events.

'Isn't your girlfriend coming along?' my mother asked at LAX.

'She has to work.'

'That's a pity. Couldn't she get some time off?'

'Who knows.'

'Are you two still getting along?'

'It's over.'

Her so-called sympathy was too meager to measure. In response to my ongoing silence she said at last, 'Just remember what my father always said: there are plenty more fish in the sea.'

I wrote to Sarah about my love, about the loss. That I had wanted to make the goodbye quick and painless, but that it had been neither. That I begged her to wait for me until I returned from my mission. If no country is home to you, than I shall make my home in love. I signed it *Odysseus* and switched off the reading light. On the other side of the door, Calypso was snoring.

At breakfast she asked about my plans. Not for today, but for the time to come. She avoided the word *future*. There had been that morning in Los Angeles when I had told her that I would go with her to Vienna.

'If you like,' she'd said, and asked no further questions.

Now the moment had arrived to ask those questions, of an early morning along the Ringstrasse in Vienna, our eyes still puffy with sleep and with a day stretching out before us for which they were predicting rain and an afternoon high of two degrees.

'In early January we're going to Prague,' she said. 'What are your plans?'

I looked past her, at the girl replenishing the buffet. She had said *we*, without including me. I hadn't shared with her my thoughts about my life as sacrifice. My mother didn't understand that I was her homecoming. I wavered, thrown off balance by her question, the need to adopt a stance.

'To watch after you,' I said then.

'Being together has to be enjoyable, Ludwig,' she said, 'you have to contribute to each other's joy in life ...'

I put my empty eggshell back in the egg cup, upside down.

'But you don't give me that feeling at all. Are you listening?'

I tapped my spoon against the eggshell. It resulted in an interesting web of fractures.

'Today I'm going to the Capuchin Crypt,' I said. 'I believe virtually all the Habsburgs are buried there, the whole shooting match. A sepulcher. A tourist attraction. Living people looking at dead ones.'

'What am I supposed to do with you, Ludwig, when you're so ...?'

'How late will you be coming back from your activities? Will we be dining together?'

'Why would you want to? You don't seem to derive any pleasure from it. You almost never talk to me, you never smile. I find it ...'

She wept. Foul play. I felt the urge to do the same. Before leaving the breakfast room, I laid my hand on her shoulder.

'Hang in there,' I said.

'Go away, you. You disgusting ... cynic.'

★

I crossed the ring to Heldenplatz, then through the arches to Hofburg. In a daze, I wandered past the inviolate, dead-as-a-doornail remains of an empire, petrified and sunken beneath its own weight.

The enormity of it! The countless tons of stone!

The perpetrators of this rank self-aggrandizement all lay in the Capuchin Crypt, domes buried beneath a church on Neue Markt, the final resting place since 1633 to the Austrian Habsburgs. After paying admission, I descended into that underworld. Sober cross vaults, the walls in pale plaster. Almost one hundred and fifty of the deceased were interred here in an equal number of sarcophagi, from newborn children to doddering emperors. Grand dukes, counts, countesses. Princes, princesses, emperors, empresses. I pictured in my mind's eye how they were carried in here amid the murmur of mourners, the shuffling monks and the wavering light of torches. A book I bought at the entrance described how that went. The funeral official knocks on the door of the crypt with his staff and asks to be admitted. The monk on the other side of the door asks who it is who wishes to enter. The official calls out the name and most important titles of the deceased, resumés that sometimes took a while, grand duke of this or that, lord of that and the other, knight in the order of so and so, et cetera. But the door remains closed, the voice says: *We know no such person.*

Again the official knocks on the door. The question is repeated, there follows a summary of the dead person's secondary titles, the minor titulature.

We know no such person.

The ritual repeats itself, again the official announces the name of the deceased, followed by the words *a poor sinner.* The door to the crypt is opened.

★

A route had been set out amid the sarcophagi. Eagles spread their wings atop coffins of lead, tin, bronze or copper, crowned skulls grinned at passers-by. Scenes from the life of the deceased were portrayed in haut-relief: a wedding, a coronation, a battle. They had succumbed to inbreeding, crib death, epidemics, venereal diseases, fevers and hunting accidents. Their hearts were removed and kept elsewhere. The eyes, brains and entrails were interred in yet another chapel.

The vanitas symbolism of skulls and bones became less profuse with time, as the empire reached its end the sarcophagi became less ornate. I saw coffins containing Ludwigs, a certain Ludwig Joseph of whom the booklet noted only that he was the son of Emperor Leopold II, and a Karl Ludwig, father of Crown Prince Franz Ferdinand and brother of Franz Joseph I. The editors had apparently seen no reason to make special mention of them.

In a nearby coffeehouse I read about the enlightened Emperor Joseph II, who had opened the royal gardens at Schönbrunn and the Prater to the public. A distressed noblewoman had complained to him, 'But Your Majesty, if you allow the people into the royal gardens, our kind of people can never gather there again!'

'My dear lady,' Joseph had replied, 'if I wished to always be among my own kind, I would spend my days in the Capuchin Crypt.'

The air outside was cold and biting, with a strong odor of manure. I was walking through a dark gallery along Augustinerstrasse when suddenly a horse-drawn carriage came racing past. The coachman wore a broad-rimmed hat, a black, heavy cape draped over his shoulders. The black coach was empty, the rattle of hooves echoed from the walls. That is Mr. Death, who rides the streets of Vienna.

That evening I took a walk along the Danube and went into a few of the big hotels. All of them had a pianist in the lobby or the bar, surrounded by the workings of the hotel, ghosts in the machine. There would be work for me here, I knew that. Something appealed to me about the idea of being a harmless parasite, living off the rich, chipping off bits of their monolithic capital. I sensed what my role would be – creating the impression of being a lost prince, stirring them up to acts of compassion.

In the lobby of the former palace where we had set up camp, an Arab woman in a headscarf was waiting amid dozens of shopping bags, printed with the nouveau-riche constellation of Gucci, Prada, DKNY – but her posture was that of the stolid female vendor amid pyramids of colorful herbs in the souk at Aleppo. An Arab hurried by on his way to the elevator, his one hand clutching that of a monstrously fat little boy, the other holding bags full of McDonald's happy meals. He had been out foraging to feed the nest. The royal households, the nobility, they all wasted away or were already extinct, now it was other people's turn to populate the palaces: porno stars and Arabs who had brought their desert ways along with them. But we would never succeed in making this life our own, we would always feel the thrill and excitement of a successful burglary; the manners and natural-born insouciance of the original inhabitants of these houses were not ours to imitate. The rabble had been admitted to the palace gardens, had descended like a plague of locusts, and the original inhabitants had been driven off to ever-smaller reservations.

In the room I dialed Sarah's number. Her cheerful voice, the summons to leave behind *something nice* on the answering machine. It was early in the afternoon there, we lived in different worlds, different times. It was the umpteenth time I'd called, she had never answered once. Silence breeds the greatest of disasters. I punched the repeat button and gave her the phone number of the hotel and our room number. It wasn't the first time I'd done that. Maybe she had accidentally erased my earlier messages. Perhaps my letters had never arrived. I had left so triflingly, with no idea of the consequences. I hadn't felt this coming. It was logical, but the heart knew nothing about that. I sat on the edge of my mother's bed and waited for the phone to ring.

Around midnight I went to bed. It was two in the morning when my mother came in. She slid the doors closed quietly, and after a while the light shining through the cracks went out as well.

The scene changed. Now the creeping graduality of Prague. Making acquaintance with a people of despondent drinkers. Women with the most beautiful legs I've ever seen. A skin flick is made in Prague each day, it is the capital of European pornography. The first week of the new year and I still haven't heard a word from Sarah. Every day I make plans to go back. I'm afraid of what I might find. I can't count on things being as they were when I left, she told me that. That could mean anything, but not much good.

We travel from one gorgeous backdrop to the other. But this time the reality is moth-eaten. Hotel Europe is on the point of collapse.

'They dreamed up those three stars themselves,' my mother says. 'I don't even have a TV in my room. What a dirty mess.'

I see our own inevitable downfall in that, in that mess. That I revel in it does not seem like a good sign to me.

Our rooms are next to each other on the first floor. The hubbub of Wenceslas Square intrudes all day and all night. A little further along is a stand where they fry sausages and hamburgers, providing the dominant aroma in our rooms. I feel more at home in Hotel Europe than I did at the Imperial, but my mother acts as though she's being taken to the cleaners. Rollo Liban is staying at a hotel down the street. She's sure that it's a much better place. The beds here are as hard as the expressions on the chambermaids' faces. My mother sleeps poorly. There are little vertical lines above her lips, creases that can't be disguised with powder, except when in a state of complete immobility. I see a few wrinkles running like the channels of a river delta from her décolleté to her throat. Here's what I think: time stood still for her once she left the limelight, but now that she has come back to it the clock has started ticking again – and faster than ever. I fantasize about vampire-like creatures who screech horribly and turn to dust as soon as they are exposed to sunlight. When we checked in I heard her ask which floor the gym was on, a question the Czech girl at the desk did not understand.

'Sports,' my mother said. 'Physical exercise.'

She imitated someone bicycling at an admirable pace, then rowing and running. This was understood, and the reply in sign language was that this was not available at the hotel. The girl behind the desk was pretty. She smiled at me while we stood waiting for the elevator.

I am bored in Prague, I count the passing hours. Atop my nightstand is an orange telephone with a real dial. In the café downstairs the pianist is busy destroying the collected work of The Beatles. The gray-haired musician has something professorial about him. Sometimes he strolls back and forth between the piano and the hall leading to the toilets in order to work the stiffness out of his joints. On occasion you actually forget he's there. Only when he stops playing are you overcome by a sense of deep fatigue, because he's been plugging your ears the whole time with a carpet of sound. It seems as though he plays from memory, songs he heard as a boy and which he is now trying to reproduce. There's always someone who will sing along with 'Yesterday'.

Although my emotional state is governed by a woman with dark, curly hair who doesn't return my calls, my senses are wide open to the melancholy beauty of the Hotel Europe. Of the way it must have looked when it opened its doors in 1889 I can only dream. It must have been a jewel. Now it smells like an old people's home. I love wainscoting and wooden ceilings. Hanging from the balustrades are plastic baskets with artificial plants – only on the fifth floor, where the poor people and students live, are the plants real; there they are

226

whipped to a pallor by the wind, gasp for breath between the balus-ters. The potting soil is covered with a white, moldy film.

The floors are all built around a skylight. You look down to the first floor, where our rooms are. The light, by the time it gets down there, is weak, like at the bottom of a well.

Someone apparently thought that red and fluorescent green would be the best colors for the stairwell. The pillars on each floor are circled by plaster garlands, ending in a wreath. Nicotine-colored moisture runs down the walls. It is a clash of styles and influences, the good old Louis-the-Something hotel style, Art Deco, the impoverished fashion of the socialist workers' paradise and the stagnation of a hotel that falls short of the demands of the modern age. The carpets are grimy, the decorative picture frames cracked, we are witnessing a monumental demise. The hotel is so *tired*, it is begging for attention, for a renaissance.

On our floor is a set of stairs, six or seven steps, that suddenly disap-pears into a wall – this is where the ghosts come out at night. It is glorious and sad, this hotel, a royal grave left unplundered.

We are sitting at a table in the Titan restaurant. From the speakers come songs by artists forgotten everywhere in the world except here. Joe Cocker. Barbra Streisand. In the middle of the restaurant is a table set for forty, but no one is seated at it.

'As though someone was going to throw a party, but changed their mind,' my mother says.

The whole thing has given her the giggles. The waiter hands us the menu. In a plastic folder is a sheet of paper bearing the words JULY SPECIAL. My mother asks for the January special. The man says it's the same as this one. I order the July special. While she tries to decipher the menu's English, she asks, 'Have you talked to your girlfriend yet?'

'She's not my girlfriend anymore. You know that. It's over.'

'Well it doesn't have to be so definite, does it? You two are so theatrical.'

'I can't reach her. Not since we left. I've talked to her answering machine so often that it must be full by now. I left the number in Vienna, the one here, slowly, so that she could write it down. But she hasn't called back or left a message.'

'Something could have gone wrong that you don't know about, sweetheart. It's possible.'

'She may be chaotic, but her principles are like cast iron. I left, these are the consequences. That's what she's trying to tell me.'

My mother sniffs in disapproval.

'Love isn't a principle. Love should be accommodating and compassionate. You can't determine the course of love, that's what Khalil Gibran says. Love itself determines the course of events for you, if it thinks you're worthy. Not the other way around.'

'Gibran, the spiritual snake-oil merchant.'

'Maybe she's not the kind of girl you can leave alone.'

'What do you mean by that?'

'There are girls like that. You can't leave them alone.'

'What are you saying exactly?'

'That things happen.'

'Such as?'

'I think you can figure that out for yourself.'

'Oh, thank you.'

'She plucked at her hair the whole time. That says something as well.'

'What?! What for Christ's sake . . .'

The waiter comes out of the kitchen, chewing on something. My July menu is served. A whole duck. Tucked away beneath it is a bed of red cabbage, white cabbage and, the great blunder of Czech popular cuisine, a pile of noodles. Boiled strings of dough. Sometimes made from potato flour, sometimes wheat. Resignedly, my fork putters about between the duck, the cabbage and the starch.

'I'm not sure this is really cheese,' I hear her say across the table.

The chef's salad, always a risky thing to order. You want to look the other way, but the bright light from the electric candles overhead reveals everything in its nakedness.

'When was the last time you smiled?' she asks.

I look up.

'Or said something nice to me?'

'You have journalists for that, don't you? Talk show hosts?'

'I'm so tired of this, Ludwig. Really, so very tired. I don't have to take it anymore. I must be crazy to have let this go on so long. That you blame me for living my life, that's your business, but I don't want to listen to it anymore. Do it somewhere where I'm not around.'

Dinner has come to a halt. It takes a little while for my mother to pull herself together.

'I've thought about this for a long time, Ludwig, but I think it would be better if you went away. Lead your own life. You're twenty years old, you ...'

'Twenty-one,' I murmur.

'You're old enough to stand on your own two feet. I'll give you money to help you get set up, but I don't want this anymore. This sour old man who comments on everything, on everything I do. I get a knot in my stomach every time I see you. It makes my stomach hurt.'

I barely hear what she's saying, until she asks, 'What are you doing here, for heaven's sake? You follow me around like a vicious little dog. Why, Ludwig?'

'To save you,' I say. 'To keep you from making a complete mess of things.'

Her shrill laugh, almost hateful.

'To save me? Do you have some kind of Messiah complex or something? Please, stop it. Save me? It's been a long time since I've felt as down as I have ever since you ... Go save yourself, buddy.'

★

229

And so came the unexpected end to my European tour with her. She weeps, again, and I remember the words from the shredded Bible I had found on the street: *Therefore shall a man leave his father and his mother, and shall cleave unto his wife: and they shall be one flesh*; I have done precisely the opposite. She tosses her knife and fork into the bowl of chef's salad and pushes back her chair with a screech. The people at the next table look up as she leaves the restaurant, bent over, wrapped in her sorrow. Then they look at me. Through my fault, through my fault, through my most grievous fault.

I went back to Los Angeles. From one defeat to the next. Between the airport and her house I died of misery. It was a stroke of luck that I hadn't returned her key before I left. The apartment had not been abandoned, as I had feared, but seemed barely occupied either.

'Hello, Dylan,' I said to the fetus.

I stood motionless amid the chaos. I had left this paradise of my own accord, my return was a clandestine intrusion, a breaking and an entering. The apartment seemed to have been left in a hurry, but then it had always seemed that way.

'Where's your mother, Dylan?'

The answering machine showed a blinking number 20. I tossed a T-shirt over it. The daylight was fading slowly, I sat on the edge of the bed and thought about the state of inertia in which I found myself. Shadows were crawling out from the objects in the room. Even putting on water for tea seemed like an effort from which I might never recover. After a little while I fell back on the bed, my hands folded behind my head. If I craned my neck I could see the photo of the fetus. I drifted in and out of sleep.

'I was in Vienna, Dylan,' I said. 'Not your kind of place. Austria is a completely racist country. I was in Prague too. In fact, I can't remember seeing a single black person. Maybe if I'd paid more attention.'

The black coach in Vienna, the rattling sound of hoof beats. *Der Tod, das muss ein Wiener sein.*

'Life is strange, Dylan. I'm trying to reconstruct the train of thought behind the stupid mistake I made by leaving your mother – what was I thinking? What kind of idea could be weighty enough to make you leave the sanctuary of love? I should make a sacrifice, I haven't forgotten about that. Maybe a self-sacrifice, to show her what that is. To set an example. You and I are both sons, we both know how difficult all that can be. What we basically need is a mother who gives herself away for us. But giving yourself away isn't exactly in my genes. I should know, because I tried. The sacrifice was not accepted, more or less as I'd predicted. I thought maybe it would bring us closer, that we would belong together again if one of us had the courage to forget his own self-interest, without restrictions, without conditions, all those things that make a sacrifice look more like a transaction. The sacrifice didn't create the orderliness I was looking for. All it brought was more distance and chaos. It wasn't the right time or the right place and, more fundamentally, we're not the right people. It might be my fault for expecting results. I took it to the market and hung a price tag on it. I wanted harmony. But that calls for dedication, and that's exactly what she doesn't have. I was going to show her how it was supposed to work. I didn't take myself into account. By leaving your mother, I scotched my own desires. But scotching your desires isn't the point. That's not a sacrifice, that's self-castigation.

'During our last supper, coincidentally or not, she asked me whether I had a Messiah complex. Maybe I actually *was* seeing myself in a sort of holy light, while in reality I was her vicious little dog. I'm ashamed of being arrogant enough to think I could be someone else's salvation. In the plane on the way here I had a lot of time to think about that. It's amazing how, in one fell swoop, you can chase away the only two people who really matter. At first they fought over me, like the two mothers before King Solomon – and now neither of them wants to see me anymore. Be glad you didn't have to go through all this, Dylan, be glad. Especially the loneliness. Sometimes that can be glorious, you soar above the world on wings of wax, above everything and everyone, with that kind of loneliness it's actually a pity not to have an audience, no oohing and aahing. But you also have the other kind, when you're buried like a stone under the earth, all locked up in yourself, and no-one comes to dig you up. You might be there, you might not, you're dead to the world. My optimism, if you can call it that, consists in not making a production of that. In not bowing to the heaviness or to the lightness.'

The irrepressible light of morning, you had almost forgotten how pure it is. The day lies before you like a swimming pool without a ripple, you're the first bather. Gradually it becomes populated with the things that were interrupted by sleep.

Where Sarah is.

My knees go weak when I consider the possibilities.

I leave the house only in order to go shopping, to get takeaway meals, grab a macchiato on Rose Avenue. That light, the glaring, open sky, I can barely stand it. I hurry back to the apartment's shadows, to my waiting room. She could come back any moment, and be gone again before I arrive.

The days faded into each other. I folded her clothes and piled them neatly in the wooden chest. My fingertips slid over cloth that had been a second skin to her. I went to a laundromat to do the dirty clothes and looked at the crotch of her panties as though reading her diary. Her underwear, the pale stripes at the crotch often in plain view, had been scattered everywhere, despite my comments. Her voice, sounding offended, 'But we're open down there, Ludwig . . .'

'Your mother's a dirty girl, Dylan,' I said. 'The sweetest dirty girl I know.'

Sometimes my heart leapt at a noise from the backyard, but no-one ever came. I lit the candle in front of Dylan's photo. Someone had to keep the ritual alive. It had to be her hands that held him, it was a dramatic gesture, I could see her doing it, and also the father's revulsion at the theatricality of it.

One afternoon I went out, to UCLA, to see whether they might know where she was. The girl who went to fetch the boss seemed vaguely amused, as though I were not the first to ask about Sarah. The boss came, looking like a man who had never been able to cash in on his college degree. She had quit weeks ago, he said, he had told her she could always come back.

'She's a good person to have around, always cheerful, even when the going's tough.'

'Do you know where she went? Why she quit?'

He raised his hands and shrugged.

'A boyfriend maybe? She didn't say anything, in fact I don't know very much about her, now that you ask me.'

It seemed unlikely that she would have gone home to her parents, but still I looked up their number in Augusta.

A woman said *hello?* I said *hello?* back.

'Hello?'

'This is Ludwig Unger, I'm . . .'

'Hello?'

I hung up and tried again.

'I guess something went wrong,' the woman said. 'It's been snowing.'

She didn't know where her daughter was.

'Yesterday I ran across a picture of her, such a sweet child. She still is, of course, but back then, so . . . You can't imagine that, that your heart breaks sometimes when you see what they were like.'

The child, a rank weed, should have grown no further, now it's too late.

'You sound too young to have children yourself. Do you have children?'

Sarah had disappeared for a while before, then she simply forgot to tell people where she was.

'Don't you worry,' she said, 'we mothers do enough worrying

already. We worry so much that it's enough for everything and everyone. That's why we're here, to carry the worries of the world. Sarah's real strong, she adapts quickly. A real survivor.'

I had made contact with a white and distant land, a woman was writing her fears in the snow.

I didn't see Sarah again. She must have wondered who had folded her clothes so neatly. Whenever the TV shows demonstrators railing against G8 summits or Olympic Games in a rogue country, I still examine the crowd. A shopping cart perhaps, with Sarah pushing it, her clenched fist raised in the air. When I dream of her, she laughs at me. *Crazy Ludwig, don't go thinking you miss me.* Shame spots my skin like a disease, in her I have passed on while she is still always in me. You only get one chance, and it's better not to end up in a position in which you have to ask a woman for forgiveness.

What I would have liked to be able to say was: I have learned to be at home wherever I am. But perhaps this comes closer to the truth: I have learned not to desire a home wherever I am. In that way, the life of a musician moving from hotel to hotel is almost tolerable. To pose no demands that exceed the possibilities of that particular place and time.

'The language of music, people speak that wherever you go, don't they?'

A sentence which people often use to start up a conversation at the bar. The commonplace is our natural habitat, the cliché our private lives. Sometimes an unexpected story follows, the trauma or the glory of a human life.

I learn how to drink without slurring my words. To beat back the drunkenness. Reeds beaten by the wind, the stalks bend over further and further towards you, the important thing is to remain upright no matter how the alcohol rages through your veins. I'm conscientious about my little jobs. It's a delicate balance, I go to the trouble of getting things just the way I want them: that is to say, I sometimes insist that they give me a room and that the hotel, if at all possible, be in a favorable climate zone. Portugal, the Caribbean, Monaco, the Côte d'Azur, cities with Dior and Chanel in their coats of arms. The palaces in which, after the nobles left, the hoteliers have taken residence.

Cannes, the Majestic Barrière – the shrouded life, the sounds muffled by the thick carpets. Time eludes us with a whisper.

Biarritz, Hotel du Palais. The dazzling Atlantic light, life that passes you by like a caravan through the desert sand.

I live in little rooms beneath the eaves, on floors where the elevator never arrives, where the staff polish shoes and copper. Sometimes I am given a real hotel room, when occupancy is low.

On the beach I say hello to people I saw in the bar the night before. The women, older than me, eyes that flash like stars. They count out the shrinking capital of their beauty. I am the investor who enhances it for them. In disbelief, they receive me in their beds. With the persistent hardness of my sex I take away their shame. It fills them with pride. They are the ones who have caused that turmoil, that boiling of the bloodstream, and they will help me to get rid of it as well. That is the deal.

In Biarritz, Abijail Falcón is awaiting her divorce. She comes out of the gym, she is wearing shiny white stretch pants, she looks healthy and hungry. I'm sure she's had her breasts done. Before I come in her, she says, 'Is this normal? Are you sure you don't have some kind of deviation?'

The Argentine uses herself against me, she doesn't believe in altruism, only in pathologies.

I don't object when she insists on buying me a new wardrobe in the shops along Avenue Edouard VII.

'You were made for Italian fashion,' she tells me, seated on a pouffe, her smooth brown legs crossed at the knees.

She was virtuous for twenty-four years – although she quotes Leonard Cohen with a malicious little laugh when she says *give or take a night or two* – but now she follows her desires.

'Life is short, dearest, shorter than you might think.'

I sport light linen blazers by Corneliani, a light gray woolen sport coat by Zegna; I have my doubts about pegged trouser legs, but Abijail says the pants make my ass look good. I enjoy making her feel like I'm some sort of erotic toy. That's what she's paying for – or at least her soon-to-be-ex, the car manufacturer from Córdoba, is: the gold card has his name on it.

After a few days she reveals her predilection for straddling my face, to ride me like that, rubbing her cunt over my mouth and nose. Then she takes possession of my member. She has little to lose, the older woman, restored like a monumental mansion, her eyes full of playfulness and defeat.

I avoid sleeping with them. To wake up beside them is an intimacy I cannot bear. Two or three times I accidentally fall asleep; by early light the dilapidation is more than I can stand. All lust then immediately reverts to its opposite.

'Stay, would you,' says the heiress to the Krause fortune in Karlovy Vary. 'I'll pay you for it.'

It proves negotiable. The repression of disgust can be expressed in cash; the start of all prostitution. But I don't stay long in Karlovy Vary, the hard, bling-bling world of the Russian mafiosi who settled there after the fall of the Wall does not particularly appeal to me.

On the volcanic island of Nevis, on the other hand, I stay for six months. I rent a well-lighted room on the outskirts of Charlestown, above an eatery where they serve excellent Creole food – beans, rice, goat meat. The jungle starts where the houses stop, my balcony is only a few meters from the edge of it. Sometimes at night you hear something heavy crash to the ground, a piece of fruit perhaps, a branch. Above the bed, which creaks like a ship in distress, a mosquito net hangs in broad pleats. I like lying under it, staring at the wooden ceiling, the fan, and thinking about the winding road that brought me here.

I play at the Four Seasons Resort, a haven of hysterical luxury. It wasn't easy finding a job in the Caribbean. I sent around a promotional CD, with a résumé and flattering photos in which you see me seated at the grand piano in the hall of mirrors at Grand Hotel Pupp. The Four Seasons' regular pianist has gone to Miami for six months, that's the slot into which I fit. Beside the pool in the evening a steel band plays, I sit at an undependably tuned piano at the edge of the patio. The sea washes in with a sigh, people walk hand in hand along the surf, which is lit up by phosphorescent plankton – you can have a good time there.

I meet Tate Bloom from New York. She's a public relations manager for the Four Seasons chain, she has an office job in New York and travels every few weeks to Nevis, the Bahamas and Costa Rica, *to maintain the local contacts*, as she puts it during an introductory dinner in the dining room. She hands me her business card. I hand her mine. I'm feeling rowdy and steal bites of food from her plate.

'Please, Ludwig,' she says, 'try to respect the process.'

That's enough to give me a hint of what the future has in store.

She has red hair, a Jewish-looking face, an Irish-American background. Tate is thirty, only a couple of years older than me, it will be nice to be normal again. We go to Eddy's Bar in my little four-wheel-drive rental. The music is loud, we can barely hear each other. A black man comes over and sits down at our table, he talks to Tate and a few times fetches us bottles of beer. He puts Tate's glass on a napkin and pours her beer slowly. His dedication is over the top. He's friendly to me. Being desired by two men does her good, she laughs and glows.

Her light slip-ons gleam like silk. The polish on her toenails is still fresh. I tell the man it was nice of him to bring us beer, but that I'd like to continue my conversation with the lady now, without him around. He gets up, starts to say something, but then leaves without a word of protest. Tate is aghast, she says, 'Do you know who that was? The owner!'

'He was putting the make on you. Three is a crowd.'

She forgets her decorum for a moment, she bursts into laughter. In the car we kiss. She smells sweet, her teeth are perfect. American. Like new.

'I have to get back to the hotel,' she says, 'I can't . . .'

The sky is wide open, its cool breath pours over us. I park in front of the Creole restaurant and she goes upstairs with me. Her resistance has an end. She whispers nasty things in my ear, words I've never heard that way before. I push into her a little ways, then there's an obstacle.

'Sorry,' she says.

I'm drunk and boundless but she refuses, the tampon stays in. She exhibits an exciting pattern of surrender and refusal. She kneels in front of me on all fours, her body floating like a pale spot in the satin of the night. I smear saliva on my sex and put it in her with short, steady thrusts. Her little cries are broken by the pillow. She holds her hand back and presses it against my pelvis, a brake. I'm dizzy with pleasure. The jungle begins to throb. A cry rings out there, then another, then the tense silence returns, the bated breath.

She moans.

'Oh, fuck. Oh, goddamn.'

We ride the rhythm of spasms. The blue mist in the room surrounds us like a shell.

She shakes me awake, frightened.

'What's that?' she whispers.

241

'Monkeys,' I whisper back.

They move in little bands along the forest's edge. Sometimes one of them will dare a leap onto the roof. They have flap-ears and black, serious little faces. I go to the window and see them in the weak, peach-like light, moving cautiously from tree to tree.

'I have to get back,' Tate says nervously. 'You have to give me a ride.'

I drop her off along the lane of palms that leads to the Four Seasons; she doesn't want the staff to see her now and know that we were together. She chooses a shortcut across the golf course, her heels punch holes in the mossy grass. She takes her shoes off, holds them in one hand and walks towards the first row of apartments, then disappears from sight.

That first night determines our routine. We sleep together, we wait till morning, the rustling of the monkeys at the forest's edge, then I take her back to the hotel. During my time on the island she flies in from New York four times, for a couple of days. The last time she brings with her a new player in the game: Todd Greene, a designer, a New Yorker like her, they're going to get married in December. The fisher-men have drawn their sloops up onto the sand for the season, you know that there is a skeleton of ancient trusses and planks beneath the thick layers of paint, the green, the blue, the yellow, the names *Praise Him, Morning Star, Light of My Eyes.*

'I'm sorry,' she says. 'I should have told you before.'

I wonder to myself whether you could swim to St. Kitts, how long that would take. Or whether you would perhaps sink halfway, in peace, swaying like seaweed.

'I wanted to be honest,' she says, 'I didn't want to keep anything from you, but you're a risk. Haven't you ever noticed that? That women want to save you? I think – I know you won't let yourself be saved. You enjoy the attention, the worrying about you, but you don't want to be saved. That's your life. I've thought about it, about a life with you, but I kept seeing scenes of people being dragged down while they were trying to rescue someone else.'

A silence. Then, 'That wasn't very kind. I'm sorry.'

'I guess . . . I guess I thought it might amount to something.'

'What do you mean, Ludwig? What exactly might it have amounted to?'

'A possibility.'

'That's not particularly reassuring. A possibility. A woman wants to hear a bit more than that, you know. What kind of possibility were you thinking of?'

It took a long time before I came up with the answer. Then I said, 'The possibility of a roof over my head.'

I went on with my life as a liability. Many things were relegated to the background. During those years I was the lover of wives, widows, women who said *but I'm old enough to be your mother.* That was what I goaded them into, to care for me, to feed and clothe me, to be my mother. The only way that could happen was along the road of sexuality. I couldn't stand them when they acted like nervous schoolgirls or when I saw them paying too much attention to their appearance before we went out to dinner at a restaurant. I preferred to have them be a bit indifferent towards my person, but to take full possession of my body.

I had, generally speaking, little to fear from them, as little as they did from me: we were not out to fool ourselves. Concerning our position with regard to the other, there was to be no doubt. Upright statements of infatuation I responded to by putting an end to relations. Emotions disturbed the process. An older woman who asks *may I hold your hand?* and then begs for your love is a terrible thing to see. It is disgusting. I was ashamed of myself then for having prompted that disfigurement, for being part of that disfigurement.

It was an equilibrium that demanded a great deal from both parties. The woman who was best at it was Lotte Augustin, a German. I met her on the Lagonissi peninsula, close to Athens. She had a life to go back to, which helped. She was the ironic beauty from the television series, who appears whenever a murder has been committed upon a wealthy industrialist – the detectives repress their awe of crystal and Japanese wallpaper as they enter the salon. As soon as the widow appears, blonde, a red suit-dress, rings glistening on her fingers and looks that are the subject of professional maintenance, you know who did the killing.

That Lotte Augustin is staying at this particular resort says a great deal, but not everything. The expenditure of one thousand euros a night for a Junior Waterfront Suite with private pool must not feel like the loss of a limb. Not even when you extend your stay twice, for a week each time. After that she goes back to her life, her work, to her marriage to a CDU federal state minister that had remained intact first for the sake of his career, then for the sake of the children, and now simply because it has already remained intact for so long. Against the tanned skin above her breasts, gleaming and redolent of suntan lotion, there hangs a little golden cross. She is not a church-goer, but sometimes she prays for her children's souls.

I feel her prying eyes in the piano bar. She smiles distantly at me from behind a magazine. Later on she says, 'I thought you were German.'

'My grandfather was German. I'm half Dutch, half Austrian. Two times almost a German. Does that count?'

She shakes her head.

'Fraternal peoples.'

She bears an air of fluid melancholy. She has sold the shares in the health-care interim management company she set up, for three and a half million euros, she still holds a position on the board of supervisors, but has turned the daily management over to a woman in her early forties – she believes that women have to help each other climb the ladder of success. She spends a lot of time phoning from her recliner beside the infinity-edge pool. I float in it and try to remain motionless. From that position the water of the pool blends perfectly into that of the Saronic Gulf. None of the people she talks to know that she is almost naked. Her heavy breasts hang a bit to one side of her chest; when you lift them, the skin in the creases beneath is pale.

Her areolas are almost black from the sun, the prominent nipples always erect. Beside the recliner is an ashtray with a layer of sand in it; a skyline of Dunhill filters marked with red lipstick. When she speaks German she is forceful and to the point – when she switches to another language her personality changes along with it. In English, she is less confident. She hesitates over certain expressions and words, sometimes she will finish a sentence in German, irritatedly. She swims without getting her hair wet. I lie in wait like an alligator. Her blue eyes glisten. Her pubic hair is thin and closely shorn, she pays careful attention to the magazines and the latest fashion. We mate on the broad marble steps of the pool. The water makes her dry, later it gets slipperier. She lays her head back on the sun-warmed marble. She wears waterproof mascara. The light makes its way into her open mouth, I see gold molars, worn fillings, I avoid the flow of her breath. All the scents of age can be masked, except for this one. The water laps against the pool's edge, sparkling drops slide from her oiled skin.

The obscenity of this intercourse excites and repels me. The longer I put off my orgasm, the longer I can keep the worst of the repulsion at bay – the confrontation with suspicions about my own perversity, the reasons for things that someone my age is not supposed to do. The shame concerning the latter, until I am back in my room, until sleep has passed. The next day the feelings of lust return unabated: the climb to the high dive, the fear and the delight just before the leap, the fall, with an exploding heart.

Lotte Augustin accepts this pattern of comfort, ecstasy and escape. She says, 'This must be a lot stranger for you than it is for me.'

It is an uncomfortable, interesting observation. Her desire for me, so much younger than her, in the flower and recklessness of my youth, is *healthy*. Everyone wants to possess youth, it is a respectable longing. That I make love to a woman who is almost sixty, on the other hand, is *sick*. But all forms of human intercourse, no matter how different in kind, tend towards a certain equilibrium. And so we cancel out her age against my sickness. Biology against pathology.

The modesty of the first few days has left her now, she takes her breasts in her hands and offers them to me, the sensation of her soft, fragrant flesh makes me light in the head. During the act her mouth is always open, with her constant keening she puts herself in a trance-like state, until suddenly her eyes open wide, as though awakening from a nightmare, and she digs her manicured nails into my flesh and moans things in German.

We take a taxi to Cape Sounion, the driver waits for us at the parking lot. On the reserve that is the hotel on the Lagonissi peninsula it's easy to forget that you are in a country with an arid climate, that the sun here splits rock. In the pale blue haze over the sea, sailboats and islands are of equal weight.

At the temple of Poseidon, perched gloriously at the tip of the cape, Lotte shows me where Byron carved his name in the pillar, in graceful letters. She is wearing a sleeveless blouse embroidered with gold thread and a skirt that does not quite reach her knees, everything white, just like the espadrilles on her feet. Her nipples, the bumps they make, press themselves on me. She bends over to read other names scratched in the pillar, and slides her sunglasses with the monogrammed C's up onto her forehead in order to see better. Her breasts sway heavily under the textile. I feel an erection coming up.

At the edge of the cape a guide wearing sandals announces in a loud voice that it was on this rock that King Aegeus waited for the return of his son Theseus, who had gone to Crete to slay the Minotaur. Theseus had left with black sails and, if he survived his mission, would return with white in the riggings. But because of the tragic end of his love for Ariadne, whom he was forced to leave behind on Naxos, Theseus forgot his promise and sailed back to Athens with black sails.

From Cape Sounion, his father saw the black sails approaching in the distance. Overcome by sorrow, he threw himself into the sea.

I recall the contours of the legend, it had been impressive even when I'd heard it in a Suffolk classroom. A few tourists leave the group and walk over to the edge, one of them says, 'It's not really all that steep. It would be more like rolling instead of falling.'

Lotte comes over and stands beside me. I know the kind of mood she's in.

'In Germany you sometimes forget how lovely the world is,' she says.

I tell her the story I just heard. We look out over the mythical sea, the line between water and sky has been dispelled, white sails float on the horizon, sons who have slain the beast and are now returning home.

The plane lands early in the morning. The passengers leave the aircraft and descend the stairs to the bus on the landing strip. It is cold, a purple veil lies over the desert. Between the layers of cold air drift the pungent, titillating odors of another world.

In the arrivals hall the flash of recognition – even far away and amid the crowd, I see from the way she moves, her silhouette among the others, that it's her. Imprint. Lorenz. And desperate love as well. That tremor, risen from the depths where the child lies sleeping, opens its eyes now and sees its mother.

My smile is untainted, nothing grinds between my teeth.

She has a cobalt-blue mantilla draped over her shoulders. She is crying a little. She throws her arms around me, I feel her belly against my body, her breasts. The repulsion, sharp as a toothache. I will never have a normal relationship with that body. Not even now that we have arrived at the end, now that her days are numbered.

'I've got a cab for us,' she says. 'Come on.'

We had telephoned occasionally. At long last she had bought a cell phone, something she had always avoided out of an unspecified fear of *radiation*.

'Tunisia,' she said when I asked where in the world she was.

'Jesus.'

'This is an island, I think. I've barely been out of the hotel.'

'And what is the island called?' I ask, as though trying to help her after she has lost her way.

'Djerba.'

I was holding a shell to my ear, listening to the hissing of the ocean.

'Hello, are you there?'

'Yes, I'm still here. What are you doing out there?'

'Where?'

'On Djerba.'

'Oh. Taking it easy. Reading a lot.'

'I mean, why are you there?'

'Oh, well, they didn't want me anymore. That's what it really boils down to.'

'Who?'

'There was a spot on my breast. You couldn't see it at all, with a little makeup, but by then they weren't interested anymore. They said the actors wouldn't be able to handle it. Just a little spot.'

My head spun. The moment you knew would come, for which in your blackest hours you had longed. Which you had feared more than anything else. My voice was flat, toneless, when I asked, 'What kind of spot?'

'A kind of cancer. An early stage. On the nipple, the right one.'

From the sacred spaces of the past came the requiems I had sung for her. The moment had come. I cursed quietly.

'Yeah, you can say that again.'

'What now?' I asked.

'Don't worry your head about it, love. It's only a little spot. Sometimes it even heals over for a while.'

'It's a open wound?'

'That's how it started. An infection. A sort of flaky little wound that bled a little sometimes. Sometimes a little pus came out of it. That healed over again but now it's been open again for a while. I don't understand it. I eat so many good things, lots of vitamin C, wheat germ. I have this really good salve that I rub on it. I've got it pretty well under control.'

'Vitamin C? Against cancer?'

'It's so good, a lot more people . . .'

250

'And the doctor? Where are you going for treatment?'

'I've heard about this wonderful orthomolecular physician, I want to make an appointment with him. And in Cologne there's a doctor who has developed a special method . . .'

And so it dawned on me that she was not planning to go to a hospital for treatment at all, that she didn't even want to think about an operation. She was placing her fate in the hands of people who called themselves healers. The greatest act one could perform on this earth was to heal another. To be Jesus.

She was on the far shore of the same sea I was looking at. I left Lagonissi as quickly as I could.

In the backseat of the taxi, with the desert awakening all around, it was as though we were racing back through time, back to Alexandria.

The subject lay silently between us, black water.

'Where did you come from now?' she asked.

I pointed at the windshield, down the long asphalt road, towards the still-invisible sea beyond.

'The other side. Athens.'

'When you got off the plane I saw that you have the same stately posture as my father. You inherited that from him. So straight and tall. Not that hulking frame that your father had.'

I saw oleanders and crooked olive trees with bluish-green leaves and occasionally, along the road, women in long, heavy skirts and broad-rimmed straw hats.

'This is where it is,' my mother said. 'It's not far now.'

Midoun was the name of the village. Then the houses of Midoun segued into more olive orchards, with here and there a house the color of dust, sometimes a few of them huddled together.

Parallel to the coastline the hotels loomed up, one after the other, countless charter flights poured into them constantly. Bougainvillea bloomed beside the entrance. A man in an emerald-green waistcoat took my suitcase. On the reception desk was a sign. *Honored guest, the algae on the beach is a natural phenomenon, we are unable to remove it completely. The algae is a part of the ecosystem. The sea will remove it by itself. The management thanks you for being understanding.*

We went down to the breakfast room. A low mist hung in the room, coming from the fried eggs, bacon, the steam from chafing dishes. We found a little table by the window. The food was spread out over a few islands, between them people swarmed with plates in hand. The conveyor toaster was of particular interest to me. You put a slice of bread on a conveyor belt and it was roasted top and bottom by glowing spirals – when it reached the end of the belt the bread fell onto a little slide and was ejected from the machine, toasted and all. An industrial, efficient process, in keeping with the mass tourism along this stretch of coast.

'Mostly Germans here,' my mother said. 'It's very inexpensive. I could spend the rest of my life here if I wanted to.'

Emotion sticking like a fishbone in my craw. The rest of her life, it might be long or short, what is clear in any event is that Death has reminded her of their rendezvous. Was she always so clumsy with knife and fork? I look at her like a collector. I collect memories.

At four in the afternoon I awoke from a deep sleep and started the day for the second time. From the window I could see on the beach the plague of algae I had read about downstairs. Dark brown, a thick layer meters wide, tossed up by the sea. Beyond that, along the remaining strip of sand, were wicker parasols.

The corridors were long and dark, from behind the doors came the sounds of human lives. The wind whistled down the hallways. I almost fell into the elevator, which had stopped a good thirty centimeters lower than I had expected.

I found her on one of the recliners along the narrow stretch of sand.

'Feeling rested, sweetheart?' she asked.

She wasn't wearing a top. I wondered whether that was acceptable in this part of the world, with its Arab prudishness, but noticed that other women were doing the same. There was a bright red spot on her right nipple. It looked scaly, infected.

'And now,' I said after a time, 'what about that?'

I nodded at her breast. She looked at it.

'This,' she said, 'is not cancer, this is a challenge.'

I shook my head slowly, in disbelief.

'Is that what the doctor said, *Mrs. Unger, you have a challenge*? It looks scary. Aggressive.'

'It's not that bad, is it? Like an insect bite or something.'

'The crab, Mother, that's what bit you.'

She shrugged.

'Those are only metaphors.'

'What are you planning to do about it? Do you even *have* a plan?'

'I have an appointment in Cologne in December. It's quite a drastic procedure, you know, it makes you very ill, but I've heard such good things about it.'

'Such as?'

'He sort of heats the cancer, those cells can't take it and they die.'

'Only those cells? The other cells can take it?'

'Don't ask me how it works exactly. If you really want to know, look it up on the Internet.'

'I already did.'

'Not well enough, apparently.'

We drank tall glasses of fruit juice at the nearest outdoor café, beneath a white latticework roof through which the late-afternoon sun threw squares of light. The saddest hour. Families at little tables ate deep-fried

253

dishes. The black waiters were the only ones who smiled. The Arabs looked down on us rather emphatically.

'So you're not going to go to a hospital?' I asked. 'No chemotherapy or radiation?'

'I wouldn't dream of it,' she said. 'Even doctors advise their wives not to do that.'

She threw up a barricade of unverifiable information that underscored the correctness of her choice, which I found reckless, and which frightened me.

'We haven't seen each other for so long, Ludwig, shall we talk about something else?'

She was planning to settle in Holland for as long as the alternative treatments took, perhaps for good. The wanderings since the loss of our house had lasted eight years, she wasn't even sure that Warren and Catherine hadn't taken our household goods to the flea market long ago.

'You're going to die if you don't do anything about that breast,' I said. 'You do realize that, don't you?'

'Not do anything? But I'm doing so much! How can you say that? I've gathered a lot of information, believe me.'

'When did you find out about it?'

'The first time I went to a doctor was in January. It just wouldn't heal.'

'This is November.'

We were silent. Through my straw I sucked up water from among the ice cubes.

'Paget's disease,' I said. 'That's what you've got.'

'I know.'

'A preliminary form of cancer, not hard to treat.'

'If they cut into you that can cause the cancer to spread, they don't tell you that.'

254

'They.'

'The doctors, that's who. In the service of the pharmaceutical industry.'

'They *have* taken an oath, you know.'

'Now you're being very naïve, Ludwig, please.'

I had hoped that, with the intercession of time, we would be able to deal with each other more mildly, but the only thing time taught was that these things were immutable, that in all things this first day stood back to back with the last one long ago, so that the mood again became poisoned by conflicts and irreconcilable differences. We had remained the same, we had not escaped ourselves or the other, not even now that the disease had taken root in her.

At eight o'clock we met in the dining room. Cooks in high white hats fried little fish and thin entrecôtes beside the pool. The luminescent turquoise of the water looked sweet and edible. There is something magical about the glow of swimming pools in the dark; if I ever have a house I want one with a pool, simply because of that edible light.

The hotel was furnished like a large sailing ship, a mast stood smack in the middle of the central lobby, ropes were slung here and there. Between the staff and the tourists there existed a strictly businesslike contact, when all was said and done each one went home and all memories were lost of this meeting of the peoples. People slipped by each other without touching; watching for a while from a couch in the lobby, one had the feeling that the ship could suddenly drag anchor, and that crew and passengers would be locked forever in this vacuum, with the Buena Vista Social Club on eternal replay.

Similar feelings of endlessness overtook me in the corridors that I moved down on my way to my room. There was an enormous difference in air pressure between the hallways and the rooms, a horrible whistling and buzzing wormed its way under the doors, pressed itself through fissures. Doors slammed violently. Once, by accident, I stepped out of the elevator too soon and wandered through identical corridors in search of my room, but the magnetic key didn't fit – lost in the labyrinth, with no thread of love to show me the way out. I follow the sandy footprints of children down the sky-blue carpet, the tracks of little prehistoric predators.

The flat coastline described a lazy curve, at night you could see the lights of Zarzis in the distance. Seen from offshore, Africa began hesitantly, without emphasis, the land barely rose above water. Very little grew on the silted soil. A dead, flat coast, without striking characteristics.

The wind came up. That night I closed the doors to the balcony. When I looked out the window in the morning the sea was restless. During the night it had washed away parasols, the water stood in puddles on the little volleyball court. And the sea had brought ashore even more algae. Tons of organic material had been shoved all the way up the terraces, the beach had disappeared completely beneath it. All was foam, chaos. In the midst of that goo stood four men, their trouser legs rolled up. Two of them were carrying shovels. To anyone overseeing the fifteen-meter-wide band of seaweed covering the entire coastline, the shovel was an absurd prop. Later a little red tractor appeared, pulling a trailer, and the men began their Herculean labor. Shovelful by shovelful they scooped up the algae. The parasols remained upturned, no-one seemed to believe anymore in the ruined façade.

The hotel's entertainer, spirited and homosexual, is standing at poolside. The group in the water at his feet is trying to keep up with the exercises as he counts down from ten to one in his shrill voice. I try to avoid him as much as possible, because of the longing glances he tosses my way. He counts down in French, German and English, the ghetto blaster roaring at his back. His swimming trunks are tiny and tight.

She is in the baths, leaning back in a recliner, her body wrapped in a white, much-washed bathrobe. Her feet are resting on a footstool, there are balls of cotton wedged between her toes. She flaps her hands. 'Have a massage,' she says. 'It's lovely, so relaxing. It would be good for you. Sit down, you make me nervous when you stand there wobbling like that. Would you like a cup of tea? What's-His-Name, you know, he'll fetch it for you. Ask him to come over, would you?'

I poke my head around the corner of the relax room and ask the receptionist to send someone over. A few minutes later a man comes gliding in, charm incarnate – smooth and gleaming brown as a waxed piece of hardwood furniture.

'*Thé de menthe* for Frau Marthe, *subito*. And this, who might this be?' He winks.

'Your brother? Someone else?'

'My son,' she said.

'*Incroyable!*'

How much feigned amazement can fit in one face. He hurries away on his white clogs.

'A real clown,' my mother says to the vacuum he leaves behind. 'And a huge flirt.'

And a little later.

'But I still look pretty good, don't you think?'

'The cancer's not on your face, that's right.'

I see her sigh but can't hear it.

'I wanted to ask you to go along with me to Holland,' she says. 'At least for the first period. If you've got the time, that is.'

'Terminal care.'

'I have no intention of dying yet!'

'Maybe you'll become ill. That's to be expected if you don't do anything.'

'But Ludwig, maybe I would have been dead a long time ago if I'd let them cut into me. You read so much about women who have a breast removed and then die because it spread to the lymph glands or brain.'

'I'm sure there also plenty of women to whom that doesn't happen.'

Two girls in white uniforms come in. One of them sits down at her feet, the other settles beside her; they finish the treatment. Visions of hospitals, the earnestness of doctors. You have only that one, irreproducible life – they see dozens come by, just like you. You don't understand how that can be, that they don't attach the same importance to your life as you do: the feeling that someone has insulted you gravely.

My mother looks at me. I still haven't answered her question.

'Of course I'll go along,' I say. 'What do you think?'

Her bathroom floor was littered with pills. Yellow pills, red and green. Pills that had rolled away, slipped through her fingers. This was how she treated herself: according to her own plan and her own insights. A yellow parachute unfurled above the sea, a minuscule nuclear explosion on the horizon.

'*Guten Tag!*' the homo quacked into the microphone.

It was four o'clock, time for belly-dancing lessons to begin. An older woman was taking part, watched from a recliner by her young Arab lover. The woman appeared each morning at breakfast in a batik skirt, her white hair still wet, her water-color face expressionless. Africa! The continent of hope for lonely women from the North. Drenched in honey, they drew swarms of starving flies as soon as they touched down.

That evening we went to a show in the Coquille Room, where the concept of *shells* was unraveled to the point of being nerve-racking. A man danced with five jugs balanced on his head. Six. Seven. The audience clapped along to the beat of the music. White children were sitting on the edge of the stage. The man was also able to balance seven jugs on the point of a stick, with the stick resting on his lower teeth. There were fat belly dancers, the flesh swaying independently of their bodies.

'So that's where all the food goes!' my mother whispered. She was amazed each day anew at the piles of food in the restaurant.

Armies were fed here, the supply lines were kept open and profuse.

The wind had died down, but I kept the doors closed, irritated by the inane hissing of the sea. The beach was a complete shambles by now – the despair and the ecstasy after the apocalypse.

I didn't understand my own feelings: even now, now that Death was spreading through her from the breast from which I had drunk of life, the heavens were aligned in fruitless, impotent hatred. I'd thought I had gained a certain autonomy, but now that we were together again it turned out that the longing for retaliation had not disappeared. The clarity had existed by grace of the distance we had maintained since parting in Prague. These days, however, I was better able to control my aversion, the bitterness and the whims that tasted of defeat remained largely behind the pickets of my teeth and the smoke screen of my eyes.

The only memories of a kind of happiness, during those weeks on Djerba, have to do with food – with the regular, copious, distracting food into which we dug with a vengeance.

Once in Holland, we settled down at a little distance from each other. She hired a holiday cottage east of the city of Groningen, outside the village of Meeden. I moved into a furnished flat in the center of the provincial capital and began my life as a Dutchman. A small, inconspicuous existence that took place within the space of roughly one square kilometer: the walking distance from my apartment on the market square to the casino (where a theater agent had found me a job), the walk along the Diepenring and the routes to the grand cafés and sandwich shops where I started my day.

All that time, it seemed, she was in no hurry at all to die, that mother of mine. Shortly after our arrival, at my insistence, she had submitted to a checkup at the hospital. A mammogram and echogram were made of breast and armpit, I sat in the waiting room and read magazines and tabloids in a language I had once known fairly well, but which time had now partly erased. I understood everything, but spoke Dutch now like a dead language; people listened in amusement to the misshapen diphthongs, wrongly stressed syllables, the faulty vocabulary; all those misunderstandings. When they switched to English to make things easier for me, I refused with the pride of an ambitious immigrant and went on failing to hit the mark, like a drunken man in a shooting gallery.

My mother came out of the doctor's office, I fetched tea for us from the machine. She was disappointed; on this of all days the wound had been producing a great deal of pus. She blamed her breast for this; it had been calm for some time, *closed* as she called it, and now, today, now that other eyes had looked at it, the breast had been disobedient. From her talk with the oncological surgeon it appeared that there was as yet no tumor in the underlying gland tissue, it had in any case been difficult to see. It was still too early to determine whether it had spread to her lymph system.

'Could I ask what you're planning to do about this?' asked the surgeon, a lively woman with braces on her lower teeth and her hair in a ponytail.

My mother told her about the course of treatment she'd prescribed for herself, the nutritional supplements, the salt treatment, the iodine she rubbed on it every morning (*that smarts, you know!*), and finally about her planned visit to the man who had entered our lives like a benedictory priest: Dr. Richard H. Kloos, a Dutchman who had his practice in Cologne. I fixed my gaze on the woman across from us. My mother's exuberance had to do with the favorable results of a few minutes earlier, the stay of execution that she celebrated as a triumph.

That was how we left the hospital, with handfuls of new life and the promise that my mother would come in for regular checkups. I walked her to the station, to catch her bus. The city was covered in uniform, milky winter light, the sun was pale as a moon.

'This was the town I longed for as a girl,' she said. 'Sometimes we went shopping here, the streets were the longest and broadest in the whole world. Anything you could think of, you could buy it here.'

In the station restaurant we drank hot chocolate with whipped cream, she ordered a slice of apple pie with more whipped cream to go with it. I knew that the chance of her listening to the counsel of medical science had decreased even further today.

'Could you pass me the sugar?'

She slid the bowl across the table to me.

'Do you want some of my whipped cream, I've got so much!'

'A little bit, thanks.'

I raised my cup.

'To a painless death.'

'Oh, Ludwig, please!'

After that I waved to her as the bus pulled away, as fervently as though we were traveling to opposite shores of a great sea.

We saw each other again when I picked her up in Meeden. We were going to Cologne. In her low-ceilinged living room was a cage with an orange canary in it. The little bird hopped nervously back and forth, a mixture of birdseed and shell sand on the floor beneath the cage crunched under my feet.

'I decided to buy myself a canary,' she said, 'but it never sings at all. The birds outside peep the same way. If something doesn't change I'm going to take him back to the shop. I wanted something I could talk to, but this is hopeless.'

That odor of holiday cottages, of musty closets, moist blankets. I could smell it right through the haze of incense and guttered candles, the smell of an abandoned place, not heated or maintained by human energy. Her appointment was for early the next morning, so we were going to sleep in Cologne. I hoisted her suitcase, heavy enough for someone leaving home for weeks, into the rental car and waited until she was ready. When she finally sat down beside me she smelled like a seraglio, and said with a touch of impatience, 'Okay, let's get going.'

As the highway opened up before us, I said, 'Could I ask you from now on to use just a little less eau de cologne? I'm feeling a bit dizzy.'

'So open your window. Come on.'

After that we remained silent until we had passed Zwolle. Then she asked, 'Have you ever seen that girl from Los Angeles again? The one you were so crazy about?'

I shook my head.

'I dream about her sometimes,' I said. 'Every time I spend the first night in a new country, strangely enough. It's like clockwork. Sometimes a little more often, but always the first night after I've crossed the border, when I'm lying in a strange bed, under a strange sky.'

'Strange, yeah.'

'I think I'm the only person in the world who has that. I've never heard of it or read about it anywhere. The Unger Syndrome.'

'There must be other people who have the same thing.'

'You're probably right. But now I've coined the term.'

'Have you ever become involved with a girl after that? For a longer period of time, I mean.'

'No.'

'You're thirty now.'

'Almost.'

Only at dinner, late that evening in Cologne, did she broach the subject again.

'So why don't you have any girlfriends?'

Because you're still alive, I thought, but I said something else.

'Maybe because I don't really need anyone anymore, as you once told me.'

'Did I say that? I'm surprised you remember.'

263

I examined her face in search of hidden meanings, but she seemed to have truly forgotten about it, the evil spell, the shadow at my back.

'I can't believe you've actually forgotten saying that.'

'Really, I have. What did I say? That you didn't really need anyone anymore? That's true, isn't it? You can't expect someone else to compensate for your defects. People should be together because they're free to do that, not out of dependency.'

'It meant something else, back then.'

'But it's not because you prefer boys, is it? That's not why you don't have girlfriends, is it? I mean, it could be, right? It happens more often to boys who are very much focused on their mother, when there's no father figure around.'

'Oh, Jesus.'

'I want so badly to be a grandmother.'

I shook my head, a punch-drunk boxer. The bite of schnitzel had concealed a clump of gristle. I raised my napkin to my mouth and discreetly spat out the meat.

'Nice?' she asked.

'Mmmmm. Could you pass the salt?'

This is how the day began:

She: I think that's such a nice thought, that we don't breathe ourselves, but that we are breathed.

I: Briefed?

She: Breathed. That we are breathed.

I: By whom, exactly?

She: Oh please, let's not start at breakfast.

A little later we were standing before the *Privatpraxis* of PD Dr. Med. Richard H. Kloos, *Arzt für Allgemeinmedizin und Naturheilkunde*, and coincidentally the world's last wearer of bowties. The body of the good doctor himself, it appeared, was seized regularly by heavy tremors. The cups on his desk rattled, the water rocked in the pitcher. The bowtie and the tremors lent him credibility, just as the seer is often blind and the shaman lame or crippled. Those are the afflictions with which the god has smitten them, so they can speak the truth profoundly. I heard my mother saying . . . *to give my own body a chance first . . . thoroughly detoxify . . . so much old pain* . . . And he: *Everything is connected with everything else, everyone produces cancer cells all day long. Back in 1912, Rudolf Steiner said . . . That's right, he knew about the effectiveness of mistletoe as well. It's so good for people, mistletoe, it's a gift. I had cancer myself, that's when I found out about the power of mistletoe, I owe my life to mistletoe! I want do something in return for mistletoe!*

And once again the storm of muscular contractions shook the table. When it was over he arranged his bleached locks and dabbed at his moustache as though it had been knocked out of place. My mother nodded contentedly. She was in the presence of a peer, she didn't have to defend herself. Dr. Richard H. Kloos didn't even have to work hard

265

in order to convince her to follow the fifty-thousand-euro course of treatment. I tried with all my might to catch his meaning when he proceeded into a lecture about Natural Killer Cells – dendritic cells, each and every one of them capable of destroying five thousand cancer cells. The armies of cancer and anti-cancer paraded around the table. The treatment he had developed boiled down to a form of *own-blood therapy* and was allowed only in Germany, Austria and Switzerland. From what I understood, my mother's blood would be tapped off and the monocytes, the *baby white-blood cells*, would be separated from it. Within seven days, Richard Kloos said, the monocytes would be converted into healthy dendritic cells and then injected back into the bloodstream. The treatment would involve six visits to the clinic.

'Two to four hours after the treatment you come down with a kind of flu. There is so much going on in your immune system that it produces symptoms of feverishness. I would advise you not to travel during that period, but to take a hotel and wait until you recover.'

When he was called out of the room for a minute, my mother said contentedly, 'A real man of science.'

He then took us on a tour of the clinic. We saw the long rectangular boxes into which the patients were put during their treatment. The temperature inside was then cranked up to a maximum of forty-two degrees centigrade; it was at that temperature, Kloos said, that the protein in cancer cells began to coagulate, while the protein in normal, healthy cells did so only at forty-four degrees. We peeked into a room where a woman was lying on a waterbed.

'She's developing an electron field,' Kloos said.

He stood in the doorway and winked at my mother. I heard him say, '. . . that's exactly what Rudolf Steiner said, isn't it?'

Back in his office we waited politely for his tremors – which had started this time in mid-sentence – to end. He resumed, 'What I can't tell everyone, but feel comfortable telling you, is that we also accept payment in cash. Off the record, if your insurance won't cover the treatment.'

We left Cologne and followed the snarl of autobahns. That part of Europe looks, on the map, like the web of veins on an old woman's leg. From beside me came a voice dipped in the bittersweetness of self-pity.

'I felt sort of sad last night when you didn't want to take my arm.'

I said nothing. She said, 'What I thought was: there will come a day when you'll get down on your bare knees and beg to be able to still give me your arm.'

Above the fields, the cloud cover roiled, veils of rain hung from the sky.

'Even in death you still manipulate me,' I said.

Six disastrous trips to Cologne followed. In addition to the patent agonies of war, torture and famine, there is also the agony of family. Along the high quays of Cologne, above the river that swept deep and wide through its channel, I thought with irksome regularity on the words Randy Newman had written with the Rhine in mind. *I'm looking at the river. But I'm thinking of the sea.* The first two times I stayed with her during the treatment in the box, that stage prop from the theater of illusionists in which Richard H. Kloos was a player as well. Her head, resting on a towel, was the only thing sticking out of it. I sat in a chair beside her and watched as she was slowly warmed up. Her face grew redder and redder. The sweat poured off her. Sometimes the skepticism and the chill in my soul left, to make way for the irrational hope that this via dolorosa would lead to healing, that it was actually possible. Kloos, after all, had said that fifteen percent of the women who came to him were completely healed by his treatment. Sixty percent showed partial remission, and twenty-five percent died anyway. One hundred percent of everyone who came here tried to wriggle their way into that fifteen percent. They all did their best. Belief was the most important condition. Anyone who did not believe had given up all hope of being healed and was lost. And so they believed, the women I saw shuffling down the hall, skinny and exhausted in their fluffy bathrobes, they believed in the magic power of dendritic cells and the magic hand of Dr. Richard H. Kloos, the mediator between life and death. They believed in the face of everything, in order to win a place in the Lucky Fifteen. I dabbed at her face with a cloth, which I had to change for another after the second time, so freely did the sweat run.

At one point she wept silently, tears mingled with the sweat. I laid my hand for a moment on her forehead, the soaked hair, and said everything would be all right. Thin, stupid comfort. A formula with no heart. Through her exhaustion I saw, for the first time, traces of fear in her eyes, like a horse sinking into quicksand. The mammal's fear of life going on without it, while it disappears into ultimate darkness. Suddenly these torments no longer constituted the road to healing, but the gates to the unspeakable suffering that awaited; tears dripped onto the towel. I raised the straw to her lips, she sucked water from the cup.

The third time we went she said she would rather have a nurse beside her.

'I can do it from now on without you there,' she said. 'I sort of know what's coming. I'd rather have someone there who's giving it their full attention. I had to ask you to wipe my face the whole time. You had such a cold look in your eye. You made me feel kind of dirty.'

Shortly after the first treatment at Dr. Kloos's clinic, a woman who had become my mother's special friend in adversity died. Her breast had been amputated, the cancer had returned after a few years, she had been living off an outside chance. My mother went to her funeral.

When she came back she said she wanted to be cremated. She repeated her phrase about *not planning to die soon, but still* . . . What she really wanted was to be burnt on a wooden platform on the banks of the Ganges, but she didn't want to force that kind of logistical feat on me.

She was waiting for a miracle. Dr. Kloos may not have healed her, yet still she felt a part of that sixty percent, the ones who exhibited partial response. There were new miracle makers, whom she referred to as *physicians* and *scientists*, one of whom lived in the woods in Drenthe Province. He said, 'Marthe, it's one minute to twelve. You have to start working on loving yourself, on your self-appreciation, right now. It's not too late.'

I asked her what he had promised.

'Does he say the cancer will go away by taking a rest, by meditating, by loving yourself?'

'It's possible to program yourself at the cellular level, that's all he says. Rather than cutting everything away, he goes to the root of the disease.'

'And that's how he heals people?'

'He's actually very modest. He says it's possible, not that it always happens. You're in control of so much yourself.'

The healers who seemed most credible, it struck me, were those who admitted they were not perfect. Precisely by not being perfect, by leaving a wide margin for failure, they allowed for the possibility of being healed.

An older woman, living in a holiday cottage with a canary. Sometimes, on the street or in a restaurant, the whispers and the turned heads were a reminder of the life that had gone before. Now she was back where her life had started, Bourtange was just down the road. She had made a long journey, at the end of it she had come home; to get there all she had to do was cross what they once called the Bourtanger Moor. Aunt Edith, Uncle Gerard, we hadn't talked about them since, we didn't know whether they still lived there, whether they were still alive. The rupture had been resolute and irrevocable. The circle had been closed to her. By moving to Meeden she had sought rapprochement, as unemphatically as possible. If asked, she would have denied it.

She did not go back to the oncological surgeon.

'Why would I do that?' she said. 'It's going fine this way, isn't it?'

'You promised you would.'

'It has to have a purpose. I don't see the use of it.'

She drifted further and further away, increasingly beyond the reach of common sense – she created her own good-luck rituals and found comfort with faith healers and anthroposophists, with the sorcerers. With their lips they claimed to have no intention of luring her away from regular medicine, but supported her in every decision that boiled down to exactly that. Fearing the law, their occult message was dissipated through subterranean vents, the sermons-in-the-field of the natural healers; they were slippery as eels in wet grass. I did not believe their intentions were malevolent. That would have been easier to take, criminal intent, hurting the other in order to reap profit for one's self. I would have understood such intentions; after all, there are enough people like that. The audacity lay in the fact that they truly believed that their laying on of hands, their home-brewed medicines, their sign-posts to spiritual transformation would make the cancer go away. Brazen claims, cloaked in false modesty and a humbly stammered *who am I that I should be given this gift?* The ill person, that weakened, halting organism, suddenly robbed of the health which it had always enjoyed so lightheartedly, is incapable of sealing the breaches. As a result, unfounded messages of hope and comfort come rolling in.

My powerlessness was total. I could locate no fissures in my mother's rejection of doctors, operations, radiation, chemo- or hormone therapy. Her opinions were as hard as a church pew. She worked actively on a world view in which doctors and hospital management teams were mere marionettes of the pharmaceutical industry. At the house in Meeden I found magazines and books that fed the paranoia. When a real and probable cause of death came into view, she created for herself an enemy worth fighting.

'The important thing for me isn't that breast,' she said. 'I could live very well with only one breast; the important thing is to listen to what this is telling me. I don't want to deny myself that opportunity.'

As principled as she was in her rejection of the physicians' order, she was opportunistic in equal measure when it came to alternative healers. A woman in the town of Noordwijk aan Zee had tested her polarity with a biotensor and concluded that she did not have cancer at all. These were viruses, and her body was riddled with them. The therapy focused for some time after that on combating viruses. This ran in conjunction with the daily consumption of huge doses of vitamins and minerals, on the advice of a doctor who adhered to the principles of orthomolecular medicine – a pseudo-scientific school of thought that prescribed huge overdoses of nutritional supplements to make up for supposed deficiencies. On his advice she had the amalgam in her teeth replaced with white fillings, in order to reduce toxic load. During meals she swallowed handfuls of pills from a flat plastic box with twelve compartments. Before breakfast she would choke down a paste of bitter almonds.

And the cancer? It didn't budge, despite all these efforts. She denied the lack of results.

'Otherwise I might not still be here,' she said.

I slammed doors and pulled out of the drive with my tires spitting gravel.

I dreamed she was dead. It cut me in two.

She was not afraid of death, she said. She believed in the eternal nature of energy, dying was only a transition from one phase to the next. The *transition*: in our talks, that was her euphemism for the irrefutable reality of death. I looked at her and I listened, and knew that my puzzlement at this strange creature would never end. I tried to figure out the background to her radical methodology, why she would ignore a medical intervention with a good prognosis. I wanted to understand the psychology of that intolerable irrationality, of that absurdity, but couldn't actually ask about it because we didn't speak the same language. I had to put on my ears crooked and tip my brain to one side in order to grasp even a fraction of her notions.

I found clues in language. *I've got it pretty much under control*, she would say. That was an indicator. I built a little theory around the word *control*, and the loss of same. To do that I first had to understand the effect on a human of revolving doors, the lobby behind them, the elevators and corridors, the desks covered in papers, the doctor with pager and pens in his breast pocket. As soon as you enter the revolving doors you begin to shrink, you stand powerless opposite the scope and efficiency of the machine. You are turned inside out, they read the message written in your organs and announce it to you in a language you do not yet understand but will quickly come to master. With electrodes on your body and machines sighing all around, you work your way to a conclusion, a diagnosis, a prognosis. The straw to clutch at, the thread to dangle by, you had never known how enormously important they would be one day. In the revolving doors you leave behind much of who you are, beneath the bleak incandescent lighting and suspended ceilings you shrivel to the size of your defect and finally become one with it. You lose the authority you never really had anyway; no-one has a say when it comes to his own cells. Then, narcosis, the ultimate loss of control. A stranger's hands grub around in your organs, scissors clip, scalpels cut, retractors prop your body open and drains suck out your juices. You are not present, you could just as well be someone else, it's not about you. All those concepts you once applied to your status as an individual no longer exist.

No history, only current events.

That was how I imagined her wordless fear.

We went back to the hospital only when she thought she *felt something* in her breast.

'Maybe it's just an infection,' she hushed.

Let it be a tumor, was the thought that shot through my mind, let the bastards be proven wrong.

But the results produced no triumph.

'We clearly see a tumor now,' the surgeon said.

There are no other sounds. Only that voice, that little sentence. The same woman as last time.

'We can't be completely sure whether it's formed secondaries yet. And I don't think it looks good, as you put it. The infiltrative mamma carcinoma, the tumor, which started in the milk ducts, has spread to the inside. And the underlying tumor has, as it were, drawn the nipple back. Made it disappear. Had you noticed that?'

'I had noticed that, yes,' my mother said.

'There are ulcerations on the breast. We'll have to deal with those right away, if you don't do anything the holes in the skin will become larger and larger.'

'Oh, but I'm not at all sure that I want that.'

Everything about Dr. Rooyaards fell silent. Except for her eyes, where an expression seemed to deepen.

'I'd really have to think about that first,' my mother went on. 'I don't want, now that I've come this far . . . no.'

She had already regrouped; the surprise, the shock, encapsulated in an instant – she had once again taken control.

'I have the impression,' Rooyaards said, 'but correct me if I'm wrong, that you think I'm saying these things because I'm somehow

274

against you. But that is not the case, Mrs. Unger, believe me. I see a malignancy in your breast, a red, tumorous tissue. It needn't be too late. You have to seize this chance. If you don't, then you will truly have given up a real opportunity to recover. That would be such a pity, Mrs. Unger, such a pity. You owe it to yourself. You do want to get better, don't you?'

For a moment I was in love with her. She was beautiful in her plea – gestures of restrained, impotent anger, a powerful force being held in check and reduced in language to the proportions of reasonability. A tour de force, a lovely thing to see. For just a moment there I thought it might work, that Marthe Unger would allow herself to be lured to this side of the fence. Then the ax fell.

'No,' she said. 'I have to remain faithful to myself. I have to . . .'

That was all there was. The judgment remained suspended in that vacuum, the decision about how she was going to die.

And I wanted her dead, oh yes. It had all taken long enough. Applause, curtains and zip back home. I would sing as I cremated her body. Her just deserts. Her faithlessness, the egoism. The whims, the irresponsibility and the recklessness; the fears which, in addition to life itself, she had awakened in me with a kiss. For all these things there was only one appropriate sanction.

You have no idea what it's like, that's why you're able to think such things. You don't know a thing about it.

I smelled it whenever I came in, the smell of rotting. Her body had already begun decomposing, while inside there, inside that skin, there was still someone living who insisted that *spontaneous remissions occur quite frequently*. She stuffed perfume-drenched handkerchiefs into her bra to stanch the flow from her nipple, but the smell came right through it, right through her clothing and the shroud of Chanel No. 5. Incense drifted through the room like a mist. Did she know that her end had come? That the net was drawing closed? I begged her not to wait any longer for an operation.

'But then I would only be doing it for you, Ludwig. Is that what you want, for me to be unfaithful to myself because you wanted me to let them cut into me?'

Once the day and the hour had been established, would the anger stop then? Perhaps one lays down one's weapons as soon as there is nothing more to be lost or won. When the days of your life are still unnumbered, you lived in a carefree eternity, it could end tomorrow or never, who's to say? Within that free space you have every opportunity to fight your wars, to defend your interests, to run amok with impunity.

Until it slams to a halt.

We were not the ones present anymore, the only things in the room were my despair and her denial. More often than that, I felt nothing at all. Then I would sit there looking at her with the cold eyes of a fish, not knowing whether her death would bring me joy or sorrow.

The windows were wide open all the time now. The canary still did not sing. The stench was unbearable. The thought of turning my back on her did occur to me, it occurred to me often, but I knew I lacked the strength for such radicalness. Why remain loyal for a lifetime and then jump ship just before the end?

'Maybe you should put some more eau de cologne on it,' I say. 'You stink.'

'Don't exaggerate, for once.'

'It smells here of the Third World. The alley behind a restaurant.'

'If you're going to start in again, then just go away.'

All you see is the current manifestation, you and her, today. Far away, invisible now, are the things that happened; she, your young mother, smoking cigarettes absently at Trianon, you with your nose up against the pastry display case, or how she brushes your hair, for a very long time and very slowly, as you lie rolled up like a cat on her lap – but those things no longer play a role in the cruel, acute *now* in which you pound away at each other's souls.

When finally, because there was really no way around it, she allowed them to operate on her breast – that breast seen by so many eyes, desired by countless, now riddled with cancer and reeking horribly – she did so under protest, as though she were being forced into it. She could not admit the defeat, the failure. She felt betrayed. The miracle had not happened. Her belief and dogged faith had not been rewarded. The cosmos, the powers, no hand had reached out to her. She felt wronged and angry, in a voice thick with emotion she said, 'It's really hard to keep believing now. Really hard.'

Her tears were called loneliness, loneliness, loneliness. She entered the night in a white hospital smock with buttons down the back.

The cone excision, whereby both the nipple and the underlying, damaged glandular tissue were removed, called for post-treatment with radiation, but she refused point blank.

'Your mother might get lucky,' Dr. Rooyaards told me. 'There's no guaranteeing it, but she might.'

She had counted on a miracle and now all she could do was hope for good luck. Two days later she was allowed to go home, out through the revolving doors, to find her life again, see if it still fit. In the car I asked how she was feeling.

'Oh, good, yeah.'

At home she lay down on her bed, asked me to bring her her glasses and a scarf. When I came back, she was sound asleep. The smell of cadaver had disappeared. I whistled quietly to the canary, unilaterally, and cleaned its cage. Then I gave it clean water and fresh seed. At the little village Attent supermarket, I did some shopping. Because of my hotel-hopping I had never learned to cook well, but I did know how to whip together pasta with anchovies and tomato.

'Sorry, sweetheart, but I'm not very hungry,' she said after pecking at her food a few times.

She went back to sleep. It was pleasant to care for her, her enfeeblement fostered a certain harmony. From the doorway I looked at her and thought about her life, about how she had cashed in on desire, twice over in fact, but that now, in the act of dying, had fallen from the pinnacle of the big top all the way to the ground, all the way to this bed.

On the nightstand a votive candle was lit beneath a little copper bowl of aromatic oil. Draperies on the walls, Oriental covers on the bed. Her bedroom was a time machine, it took me back to the parts of my biography that were closed off with curtains.

She opened her eyes. Her hospital voice, 'I guess I must have dropped off.'

The skin on her face was full of fine lines, as though she had walked through a cobweb.

'Would you like some tea?'

'Please. Nice. And a paracetamol, please.'

'Are you in pain? All we have is ibuprofen.'

'My head hurts, a little. Ibuprofen is okay.'

The most pleasant memories have to do with time running short, with days that are numbered. Those weeks after the operation, the waiting at Kings Ness. The hallowed, white mood in the house. Finiteness is the precondition.

On the table lay a plastic folder with the punch card of patient M. Unger, and the confirmation of our appointment. The date was crawling closer, you could hear it breathing. Again that desk at which we sat side by side, and Dr. Rooyaards behind it. Her glasses were on the table. What it boiled down to was this: the scan showed metastases in the brain. My mother nodded. Kept doing that, a toy dog on the rear shelf. The voice from the other side, 'I wish it could be different.'

The standstill of that moment, a frozen throne room, blue as the heart of a glacier; the king has icicles in his beard, the wine stands slanted and hard as steel in the chalices, the queen waits sadly for spring to arrive.

'We all have to go sometime,' my mother said.

My record button had been pushed; later – when I was once again present – I would play it all back again. *How long?* was a question, because *nothing to do about it* was a certainty now. Hesitation from across the desk, *depends on so many factors, for example* . . . My mother was immediately decisive about forms of therapy that could prolong life. *Oh no, not now, all of a sudden . . . no, absolutely not.*

A phrase came to mind, one I didn't even know I knew: lingering terminal course.

It was the last time we went out through the revolving doors. Heading for the big thaw.

Which was then followed by life as predicted. The headaches. The infernal headaches. And, after a few weeks, the vomiting. Each morning the heartrending retching. With every passing day there was less of her left, it seemed as though she were being eaten during the night. There were conversations with the general physician, the making of preparations. The unthinkable. The GP dressed like an Englishman, drove a Land Rover. Dantuma, no first name. He would have preferred to express himself solely in punctuation marks. No more than three months, he told me.

'I'd be surprised if it was any longer than that.'

If he recognized her at all, he never let on.

One morning I took the car to Bourtange. I had found the address in the phone book, I knew what I was looking for. I drove slowly along the canal. My memories took place in a different season, but I was that little boy on the scooter. The farm, the dismal bricks. I climbed out like someone in a film, and the events that followed were also part of the scenario I'd anticipated. A dog begins to bark, after a little while a stable door opens. A man comes out. Blue KLM overalls, leather clogs on his feet. It almost has to be him, but I don't recognize him.

'Uncle Gerard?' I say.

A movement at the periphery of my vision, a face behind the kitchen curtains. I recognize that one.

'It's me,' I say. 'Ludwig, Marthe's son.'

'Ludwig. My oh my. Ludwig. I'm flabbergasted.'

'Uncle Gerard.'

We shake hands. He, the giant, is as tall as I am.

'Gerard?'

The woman pokes her head out the door. My aunt Edith.

'It's Marthe's boy,' he says.

We sit at the kitchen table. Only the people here have grown older, the oak furniture and thick tablecloth are ageless. Are the children of black sheep automatically black sheep themselves? I drink weak coffee from a cup that recalls the coronation of Queen Beatrix. Our lives in broken sentences; the locations, not the deeds.

'My oh my oh my,' Uncle Gerard says a few times.

My aunt says nothing, keeps her hands folded on the tabletop as though praying. They still farm, *but a lot less than before*. They've leased out some of their land, it was too much for them to keep up. The Natural Heritage Foundation bought a large chunk of it, which has now been left to grow wild.

'Such good soil . . .'

During a silence I say, 'But the reason I came here . . .'

The diagnosis, the prognosis, a few details from the files. They don't know what to say.

'And in Meeden all that time. Just up the road,' Uncle Gerard says, shaking his head.

'But what do you expect us to do?' his wife says. 'After all these years . . .'

'I understand that,' I say. 'But I just thought maybe the two of you would want to know. And now – there's still a little time left.'

Uncle Gerard walked me to the car.

'It's a shock to her,' he says.

A man accustomed to explaining his wife.

'She just needs some time. We'll call tomorrow.'

That is what happened. They wanted to see her, my uncle said on the phone.

Now I had to tell my mother. She was sitting on the couch, a magazine beside her, a shawl draped over her shoulders. She was cold all the time now. It was April, life outside was bursting at the seams.

'Those people,' she said. 'What would they do here?'

And then that afternoon, out of the blue.

'Let them come. If they want to so badly.'

An artery pulsed at the side of her neck, like a lizard's. The heating was set at twenty-three degrees. She ate little, less all the time. We didn't talk about what had gone before all this, it seemed never to have existed. We lived in the here and now-pain, now-tired, now-vomiting, now-tired-again, now-headache, now-sleep. *We*, because powerlessness is also suffering, a derivative form.

In the evening the couch was mine. I would wake up in the same position in which I had fallen asleep. Her shuffling about woke me. She was clutching the toilet, it seemed as though her body were doing its utmost to rid itself of its organs. I gagged with her. The pressure in her brain meant she could barely read. That was how it went, you stood there and watched. The devastation. This was what the end looked like. It was cruel and disgusting. And no-one anywhere with whom one could file a complaint. In how many houses, behind how many front doors, did this take place?

'Try eating a little bit,' I said.

'It doesn't appeal to me.'

'As long as you eat more than the cancer, we're still ahead of the game.'

She did her best. A few bites to humor me. I bought apple sauce, she liked ice lollies. Yogurt and custard pudding were often too rich for her. I ate the custard and searched the kitchen drawers for a bottle licker, which wasn't there. Beneath her skin the anatomical model began to appear, the tendons, veins, bones. Slowly, the sick old woman shuffled around the house. The heat had already left her. Along with the heat, the color had disappeared as well. The layers were being peeled off, further and further.

'Without the headache, this would be bearable,' she said. 'The headache is the worst part.'

'You could always go in for radiation. That would ease the pain.'

She smiled faintly, shook her head. Echoes of the old struggle.

'There they are,' I said one Saturday morning.

An Opel Astra, gleaming in the sun. I opened the door, a rustle of springtime slipped past me into the house. Uncle Gerard was carrying the flowers. My mother had dressed for the occasion. (Unsinkability.) She got up and walked to the door. They were shocked when they saw her, how could they not be? The last time he had seen her was beside the canal where she had been swimming; I knew he was thinking back on her body.

A meeting like this, an event from which you withdraw, back into your shell, rattle my cage when it's over. But that's impossible! You're the intermediary, the man in the middle, fluff pillows is what you have to do, make coffee, green tea, you've bought little cakes with pink icing because that's what they served you. They sit around the table, the subject lies between them. Conversation as though someone's walking on glass.

'So what now?' says my mother, echoing her sister's words. 'Now I'm going to die.'

The old feuds mobilize new forces within her.

'I did everything I could. It just wasn't supposed to be.'

'Mostly alternative things, though, weren't they? That's what Ludwig said.'

'*Alternative* isn't really the right word for it. It should be standard, and the other stuff should be the alternative.'

My uncle and aunt remain silent in order not to have to say that she's dying now of a cancer that could have been treated easily, because that's what I told them.

'If you think you did the right thing, then that's the way it is.'

(Aunt Edith signs the Treaty of Versailles.) Then they talk about the old days. Their father's farm. Aunt Wichie is still alive, she's eighty-eight, she's already outlived him by almost ten years. An outsider would think he was looking at two families flashing each other bits of history from behind glass. Uncle Gerard mostly keeps his mouth shut. So do I. It's about the two of them. Whether she's planning to stay here, Aunt Edith asks. My mother looks at me and smiles.

'That depends,' she says.

Then it's time for them to leave. The fruit trees across the way are in blossom. Blackbirds chase each other, cackling beneath the barberry. The people are tired to the bone.

The pain she talked about was not the pain she felt.

'As long as it's bearable, it's bearable,' the GP said.

We talked about my role in nursing her. Terminal care, Dantuma said, was a completely different story.

Uncle Gerard called, asked me to come, they needed to talk to me. I got a shortbread biscuit along with the coffee. Aunt Edith started.

'We've been thinking,' she said, 'Gerard and I . . .'

He nodded.

'. . . and first of all we want to say that we think it's really good what you're doing there all by yourself, we admire that. But we think it would be better for her to come here. For as long as she has left. Then you don't have to do it all on your own. It's going to get really difficult. Nobody can do that alone.'

'Maybe Dantuma can arrange a place in a hospice,' I said. 'And besides, I don't know whether she'll want to. She's not' – and here I couldn't help laughing – 'the easiest person.'

'Marthe will realize that it's the best thing for her and for you,' Uncle Gerard said. 'She can't leave this up to you on your own.'

'But where would I stay?' I asked. 'I don't want to drive down here every day from the city . . .'

'Plenty o' room here,' Uncle Gerard said.

That was the message I took back to Meeden. She wasn't in the living room. I poked my head into her room. She was lying on the bed.

'So glad,' she panted, 'you're back.'

Tears were running down her cheeks. The nightstand had been knocked over, the flame under the oil had been extinguished in the fall. An epileptic seizure. The first. She couldn't be left alone anymore, not even to pop out for some shopping, the risk of another seizure was too great for that. It didn't take me much effort to convince her to move to Bourtange. Maybe she had only been waiting for someone to ask.

She lay in the guestroom, where the blue-flowered wallpaper was the same as ever. I sat on the edge of the bed, bending over her the way she had once bent over me, when she'd said goodbye before her big trip. For the first few days she still came down the stairs at times, but that soon stopped. She no longer had the strength to get out of bed. The bedroom smelled of urine, Dantuma inserted a catheter and gave her morphine. The pounding pain in her head obstructed the blessing of a deep, uninterrupted sleep.

The poplars along the canal wore exuberant, fresh green. I walked down to the locks, it wasn't far, not the Homeric journey of my memories. Once she was no longer around, I would have no-one left. Only a father in the jungle. No more shared past, not a single *remember when. The Last of the Mohicans* meets *Alone in the World*, only now you're crying for yourself and not for some dead Indian or for a little orphan boy roaming the back roads of France. Not my kind of thing, crying; I always feel like someone's watching. I always cry in tandem.

This morning she thought we were on Kings Ness, she was worried and sad because we were going to lose everything. Now, in her terminal unrest, those things affect her more than they did at the time. She groans quietly in pain, like a little dog. She can barely work down her pills. With angelic patience, Aunt Edith feeds her little sips of water. I'm glad we came here, that her deathbed stands where her cradle once stood. Sometimes Uncle Gerard and I are cheerful – just the two of us, Aunt Edith is not equipped with that particular feature – and laugh loudly at jokes that aren't even that funny. A herald of relief?

The canary's cage is hanging in the front room. The bird is silent as the grave.

She's so afraid sometimes, from the inner depths her demons are now freeing themselves. I sit in a chair beside her bed and watch her body withdraw from life, as Elias Canetti wrote: the dying take the world with them. Where to?

Dantuma injects her with sedatives, and an antipsychotic to ease her confusion. She crawls back into herself, deeper and deeper all the time.

Sometimes, like a swimmer, she surfaces for air.

'Ludwig,' she says, 'my faithful Ludwig.'

Then she's gone again, back into the depths where no-one can follow.

One time she awoke with a start.

'Come! Come!' she said agitatedly.

I leaned over her, she threw her arms around my neck and pulled me down with unexpected force. Her mouth was on my neck, the dry, cracked lips, sucking greedily at my flesh. A lover's kiss, the last attempt to return to life – with a scream I pushed myself away from her.

'Jesus Christ!'

I rubbed my neck, where the vampire kiss still burned.

Aunt Edith came running up the stairs.

'It's nothing,' I said, 'I was only startled.'

She lay in bed grinning, her obscenely large teeth bared.

Dantuma boosted the dosages of Dormicum and Haldol. Above her cheekbones was a gauntness, her temples had receded to hollows. The emerging pattern of her skull. When we saw the dark spots appearing on her arms, the prognosis became more precise. Her calendar was reduced to days, hours. One more time she raised her head above water. She saw me, around her lips appeared the shadow of a smile.

'Are you all right, sweetheart?' she whispered.

Through a clump of tears I said, 'Yeah, Mama, I'm all right.'

She closed her eyes, frowned slightly.

'Funny,' she murmured. 'You never called me Mama before.'

The crematorium in Winschoten. The female funeral director, Aunt Edith, Uncle Gerard and me. Sitting at the back is a man we don't know. Aunt Wichie has written me a card. Aunt Edith hands it to me. Regular, thin handwriting, the way she was taught eighty years ago at a village school in the peat district. I put the card in my inside pocket. First the funeral director, who tells us what we are going to hear. I already know, I picked it myself. Moody Blues, 'Nights in White Satin', an abridged version. Then 'Bridge over Troubled Water' – songs she sang on the streets of Los Angeles. I step up to the front. I'll call you Mama. Ignore the embarrassment. I will tell the people how beautiful you were, honeysuckle, roses. Don't worry, I won't go too heavy on the mush; your life, after all, is reflected painfully enough on this day. This is your audience: a man we don't know, your sister and brother-in-law with whom you weren't on speaking terms and me . . . well, you know how that was. It takes two, and we never pulled our punches. Too heavy, this? An anecdote then, the light touch. About your vanity. That once, deeply insulted, you told me someone had guessed your age as forty-five. *But you are forty-five, aren't you?* I said. You: *But then that's still no reason to say it!*

Canned laughter, please. Uncle Gerard's chuckle is really a bit too paltry.

Of all the requiems I've come up with for you in my life, this final one is truly the most wretched. It's so prosaic, real death doesn't sound at all like a requiem, it doesn't echo at all. A requiem is thinking about death, not death itself. Sometimes I used to tell you the texts of my funeral orations, a game, a charm against misfortune. As long as I could tell you about it, everything was as it should be. One time I accidentally predicted what would actually happen much, much later. I told you what I would say if you would die after a long illness. I used the word *strong*. You bridled. *Strong? You could say that about anybody who's been sick a long time. A little more special, if you please.* I replaced it with *fearless. Much better*, you said. *Do that one.* This is your day, Mom, here is your word, you fearless one. You chose it yourself.

But that I, in my youthful impetuosity, called you an *angel*, I take that back. You were not that. Or at least no more than half. The other half truly consisted of more warm-blooded material.

Well then, it's now up to me to determine how you will be remembered, the counterfeiting has begun. You no longer harass me with who you are. I can love you better that way. Peace, Mother, peace. The loveliest lie wins, as it always has. Too much truth isn't good for a body. The same thing goes for loss. And now that I have no-one left to lose, I prefer to have you around in my memories as good company. If you have trouble going along with that, then please try a little harder. Try to humor me a little for a change.

I am now someone without you. That knowledge . . .

Better to play something for you. I've chosen Beethoven's *Marcia Funebre Sulla Morte d'un Eroe*, especially for you. I'll play it for you as though I were in the Royal Festival Hall. And if you sort of close your eyes and peek through your lashes, then that's where we'll be. I'm waving to you. You're moving further away, you're all the way at the back of that dark concert hall now, I can barely see you. Goodbye, Mama. Goodbye.

After laying a hand on the coffin and mumbling things, we left the auditorium – the dispatch would take place in our absence. We stood together in the reception room, a bit bedraggled. The unknown man came up to offer his condolences, his eyes averted,.

'Thank you,' I said. 'Nice of you to come.'

And then, to his back, while he was already walking away, I asked, 'Excuse me, sir, but could I ask your name?'

He turned around, took a few steps towards us.

'Boender,' he said.

The Rolodex, and fast! Boender?! Boender!

'The musician!' I said. 'You went with my mother to Los Angeles . . .'

He nodded.

'A long time ago, yeah.'

The local dialect. Aunt Edith and Uncle Gerard stood there, staring blankly at this encounter that moved me for reasons I didn't quite understand.

'Guitar player, right? Route 66?'

'Yup,' he said.

A farmer's hands, ashamed of themselves. Dark, callused lines on the fingers.

'Do you still play?'

'Oh, a little rockin' in the city. Bars and cafés. Nothing special.'

I wanted to talk to him about her, about how she had been, that mother of mine, before I was there, when she was still young, not quite a girl anymore, but I could feel the situation slipping away from me. He took a step back, with his eyes fixed on the carpet, and said, 'Well, take care then.'

And disappeared. The ghost who had accompanied her to the City of Angels, tossed aside once the light focused on her. I suddenly realized why he touched me: the convoluted thought that he could have been my father.

MEDIOHOMBRE

Why the hell isn't there a flight to El Real? The man from Aeroperlas raises his hands in surrender: next week, if I understand correctly. It's nothing but a ribbon of asphalt in the jungle, that airfield at El Real, where I have to go to find him. Aeroperlas runs a sporadic service there with little prop planes. I feel like kicking something to bits. I walk away, then back to the ticket counter. Is there any other way to get there? He consults with a colleague. I would have to travel to Yaviza, I hear. From there downriver to El Real.

I go back to my hotel in Panama City. The thought of staying here for a week is a burden. I have no sightseeing plans, and I can't motivate myself to come up with any, either. What had quietly waited in the wings all those years has suddenly become urgent.

Very early the next morning, I deposit my bags in the trunk of the taxi. The new bus terminal: from there, they've assured me, buses leave for Darién, the eastern province that borders on Colombia. There's no road between the two countries, the Pan-American Highway is chopped in two by rivers, mountains and virgin rainforest. With all the horrors that go along with that. In any case, I can almost certainly catch a bus as far as Metetí.

Darkness still. A sliver of moon, light clouds. I'm much too early, no buses leave before nine. I eat breakfast at the terminal. Mr. Chen fries banana-and-honey pancakes for me, he says, 'El Real is just like Macondo. Why do you want to go there? Nothing but wilderness. I was born there, but I haven't been back in twenty years. Not my kind of place.'

A black woman slides up to the counter, moaning and sputtering. Shopping bags everywhere, her broad lap is covered with them.

'You're going to Darién? Oh my God! Are you sure? The Indians there eat people! I'll keep you in my prayers. But right now I could use a soda.'

The bus stops at a filling station, men are rocking their cars back and forth to get more gas into the tanks. As the day wears on, the thinking stops. You become a sack of flour, a bale of cloth, you wait for them to come and unload you. Trees are dropping big, brown leaves.

The Policía Nacional at Cañazas, all two of them, make me get off the bus. In their little office they jot down the information from my passport. Flipping the pages, turning it sideways, peering at stamps. I know just enough Spanish to get by.'

'What is your destination?'

'Yaviza.'

'That's off limits. You cannot go to Yaviza without permission from the ministry.'

'So I'm going to Meteti.'

'Okay, that's fine.'

Trucks laden with red logs for the civilized world behind us. Huge trunks stripped of their bark. A routed army, humiliated and sent on transport – a cloud of dust in its wake.

At Agua Fria the asphalt stopped. People climbed off the bus. People vanished. The driver pointed at a waiting Toyota Hilux pickup with men sitting in the back. The truck pulled away. I ran after it, shouting, 'Yaviza? Yaviza?'

'*Yaviza, si!*' the men shouted back.

They grabbed my suitcase and pulled me up onto the bed. Nodding, laughing: that was a close one, gringo. In the cab, the driver ties a bandana around his face to keep out the dust. We hold on tight, the truck jolts, slams into potholes and rolls up out of them again.

Children with slingshots are walking along the road. Their fathers are carrying rifles. Indians with machetes, their hair stiff with dust. The end of another day. I wrap a T-shirt around my head. The men toss me an occasional, worried look, a stranger in their country. Nothing they are wearing or carrying is new. Around here, adapting means fading, becoming drab, wearing thin. It goes automatically, the heat and the humidity eat away at everything. It happens before you know it.

The village at the end of the road. Yaviza. The last stretch driven by starlight. The moon wasn't showing its face yet. Only one hotel, and I keep my suitcase closed to shut out the vermin. From now on, I vow, I will shake out my shoes every morning. (National Geographic Channel wisdom.)

Across the dark river, the Chucunaque, the shadow deepens, a sheer wall of plant life; somewhere there, *in that*, is where he is. I stand on the wooden dock above the river, where the boats moor at high water. The water is low now, the pirogues are bobbing around at the bottom of the pilings. I hear the Indians mumbling down there. The feeling that the darkness is slowly inhaling, expanding. Its voice of countless insects singing clearly. The Indians are sitting in the dark, murmuring, in their long canoes along the bank. Voices kept small, like those of refugees. What are they talking about? The river races by without a sound, carrying the gleam of onyx. The light of the stars refracted in its ripples.

Beneath a pair of glaring lights, dozens of men have gathered for the cockfight. An impromptu arena around a circle of sand, lined with wooden benches. They're waiting for the second rooster. The first one is already in the ring, picking at the sand, nervous, worked up. His opponent is having the spurs tied on. It's not a fair fight; the first cock is angrier, he leaps in the air aggressively and chops at the second one. His opponent gets slaughtered. After a few attacks he lies bleeding on his side, his head raised, watching fate descend on him.

A canoe is taking me to El Real. I sit on a crosspiece in the middle, the boat isn't much more than two feet wide. Tito is at the helm, his wife and child with him. An old woman is sitting in the bow. Downstream goes easily enough, we barely need the motor. Close to the bank, a man in a little pirogue tosses out his net. Early-morning mist is hanging between the trees. In front of us, a dusky mountain ridge rises up above the jungle. He is beginning to make himself known. He was here. The trees remember him, the river's memories float to the surface. Along the dark banks you can see how high the water reaches at times. The sun leaps up above the trees, is catapulted into the heavens. The old woman covers her head with a towel on which a map of Panama is printed, Darién covered by a giant toucan. The family behind me disappears beneath umbrellas. The occasional hut with palm-frond roof along the high banks. Astride the serpent's back we go deeper, for that is how it is, we don't go further, we go deeper and deeper. The Indians pay no attention to me. I fill the emptiness with thoughts. I ready the emptiness for his arrival. In which of his guises should I expect him? The father? The god-slayer? Will we recognize each other, sniff at each other, fangs bared like predators? Has he been waiting for me, will he welcome me as though it weren't him, but me, who was lost?

Ripples patter against the hull, my hand cuts through the water like a keel. The canoe turns, crossing the current for a moment, then moves up a narrow tributary. The water soon grows shallower, the old woman calls back to Tito to warn of obstacles. This is how El Real died; the river silted up, goods and people could no longer reach the town. Transport is possible only during the rainy season, when the water is high. A pallet across a brace of pirogues, the platform on which a car, a truck or a generator can be conveyed.

The river grows ever shallower. The muddy bank is covered in a layer of algae, of a greenish hue I've never seen before. The old woman sounds the channel with a stick, the canoe scrapes bottom. Big white herons fly off, croaking. The woman spits into the rusty brown water. Sticking up out of the mud, close together, are straight stalks topped with a heart-shaped leaf. The sun blasts its flames in your face, my shirt is soaked, it's like inhaling burning air. Stumps, amputated and deathly, block the way. The steaming forest on both sides, a tangle, a knot. Prismatic dragonflies chase each other above the mire. Now the women are pushing the canoe through the mud with long poles, Tito guns the motor. That is how it goes, meter by meter through the muck that belches forth its rotten breath. The jungle summons up abhorrence and enchantment, a greenhouse full of increase run amok. Ibises step calmly through the mud. The young woman climbs into the water to push. I take over her punting-pole, but soon we all have to leave the boat, all except for the child. They go barefooted, I keep my socks on. I sink deep into the mud. The Indians think that's funny, they laugh. I'm afraid of the hard things I feel beneath my feet. *Guerrilleros* swallowed up by the mud? The bones of conquistadors? We push the canoe upstream in silence, slaves of the infant king. Huts on poles rise up along the shore, the shadows of human forms inside them. The thin smoke from smoldering fires. The forerunners of El Real. We guide the bow of the canoe towards the bank, where more and more dwellings huddle. Just before we leave the water I step on something sharp with my right foot, it cuts deeply into my heel. I climb onto the shore quickly, pull off my sock and see bright red blood welling up from the gash. Standing around a barrel, the Indians rinse away the mud. I hop over to it and wash my foot. A long, deep wound, I can see the meat beneath the colorless callus. They bring my suitcase ashore, I put on clean socks. Between houses on stilts and the walls of corrals I hobble into town.

A few paved pathways lined with houses, here and there a shop, an open, horizontal shutter to provide shade, on display a smattering of toilet paper, insecticide, soft soap, sweets and canned food. When evening comes the shutters are lowered and locked. People point out to me El Nazareno, a wooden hotel on the main street with rooms on the top floor. The key is with the boy in the shop next door. I have the room facing the street. Before the window hangs a little red rag.

At the edge of El Real I find a Red Cross post. A nurse looks at my foot but can't do anything to help, it will have to heal by itself. She gives me a bottle of iodine, a roll of gauze and adhesive bandages. The prospect of delay depresses me; for the time being there is no way I can hike on through the jungle as planned. And so I go limping back to El Nazareno.

In the days that followed I tried to find out about Schultz, about where he might be holed up. It had to be somewhere in the jungle around El Real, the research I'd done back in Europe had shown me that much. It was there, after the completion of *Abgrund* (*completion* − a strange word for something that had been actually made to disappear), that he had started on *Titan*; he had been able to summon up enough vital hatred for yet another act of destruction. To get there, though, I needed a guide. From the travelers' handbook to Panama I had drawn the name of one man, Edmond Solano, who was apparently the best guide around. But when I asked the rangers at the Agencia Ambiental about him, the man talking to me mimed a pistol with thumb and forefinger, held it against his temple and pulled the trigger.

I lay on my bed, tangled up in the rotations of the ceiling fan. It was dark outside, a powerful chirping rolled in over El Real from the surrounding forest. What I knew: five hundred years ago conquistadors had built an outpost here, along the banks of the Río Tuiro, to ward off the bandits who preyed on the gold kept upstream at Santa María. Even deeper into Darién, to the south, lay the Cana Valley, where the gold mines were. In Santa María the gold piled up until there was enough to warrant putting together an armada and taking it to Panama City.

The bed sagged like a hammock, a drab, membrane-thin blanket was all I had over me. The temperature had barely dropped at all.

Past the army post, a canopy under which drowsy soldiers lay on cots, was the office of the Agencia Ambiental. There I was given the cold shoulder. The rangers' faces froze when Schultz's name was mentioned. I limped back and forth, back and forth between the hotel and the settlement. The wooden houses stood on pilings of wood or cement, underneath them chickens pecked amid the garbage. In the shade of the palm and mango trees, men were training their roosters for the cockfights. With a rapid movement they would toss the bird to one side, to teach it to regain its footing quickly. They would lay their rooster on its back, to see how quickly it was back on its feet, again and again, dozens of times in a row. Then they staked the bird by one leg in the shade, a tin can of fresh water beside it. Sphinx-like old folks watched from porches. Screens at the windows, fans slicing the thick, hot air. I had taken the laces out of my shoe to give my foot more room. The blood pounded in my heel, I hopped along on the ball of my foot. The walking wounded.

After a few days my hands began to swell and go numb, I was worried about infection. I spent the hottest part of the afternoons lying in my room; I could see it, I would have to be airlifted out to Panama City, delirious. My right hand amputated, the left one saved only in the nick of time. The foot would have to be treated for gangrene. In the water stains on the ceiling I saw deformed babies. My eyes slid lethargically over the details, a nail in a plank, little mounds of sawdust on the floor. The beams were eaten hollow, you could see the round entrance and exit holes. Some of the beams were nothing but a tube filled with crumbly sawdust, held together by the paint. If all the other noises were to stop, the vibrating zoom of insects, the crowing of roosters, all you would hear would be a close-set, uninterrupted gnawing. One day this room, this hotel, would be devoured whole.

I dream of her, my living, sorrowful mother, she says, 'You're starting to look less like me all the time! Look at that . . .'

'No! No! I look like you, here, see!'

Like waking up bleeding. No mercy, godforsaken. My hands feel like they're going to burst, they bob on the strings of my arms like Disney balloons. I miss her the way I used to miss her, at moments when I had hurt myself badly and all my childish soul became a scream of desolation, a scream for my mother who wasn't there.

I started asking passers-by whether they had heard of Schultz. An old man nodded earnestly and walked on. A woman began rattling away in Spanish. I tried to calm her; I had noticed that I could understand some things when people spoke slowly.

'She says he was here,' I heard a voice say in crystal-clear English.

As though, after swinging the dial back and forth for a long time, you suddenly hit upon a radio channel with good reception.

'You speak English!' I said to the young man who had entered the conversation a bit aloofly, but not unwillingly. 'Could you ask her what he was doing here? When he was here? Does he come here often?'

The woman had seen him, she had heard stories, she couldn't understand why the men of El Real hadn't rushed out and chopped him to pieces with their machetes. Señor Schultz had been drinking in the bar, he had turned the whole place upside down, everyone was drinking on his tab. They had started fighting, ever since then Jorge Valdez's nose had pointed in a different direction from where he was headed. They had broken in to Pilar's store to get more alcohol.

'What was he doing here?' I asked the young man.

He interpreted for me patiently. The woman didn't know why Schultz had come. She picked up her basket as though to move on.

'One more question,' I said excitedly. 'When was he here? Did he come here often?'

He had been here two or three times, the last time was long ago now. I was delighted, her eyes had seen him, it suddenly brought him closer than he had ever been before.

The young man's name was Aldair Macmillan, he was the first person I'd talked to in a long time.

'Did you come to El Real to find that man?' he asked.

'That man. Yes. It's not exactly easy.'

'Almost nothing is, here.'

'Shall we move over to the shade?'

Beneath the luxuriant foliage of a mango tree I talked to Aldair Macmillan, who studied tropical forestry at Punta Culebra. Aldair was in El Real at the moment to visit his mother. I poured my relief out over him like cool water. Nothing in his replies made it seem as though he found anything strange about my dashing off to El Real in search of a man in the jungle.

'I have three problems,' I said. 'I barely speak the language. I don't know where he is exactly. And if I did know, I wouldn't know how to get there. These are the things that are blocking my way, you understand?'

I saw him squint, and hoped it wasn't skepticism.

'Problems, problems,' he said.

'Problems, that's right.'

'I could ask around for you.'

'Really?'

'To see if there's someone . . .'

'Someone?'

'Who could help. I could . . .'

'Oh, that would be fantastic!'

A few minutes later he had disappeared among the houses. I had forgotten to say where he could find me.

The day began with a thousand cock crows. I dripped iodine into the wound, which was closing up quickly now. A pretty black girl carrying an umbrella drifted through the streets, holding a sheet of stationery on which one could enter one's name for the local lottery. The prize was a Geneva wristwatch. I put my name down; I wanted this to be a lucky day.

The jungle began directly behind the last row of houses. Protruding from the greenery were the blunt noses of three Dodge trucks, overrun by vines, their windows misted over with moss. Before long they would be completely swallowed up by the undergrowth. At the little store I bought a roll of toilet paper, batteries and a bar of soap. The old man groaned as he counted out my change. Aldair Macmillan and I didn't cross paths again till late in the afternoon. I was eating chicken and rice at a makeshift restaurant, three plastic tables outside, beneath a pergola of flowers. My table was beside the brown creek, where a little Emberá boy was moaning as he emptied his bowels. Along the banks lay the dark trunks from which pirogues were carved. The stilt-houses were closed off only by one or two walls, I wondered whether Indians said things like *have you ever seen a mess like the neighbors' place?* Then, suddenly he was standing beside my table: Aldair Macmillan.

'How did you find me?' I asked.

'I wasn't trying to find you.'

He nodded towards the black woman behind the low door to the charred kitchen.

'She's my mother. Are you enjoying your food?'

304

'It's very good. Your mother's a good cook.'

Aldair nodded contentedly.

'I grew up without a father,' he said, 'but my mother's cooking brought a lot of fathers to this table.'

The backdrop to our conversation consisted of a black woman pounding grain on the muddy riverbank. The pestle pounded dully against the hollowed log. Africa, carried forward in a dying settlement in the jungles of Panama.

'I found someone who can solve two of those problems for you,' Aldair said. 'There's a man, his name is Ché Ibarra, who knows how to find the man you're looking for. He knows the way through the jungle. Unfortunately, he only speaks Spanish and a few lines of German. He's a communist. He listens to Mozart all day long. Do you like Mozart?'

'Sometimes he moves me, sometimes I think he's an overrated Alpine composer.'

'Then it's even more of a pity that you won't be able to talk to Ché Ibarra.'

'So he really knows where Schultz is?'

'He says he's guided shipments of material there.'

The woman on the bank shoveled the grain into a wooden bowl, raised her arm and let the grain run back into the mortar, the chaff blew away. I put a few dollars on the table and we were off, in search of the man who could say the magic words and untangle the jungle's web.

Chickens were scratching about on the thatched roofs. In a few minutes the gas lanterns would go on and here and there little generators would begin thrumming.

Anyone seeing Ché Ibarra for the first time would think he had met his own murderer. But, apparently, inside that exterior of riffraff from a Mariachi film was housed the soul of a poet. His lips knew the

305

shape of the libretto to *Le nozze di Figaro*. Aldair Macmillan acted as our interpreter. Ibarra glanced at me only briefly, dead eyes in a craggy face shiny with salt and grease. He had the moustache of a Chinaman, its hairs implanted sparsely across his lip. The fireflies gleamed in the bushes behind his house. He nodded in reply to my questions. He knew the way. He had seen Schultz in real life. He was still there. A day's walk if you left before sunup, otherwise two. He didn't seem to care at all whether we went or not. When asked what it would cost to lead me there, he shrugged, then said, '*Doscientos dólares*.'

The prospect of being alone with this man in the jungle frightened me. I could see myself dead, buried carelessly beneath a layer of leaves. That someone like this could love Mozart seemed a comic misunderstanding.

'Two hundred is okay,' I said. 'When can we go?'

Again, indifference. I said I'd like to leave the day after tomorrow, before sunup. His hands lay motionless on the table in front of him. Did I need to bring things, food, water? Ché Ibarra shook his tired head – that would not be necessary.

Thirty-six hours later, almost empty-handed, I found myself at his door. A backpack containing a few odds and ends. The house was dark. A lemon-yellow moon was lingering over the trees. The chirping of geckos, and the impression that the buzzing and shrilling of insects must be loudest just before dawn. You could lose yourself in that noise, an electrifying tapestry. Just as I started climbing the steps to the veranda, I heard footsteps on the road. Ibarra had already left his house, perhaps he had been picking up a few necessities for the trip. He was wearing a half-filled backpack, he looked like nothing so much as a soldier.

'*Venga, vamos*.'

Then he gave me my first view of the prospect that would lie before me all day long, the army-green backside of a man who seemed to consist entirely of sinew and stolid willpower. I felt lucky, and I was on my way, it was going to work out. We plunged into the head-high elephant grass. The last stars in the sky were growing pale, we were rotating again into a new day. The pain in my foot was bearable, the skin had healed over. I picked up the pace, but he was far out in front of me. We crossed a path lined by a dyke that seemed built for irrigation and disappeared into the blue embrace of the forest. Ibarra put in the earbuds of his Walkman. Every once in a while he looked back. The final shadows of the night had tucked themselves away amid the trees, they would quickly be chased away by bundles of sunlight falling through the high crowns. I barely realized that I was on my way to my father. The effort it had taken to get there had relegated my goal to the background. But now every step was taking me closer to him, every meter counted; the less I thought, the better off I was, that would help me to ignore the pain in my foot that was acting up now, the short-ness of breath and the sweat seeping through my shirt – I counted my steps, up to one hundred and then back down again. The fanatical hiss of insects had subsided, as it grew hotter that sound was replaced by a low, constant drone. We arrived at a brook that could easily have flowed in England, silver water rolling over a copper-colored bed, to cross it was an act of blasphemy; clouding the holy water, muddy feet on the gold brocade of the temple garment.

We clambered across the mossy, moist roots of trees, climbed hills of mud, stones shot out from under the soles of my shoes. We still had not stopped for a rest. My mouth was dry. Ibarra warned me not to step on a coral snake that was almost completely hidden beneath leaves and humus. My hands began swelling again and itched. I did my best to keep up with him, while he listened composedly to piano concertos or the requiem *Dies irae* – baroque absurdities of this continent. I was no longer worried about him gutting me with his knife, I was too exhausted to be afraid. We stopped beside a dark pool amid the trees, a place where elves and sorcerers wrote the course of lifetimes on the black mirror of the surface. Ibarra handed me a bottle of water. He put the earbuds back in and stared into space. Later he gave me a banana. Then a piece of bread and a can of sardines. I dunked the bread in the leftover oil. Ibarra stood up. Apparently he was not planning to take the rubbish with him. Conscientious European that I was, I put it in my backpack.

The forest showed itself to me as an entity, an organism specialized in brief, flagrant blossoming and sudden death. Minor revelations flared up between the trees, birds like hellish-red flames. I was startled by the fleshy wings of a butterfly that fluttered in my face. I slapped at them. There were animals – insects? – that sounded like a plane flying over, there were others that made the sound of a chainsaw, a dying lamb, marbles knocked together. This was how the forest sounded at a noon hour giddy with heat. My thoughts took on the form of hallucinations. Flowers fell from the sky, in front of me walked a man who, I was suddenly certain, had served with the FARC, a runaway *guerrillero* – so light-footed and purposefully did he move through the trees. A new storey was built onto my fear: what if he were taking me to a rebel camp where I would be held hostage? Did the FARC operate this deep within Panama? What time was it? Was this the day that I was going to meet him, the man of whom I had no other memory but the rustling of his trouser legs? And what day was that then?

Ibarra was waiting for me beside a little waterfall. Kneeling, he drank from the stream and gestured to me to do the same. He sat down on the stones and unlaced his army boots. Then he undressed and dove into the pool under the cascade. He swam like a little dog. My sock was red with blood. The sole was soaked. From the rocks along the bank I slid into the water. Little fishy mouths nibbled at my flesh. I went under and drifted over the smooth stones at the bottom. When I resurfaced, we were no longer alone. A man was looking at us. Soiled T-shirt and fatigue trousers, a machete hanging from his belt. They were talking, Ibarra and he. Ibarra was standing naked on the bank, solid as the trunks along the banks of the creek at El Real, seeming completely at ease. They tossed the occasional glance in my direction. While Ibarra was getting dressed, the other man shook a cigarette from a crumpled pack. I climbed onto the bank and caught a whiff of sulfur. An unpleasant kind of watchfulness had settled on the things that happened.

'*Hombre*,' the unknown man said to me.

He shook his head and said things I didn't understand. A gate was being closed, I understood that much. I breathed deeply in and out to ward off a panic attack. I understood the word *prohibido*. An obstacle, no more than that. An obstacle.

'No,' I stammered. '*No es imposible.*'

He raised his chin.

'*Vamos a señor Schultz,*' I said.

The thin valor of those words, spoken to two men who had only to walk away in order to ensure my certain death. I began speaking in English. That I sure as hell had not come to Darién just to let myself be turned away by the first hillbilly I ran into. That I was his son, that he was expecting me, that he had been waiting for me all his life, that's right, sir! Waiting for me, his son, the *hijo* of *señor Schultz*, and now you – my hand cast lightning bolts in his direction – are not going to try to tell me that I've come to the end of the road here, oh no, you are going to let us through, what's more, you're going to take us there, me, *hijo de señor Schultz*, and my man Friday here.

His head moved slightly, doubtfully, he asked, '*Usted es el hijo de señor Schultz?*'

I tapped my finger against my chest.

'*Hijo.*'

I pointed to the countryside behind him.

'*Padre.*'

He took a drag of his cigarette, then squished the glowing cone between thumb and forefinger. It was impossible to tell whether he was thinking about a great many things at the same time, or thinking very slowly about one little thing, stuck between his teeth like a bothersome piece of gristle. The smoke from his cigarette hung between us. When it had drifted away the man shrugged and said something to Ibarra, but against the rocky surface of my guide's expression all announcements dashed themselves to pieces. We started moving. First the unknown man, then Ibarra, then me. That was how we moved through the forest, like the ants at our feet, who carved out narrow roads with snippets of bright green leaves on their backs, heading home to their republics. A shiny blue butterfly flew out in front of me, amid the treetops the embers of the day died out. Dull pain wedged itself between my temples, every single footstep resounded in my head.

By the time we headed for a spot of light amid the trees, I was counting on nothing. A clearing, columns of smoke rising skywards between the stumps. We stepped out of the shadows into the last daylight – I took a deep breath. Between a handful of huts lay dogs, there were no people anywhere. We walked past the paltry thatched shelters. There was washing hanging outside them. The settlement was suffused with the general messiness of temporary, improvised living. All the trees around the plot had been cut down, elephant grass was shooting up between the fallen trunks. This was an outpost, they were taking me further. Uphill we went now, again we slipped into the trees, this time along a winding path of footprints on the moist ground. Night was falling, I heard loud, mechanical sounds. The song of stone against steel, the strain of powerful engines. Then we were standing at the edge of a scene that would come back in my dreams – a grated, tortured landscape, a work of systematic hatred. A lone, steep mountain, the face of which on our side was eaten away by a malicious brand of erosion. A bulldozer labored across the violated surface of the earth, a plain of ground stone. A truck was flattening out the mountain's remains. Fires were burning in oil drums, smoking, flaring. Above all this, at the edge of the quarry, was where we stood. We descended along a winding path into the depths. I felt numb and without expectations. He might be there, he might not be. What had I hoped all this would lead to?

We were heading towards a central barrack. The bulldozer came to a halt, only the one yellow eye of the truck still crept over the terrain. Ibarra and I waited outside the long hut as the workers entered, drawn by the paltry light that burned inside. A few men came out again, tattered and dirty from head to toe like mineworkers. They looked at me, as though trying to see a resemblance with him. They exchanged words, seemed to hesitate about what to do. One of them had to take me to Schultz, none of them was eager to do so. In the end, an old Indian – his face weathered as a gravestone – was given the task. Beneath his unbuttoned shirt you could see his hairless chest, the wrinkled, round belly beneath that. He was my escort for the last stage of this journey. He walked away without looking back, the men pushed me after him. We crossed the dead ground, there was a slope we climbed, I saw the contours of a little building in the darkness. Reddish light inside. I stumbled after the Indian. My heart leapt in my throat, a boulder rolled down the slope. At a little distance from the hut, the Indian stopped in his tracks. In his frail, lonesome voice he called out, '*Señor Schultz, discúlpame!*'

It seemed that all the currents in my life had been meant to arrive at this moment, here, under the forest at the top of the slope, up to the red half-light coming from the windows and the cracks around the door of flattened tins; it was for this that it had all existed. *Señor Schultz, discúlpame* . . . the open sesame that would reveal a father, the veils would be parted. Bumping around, then the door opened, shrieking softly on its hinges. A man peered into the darkness and said, '*Qué hay? Qué quiere?*'

The Indian stepped back and disappeared quickly. The man took a step forward, mumbling, uncertain about the shape in the darkness.

'Mr. Schultz,' I said.

'Who's there? Who are you?'

I broke the inertia by taking a step, by saying, 'I've come here to talk to you.'

We were facing each other now. It occurred to me that he might be night blind, or simply nearsighted as all get-out, because he still seemed to see nothing but shadows.

'Shall we go inside?' I asked.

He backed through the doorway, I stooped and followed him. I found myself standing in a shabby, low-ceilinged room, the hut of a castaway. A man, my height, his beard streaked with gray. He said nothing, just looked. My voice was even and clear when I said, 'I'm Ludwig Unger.'

And, as though to refresh his memory, 'Your son.'

The silence reverberated between my ears. The man ran his hand over his beard, then laid it on the back of his neck. He walked to the table and sat down. The back of the chair creaked, his gaze swept the ceiling, the kerosene lamp above the table. I thought I heard him making a sound beneath his breath, a thought that couldn't make it past his lips. There inside him an arranging was going on, the disposition of the things that, on one evening out of a million, had fallen on his head.

'You look like her,' he said then.

Again he withdrew inside himself, looking for words, for something to say.

'You always were your mother's baby.'

His shack was that of a cynical philosopher, a cur.

'Cat got your tongue, boy? Sit down.'

There was another chair in the room, beside the bed, covered in clothes and papers. Next to the mattress was the butt of a candle in a tin can, and an almost-consumed green spiral to ward off insects. Now we were sitting across from each other, Bodo Schultz and Ludwig Unger, separated by a lifetime, my lifetime, and it was at that of all moments that my tongue seemed to lie paralyzed in my mouth. He was so much older than I had imagined him. Father, is that you? He filled two glasses from a bottle with no label.

'Maybe this will make you a little more talkative.'

Ay, the burning in my guts! He assessed me, squinting, as though his eyes were indeed bad.

'How's your mother doing?'

I exhaled loudly through my nostrils.

'Not good,' I said. 'She's dead.'

'Dead,' he echoed.

'Cancer.'

He nodded like a turtle.

'Marthe dead. When?'

'May of last year.'

'May. What month is it now?'

'January.'

'Did she suffer?'

'She suffered.'

'There isn't any other way.'

'Perhaps not.'

He drank. Drops remained hanging in his beard.

'That's fucked,' he said.

And a little later, 'How did you get here?'

'A man brought me. He showed me the way.'

'It's hard not to be found in this world.'

I had no other repertoire at my disposal but the primal questions. They were burning in my soul like phosphor.

'Why did you go away? From Alexandria, I mean. Without . . . anything.'

A laugh, scornful, insulting.

'Did you come all this way just to lecture me on marital ethics, boy? Is that it? Then I can probably expect a few more of your sort to show up here, don't you think?'

I drew in my breath.

'I don't know about your life. I just have a couple of questions. Then I'll go away.'

'You could have called.'

He nodded at the satellite phone on the shelf behind him.

'I didn't have your number, I'm sorry.'

When he grinned you could see the black holes in his teeth.

'You came here because you want to find out something,' he said. 'Do you want to know what you could have figured out anyway, or do you want to know about what you can't even fathom right now? The point where nothing's left. Beyond that. Beyond people. Beyond everything. Where cosmic loneliness is your reward. Knowledge in its most supreme form. No more prospects, only chasms.'

'All I want to know is what reason was good enough to leave your wife and child alone.'

He refilled the glasses. His hand shook.

'Siddhartha Gautama looks at his sleeping wife and child. Rahula, that was the child's name. Ball, chain. Gautama sneaks out of the house and never comes back. He becomes an ascetic in the wilderness. Some people become Buddha. Others anti-Buddha.'

'Ball and chain.'

314

'Your mother got pregnant. Dozens, hundreds of men had poured their seed into her, I made her pregnant.'

'You were married.'

'No children, I told her that. Absolutely not. Women's little accidents, phaw!'

'I was unwanted . . .'

'No sad little songs here. Don't bellyache. She screwed me into it. Lesson one: never underestimate the hunger of the womb. The female animal is ravenous. She punches a bunghole in your flesh, your strength runs out. Your mother? I wanted a woman, I got a household. She kissed as though trying to suck the life out of me. She didn't kiss, she sucked.'

Oh, horrible flash – her lips on my neck, the kiss of death.

'Spare me the gruesome details,' I said.

His sardonic laugh.

'My answers already stuck in your craw? You just got here. Aw, did he come all that way for something he doesn't want to know about? Prometheus with his smoking matchstick! Hahaha!'

A black, exploding star at the center of my chest. He slams his glass down on the table. He says, '*Love* is what she called it, and played the flute on my hollow bones. And you, you belonged to your mother. She even gave you her name, or so I hear. Praise the day I left, that way you had her all to yourself, that's what little boys want, isn't it? Mommy all to themselves? With no one to interrupt their dirty little fantasies? When you're playing with your little weenie?'

I leaned across the table, my fists clenched.

'You're going too far now.'

My breath caught.

'You have no right . . .'

He shook his head.

'You should have more of me in you. This is pathetic. Tiring. Please just go away.'

315

I stood up, holding on to the edge of the table, and shut my eyes for a moment. I took a deep breath.

'One more thing,' I said. 'You sent me a postcard. I'd just turned fifteen. You wrote that I was supposed to love you. Why?'

'I wrote that?'

'*Love me*, on a postcard from Colombia.'

He frowned and puckered his lips in disbelief.

'Says nothing to me. Must have been someone else.'

The expanding star filled my chest, my body. To kick the life out of him, slowly and methodically, singing euphorically all the while.

'You're not the first,' he said. 'Trying to define yourself by giving me a whipping! So that's why you came.'

O delirium! O infernal tumor in my head!

He swung his arms and parried like a boxer.

'Ho! Whoa! Ho! Came here to make mincemeat out of your old man, huh? Well just try it, patsy boy.'

I shook my head.

'Look at yourself. Disgusting. I don't have to whip you. You did that yourself a long time ago.'

'Whoo! Right to the head! Drink up, boy. Talk to me. Months go by around here without me hearing one intelligent, well-put word. Everything around here's a commodity, every rock, every shoelace, every word. I don't understand the Indians, and what I do understand I don't like. I'd rather have Negroes. They're stronger, better, but almost impossible to get. The Negro doesn't like it here, the interior. They stay on the coast. And you can hardly blame him, the Negro, for wanting to be at liberty to fry his fish and fornicate at will. Around here we all rot away. Everything. It's a digestive tract. Illiterate insects eat your books, grind *Der Wille zur Macht* and any old operating manual into the same powder. Your watch and a truck crumble away under the same corrosion. It's fascinating. In this world, where you're dead to the world, you can actively take part in your own nonexistence. In fact, you're not even there anymore, you look around in amazement at everything that's still standing, at everything that keeps itself going on the last shreds of rage and willpower. The idealist and the believer see beauty and meaning in that, in nature, but those things can be conquered by the will. The focused will. That destroys them. But indifference, indifference always beats you in the end. Always. That's the armor the gods have adopted, indifference. Stone for stone, I blow those thrones right out from under their asses. They've scared us so badly with their abysses! The gods on high, they laughed themselves silly. But they weren't expecting to see a horizontal abyss, the abyss that stretches out like a yawn! All his life a person fears the depths, but dies on the flats. You understand, boy, that's my meaning, that's the meaning of all destruction. Only destruction has a permanent character.'

How long must I have listened to that crackling broadcast? I had already heard the sacred earnestness of his words outside there, in the scream of stone. I drank and listened and went under in the man who was my father.

Later we left the hut, into the humming night, beneath that big yellow moon come out to play. In the depths below the fires were going out. He was staggering out in front of me, down the slope, towards the only place where a light was still shining. We climbed the steps to a half-open barrack where a pockmarked Negress was serving *aguardiente* to the last of the workmen. When he stepped out of the dark onto the rough plank floor, they all fell still.

'*Hola, campesinos!*' he roared.

They nodded. The woman filled two glasses. The men were sitting at wooden trestle tables covered in glasses and bottles. The generator behind the building was throbbing off-beat with the Vallenato from the speakers. On the makeshift counter, beneath a bright light, was a bowl containing chunks of meat in red sauce. Occasionally the woman waved a flyswatter over it.

'*Maria, donde están las chicas?*' Schultz asked.

The woman shrugged, then shouted something to one of the men. Shuffling to his feet, he disappeared from the circle of light. Later they arrived, the camp followers. Fatigued faces, their dark eyes thick with sleep. Schultz's favorite was a Creole girl with thin calves and little breasts that were round as balls. He bared his ruined teeth.

'I taught this one to eat with a knife and fork.'

She sat on his lap and called him *Papita*. Beneath her petticoat you could see her panties. The other two aimed their attentions at me, but when the conversation died after only a few words, they left me alone. The men seemed to breathe easier now that there were women around. Schultz grabbed his girl by the scruff of the neck. She thrashed about like a wild kitten. I tried to keep my eyes open for danger, but the burning in my gut made me careless. I stamped on the plank floor in time to the music.

'These here are the stupidest assholes in the whole world!' Schultz called out from behind the girl. 'They don't know a damned thing, but give them a bottle and they think they know it all.'

When he laughed, all conversation stopped.

'As soon as it's got Indian blood in it, it's fucked. No use for anything. Listless slaves. Not a thought in their heads. Aimless, tragic peoples. Maria!'

She filled his glass, the captain of this ship of the damned.

'Take Conchita!' he shouted. 'A pussy like a baby's. You do like pussy, don't you, boy? You're not a faggot, are you? Hahaha! *Tengo un hijo maricón!*'

The women chattered with laughter, the men flashed their teeth uneasily and avoided my eyes.

318

'Did your mother make a faggot out of you, boy? Is that what you came here to tell me? Daddy, I'm a turd-burglar? A chip off the old block, that boy, maybe he's more like me than I thought. I fucked that mommy of yours up the old poop-chute too. That changed the expression on her face, put a little color in that pale complexion!'

My fists shot out like stilettos, one, two, three times, left and right, he fell backwards onto the floor, girl and all. He lay there laughing on the planks, the blood running from his mouth. The girl scrambled to her feet and ran away. No-one did anything, no-one dared to do anything, an icy calm had descended on me. He tried to pull himself up on a table leg.

'You've got a mean punch for a faggot.'

My foot shot out and caught him in the ribs. He writhed like an eel on a glowing grill.

'Filthy little bastard!' he panted. 'Tell that slut to come back here. Tell her to come back, goddamn it!'

Lying on the planks he looked up at me, the dying cock in Yaviza flashed through my mind. The men kept their eyes averted, no-one looked at us, a fallen emperor is more dangerous than an emperor on horseback. I went back and sat down. Groaning, he maneuvered himself into a sitting position. Maria brought him another glass and filled mine. I wiped my fist on my trousers. Bent over, holding a hand against the side of his chest, he sat there spitting gobs of blood onto the floor. The girl knelt down in front of him, he slapped her hand away when she tried to stroke his face. I pulled my chair over, put my face down close to his.

'I waited for you the whole time,' I said. 'I looked for you everywhere, I thought I saw you everywhere. Is that him, does he look like that? No, he doesn't walk that way. He has to be a lot taller. Brown eyes, not blue ones. When you're missing something as major as a father, you're always cutting and pasting, wherever you are. You believe in miracles. Who says I'm not going to run into him here, today? You dream up things that might give him a reason to show up. The story always makes perfect sense, except he never shows up, that's the only thing wrong with the stories, that he refuses to show up.

'Even earlier than that, the years when you wonder: does he think about me like I think about him? Am I in his thoughts? If I listen closely, can I hear him whisper? Are we able to get in touch with each other in some magical way, through dreams, telepathy? But I only dreamed of you as a phantom, as the silent ghost from *A Christmas Carol*. Never a face, never that. These, I knew when I woke up, these were the ghosts of impotence and frustration. That's the half that's missing. That's what you left behind. Nothing but sorrow and misery. And this, this here, is nothing but the same thing to the umpteenth degree. You spread that nihilistic trash of yours like some contagious disease. The only thing you believe in are the things that are broken. In things that are ravaged. The only thing you can count on is the blackest of the black. Mishmash of moral colorblindness and poignant simplism. *Mediohombre*, that's what I called you. How fitting that turned out to be!'

'Let's drink to that!' he shouted. '*Mediohombre!*'

'Half a man . . .'

'*Mediohombre!*'

His hand had disappeared under the girl's skirt. She pushed it away, but it kept crawling up between her legs. He was strong, he was capable of *bearing* things. That was the one thing I admired about him, the kind of admiration that's tied up with fear; that he endured his life, spared no-one and nothing, and never looked back. And from the maelstrom of the night I fished up yet another clear thought – that finally, once I had returned out of this wilderness, I would no longer have any desires in which he played a role. Not a single expectation would survive this night. Where all feeling has been crushed there opens up a luxurious amount of space for the horrific, delicious mercy of indifference, that guise worn by the gods.

I awakened with a start because of something moving beside me. We were lying in the corner of a hut, through the thin mattress I could feel the hard dirt floor. She rolled onto her other side. On her brown back was the tattoo of a shackled hand, clenched in a combative fist. The heat pressed me against the mattress. I struggled my way out of that nest of fleas and venereal disease and dressed quickly. I left thirty dollars behind on the spot where I had lain. Shoelaces untied and shirt unbuttoned, I left the hut in search of water. By the barrack I saw Ché Ibarra, standing in the shade of the wall. The scraping of metal claws grated in my ears. The mountain looked down on us and bled. Forgive my father, for he knows not what he does.

'*Una hora más,*' I told Ibarra.

In the barrack I drank three mugs of cool water from a barrel. This was what the river's song was about. I climbed the path to his house. He was sitting in a chair, in a dingy pair of boxer shorts too baggy for his legs. It was impossible to tell where the piss stain stopped. The skin around his eyes was black and swollen, I had hit him squarely. He was holding one hand to his side.

'I think I broke a couple of them,' he said.

His white calves were covered in sores. The jungle was in the process of devouring him. There was not much left of the big man from the stories. The Creole girl was making coffee over a fire outside. She squatted there, waiting for the lid of the dented kettle to start rattling. I picked up my backpack and put it on the table.

'I was supposed to give this to you,' I said.

From the bag I produced the plastic box I had carried with me throughout that long hike. I put it down in front of him and zipped up my pack.

'What is it?' he asked.

'It's for you.'

His red eyes shot back and forth between my face and the outsized sandwich box. His hands shaking, he took the rubber band off the box, removed the lid and looked in it.

'What's that?'

'What do you think?'

'Ashes?'

'Ashes.'

'Not her ashes . . .?'

'Her ashes.'

He pulled his hand back as though the box contained a deadly adder.

'Jesus Christ . . .'

'It was her dying wish.'

'Just like Marthe,' he whispered. 'Just like her . . .'

'She never understood why you went away,' I said.

He doubled up even further.

'She never stopped loving you.'

And with those words I put on my backpack, said *Bye now*, and pulled closed behind me not one door, but many.

That was more or less the way I told it to Linny Wallace. Some things I left out, others I toned down, but it was along those lines that the story spun itself out. In the restaurant they were setting the tables for breakfast. A man walked down the corridor, pulling a vacuum cleaner. We both felt like a gas station that is open twenty-four hours a day; even our clothing, our hair was *tired*. We climbed the stairs, at the door to her room there was a moment's hesitation, then she took my hand and said, 'Come.'

We undressed, on far sides of the bed. We averted our eyes from each other's nakedness. I lay curled up slightly, my back to her. The light smell of soap when her body moved against mine. She put her arms around me. Then the shaking started. It came in bigger and bigger waves. I lay there shaking like a Parkinson's patient, my teeth chattering, dug up out of an avalanche, defrosted. It seemed like it would never stop.

'Shh, shh, oh, take it easy now,' whispered the woman who was holding me.

Gradually the trembling decreased, her soft, soothing hands caressed my upper arms and chest, she stroked the tremors out of me. And that was how we fell asleep, the gray morning light leaking through the curtains.

The cemetery around St. George's had been full for years, but Warren received a spot in the Feldman family grave, a stone sepulcher sealed with iron doors. The outside walls and tower of the Anglican church were built from the round pieces of flint which the sea brought ashore; it was a large church, the largest building in Alburgh, like a mother hen spreading the down of eternity over the last of the believers. I was the first to arrive. I had on my charcoal-gray suit with a black tie. I was welcomed by the priest, Lindsay Temple, who didn't seem quite sure she recognized me. My mind was almost sagging out of my body with fatigue. We ran through the program, between the prayer and the reading I would go to the piano and play the *Marcia Funebre Sulla Morte d'un Eroe*. She wrote down every word.

'Beethoven, right?'

'Ludwig von Beethoven, yes.'

At Catherine's request, her own parish priest was also taking part in the ceremony. My head was a bowl full of sparkling wine. Catherine nodded and sat down in the pew in front of me. She was flanked by two daughters, dark as shadows. In the row across the aisle was Joanna, sitting between two Titans and a Titaness. The question of the day: who had most right to the deceased? Who got to claim his memory? Rustling, shuffling, the church was filling up. I saw Terry Mud, wearing his tie as though he'd used it to hang himself. I'd ask him later whether I could stay in his caravan for a while.

The rose window behind the altar was weeping holy tears of stained glass. Arrows pierced a martyr. The people sat down, the doors closed. Lindsay Temple began to speak. Resurrection, eternal life. He who today we are bearing to his grave. His life in a nutshell, a nod to his second, a nod to his first wife – strict protocol. The chuckling in the pews when his seawall was mentioned. I was dreaming with my eyes open. How once I had left my sleeping body and shot to the clouds like an arrow, higher, past the spheres surrounding Earth, like light past other heavenly bodies, a journey without return, until suddenly her voice sounded, my mother calling *Lud-wig!* With a start I fell back into my body, straight up in bed; startled, I shouted *Yeah?*, but nothing but silence and darkness surrounded me.

'I would like to ask Ludwig Unger, a good friend of the family, to come up, he will play for us . . .'

I play the funeral march faultlessly, I could play it in my sleep. Frozen butterflies extend their wings – melting into tears they rain down on the people. For Warren, for Marthe, I have nothing better to give.

More Bible readings, the words and formulas like lids too small to contain the bulk of absence. Catherine turns to me and smiles so that my heart breaks. *The Lord's Prayer*, we stand up, I hold on to the pew in front of me.

Amid the sunken graves, the Celtic crosses, stones carved with ships, the people form a hedge, row after row, not everyone is able to see how the coffin disappears into the crypt. People pat my arms, pat me on the back, *nicely played, nicely played*. The bearers return from the darkness, Catherine and her daughters have remained. The cold bites my face, the wind coming off the land rustles between the graves and the bare, gleaming branches. Women sniff. Catherine takes an eternity, after this there will be nothing but dream and memory. The final touch, skin on wood. Shrunken, waxen, she returns from the underworld. Now Joanna and her children disappear into the grave. When they come back, a voice announces the further proceedings. The crowd disperses, later there will be whiskey and music, *Catherine and the children would appreciate the pleasure of your company.*

Before I could drink to the dead, before I could stamp my feet to the music and enter into loud conversation, there was something I had to do. I went back to the Whaler. In my room I opened the wardrobe and pulled down my suitcase. I took the plastic bag with the urn out of it. Then I left the room.

At the Readers' Room I walked up onto the esplanade. The sea lay glistening calmly below. I walked up past the pier and the winter storage area for the beach cabins to the start of Kings Ness. Warren Feldman's hill, the realm of King Knut. Sand and stones crunched beneath my leather soles. I didn't follow the curve of the road but cut straight through, through the tall grass towards the rampant growth of thorn bushes in the distance, atop the cliff. A house had once stood there. It was there that I brought her, and I thought back on that other inurnment, that plastic box full of ashes from the kitchen of Aldair Macmillan's mother, who had consented in surprise when I asked to shovel them from her oven. A flash of intuition, perhaps, to burden whatever remained of his conscience, to force him to *remember.*

A few yellow flowers amid the gorse, flashing like medals on a uniform. From far away, a voice was carried on the wind, someone bellowing *Mol-ly!* I walked close to the edge; there below you could see the remains of Warren's seawall. After him the deluge. I needed to ask Catherine about precisely how he handled all that later, when things quieted down a bit.

Here it was, sticking out of the cliff here were the pipes that had carried water and gas to our house. Never had we been more at home than we were here. I took the urn out of the bag and set it in the grass. On the horizon was a pale blue streak of light. The sky was open, you were never sure just how far you could see. At this spot, later, I would have a bench installed. *For Marthe Unger. For Warren Feldman. This place they loved.* Something like that. I broke the seal, the lid was on tight. I unscrewed it and walked as close to the edge as I could. The beach was empty. As for man, his days are as grass, as a flower of the field so he flourishes, for the wind passes over it and he is gone, and the place thereof shall know it no more.

I upturned the urn above the abyss. Part of it fell straight down, another part was caught by the wind – there you float, Mother, there you float.

I stepped back. With the urn in my hand I looked out across the water. So this was where we said goodbye, at the edge of the world, beside the glistening sea. Nothing had remained undone, there was nothing I desired. I was alone. And everything was beginning.

Little Caesar

Tommy Wieringa

ABOUT THIS GUIDE

We hope that these discussion questions will enhance your
reading group's exploration of Tommy Wieringa's
Little Caesar. They are meant to stimulate discussion, offer new
viewpoints and enrich your enjoyment of the book.

More reading group guides and additional information,
including summaries, author tours and author sites for other
fine Black Cat titles may be found on our Web site,
www.groveatlantic.com.

1. This moving novel charts the destruction that can occur within the heart of families and the ensuing strength of the human spirit to overcome it—or to pursue another path, at least. Did you find this novel ultimately redemptive? Discuss your reactions.

2. Consider the theme of erosion that weaves through the narrative, constantly undermining the characters and causing them to reassess their lives. Discuss the many guises erosion takes: the sea and wind against the landscape; time, love, hope, and illness. Did you find other guises? Consider this quote: "When you look up from the beach you can see the web of roots clutching naked and panicky at the yellow sand" (p. 85). How does this imagery of roots compare to the people in the novel?

3. Ludwig Unger tells his life story to a woman he meets in a bar after returning to Alburgh, his childhood town, for a funeral. How is this narrative device effective? How did it deepen your understanding of Ludwig's character? Did he evolve during the long hours of telling this story? Is Linny Wallace important to the story, or is she merely one woman in a particular time and place in Ludwig's life?

4. Ludwig views his life story as a confession: "The reason for my confession ... lies in the desire to impose order" (p. 78). Why do you think he feels this way? Was he searching for absolution through its telling? What do you think "imposing

order" suggests? Do you agree that he achieves order through his narration? Discuss how and why he views his life as unstructured, beyond his control, or out of order.

5. In many ways Ludwig considers himself unanchored or adrift in the world because of the physical loss of his childhood home on Kings Ness, taken from him and his mother by the raging wind and North Sea. Discuss what this home meant to him as an adolescent. How was it a sanctuary for him and his mother, a refuge from the constantly threatening world? What does the home—and its loss—mean to him as an adult?

6. Discuss the many ways in which the ground beneath Ludwig's feet collapses (literally and figuratively) throughout his childhood, and examine why he considers his relationship with his mother the bedrock of security.

7. The complicated relationship between Marthe and Ludwig—as seen through Ludwig's eyes—lies at the heart of the novel. Discuss the intensity of Ludwig's gaze and why his mother held such sway over him. How does the father's abandonment affect them? Do you think Marthe was aware of her son's confused sexual feelings for her? Why do you think she dresses him and puts makeup on him?

8. Discuss how loneliness impacts both Ludwig and his mother. How often do they interact with others? Do you agree that they are an island unto themselves? Is this a result of Ludwig's blinkered vision of his childhood with Marthe? Did

Ludwig—a Dutch-Austrian boy, born in Alexandria, living in England—feel like an outsider?

9. "My mother has led so many lives already, her life with me was merely one manifestation. That makes you unsure of yourself" (p. 99). Is Ludwig's discovery that his mother is the renowned porn star, Eve LeSage, the culmination of his childhood fears that he is not the center of her life? Why or why not? Find earlier examples of his attempts to make her his alone. Did he ever succeed?

10. How, if at all, does Ludwig's relationship with his mother change after this discovery? In what ways does his self image change? What does he mean when he states that "my history was in need of rewriting" (p. 91)?

11. Marthe Unger is portrayed through the lens of her son, through the screens and veils of his all-consuming adolescent love for her tinged with his present-day adult perspective. How do Ludwig's feelings for his mother change throughout the course of the novel? How do his feelings remain the same? Consider how the author presents both sides in the same narrative voice.

12. Throughout the novel Ludwig attempts to hold onto his past as a proof of his existence, of his passage through life. Discuss this preoccupation in terms of the theme of death that permeates the novel. Using the following quote as a springboard, elaborate upon the reasons for his need to spend time with his mother: "Although I had lost her any

number of times, she was indeed the only one I had. There couldn't be anyone else, we were the sole witnesses to each other's lives" (p. 212).

13. Why does Ludwig take his parents' life histories so much to heart, and why does he feel so responsible for them, viewing himself as an extension of both? Is he ever able to view himself apart from his parents, and especially apart from his mother?

14. In leaving his girlfriend Sarah and following his mother back to Europe, Ludwig believes that he is protecting and saving Marthe. Do you agree with this? How true was Sarah's belief that he had grown too dependent on Marthe? Ludwig states: "The life of a porn star is her point of departure, I will be her return" (p. 132). What are Ludwig's points of departure and return?

15. As cancer invades Marthe's body, she staunchly refuses to follow conventional and potentially life-saving treatment in a desire to "remain faithful" to herself (p. 275). What is this truth of self to which she clings? Do you consider her decisions admirable or self-centered? Did you regard her death an act of self-destruction?

16. Discuss how the novel explores the role of marriage: Marthe and Bodo's, Warren and Catherine's, and Warren and Joanna's. Consider whether or not happiness within a marriage is attainable in this novel. If so, must it always come at the expense of other people's (particularly the children's) happiness? Consider this quote and discuss how it applies to the novel's

theme of marital and parental responsibility: "should you stay where your love is buried, is that where your home is? Or is it with your children?" (p. 20).

17. As an adult, Ludwig lives without roots, without permanence. He interprets his mother's words, "In fact, you don't really need anyone anymore" (p. 103)," as a call to a life of loneliness, to meaningless relationships with a succession of women. What do you think his mother might have meant instead?

18. Continue your discussion of Ludwig's meaning of home by considering his statement: "I have learned not to desire a home wherever I am" (p. 237). How does he achieve the "delicious mercy of indifference" (p. 321) that his father prized so highly? Consider his poignant words about his relationship with Tate in the Caribbean: "[It] might amount to something. . . . The possibility of a roof over my head" (p. 243).

19. Discuss Bodo's role in the novel, and the effects of his absence in Ludwig's life. Why does he remain such a powerful influence over the years? Consider the private destruction that he wreaks on his family, and contrast it to his public artistic destruction, Abgrund (p. 154). What do you think about Bodo? Do you agree with his statement: "Destruction is the only thing with permanence" (p. 80)?

20. Warren Feldman's response to nature's adversity is to build a seawall to protect the homes and families he loves. Compare his reaction to those of Bodo Schultz, who launches a campaign against the gods in tearing down a mountain. Warren's

seawall fails, yet Bodo claims victory. What is the ultimate prize for winning? How do these two responses affect Ludwig's attempt to live his life?

21. Why does Ludwig feel the need to visit his father after his mother's death? What do you think he hopes to achieve through his visit? How does the presentation of Marthe's fake ashes affect Bodo, and why does Ludwig consider this a moral victory? What does Ludwig mean when he says he "pulled closed behind me not one door, but many" (p. 322)?

22. Discuss the end of the novel, when Ludwig is finally able to let go of his mother's ashes. Analyze the sense of relief that this brings him. What future do you envision for him as he moves forward with these words: "Nothing had remained undone, there was nothing I desired. I was alone. And everything was beginning" (p. 327)?

Suggestions for further reading:

First Light by Charles Baxter; *Winterton Blue* by Trezza Azzopardi; *Almost Innocent* by Sheila Bosworth; *Mothers and Sons* by Colm Tóibín

TOMMY WIERINGA was born in 1967 and grew up in Aruba in the Dutch Antilles off the coast of Venezuela before returning to the Netherlands when he was ten years old. He has written several books; his novel *Joe Speedboat* won the Bordewijk Prize, was long-listed for the 2011 International IMPAC Dublin Literary Award, and was nominated for the AKO Literature Prize. Wieringa is a columnist for the Dutch *NRC Handelsblad* daily newspaper.

SAM GARRETT studied journalism and philosophy at the University of Oregon in the wild and woolly 1970s. He currently divides his time between the Netherlands and France. Two-time winner of the Society of Authors' Vondel Prize for Dutch translation, in 2003 and again in 2009, he has translated a number of Holland's most popular authors into English.